"I AM STAR CAPTAIN MARILEN OF CLAN SMOKE JAGUAR.

"You used dishonorable trickery to lure us here. But I offer you the chance to redeem this shame—I will grant you the honor of one-on-one combat against me. We fight for the right of free passage from this place and the chance for you to regain honor by facing us again on a warrior's field of battle. What do you say, Major Loren?"

Loren stared at her *Koshi* 'Mech on his primary display and winced. The fangs and white eyes of a jaguar had been painted around the head/cockpit, adding to the menace the huge fighting machine represented.

"Star Captain, your call for one-on-one battle is refused. You yourself are here on a mission of questionable integrity and honor—coming to kill our officers only. Headhunter missions are no less unbefitting a true warrior. Surrender, and you will have a chance to fight again another day, and perhaps regain *your* lost honor."

"You do not fully understand the way of our Clan," Marilen said, even as her *Koshi* opened up with a laser blast from its left arm.

Several hot streams ate away at Loren's *Penetrator* replacement armor, digging deeply into the 'Mech's center torso as the big machine reeled under the hits, bending at the waist. "Engage!" he ordered. . . .

BATTLETECH®

IMPETUS OF WAR

Blaine Lee Pardoe

A ROC BOOK

ROC
Published by the Penguin Group
Penguin Books USA Inc., 375 Hudson Street,
New York, New York 10014, U.S.A.
Penguin Books Ltd, 27 Wrights Lane,
London W8 5TZ, England
Penguin Books Australia Ltd, Ringwood,
Victoria, Australia
Penguin Books Canada Ltd, 10 Alcorn Avenue,
Toronto, Ontario, Canada M4V 3B2
Penguin Books (N.Z.) Ltd, 182-190 Wairau Road,
Auckland 10, New Zealand

Penguin Books Ltd, Registered Offices:
Harmondsworth, Middlesex, England

First published by Roc, an imprint of Dutton Signet,
a division of Penguin Books USA Inc.

First Printing, December, 1996
10 9 8 7 6 5 4 3 2 1

Series Editor: Donna Ippolito
Cover art by Bruce Jensen
Mechanical Drawings: Duane Loose and the FASA art department

 REGISTERED TRADEMARK—MARCA REGISTRADA

BATTLETECH, FASA, and the distinctive BATTLETECH and FASA logos are
trademarks of the FASA Corporation, 1100 W. Cermak, Suite B305, Chicago, IL
60608.

Printed in the United States of America

To Victoria Rose, my loving daughter, for her inquisitive mind and loyalty to a father who spends far too much time in front of a PC. To Alexander William, my wonderful son, for the joy he has brought my life. To my beautiful and loving wife, Cyndi, for her love, devotion, patience, understanding, support, and everything in between. She's a wonderful woman, in this or any century, and I thank the great Kerensky every day that I found her.

The book is also dedicated to my parents, Dave and Rose, my grandparents, Corwin and Letha, not to mention Chris, Donnie, Jim, and Deb. I'll get the rest of the family in the next book.

Also to Daniel Plunkett for his numerous runs to Taco Bell. Bill Nemanick, thanks for the title, which came before the idea.

Finally, to Central Michigan University; the lads and lasses of Alpha Kappa Psi, Phi Chi Theta, Delta Gamma, the CM Life, and a million great memories therein. . . .

Special thanks to Donna Ippolito for her patience and to Sam Lewis, who helped hammer out a good story line—and for letting me make the Smoke Jaguars look *real* sinister.

Also thanks to the Virtual World Centers in Chicago and Dallas for letting me spend some time in the cockpit. And to the Virginia Rail Express, where most of this book was written on the daily hike into the District.

Finally, to all the BattleTech writers who help forge this universe with every book. Especially Bill Keith, who reminded me at GenCon just how much fun this really is.

When wars start, the devil makes more room in hell.

—A Germanic proverb

MAP OF WAYSIDE V

Seas

Forests

Mountains

Continents

Dried up Sea Floors

New Scotland Continent

McCormac Sea

Kearny Sea

Jaguar Base

Jaguar Air Ship

New Sherwood Petrified Forest

Takashi Straits

New Northwind Continent

Marion Sea

Kurita Prime Continent

LZ

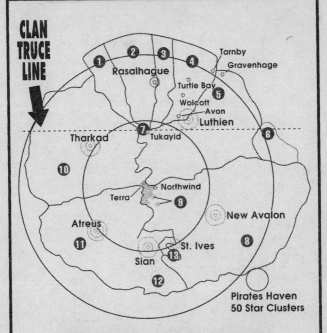

CLAN TRUCE LINE

Rasalhague

Tarnby
Gravenhage

Turtle Bay

Wolcott

Avon
Luthien

Tharkad

Tukayid

Northwind

Terra

New Avalon

Atreus

St. Ives

Sian

Pirates Haven
50 Star Clusters

MAP OF THE INNER SPHERE

1 • Jade Falcon/Steel Viper, 2 • Wolf Clan, 3 • Ghost Bear,
4 • Smoke Jaguars/Nova Cats, 5 • Draconis Combine,
6 • Outworlds Alliance, 7 • Free Rasalhague Republic,
8 • Federated Commonwealth, 9 • Chaos March,
10 • Lyran Alliance, 11 • Free Worlds League,
12 • Capellan Confederation, 13 • St. Ives Compact

Map Compiled by COMSTAR
From information provided by the COMSTAR EXPLORER SERVICE
and the STAR LEAGUE ARCHIVES on Terra

© 3058 COMSTAR CARTOGRAPHIC CORPS

Prologue

The Fort, Tara
Northwind
The Chaos March
30 April 3058

Major Loren Jaffray stood before the door leading to the office of his commanding officer, but gave his uniform a last once-over before raising his hand to knock. Crisp and correct, his drab green Highlander fatigues were pressed as carefully as any dress uniform, a matter of pride for Loren. He also meticulously removed his red beret, trademark of the Kilsyth Guards Battalion, and tucked it tightly under his left epaulette. Only then did he knock at the door of Colonel Andrea "Cat" Stirling's office here in The Fort, the massive complex that served as headquarters of the Northwind Highlanders on their homeworld.

The hard wood stung Loren's knuckles as it must have done to so many in the four centuries since the venerable oaken door had been hung. He looked both ways down the corridor and remembered the first time he'd seen these same halls upon arriving for the first time on Northwind, some eight months before. The place had seemed much larger then, even awe-inspiring. A moment later he heard a voice call for him to enter.

Andrea Stirling's office was as distinctive as those of the other three Colonels commanding the four regiments that made up the Northwind Highlanders. The images on her walls, captured field maps from battles and wars won and lost decades—even centuries—before seemed to set the tone for the feisty woman who led the Fusiliers that bore her name. Loren stepped in and snapped a salute while Colonel Stirling continued to study the two monitor screens before her. Still without lifting her gaze, she motioned for him to sit down.

Despite her youthful appearance, Andrea Stirling had a full twenty years on Loren's thirty-three. The jet black of his spiked crew cut was beginning to show some premature white, while hers was as dark as it must have been at his age. Loren tried to ignore such things, preferring not to acknowledge how feminine she was in her lean, tight way. He admired her greatly as an officer and a soldier. That seemed more than enough.

She finally pulled herself away from the screens and looked up at him. Like his, her eyes were green, her gaze sharp. "I was just going over today's reports," she said. "And I see you've got Craig's Battalion slated for underwater operations over the next forty-eight hours, is that correct?"

"Yes, sir." Loren kept his voice neutral, but he knew that she was really asking for a good reason why. "When it was just the militaries of the Inner Sphere fighting each other, we usually knew what to expect in battle, and we even honored certain rules of war. But now we've got the Clans hanging over our heads, and we can't assume anything about them. Truce or no truce, sooner or later we'll be going head to head with them again, and I say we'll never beat them unless we're ready for anything."

They'd had this discussion before, of course. Many times. Loren had studied every military report he could get his hands on concerning the Clan invasion of the Inner Sphere that began eight years before. He believed too many commanders viewed them as a monolithic force rather than studying the strengths, weaknesses, and idiosyncrasies of each of the seven invading Clans.

"You don't have to sell me on the threat of the Clans, Major. I've fought them before." Her tone was sharp.

"Then the Colonel understands that we might have to use any and all tactics, including underwater operations."

"Yes," she said slowly, as if gauging her words carefully.

Loren wondered if she had more on her mind than the Battalion's training program. "Is there a problem, sir?"

She looked at him hard with those green eyes for a moment before speaking. "Major—Loren . . ." The sudden shift to an informal tone caught him off guard. "You've been my Executive Officer for some eight months now, correct?"

"Yes, sir." *Only eight months?* Loren thought suddenly. Was that all? It seemed more like he'd spent his whole life among the Highlanders.

"Everyone knows you were a House Liao Death Commando before you joined us. And by now everyone knows that hasn't stood in the way of my appreciating your abilities, but some of my officers are still having a hard time accepting your authority."

How Loren Jaffray came to be standing here today wearing the rank and uniform of an officer of the Northwind Highlanders was no secret to anyone. He'd been raised by his grandfather, one of the Highlanders who had not come back to Northwind when Prince Hanse Davion of the Federated Suns returned the planet to the mercenary unit three decades before. In exchange, the Highlanders had agreed to work for him instead of Chancellor Maximilian Liao. They'd jumped their long-standing contract with Liao in the midst of the Fourth Succession War, abandoning the Capellan Confederation to the mercy of Davion's powerful armies.

His father had become a military man, too, a member of the elite corps known as the Death Commandos, a unit answerable only to the Capellan Chancellor himself and sworn to follow his orders to the death. It had been a secret Death Commando mission that had brought Loren to Northwind in the first place, though no one could ever have guessed the way it would turn out. Instead of destroying the Highlanders, which had been his mission, he'd ended up joining them and reassuming the Jaffray colors among the Highlander clans. Loren had fought alongside them for their independence against the Davions last fall, but he knew many Highlanders still didn't trust him. He'd overheard the remarks, the whispers, the rumors. *There are those don't understand, and never will, that one man's terrorist is another man's patriot.*

"I know some are still having trouble accepting me," he said wearily. "Only time will prove my honor and my loyalty. But I wonder if that's really why you called me in today?"

Cat Stirling gave a small shrug. "Let's talk about this training regimen you've set up. From what I can see, you've got the bulk of the Fusiliers in classrooms, running simulations, and even undergoing survival training. According to the schedule, you've got over thirty of my best MechWarriors slated for ten hours of hand-to-hand combat, demolitions, and pistol practice today alone."

Loren nodded slowly. "As your Executive Officer, I'm tasked with maintaining preparedness of the regiment, and that includes all training. If you don't approve of the program, Colonel, you've got the authority to order me to change it."

Cat Stirling shook her head sternly. "You're missing the point, Major. I don't necessarily want to change it. I just want to know what you're up to."

"You've read the reports I've compiled, seen the tactical database models, sir. It's only a matter of time before all or some of the Clans come at us again. If they decide to break the truce and drive straight for Terra, what happens then? The regiment's got to be ready." Loren had thought about this a lot. Northwind lay only one jump from Terra and now that the whole surrounding region had gone up for grabs, who knew what might be next? What had once been part of the Federated Commonwealth was so splintered that everyone had starting calling it the Chaos March.

"We're talking about training MechWarriors here, Major. Why all the survival skills and field tech classes? They got that kind of training years ago either at some academy or in basic."

Loren had been expecting this question ever since he'd started down the path he was blazing for the Fusiliers. "It's been years since most of these personnel have had to rely on those skills, Colonel, and many have forgotten them altogether. But from studying the Clans, I've seen that survival skills are exactly what Inner Sphere forces have often had to fall back on when facing them. We've seen the same scenario a number of times. A battle is fought, the Inner Sphere force is injured or crippled but survives. They're forced to go to ground as guerrillas until relief arrives or they can be evacuated." Loren had devoured every existing report, and they told a chilling story.

"Prior to the start of my reorganization, we were geared to fight standard Inner Sphere units—warriors with the same training and beliefs as ours. But what I've been doing is training our people for survival in every possible kind of environment I can imagine. I've also increased our repair-parts supplies and cross-trained everyone in field-combat repairs, so we'll be able to keep our BattleMechs operational if we're ever forced to operate as a guerrilla force. And I've been re-fitting our weapons in favor of energy-based types to reduce dependence on systems that require reloading. If we lose our 'Mechs, our people can still fight as infantry—if we must."

"Ah, yes, your overhaul of the Fusiliers' technical element," Stirling said, pulling several sheets of hardcopy from a file on her desk and scanning them. "I'd be the last to disagree that the regiment runs on its technicians. But you've also got to realize that there's resistance to change, even when change is good. Your promotion of Mitchell Fraser to Regimental Technical Chief, for example."

"You approved that promotion, sir."

"Yes. I've known Mitch and his family for years. Hell, at some point we trace back to the same Scots blood. He's good. But coupled with your other innovations, some of our officers are questioning why. The same could be said of Lovat's posting as the new Regimental Intelligence Officer. Both men are excellent at what they do, but this regiment is centuries old. The established officers don't understand the need for so much change so fast."

Loren found himself biting his lip, holding back his words. *On one hand she approves everything I've done, yet now she questions the changes. Mitch Fraser was an ideal choice—a tinkerer to the point of genius. And Lovat knows more about intelligence than some of the best black ops people in the Death Commandos.*

Cat Stirling gave him a thin smile. "Don't think I don't understand. An XO has to have people who're loyal to his way of thinking and acting, and I know both Fraser and Lovat are both that for you. It wasn't so different for me when I assumed command of the Fusiliers from McCormack six years ago. There was resistance to the changes I wanted to make even though I spaced them out over several years. I agree with your analysis of the Clan threat, and that's why I've approved your innovations. The Truce of Tukayyid doesn't look like it's going to hold a full fifteen years. The real question is whether we're simply pressing too hard too fast."

"Have there been complaints, sir?" It was a risky question, but Loren had to ask.

Stirling did not waver. "There have."

Loren didn't even have to guess where they'd come from.

It had to be Majors Cullen Craig and Kurt Blakadar, and probably some of the others in their ranks. The techs he already knew about, but at least they understood the need to go through proper channels.

"I apologize that my officers haven't followed the proper chain of command in raising such matters, sir." Where Loren came from, such infractions would never have been tolerated. And even now among the feisty Highlanders he experienced it as an embarrassment.

"I can see that you're upset, Major, but remember this. Here in the Highlanders we are family first. This was not a breach of protocol; independent thinking is encouraged within our ranks. That door"—she pointed to the one through which he'd come—"is always open to those in the regiment."

"Understood, sir," Loren reined his feelings and drew another deep breath. There was more to this than him being a former Death Commando or pushing those in his command too hard. *It's time we cleared the air, time she heard it said out loud.* "Sir, permission to speak freely."

"Granted, Major."

"Major MacFranklin was your Executive Officer for six years prior to my assuming this position. I don't run the regiment the way he did, and that's what these complaints are about—you and I know it. He was an apt tactician and 'Mech pilot, but he depended too much on favoritism, family connections, and other kinds of politicking. I mean him no discredit, Colonel, but I'm different. I think the Fusiliers are too good for that."

Cat Stirling stared at Loren with an unreadable expression for a moment. "I know that, Major. That's one of the reasons I wanted you as my exec instead of promoting Craig or Blakadar. Everyone was impressed with you in the fight for Tara last fall. MacFranklin, God rest his soul, was definitely becoming a problem. He was a fine commander on the field, but he had so many scams running behind the scenes it was a miracle he didn't spend his life in the brig."

"You knew then?"

She smiled like a cat. "Of course. No matter what, never forget that I am in command. If MacFranklin hadn't died, he'd have been busted out. You were the right person at the right time. Some of the old-guard officers want things the way they used to be, more of a free hand, less focus. Favoritism rather than performance.

"We both know one thing; the Clans are *the* threat. I can read a map too. If they ever manage to drive all the way to Terra, we're only a short jump away."

Stirling smiled even more broadly. "Never assume anything with me, Major. They don't call me 'Cat' because I'm a fool. On the other hand, I don't want to exhaust our forces in training and preparing. I need to confirm that your plan is moving at the right pace to make this the hardest-ass outfit in the Highlanders, not a bunch of burn-outs."

"There's only one way I know of to test the mettle of a MechWarrior, Colonel," Loren said.

Andrea Stirling nodded in agreement. "Yes, on the field of combat. And that's why I'm proposing a test of your training program. Bill MacLeod has agreed to run a test between his command battalion and ours. The Highlanders are expecting a visit from a potential employer any day now. I want that visitor to see what stuff we're made of."

"This potential employer, will they have an interest in our anti-Clan tactics?"

Cat Stirling nodded once, slowly and carefully. "You could say that. The Draconis Combine has weathered the brunt of the Clan invasion, and the bastards are still poised over their heads like an executioner's axe.

"For the first time ever, Major, the Northwind Highlanders are considering an offer of a contract with the Combine. Theodore Kurita wants to take the fight right to the doorstep of the Clans, but he's going to need a lot of help doing it."

BOOK I

Visions

An empire founded by war has to maintain itself by war.

—Montesquieu

There is no victory except through our imaginations.

—Dwight D. Eisenhower

═══ 1 ═══

Horne Plains
Avon
Smoke Jaguar/Nova Cat Occupation Zone
1 May 3058

Star Colonel Devon Osis cut a path through the wind-whipped grass of the Horne Plains, crushing reed-like, meter-tall grasses with each step. Before him was the tent of the Khan of the Smoke Jaguars, and beyond that he saw the sky reddening as Avon's sun slowly sank from view. Also visible on the horizon were the menacing outlines of two Stars' worth of the Jaguars' most fearsome weapons, their Omni-Mechs. Each one of the ten-meter-tall war machines bristled with pod-mounted weapons, though from here they looked more like statues silhouetted against the dying light, sentinels guarding the vast plains from a foe nowhere to be seen.

When Devon Osis had first arrived on Avon, the sight had been a splendor to him. Now it only reminded him that he was a warrior without a war. Continuing on to the tent's far end, he pulled open the flap to enter. Dominating the space within was a portable holographic projection table. On it was a green-lit projection of the plains Devon Osis had just spent the last half-hour crossing. Standing at the table was the unmistakable figure of Lincoln Osis, Khan of the Smoke Jaguars. He rested his black-skinned hands wide on the edge of the table as he leaned over the projected display.

The Khan's long face was as serious as ever in the gloom as he looked up at his visitor, those hard, dark eyes seeming to burn with some deep inner fire. Despite the losses and humiliation the Jaguars had suffered in the monumental battles of Luthien and Tukayyid, Lincoln Osis had prevailed and with him the spirit of the Smoke Jaguars. He had taught his warriors that survival was the key to victory. That was why Devon saw his Khan as the leader who would carry their Clan on to a greater future—one where the Smoke Jaguars dominated not only the other Clans, but the whole of the Inner Sphere as well.

Star Colonel Devon Osis stood at attention while the Khan continued to study the table. The holographic image showed the placement of the OmniMechs seen in the distance as well as their opponents at the other end of the table.

"My Khan," Devon said in a crisp military voice, dipping his head in reverence.

"These sibkos are preparing yet another drill." Khan Osis spoke tersely, almost angrily. "They lack boldness in their bidding."

Devon looked over at the holographic table and nodded, not fully understanding. Lincoln Osis shot him a look. "Time is our greatest enemy these days," he said, half-under his breath. "A greater foe than any of our fellow Clans are willing to admit. It hangs about our necks like a hangman's noose, getting tighter with each passing day." Devon Osis could not tell whether the Khan was addressing him or talking to himself.

"Heed my words, Devon, it is not a treaty line that holds us in place, it is time. In the end, time is the enemy we must defeat."

Devon nodded. "What is your command of me?"

"You remember our discussion of the Tau Galaxy a while back, quiaff?"

"Aff. They were months from being ready, as I recall," Devon said. The discussion was one he remembered well for the handful of secrets the Khan had opened to him. Forged on the Jaguar homeworld of Huntress, Tau Galaxy was a newly formed unit. Its warriors were much-needed truebirth replacements, engineered from the best of the Smoke Jaguar genetic heritage. And the formation of this new Galaxy was, for the most part, a secret.

"Like the hunting jaguar, we will stalk this enemy that is time, and defeat it. The Tau Galaxy is not just a dream, but a reality that is on its way to the Inner Sphere as we speak. It will give our Clan the savage bit needed to win eventual victory." The Khan's eyes glittered with battle-lust.

"Their arrival will mark a new era for the Smoke Jaguar," he went on. "The time has come to right the wrongs of the past. First, we were forced to share our invasion corridor with the Nova Cats, who promptly stole some of our worlds. Then we lost many brave warriors at Tukayyid and again in the battle of Luthien. The Nova Cats held us back at Luthien, and now the Wolves try to prove that we are a weakened Clan and carry out attacks against our worlds. We must no longer be at the mercy of events, but take bold action. And the time for action is now."

Devon Osis nodded slightly, drinking in each word. The Tau Galaxy was fresh and powerful, the best of the Smoke Jaguar genetic legacy. Its arrival meant that the Draconis Combine and the rest of the Inner Sphere were ripe for the taking. All that separated the Clans from the prize of the Inner Sphere was the imaginary truce line at the planet Tukayyid, and that line became more blurred with each passing day. "The Combine worships the Dragon, but we will crush these barbarians like the paper tigers they are, and the path to Terra will be ours to take."

The Khan of the Smoke Jaguars bristled at the words. "Negative, Star Colonel. You must look beyond the Combine in your thoughts. Clan Nova Cat, that is our target. Ulric Kerensky hung them around our necks like an albatross. They stole our worlds, then their fighting manner cost us victory on Luthien. We have shouldered the burden of them for too long now. They were brought here to drain us, like a leech, so that when the time came to move, we would be too weak to seize Terra, too weak to assume our rightful destiny as the ilClan."

Devon knew that Lincoln Osis was right. Clan Nova Cat had been given the Smoke Jaguar assault corridor to share during the latter part of the invasion of the Inner Sphere. After stealing several worlds away from the Jaguars, they had dug themselves in. When the Treaty of Tukayyid did expire, they were poised to give the Smoke Jaguars a swift race toward Terra. Devon found himself admiring his Khan even more.

"We will crush the Nova Cats," he said, his blood beginning to race.

Lincoln Osis nodded. "The Tau Galaxy is fresh and from

the finest of our genetic pool. I have spared no expense to train and equip them with the best equipment our Clan possesses. They have been pawed and mauled hard, and have now been blooded by only the best." The words gave Devon a kind of thrill, almost like what he felt when Lincoln Osis put on the ceremonial mask and became the Jaguar himself.

The Khan placed his hands on Devon's shoulders. "You have tested to the rank of Galaxy Commander but have no Galaxy to command, Devon Osis. You have carried your old rank until a new unit was available. Now one is. I grant you the Tau Galaxy."

"I will not disappoint you, my Khan."

"There is no room for the failures of the past. The Wolves are frothing at our door, striking at us to regain the honor the Jade Falcons beat from them. The Falcons play games with their sibkos, trying to prove their strength. The Steel Vipers are coiled and prepared to strike at any moment. The Ghost Bears huddle in their caves, waiting and watching.

"And then there are the Nova Cats. They are a cancer on us, draining us of our strength." The Khan paused for a moment, his face contorted in disgust.

"Like freebirth mystics, they stare upward into the night, seeking counsel from whatever spirits they imagine reside there. They consult the seers and the stars to see their way. Tonight, when the Khan of the Cats looks into the night sky asking for a vision to guide him, he will see the Smoke Jaguar. You will be that Jaguar.

"Tau Galaxy will arrive shortly on our base at Wildcat. You will go there, and take command from Star Colonel Roberta, who has brought the Galaxy here from the homeworlds. Complete their training and draw up a strategy for making use of them. I will tell you when the time is right, and when it is—the Jaguar goes hunting once more."

The cool night breezes brushed against Star Colonel Santin West, but the heat of the roaring bonfire beat back the cold of Mount Neyzari as he sat huddled there under the dark skies of Tarnby. He shifted slightly, adjusting his stiff crossed legs as he stared into the roaring flames. He was not tall by Elemental standards, just under 2.5 meters when standing. His bleached white hair was cropped like a porcupine's quilled back, and despite the cold up here, he wore only shorts and the skin of a female Nova Cat around his shoulders. The deep circles under his eyes looked even darker in the flicker of the bonfire.

He stared into the flames and felt his body list slightly, then correct itself. It had been six days since he had last eaten, and at least forty-eight hours since he had slept. His strength was fading quickly, but as the Oathmaster assured him, this was the best way to catch a vision. The Rite of the Vision was one of the most honored and mysterious of the Clan Nova Cat rituals, and he did not want to fail—again.

Santin West's previous attempts at the Rite seemed like a lifetime ago in his mind. One had come after Luthien, when he had hoped to learn what the future might hold. But no vision had come. Then came the bloodbath of Tukayyid. The death of sibkin who had grown up with him and survived the grueling warrior training of their sibko had hurt him in ways he still did not totally understand.

This time was different for him. He lusted to know the future—not just for himself but for the Clan as a whole. The past could not be changed. But to see into the mists of what was yet to be could give his people power to shape the present.

His eyes wandered down to the small pile of relics in front of him. These were his *vineers,* mementos of battles past. Each Nova Cat warrior kept such relics of great battles in which he or she had taken part. Usually they were stored in a leather pouch and worn only during ceremonies, but the Rite of the Vision demanded that the vineers be sacrificed to the flames. They were not mere trinkets; each one served as a spiritual focus for a warrior, preserving a memory and, more important, the reason the memory was important. To a Nova Cat, the vineer was topped in importance only by the codex bracelet that carried his or her official service record and everything else of importance, down to the warrior's DNA code. The difference was simple. The codex was an official record, the vineer carried that which was personal and beyond record.

Santin West saw the small piece of Elemental armor he had taken from his final opponent the day he had won his Bloodname. It was twisted and mauled, recalling the joy he had felt at winning the contest. There was also a torn bandanna, a relic of the warrior he had bested in the Trial of Position for the rank of Star Captain. Next to it, he saw the small finger broken off his first Elemental suit during the

Trial of Position that had earned him the rank of Star
Colonel.

There was also a thin strand of myomer cable, the material
that served as the "muscle" of a BattleMech. Looking at it,
he remembered the battle on Caripace and the fight the Combine MechWarrior had given him. There were also pieces of
cockpit glass among his vineers, each taken from other opponents he had bested during the invasion.

Also among the vineers was an earring, charred black and
half-melted. Santin West had taken it from a Kell Hound
when his own unit was destroyed in the Kadoguchi Valley
during the fight for Luthien. But he felt no shame for that
battle despite the loss of his comrades. They had fought well,
meeting death just as he hoped to one day, fighting to the end
and beyond. Such was the way of warriors.

There was one icon in the pile of vineers that seemed to
stand out. The patch showed the ComStar logo and the golden
and white symbols of the 244th Division. *Tukayyid.* He had
been there, and this was his link to that battle. Seeing the
wrinkled patch, burned slightly on one edge, brought back the
roar of the autocannon and the shrieks of battle as he remembered the slaughter.

Santin looked up from the vineers, his mind still lost in
memories of the past. The Oathmaster was standing next to
him. She sprinkled a white powder into the flames, then
added several hardwood logs. The powder crystals flashed
brilliant green, blue, and blood red in the flames. Oathmaster
Biccon Winters dropped several pellets into the roaring
flames as well. These were incense, and their heady aroma
seized and held Santin West's senses. The logs, some still
holding moisture, popped and sent sparks into the night air.

His eyes moved to the source of the raging bonfire, and he
fixed his gaze on the glowing orange coals at the base of the
fire. Spotted black with carbon from their burning, the embers
seemed to shimmer with radiating heat. Continuing to stare at
them, he felt a sense of vertigo, but could not tell whether he
was falling or being pulled into the heart of the fire.

In the glowing embers he saw a dark shape. As he held it
with his gaze, it seemed to take form, becoming a pouncing
cat. Santin West's eyes were wide with excitement as he
stared at it. Following the outline of the cat, he began to see
another yellowish-orange figure appear among the coals.
Again, he saw a hunting cat, this one seemingly in mid-leap.

From the bottom-most layer of the coals he saw yet another outline—this time only the head of a cat—come into focus. The three images shimmered in the waves of heat rising from the fire, all seeming as real as if they were alive.

Suddenly the logs shifted and dropped down over the embers. The movement and the sound shattered his concentration for a moment, and when his eyes blinked open again he saw that one of the images had been destroyed by the slight cascade of logs in the fire. The first dark shape remained, but it did not seem to be fighting, only standing. The other, the cat's head, was undamaged but now seemed to change before his eyes. Santin's breath raced, his heart throbbing like a horse in mid-race, yet he was unable to move, suspended in time and space before the fire.

The cat's head seemed to darken and take on the visage of a grinning skull. It bowed to him, as if offering a concession. Santin West reached out for it, but the logs shifted again, this time destroying the cat's skull that had grinned so devilishly at him. He dropped his hand back to his knee and shook his head softly.

"You had a vision, Santin West, aff?" a voice asked from beyond his field of vision. He knew it to be Biccon Winters, Oathmaster of the Nova Cats and warden of the Rite. Her voice gave away a touch of envy.

"Aff," he said in a barely audible tone, his eyes still glassy and fixed on the flames in hopes the vision would return.

"Excellent. This is your fourth attempt, Star Colonel. I congratulate you. Many who undertake the rite never fully meet their goal. We Nova Cats understand the value of such visions. Ever since our founder, Nicholas Kerensky, had the vision that led to our genesis as a people, only the Nova Cat warriors still undertake such quests. It is both a link to our past and a bridge to our future."

Santin West felt lightheaded, his stomach aching and his muscles yearning to stretch. "My vision—it was . . ." His words trailed off as his mind sought to explain what he had seen.

The hand of the Oathmaster came to rest on his shoulder. "I am the keeper of the rede for our people and the warden of this rite. A vision is sacred, and often will reveal its meaning only with the passage of time."

Santin shifted and uncrossed his legs. For the first time the cool of the night air seemed to sting him as he moved. "You

do not understand. I must comprehend what I have seen."
His mind danced with the image that already seemed to be
fading from his memory. *The two cats entangled, that I
understand. The Smoke Jaguars and Nova Cats have been at
each other's throats for centuries. But I saw another, one
that became a death mask, the one that bowed to me. The two
warring cats were crushed and all that was left was the
death-grin of the third. I must understand what I saw. Is this
my future, or that of my Clan?*

Oathmaster Winters shook her head. "Neg, Star Colonel.
Nicholas Kerensky and the founder of our Clan, Khan San-
dra Rosse, both taught us to wait with patience as the meaning of a vision gradually unfolds. Let your understanding
ripen, and then we will talk more of this. If what you have
seen is a portent of our future, I will make the Khans aware
of it. Such is my duty and honor."

Santin West rose to his feet slowly and wobbled. At
that moment the days and nights of fasting and concentration caught up with him. He took one feeble step, then suddenly collapsed at the feet of Oathmaster Winters. West lay
sprawled out over his prized vineers, passed out from exhaustion and exertion.

2

Hall of Warriors, The Fort
Tara, Northwind
The Chaos March
2 May 3058

The Assembly Hall of Clan Elders was the chief government
building in Tara, and the heart and soul of Northwind's planetary government. Despite the fact that the Highlanders were
only a fraction of the planet's population, they were
the only real power and authority on the world. That was even
more true now that the Highlanders had won this planet away
from the Prince Victor Davion and the Federated Commonwealth.

Set in the center of Tara, the Assembly Hall was part of a whole complex of buildings that had been known as The Fort ever since the Highlanders had come back to Northwind in 3028. The returning elders had declared that they would defend their beloved planet from the fortress of these walls against any and all who threatened.

Once a year the elders of Tara and all the chiefs from the outlying provinces met in High Assembly to decide matters of planetary importance, but the day-to-day decisions were made by various sub-assemblies. The largest, and most prestigious, of these was the Assembly of Warriors, which was charged with governing the Highlanders' military. Composed of exactly one hundred proven Highlander soldiers, the Assembly of Warriors was the cornerstone of Northwind.

Unlike the rest of The Fort, the U-shaped Hall of Warriors was constructed of wood. At one end was an elevated platform with a table for the four Colonels commanding the four regiments of the Highlanders. Flanking the platform, the one hundred warriors sat at solid oak tables equipped with computer terminals and other sophisticated equipment. Most wore the traditional kilts and heavy boots favored by Mech-Warriors and aerospace pilots. Dress uniforms were considered inappropriate for the Assembly of Warriors.

The lighting built into the walls was dim but adequate as Loren descended the few steps leading down to the sod floor of the chamber. All around him other members of the Assembly were also filing in and finding their places on the wooden benches behind the tables. In addition to a monitor, each seat had access to high-speed communications arrays for accessing presentation data as well as casting votes on matters brought before the Assembly. Right now the displays were blank.

Loren sat down and adjusted the woolen tartan kilt around his legs. Wearing it had been the thing hardest to get used to since joining the Highlanders. The rich wool of the kilt often made his legs itch during stuffy formal occasions such as long meetings, and worse was the fact that the traditional uniform did not call for undergarments. The black shirt had long tails that could be tied in the crotch for some degree of "support," but the sensation was drafty, and always would be uncomfortable.

He caught sight of Chastity Mulvaney looking around for

a seat. "Major Mulvaney," Loren said, smiling and gesturing for her to take the empty place next to him.

She walked up, then stood there for a moment, arms crossed over her chest, narrowing her eyes slightly. "Don't be so smug, Loren. I've seen the regimental combat assessment. You won, I lost. Let it drop or I'll drop it for you."

Theirs had been a love/hate relationship from the start, and that hadn't changed over time. She was the perfect match for Loren, both on and off the field of battle. His command battalion had beaten hers in the recent exercise between the Kilsyth Guards and MacLeod's Regiment, but that didn't mean she wouldn't beat him next time. *Some things defy words. I don't have to tell her how I feel, she knows it. Just like I know her feelings.*

Loren shrugged, but before he could say anything more their attention was drawn by the arrival of the commanding officers of the Northwind Highlanders. As the four Colonels filed in, Loren thought how different each one was from the rest. Where MacLeod's Regiment was known for its wildness and recklessness, Colonel Edward Senn's First Kearny Regiment had a reputation for conservative stubbornness. Loren smiled to himself, thinking of his time as one of MacLeod's "Bad Boys" in the recent battle for Tara. The Second Kearny, under the stone-faced Colonel James D. Cochraine, was considered the most impassioned of the regiments, often rushing into battle more on emotion than common sense. Colonel Andrea Stirling had been raised in that unit before taking command of the Fusiliers from Henrietta McCormack. It was Stirling's cunning and inventiveness on the battlefield that had earned her regiment the same reputation.

The four proceeded in single file to the commander's table, then turned to face the gathered warriors, who instantly stood, snapping to attention. Loren felt a rush, a slight pounding in his ears, the kind of warm pride he used to feel when in the presence of the Chancellor.

"As you were," Colonel Senn said. As commander of the senior regiment of the Northwind Highlanders, Senn presided over the Assembly of Warriors when not on active duty.

As all took their seats, Senn waited for the sounds to die down before speaking again. "I remind you all that the proceedings of this Assembly are sealed by covenant, and since this is the formal opening of contract negotiations, you are all bound by the security accords of the Mercenary Review and Bonding Commission."

All four Highlander regiments were currently on Northwind because the unit had not been taking assignments while trying to rebuild after losing almost a full regiment's worth of troops in the fighting with the Davions. Colonel James D. Cochraine had taken a seat at the far left of the table. Next to him was Colonel William MacLeod. Then came Colonel Senn, and finally the seat on the far right was occupied by Loren's own Colonel Stirling.

"Sergeant at Arms," Colonel Senn said to the Warrant Officer who stood at the door. The man opened the door, admitting three people all dressed in their most formal garb.

"Welcome, honored guests," Senn said and motioned the group forward.

Of the three emissaries, the obvious leader was a female of medium height, wearing a blue and green silk kimono. She moved with an air of regal grace, her shining black hair drawn back from her pale skin in a style that was at once severe yet elegant.

Loren recognized her instantly. *Omi Kurita.* Daughter of Coordinator Theodore Kurita of the Draconis Combine. Her presence on Northwind was an unofficial acknowledgement of the planet's newly won independence. As she gracefully took the steps leading to the platform where the Colonels sat, Loren studied the other two dignitaries. One wore the white uniform of a Combine MechWarrior, her stature and regal posture falling just short of Omi's The rank insignia on her uniform collar marked her as a *Sho-sa,* the DCMS equivalent of Loren's own rank of Major. The brilliant blue emblem on her shoulder told more of the story—it was the raging tidal wave of the Genyosha Regiment.

Loren didn't need the Warrant Officer's introduction to also recognize the second woman instantly, though for a very different reason. Anyone who'd ever studied the Battle of Luthien in which the Combine military and some of the Inner Sphere's best mercs had defeated a Clan attempt to capture the Combine's capital world would know that this was Ruth Horner.

Loren had found her writings on Clan tactics eye-opening, and he thought her book and other papers could easily serve as a bible for field officers. Six years ago on Luthien she'd been a *Tai-i* in the Genyosha and had led a stunning raid against the Smoke Jaguars in the Waseda Hills outside of Luthien. Loren only hoped he could do as well when his time came.

The third figure wore a gray jumpsuit bearing the star symbol of ComStar on her left chest, over the heart. The piping on her rounded collar showed the insignia of the Com Guards and the rank of Precentor. The Warrant Officer introduced her as Precenter Mercedes Laurent of the Explorer Corps as she also took her place on the stage.

Loren leaned over and spoke in a whisper to Chastity. "Omi Kurita, here, on Northwind. This has to be something important, something really big." A few short years ago, before the Clans arrived, it would have been unthinkable for a member of the Combine's ruling house to show his or her face on Northwind, a world the Combine had attacked and tried to take during the Fourth Succession War. Times had indeed changed, and with them, the Highlanders as well.

Chastity nodded. "They asked to meet with us here rather than on Outreach." Outreach was the world where mercenaries arrived from near and far seeking employment under the official auspices of the Mercenary Review and Bonding Commission. It was also the home of Wolf's Dragoons, the famous mercenaries who'd once been Clansmen and who'd tried to teach the militaries of the Inner Sphere how to fight the seemingly invincible invaders. That Theodore Kurita had bypassed the usual hiring procedures and channels was noteworthy.

Omi stood with hands at her side, her posture erect yet somehow relaxed. She let her gaze travel around the room, then brought it back to the table of Colonels. "Members of the Northwind Highlanders and esteemed commanders of the unit, I bring you warm greetings from Coordinator Theodore Kurita of the Draconis Combine."

"Thank you, Kurita Omi-*sama*," said Colonel Cochraine. "This is the first time the Assembly of Warriors has ever entertained a representative of the Combine, and your presence and purpose here surely signal the beginning of a new era in relations between our peoples. We are honored to have a visitor of such distinction as our guest on Northwind."

Loren knew there was much in the Colonel's words. Only recently had Northwind finally managed to gain its full independence from the Federated Commonwealth, though it was not clear whether Victor Davion acknowledged that status or not. This visit by Omi Kurita gave validity to their independence, even if it was not an official recognition.

The Federated Commonwealth—whatever was left of it—and the Combine had buried the hatchet ever since deciding to join together against a common foe. Only a fool would believe that Theodore Kurita would send his daughter here to Northwind without first letting Prince Victor Davion know of his intent. Maybe Victor would overlook this breach of formal diplomatic channels taking place under his very nose because he knew it concerned a mission against the Clans.

"Colonel Senn, your words are welcomed by both myself and the Coordinator. I assure you that we do not view your newly won independence as a threat, but rather as an opportunity for us to know each other better." Omi spoke in controlled tones, carefully measuring each word.

"The Coordinator sends a gift to the Northwind Highlanders, a gesture of goodwill," she went on, beginning to unroll a bolt of cloth that *Sho-sa* Horner handed to her. The cloth was red and yellow and bordered with green. At the apex of the banner was a distinctive inverted triangle with the green outline of a bagpiper—the symbol of the First Kearny Regiment. As Omi Kurita lifted it high for all to see, it was obvious that it was a battle standard, a flag carried by a command post in the field. This one was old, faded and worn and torn in one corner.

"This battle standard was once carried by your First Kearny Regiment. During the battle of Lincoln in 2802 our forces managed to capture it. Winning a battle against the Northwind Highlanders was a matter of great pride for our troops. The Coordinator has asked that I return this to its rightful owners as a gesture of good faith from him personally and the people of the Draconis Combine. He also asked me to give you this message: May we never again face each other across a field of battle, but stand together against our common foe. We are both people who appreciate honor among warriors. Please accept this in the name of that honor."

"A common foe . . ." The Clans.

Colonel Senn rose from his seat and walked, slowly and methodically to where the Coordinator's daughter stood. It was his regiment that had lost the standard in the fighting on Lincoln centuries before his birth. He took the antique banner and folded it with great reverence over one arm, then stood looking at Omi Kurita for a long moment, unmoving, unspeaking. When he finally reached out to bow and kiss the young woman's fingers, the gathered warriors let out a spontaneous roar of applause. Loren joined in, as did Mulvaney.

The clapping subsided as Colonel Senn returned to his seat, laying the banner carefully out in front of him as if it were a holy relic. "On behalf of the Northwind Highlanders, please express our deepest thanks to the Coordinator for this gift. We accept it in the name of those who have gone before us, in honor not only of the warriors of Highlander blood, but those honorable samurai of the Draconis Combine."

It was Colonel Stirling who broke the formality of the proceedings. She was well-known for playing the role of rebel, wild and unpredictable. "I honor the gift ye've brought to us," she said, her Scots burr suddenly more evident than usual. "You have brought something else of interest to this esteemed Assembly, though. You came to discuss a contract, did ye not?"

Loren smiled to himself. *She is indeed a cat through and through. She uses her accent when it suits her needs, to keep her victims always wondering just who they're facing.*

Omi smiled slightly too as if acknowledging something she had heard about Stirling's boldness. "Yes, Colonel Stirling, I have brought an offer of contract for the Northwind Highlanders. *Sho-sa* Horner of the Genyosha will go over the mission specifics." She handed a small optical laser disk to Colonel Stirling who slipped it into the arm of her chair. Then Omi Kurita stepped aside as Horner came forward. On the table monitors in front of each officer, maps and displays came up for them to scroll through.

"As you probably know, the Coordinator has been working with ComStar's Explorer Corps, hoping to locate the homeworlds of the Clans." Ruth Horner glanced over at the ComStar Precentor, who nodded in confirmation. It was really no secret that Theodore Kurita's one and only aim was to beat the Clans.

"That is how we came to identify the planet I have come to talk to you about today. Its name is Wayside V. Planetary topographical data is coming up on your screens now."

The faces of many showed puzzlement when Horner spoke the world's name. *Wayside?* Loren thought he'd studied virtually every world in the Inner Sphere, but this was not one he'd ever heard of. Judging by the expressions of those around him, he wasn't the only one.

Sho-sa Horner read their faces and quickly explained. "I realize that none of you has ever heard of Wayside V. That's because the planet is not in the Inner Sphere. The mission I come to offer you today is a chance to take the fight to the Clans themselves."

A long silence followed that announcement until Colonel MacLeod shattered it with a question directed at Mercedes Laurent. "What is ComStar's position in all this, Precentor? It was ComStar that negotiated the Treaty of Tukayyid that's supposed to keep us and the Clans from attacking each other for fifteen years. The Highlanders don't want to be party to anything that would spark a new war with the Clans."

"A good question, Colonel," the Precentor said. "But Wayside V is not in the Clan Occupation Zone here in the Inner Sphere. It is a Clan holding in the Deep Periphery. I have been authorized to turn over all Explorer Corps data gathered on this world, as well as mappings of jump points to and from the system."

Her words explained much to Loren about why none of this was happening on Outreach. Such an important mission was not the kind of thing either Theodore Kurita or his ComStar associates would want leaked. Using the table-monitor controls he quickly found a star map showing the location of the world, weeks by JumpShip from even the most remote world in the Combine.

Ruth Horner was speaking again as he brought the map into focus. "Wayside V is apparently a Smoke Jaguar supply base, and one we suspect might be part of the route back to the Clan homeworlds. The contract I offer is for a regiment of Highlanders to lead an assault on Wayside, plus one relief battalion for garrison duties once the mission is achieved. The goal is to engage and destroy the Clan force there and claim the planet for the Draconis Combine."

A buzz of commentary immediately rose up among the gathered warriors, but Colonel Senn broke through the murmurs with his own crisp voice. "You are asking us to seize an uncolonized world that no known person in the Inner Sphere has even visited before, is that correct?"

Everyone understood only too well what he was saying. For the past three centuries the Highlanders had fought all their battles on planets that had been mapped thousands of times, with dangers and hazards all known and understood, right down to the weather patterns.

Sho-sa Horner smiled. "That's right," she said. "From the satellite recons we and the Explorer Corps have been running, we know the Jaguars have set up structures that undoubtedly serve as warehouses for supplies. Hitting this planet and taking it from them is important to the Combine. For one thing, it would force the Jaguars to divert resources into setting up another supply base. And every Clan unit involved in such activity is one less sitting poised to strike along our border."

Horner took a step forward as though to impress her listeners with the urgency of her words. "The Combine has lost many worlds to the Clan invasion. Thus far we have fought on our own worlds to regain them. This would be different. We would be taking the fight to the Clans, taking back one of their planets. This Wayside V may or may not be of major importance to their overall operations, but taking something they claim would have a profound effect on our people."

Loren knew she was right. Wayside V could serve as a glimmer of hope, a rallying point. Such symbolic victories were often as crucial as major military ones.

"From data gathered by the Explorer Corps, the planet seems to house a single Provisional Garrison Cluster. As you can see, our computers have tagged the 'Mechs present as second-line Clan models. No OmniMechs and no aerospace elements were detected."

"You're proposing to send in quite an army to take on one second-line Clan cluster, are ye not?" Colonel Stirling asked.

Horner nodded firmly. "Going in with a full combat regiment and reinforcing it afterward with a battalion is our only hope of taking the world, given the age of our intelligence. If we fail in the first attempt, the Jaguars will simply increase the size of their garrison. We would never get another chance."

Loren looked at the data. The 'Mechs were older Clan models. That didn't mean they weren't every bit as deadly, but they wouldn't be the top-of-the-line 'Mechs the Clans deployed in their front-line units. His eyes shifted to the overlay maps of Wayside V, his eyes widening in disbelief. *This information has to be wrong, no world is laid out this way.*

Ruth Horner was still talking. "The terrain of Wayside poses a challenge of its own, as I'm sure some of you have already noted. At one time in its history it suffered a meteor or comet strike that stripped away the upper atmosphere to almost nothing. The continents themselves were laid waste and are very cold, oxygen-less environments still.

"The former ocean floors became the only places capable of supporting life. When their water levels plummeted, the continental surfaces became uninhabitable. Only the deepest parts of the former ocean beds still contain water; the rest of the former sea bottoms represent the only habitable areas. The Jaguars have set up their operations in one of these former ocean on the shore of one of the few water bodies that still exist on the planet."

Mulvaney leaned forward and whispered into Loren's ear as he stared at the display. "The damn place is upside down. 'Mechs could operate on those airless continents, but all it would take is one cockpit hit and you'd be toast in a matter of minutes."

"Fighting there will be *unique,* to say the least," Loren whispered back.

"A masterpiece of understatement," Mulvaney said.

3

The Fort
Tara, Northwind
The Chaos March
13 May 3058

Loren Jaffray shuffled through some of the hardcopy reports he had spread out on a back corner table of The Pub that had unofficially become his office. The small Pub, which also served as the Officer's Club for the Highlanders, was one of the places in The Fort where he felt most at ease. The dark wood panelling and timeworn furnishings gave him a sense of warmth and comfort, perhaps because it was here that he'd first understood his true place within the Highlanders. And as much as the Pub was an icon in the hearts and minds of the Highlanders, her bartender was an icon of the Pub.

Mr. Pluncket brought over a pint of Northwind Red Ale, limping heavily on his artificial leg. So engrossed was Loren in his work that he only looked up when he sensed the ageless bartender and former Sergeant Major looking over his shoulder at the reports he was studying.

"We've known each other fer a while, haven't we, laddie?" Pluncket said.

"Yes, Mr. Pluncket, that we have. You're one of the first people I met when I came to Northwind." Loren knew this was leading somewhere.

"And we are friends, true enough?"

Loren nodded. The two had fought side by side against the Davions, in the process also saving the lives of many in both MacLeod's and Stirling's regiments. "Yes, you're one of the handful of people I can call friend."

"Perhaps you can tell me then, one friend to another, what in the name of St. Richard's ghost is goin' on around here?" Pluncket threw up his hands in frustration.

Loren smiled and shook his head. Sergeant Major Pluncket was the self-appointed internal intelligence officer for the Northwind Highlanders—a gossip. He kept his ears tuned for anything and everything. The injuries that kept him from active duty only made him all the more hungry for information. "I'm not sure what you're referring to, Mr. Pluncket," Loren said, all innocence.

"You know bloody well what I'm talking about. The spaceport is sealed up tighter than a drum of toxic waste. The Assembly building has double the normal guards, and even the local media wags are being kept outside the gate. Security people—not ours, but strangers—have been seen even inside the Fort. But everybody's lips are buttoned up even though I know the Assembly has been holed up in debate. I think there's some sort of contract negotiation going on, and I want to know who it's with."

Loren understood Mr. Pluncket's frustration, but he couldn't violate the sanctity of the Warrior's Assembly, not even for a friend. "Mr. Pluncket, sometimes security is necessary, you know that. And maybe you're reading too much into a few coincidences." The truth of the matter was that the Assembly had completed its deliberations over the contract with the Combine, and the question had passed to the Highlander regimental officers for final recommendation.

Once the decision was reached to proceed formally with

the talks, each of the four regimental commanders had weighed the pros and cons of his or her unit taking the contract. The First and Second Kearny Regiments were the freshest of the Highlanders, not having engaged in combat for over a year. MacLeod's Regiment had been badly mauled during Northwind's brief fight for independence from the Federated Commonwealth. Stirling's Fusiliers had also been hit hard in the fighting. Both had taken several months to rebuild, stepping up recruitment and using the fallen FedCom booty 'Mechs as a source of resupply. Theoretically, any of the four regiments was up to taking on the mission, but Loren was sure that MacLeod's would not be in the running. It was still too early for them to accept any contracts other than relief or garrison duty, not until their new recruits had more time to become integrated into the regiment. So it was between the two Kearny regiments and the Fusiliers.

"It'd better not be any of these little crap governments springing up in the Chaos March," Plunckett fired off, still fishing for some clue. The recent split of the Federated Commonwealth and the brief war with Houses Marik and Liao had left the former Sarna March a hotbed of independent worlds, each struggling to retain some identity and to survive attempts by the various factions to seize them—either overtly or covertly. Plunckett was expressing an opinion that many Highlanders felt. It was better to stay out of the petty dirty fighting that was going on. The Highlander regiments had a long and glorious reputation of service—and they preferred to win honor by serving one of the large House governments.

"Sergeant Major, I think I can safely say, without violating security, that none of us is going to be shipping out to the Chaos March," Loren told him.

Sergeant Major Plunckett leaned down over the table as Loren covered up the logistics planning sheets he'd been working on. "Laddie, you can tell me. Who are you officers entertaining up there in the Assembly?" So intent was he on being conspiratorial that he never noticed the figure moving silently up behind him from the rear of the dimly lit Pub.

"Perhaps," the figure said, "you should ask me, bartender." Plunckett spun at the sound of the voice that he must have recognized instantly as that of Colonel Andrea Stirling. Loren suppressed a smile at the sight of the portly bartender flushing beet red but trying mightily to recover. "Colonel Stirling, sir, I didna see ya enter, lass."

"I came in the back door," Cat Stirling said, sliding into the seat between him and her Executive Officer. "Colonel's prerogative," she added, a bit acidly. "Now then, I need a few minutes alone with my XO. Regimental business." Plunckett bowed his head in acknowledgment and backed away from the two of them. Stirling did not lift her gaze from the man until he was out of earshot, then she turned to Loren.

"Remind me sometime to tell you how he lost his leg," she said. "But for now, let me ask you what you think about the contract we've been offered."

"Colonel, more than anything else, I want to go up against the Clans and beat them in battle."

Stirling smiled. "That bad?"

Loren only nodded in response, once, slowly.

"Me too. You want this job to test the training program you've put together. And I want it to test my troops in a fight after all the rebuilding."

Loren nodded. "To be frank, Colonel, I also want this for personal reasons that are beyond the training and simulation missions we've been running."

"Having a hard time adapting to life as a Highlander, Major?"

"At times, yes. There are those who still see me as a Capellan officer first despite everything that's happened since I first came to Northwind. Then there's the politics of running a regiment. Politics has never been my forte. But let me loose on a battlefield in the cockpit of a BattleMech, and I'm in my natural environment. I think a mission like this will bind together our regiment, will forge the Fusiliers into thinking and acting as one." *Let me do this because it is what I am good at.*

"You set your goals high, Major, and that is admirable."

"Thank you sir," he returned. His mind danced with her words. *This is what I am and what I do.* There were only two things that would stand in his way, the two other Majors in the Fusiliers.

Stirling must have been reading his mind. "Something wrong?" she asked, cocking her head to study his face.

"No, sir, nothing I can't handle."

"Then it must be you're thinking about Craig and Blakadar," she said, giving him a knowing smile.

He sighed deeply. "They've resisted me on every front thus far. And now I know they've been coming to you, behind my back. I don't expect them to like me, but they're attempting to undermine my authority."

"As I've said before, Major, my door is always open."

"I understand sir."

"They are good officers. They see you as an outsider still. You'll see just how good they are soon enough."

Loren sat up straighter, unable to hide his excitement. "Are you saying that we're going to get the assignment, Colonel?"

"We four Colonels have been strong-arming each other for hours, but I think it's safe to say I've drawn the mission. You'll have a lot of work to do. That map the Explorer Corps gave us, I want some names thrown on it. Highlanders don't die for terrain marked with numbers. And we're going to need a plan, one hell of a plan, for pulling this off."

Loren felt his whole body and mind race with excitement. "Sir, I've already got a plan in mind. It's called Case Granite . . ." He gathered up the papers spread out on the table and began to show her just how he intended to beat the Smoke Jaguars.

Ruth Horner and Precentor Mercedes Laurent sat facing the four regimental commanders of the Northwind Highlanders. The Executive Council meeting room was small, and the lone oblong table made the meeting seem unbalanced as the two sides squared off against each other in the negotiations. Only a few meters away was the door leading to the Hall of Warriors, where they'd first met what seemed like days ago.

"*Sho-sa* Horner, I thank you for meeting with the Executive Council," Colonel Senn began. "The goal of this discussion is to determine the terms of the contract, should the Northwind Highlanders opt to undertake it."

"Thank you, Colonel. I trust you and your other commanding officers have reviewed all of the data that I have provided?"

"Indeed we have," Colonel MacLeod said. "I was a little surprised by the information you've been able to gather thus far on the Smoke Jaguar world in the Deep Periphery. The stellar navigation charts provided were most useful." He cast a quick glance at the ComStar Precentor, who only nodded in reply. "Especially when we saw that Clan Nova Cat is only a few jumps away with their own string of supply posts."

The maps the Explorer Corps had given them provided a picture of deep space beyond the Inner Sphere that few people had ever seen.

"Colonel MacLeod, I come here with no hidden agendas. Everything we have is open to you." A nod from the Explorer Corps Precentor confirmed that the two organizations were of the same mind on the mission.

"My fear, lass, is that the Nova Cats might move in to attempt to help their fellow Clan. Despite their differences, the two Clans have worked together before. Can we be sure the Cats won't jump in and try to aid the Smoke Jaguars?"

Horner shook her head. "The two Clans have a strong dislike for each other. They only work together when forced to. Our analysts believe that even if the Smoke Jaguars were on the verge of losing every planet they've conquered, the Nova Cats would not intervene to aid them. Remember, each Clan is bent on one goal—getting to Terra first and re-establishing a new Star League. In this effort, they are at odds with each other."

"Well spoken," said Cat Stirling, pushing a hand back through her dark hair as she spoke. The edges of her hairline were shaved at the points where neurohelmet connectors would be attached, the mark of a MechWarrior. "My concern deals specifically with the issue of salvage. Your original proposal to the Executive Council indicated that the Combine wishes all salvage rights from this mission."

"Our contracts with mercenary units thus far have always ensured that we take ownership of everything recovered," Horner said calmly. There was a reason for that provision of the contract. The Combine military had been badly mauled by the Clans. Their capital world almost fell to their might. The advanced Clan technology that had been recovered was helping to re-equip the DCMS.

Stirling's Scottish drawl seemed to emerge again, a hint of things to come. "You're askin' us to undertake a mission into the unknown, with intelligence information already out of date. We understand yer government's need to recover battle tech, but we're sure to take damage in this unusual mission. I recommend we split the salvage."

"Splitting some tangibles is difficult, Colonel Stirling. How does one divide a PPC or a laser into equal parts?"

Not one to let go, Stirling locked her jaw like a pit bull engaged in a biting spree. "What I suggest is not a percentage, *Sho-sa*. Anything recovered as a result of battlefield operations becomes our property. Anything in the warehouses, the real targets of this operation, belongs to the Combine."

Ruth Horner considered the point long and hard. "I believe I can get my government to agree to those terms, provided the Highlanders pay the costs of transportation."

Colonel Senn leaned over and huddled with his fellow Colonels. After a minute or so of whispered discussion, Colonel Cochraine turned again to Horner with their decision. "Agreed. As long as the Combine agrees to underwrite any costs incurred by our DropShips on this mission and the recovery op and also agrees to provide us loaners if our ships are unable to move the recovered goods off-planet."

Ruth Horner listened, paused, and made a series of notes on her pad. "I believe that I can agree to such terms."

"And on the issue of transportation," Colonel Cochraine said, looking at the copy of the contract he had in front of him, "I just want to make sure I fully understand. The Combine will arrange for a command circuit into the Deep Periphery and will provide JumpShips for the trip to and from. The Highlanders will foot the costs of everything from the Periphery and back; your government will cover everything else."

Horner nodded slowly. "A command circuit is already being put into place in anticipation of the successful conclusion of these talks. Wayside V is sixty-five light years from the Combine border, but the route we must take is roundabout and we don't want to lose precious time. We will pay for all travel in the Inner Sphere. Beyond that, we will provide the hardware; your unit will pay at a modest per diem."

Stirling shook her forefinger in front of her. "This contract still isn't sealed, *Sho-sa*. It isn't over until *we* say it is."

Horner bowed her head slightly. "I did not mean to offend or assume, Colonel Stirling. I merely wished to point out that, thus far, we have not stumbled into any minefields in terms of negotiations."

"The day is still young, lassie," Stirling returned with her cat's smile.

"Which brings us to one other point we need to resolve,

and frankly it is a pressing one as far was we are concerned,"
Colonel Senn added. "That is of the role of the PSL on this
mission. The Northwind Highlanders must be fully in control
of the operation, not reporting to a representative of the Provisional Soldiery Liasion. We're going to be too far from
headquarters and a real chain of command to have that kind
of relationship."

"And," Stirling put in, as usual seeming to thrive on adding
tension to the discussion, "we'll want none of your ISF types
in the PSL team. The last thing we need are commandos
attempting to call the shots in the middle of battle."

"This is a sensitive subject," replied the Combine negotia-
tor carefully. "The role of the PSL is to ensure that the objectives of the Combine are fulfilled to the best of your ability."

William MacLeod spoke up at the insinuation. "We're not
wet-behind-the-ears cadets here, *Sho-sa* Horner. You're recruiting the Northwind Highlanders. We're one of the best
units in the Inner Sphere." His tone made even the Precentor
squirm slightly in her seat. "Having a watchdog is one thing,
having a boss there is another."

"I understand, esteemed Colonels." Ruth Horner gave
them one of her inscrutable smiles. "The PSL rep is there as
an advisor and observer. He or she has no authority to command your forces on Wayside unless you defy the terms of
the contract. However, he will bring a company of Combine
troops with him to assist in any way possible."

Stirling cocked an eyebrow and leaned forward. "That
sounded like a concession to me."

"It is," Horner said. "As long as you agree to the terms
laid out in the original offer." From her tone, she was not
looking forward to any other negotiations.

"The price was never an issue, *Sho-sa*," replied Colonel
Cochraine. "You'll find that with the Highlanders, self-
determination is more important that money. We fight for
our own reasons. In this case, we too recognize that the
Clans represent a clear threat to our own world. Not now, but
in the future."

"May I inquire then, what is the next step for approval of
the contract?"

"A quick vote, a formality really. With the four of us supporting it, only a unanimous vote by the Assembly could
stop it. And that won't happen."

"Excellent," she replied. "So that I will know what to include in the final draft of the document, what regiments have you chosen to fulfill the operational requirements?"

"Stirling's Fusiliers will lead the assault," Colonel Senn told her. "The Command Battalion of MacLeod's Regiment will follow them by thirty-six days as rotational relief and garrison. Stirling will take care of this second-line cluster you say is there, and MacLeod's people will help with the clean-up if it's needed—otherwise they can relieve the Fusiliers and let them come home. I think it's safe to say that these Smoke Jaguars are no match for what we'll be tossing at them."

4

The Fort
Tara, Northwind
The Chaos March
14 May 3058

Major Kurt Blakadar, the commanding officer of the Fusiliers' Second Battalion, The Black Adders, entered Loren's office first. He was tall and wore his light brown hair in a crew cut that helped conceal his true age. He wore reading glasses when not in the cockpit of his BattleMech and had them on now for the meeting Loren had called of the Fusilier commanders.

Blakadar virtually ignored Captain Colin Lovat, who sat at the far end of the small conference table. Colin's recent promotion to Intelligence Officer was seen, like Mitch's, as an unwelcome change in the eyes of the older staff officers.

Loren tried not to let it get to him, knowing he needed to keep his focus on the job at hand. Mitch and Colin were both good officers. They didn't play regimental politics, and they knew their stuff. If Blakadar and Craig really cared about the Fusiliers, why did they keep wanting to play it by the old book, the old ways?

He took his usual seat as Major Cullen Craig came in next. Cullen was much shorter and broader in the chest than either of his fellow Majors. Commander of Third Battalion of the Fusiliers, he behaved with an arrogance that was almost palpable. He looked straight at Blakadar and smiled thinly, as if amused at some joke understood only by the two of them. Loren knew that the whole little display was for his benefit, but he was content to let them think they had the upper hand for a few moments more. They'd find out soon enough that these games of power politics had no place in his command. The time had come to remind them of rank and position, of honor and duty.

"I assume you've both looked over the reorganization and battle plans I'm putting together."

Kurt Blakadar glanced first at Mitch Fraser, then at Loren, then quickly at Major Craig, who shared his puzzled expression. "Major, I take it you're going to dismiss our Chief Technician before we begin?"

Loren shook his head. "No, Major. Captain Fraser remains for the debriefing."

"Sir," Craig cut in. "We've never had technical staff sit in on our command meetings before. I know you're still getting settled in, you had no way to know."

"Actually," Loren said calmly, "I'm completely aware. I decided that Captain Fraser should participate in this meeting because it directly relates to the performance of his team." The two Fusilier majors exchanged quick glances, but held their tongues.

"Now, then, what about the BattleMech reallocation plan?" Loren went on smoothly. "Are there any issues we need to address before we initiate this phase of the prelaunch?" Both Loren and his Chief Tech had worked on the reallocations into the wee hours of the night. Loren had conceived the plan, but Mitch was the one who would have to make it work both on paper and in action.

Craig spoke again, adjusting his glasses as he began. "With all due respect, Major Jaffray, Blackie and I believe that reallocating 'Mechs at this time is not advisable. Some of our people won't have time to get acquainted with the new hardware. We propose pulling some of the extra field-repair units out of the DropShip loads and replacing them with extra ammunition. This will still meet Colonel Stirling's objectives, as outlined in your report, without shuttling around all that equipment."

There was a long pause. Loren rose from his seat and

walked around the room, circling the table like a hawk seeking prey. "Captain Fraser, you've reviewed the allocations I propose. Will it be any problem for your technical staff to handle it?"

Mitch Fraser leaned on his elbows, head in his hands over the middle of his retreating hairline as he studied the report in front of him. There were notes scribbled all over the hardcopy. "I've put together several recommended changes. Mostly upgrading to 'Mechs that have jump capability. From the tactical database information you've provided on the Clans, it sounds like they don't really favor jump-capable 'Mechs. Having a few more in the field will help us."

He handed the report to Loren, who looked it over, taking his time reviewing the data. "Excellent analysis, Mitch. I think you'll find that Colonel Stirling and I have already taken that into account. In most of these cases we'll be putting in jump-capable 'Mechs whose weapons are energy- rather than ammo-based, or are just less tonnage."

Loren understood the risk if they did not swap out their 'Mechs. Wayside V was a world with no place to resupply expended ammunition. Added to that, the Jaguars were traditionally short on jump-capable 'Mechs. *We need the jumpers for the tactical battles and the 'Mechs favoring energy weapons so we can outlast the Jaguars.*

"Let's let our Intelligence Officer run through your recommendations." Loren handed the sheet to Captain Lovat at the end of the table, who began to dutifully compare the listings against his own prepared roster.

Kurt Blakadar's face flushed angrily. "Major Jaffray, I don't think you fully understand the implications of what I was saying earlier. Just carrying out these 'Mech swaps is going to stretch our resources thin."

Loren cut him off, his voice sterner and more forceful than before. "Actually, Kurt, I understand the implications precisely. It may shock you, but I have coordinated large-scale operations before in my career. You'll simply have to step up training for the affected troops between now and the time we take off." Loren's use of Blakadar's first name was intentional. *Let Craig think that Blakadar and I are closer than he knows. It may keep him thinking about that rather than me.*

"Almost a quarter of my troops are on leave after our last training exercise. There's no way I can make these swaps, as short-staffed as I am," Craig said, trying another tack.

Loren was unmoved. "Then I guess you'll have to cancel their leaves immediately and have them recalled to the regiment."

"Major, the ink isn't even dry on this contract," Blakadar said. "Maybe we should hold off, draw up some alternatives and then hammer out the details. There's still some time before we leave."

Loren kept his face neutral. "I have my orders and now you have yours. You *will* swap out the 'Mechs as ordered. If that requires you to recall your personnel, I suggest you get started as soon as this meeting is concluded."

"Major Jaffray, maybe we should take this matter up with the Colonel," Cullen Craig said. The implication was clear. Craig was insinuating that Loren had either withheld information from Colonel Stirling or was operating without her authorization. Either way, it was a challenge Loren had no intention of ignoring.

"No, Major Craig. I'm following the Colonel's orders. And just between us, I think there's already been enough overriding of the chain of command. BattleMech allocation is totally in the jurisdiction of the Executive Officer. Colonel Stirling told me to get the regiment ready and that's exactly what I'm doing." Loren could see from the surprised looks on the faces of Craig and Blakadar that they hadn't known he'd found out that they'd gone to the Colonel behind his back.

But Craig just wouldn't give up. "I think that if the Colonel knew some of the—"

"Enough!" Loren barked, pounding his fist on the massive table with such force that even the heavy oak seemed to quake under the impact. "I'm going to say this once, and only once, so I'm going to make myself perfectly clear. I am the Executive Officer in this regiment. We three hold the same rank, but you report to me for operational and administrative issues. My orders come directly from Colonel Stirling and it is our duty to execute them to the best of our ability. Now, I've given you an order. If you refuse to follow it, I have no choice but to have you arrested and court-martialed. Do I make myself clear, Majors?"

Kurt Blakadar shifted nervously in his seat for a moment. "Major Jaffray—"

Loren cut him off. "Is that clear, Major Blakadar, Major Craig?" There would be no more discussion.

"Sir, I request permission to speak freely," Blakadar said stubbornly.

Loren looked at him and crossed his arms in defiance. "Request denied."

"Major Jaffray, your changes are coming too quickly," Craig put in quickly. "We had a smooth-running system under MacFranklin."

Loren leaned midway across the table, dominating the space above Major Craig. "Allow me to be blunt, Major. MacFranklin is dead. I am the XO of this regiment now. You follow my lead. I will *not* adapt to you, either of you. I was put in this position for a reason. It is you who must change."

Craig muttered under his breath, barely audible to those in the room. "This isn't the Capellan Confederation . . ."

"You are correct," Loren returned. "Nor is it the same Fusiliers as before I assumed command. And this is the last time I will tolerate any insinuations about my past affiliations. Think on this—" Loren opened his sidearm holster and placed the Sunbeam laser pistol on the table in front of them. These two had sniped at him from behind long enough, doing everything they could to hurt his assimilation into the regiment. Their biggest gun in painting him as an outsider was Loren's previous affiliation with the Death Commandos.

He knew what people thought about the Death Commandos, that they were ruthless fanatics trained to kill upon command. Loren decided it was time to take that reputation and use it to his advantage. *Let them see that I'm willing to take any and all measures necessary. Let them understand that I'll neither yield nor let up. I want their respect, but for this mission, I'll take their fear.*

He scanned the room quickly and saw that Fraser's eyes were nearly twice their normal size and that Captain Lovat was squirming in his seat. Blakadar's mouth hung open in dismay, and Craig looked nervous about the fact that he too was wearing a pistol. "If this were a Death Commando unit, your actions would have been viewed as attempted mutiny. I would have the authority to either place you under arrest or eliminate you as a threat to the safety of the unit and to the Chancellor." Loren reholstered the weapon. "I'm not ashamed of what I did before becoming a Highlander. I don't expect you to understand that; I *do* expect you to show me respect, however."

He had their attention now and wanted to get on with the

real point of the meeting. "Now, gentlemen, I take it you've reviewed Case Granite." Case Granite was the name he'd given to the plan he'd drafted for the attack on Wayside V.

There were quick nods. It was Captain Lovat who broke the tension. "Given the Jaguar fighting tactics, sir, I wonder if we shouldn't just drop right on top of their base and hit them fast. Seizing the base is critical to our long-term success on the planet. The Jaguars have shown the ability to formulate effective strategies when given the time to do so. If we drop onto the far side of Wayside V, as your plan has us doing, it gives them a chance to mount a pursuit, putting us on the defensive."

"And your thoughts, Mister Craig?" Loren asked.

"Intel has a good point. The Jaguars are known for their skill in offensive rather than defensive tactics. Your plan will give them the time and enough advance warning to mount an offensive operation against us. And if I read your intentions rightly, we're going to have to carry a latrine-load of supplies along with us. The way you've got it, we'll have to lure them out, outlast them, and *then* drive on their base."

Loren nodded. "That's the idea and that's exactly why I want the 'Mech swaps we've been debating. The new 'Mechs won't require all the autocannon and missile reloads.

"I'm counting on the Clans being blinded to our initial position because we'll land on the other side of the planet from their base. And when they do come for us, we'll be the ones who control where and when they can engage us. That's the key to Case Granite. We must retain full and complete control of every facet of the mission at all times. Let them expend energy coming after us. Let them waste time trying to pin us down. Let them draw further away from their supply base. They can't just ignore us, they'll have to come after us. And when they do, we'll turn it against them at every chance."

"Counter-punches?" Major Blakadar said.

"Yes. We'll make them think they've got the upper hand, then frustrate them at every turn. And the more frustrated they get, the more likely they are to make mistakes. Look over the accounts of what happened during the operation on Luthien that Ruth Horner brought us. When the Smoke Jaguars are forced into fighting on anything but their own terms, they rush in blindly. That's our advantage."

Loren closed his valise and looked at them squarely. "Know this. I really don't care what you think of me personally. Remember what the Jaguars did to Edo on Turtle Bay. They destroyed the city, boiled it off the face of the planet in retaliation for a simple civilian uprising. The Wolves may be cunning. The Falcons may be ruthless, but the Jaguars are worse than that. They're vicious. They're relentless. And they stop at nothing."

5

The Fort
Tara, Northwind
The Chaos March
15 May 3058

"Colonel Stirling?"

Cat Stirling recognized the voice of Cullen Craig, but she didn't look up immediately from the report she was studying. Her office was dark but for a reading lamp and the dim glow of two computer screens.

"It's late, Major," she said, leaning back in her chair and rubbing at one temple as if it would somehow restore the vitality she'd possessed earlier in the day. "What brings you here at this hour?"

Craig entered the office and closed the door behind him. "Sir, it's Major Jaffray . . . again."

Cat Stirling's eyes narrowed slightly. "I see."

"It's these new 'Mech assignments, sir."

"What about them, Major?"

"Well, it means requiring some of our people to switch BattleMechs only days before we're to leave Northwind. I realize we can use some of our travel time for simulator training, but I question the wisdom of pulling this switch right now. It's also going to be a lot of extra work. We'll have to load up the simulators and pull folks off leave to get them up to speed on their new 'Mechs. I think he's asking too much."

"Do you believe the safety of the regiment is at risk because of this?" She templed her fingers and leaned back in her chair.

"No, it's not that. It's just that the complaints from some of the men and women—"

"Major, let me make one thing clear," she cut in. "This order was recommended by Major Jaffray and I fully endorse it. If the safety of the regiment is endangered, that's another story. But the day I reverse an order because of some gripes among the troops is the day I step down from command."

She rose to her feet and leaned across the desk on her palms, voice rising with each word. "I never thought to see the day someone in my command would come to me with such a request. Remind your people that they are Northwind Highlanders and that these are orders, not requests. Jaffray speaks for me; he represents my intentions when it comes to the running of this unit. If anyone, including you, doesn't want to accept that, they're welcome to resign their commission right here and now. Otherwise they should pull themselves together and get to their duties. And I suggest that things will go a hell of a lot smoother if you start leading your battalion by setting an example rather than bringing me tales about the troops complaining about doing their jobs."

Craig offered a weak salute and turned to leave the room, obviously shaken by her verbal lashing.

Cat Stirling sat watching until he was all the way out before returning to her work. She knew Craig would go straight to Blackie with a report of this little meeting. And then the word would spread quickly, if she knew her troops. It would make Jaffray's life a hell of a lot easier if everybody understood once and for all that she was behind him one hundred percent. The enemy was the Jaguars, not each other.

Loren walked slowly up the winding path through Peace Park, near the center of Northwind's capital city of Tara. For centuries, despite the struggles and hardships of the Succession Wars, the park had remained untouched by the bloodshed and war that had consumed the Inner Sphere. Ironically, it was in this park named for peace that Loren and his new family had fought the Federated Commonwealth for control of Northwind last year. No longer a place commemorating peace alone, the park now represented the price of freedom for the Highlander regiments.

Scars of the battle were still evident in places where coolant had poisoned the soil and left only dead grass, or where stray laser and PPC shots had burned the trees. The occasional statue was also damaged or battered. Loren often came here at night to walk, hands stuffed in the pockets of his jacket, and to think.

Another figure stood under one of the lights lining the walk. The shadows concealed the face, but Loren would have known her anywhere.

Chastity Mulvaney walked toward him from the shadows and slid her arm around his waist. Then she matched her stride to his as they continued on slowly.

"You're thinking of those blasted Clans again, aren't you?" Her voice was almost scolding.

He nodded. "Training and studying the briefings can only do so much. The real test comes when we actually face them."

"I was wrong about you when I first met you, Loren. Hell, I hated you. And unlike you, I *have* fought the Clans in my time. I almost didn't live to tell about it. One thing you've got to remember is that they're killing machines."

"I'll survive the Jaguars, Chastity," Loren said, pulling her closer for a moment. "As much as the Clans are unknown to me, I am unknown to the Clans."

She stopped walking and turned to face him. "Loren, you'll be confronting an enemy that's genetically created for the sole purpose of warfare. From the time of their birth they're raised in sibling companies that hone their combat skills. They're like the old Spartans . . . the weak are cast out and the strong become warriors.

"I know you're very good—hell, you may be one of the best. I've never met anyone with such a fast-thinking tactical mind. But this is different. You're going to have to call on skills and capabilities that are definitely in you but that you don't like to use. I'm telling you now you're going to need every trick you've got to survive and defeat these Jaguars."

"I'm not afraid of the Jaguars," Loren said.

"I know that," she returned. "But you don't make use of your political skills even though you could. Once you get to Wayside, you'd better be ready to use politics, deception, or anything else to win."

"Politics?" Loren laughed softly, and gave her an affectionate squeeze. "We're going after the Smoke Jaguars on an isolated world in the Deep Periphery. There's no politics out there."

She stopped again and took both his hands in hers. "Listen to me, Loren. This isn't a joke. You yourself have been telling me about Blakadar and Craig's maneuverings behind your back. I've been the XO for MacLeod's Regiment for years now. Trust me, it gets worse when you're on a mission. And let's not forget that none of us are experienced at dealing with a PSL. You're going to need political savvy to keep him from getting in your hair or in your way."

Loren knew she was right about the Professional Soldiery Liaison. The Kuritas usually sent a representative as a watchdog over their interests anytime they hired mercenaries. The mistrust of mercenary units was still strong within the Combine military, despite the fact that Theodore Kurita had no choice but to use them.

She nodded more to herself than him. "Trust me, Loren. And when you're out there, far away from me and Northwind and the rest of the Highlanders, try and remember what I'm telling you now."

Loren shook his head in mock despair, then gave her a hug. "Don't worry about me, Chastity Mulvaney. Smoke Jaguars or no Smoke Jaguars, you're not going to get rid of me that easy."

They laughed together then, and continued walking hand in hand down the shadowy, tree-lined path of Peace Park.

DropShip **Claymore**
Nadir Jump Point, Gravenhage
Draconis Combine
2 June 3058

The DropShip *Claymore* was already beginning to feel cramped and claustrophobic by the time the JumpShip carrying the Fusilier task force arrived at the Gravenhage jump point on the farthest border of the Draconis Combine. Their three *Overlord* Class ships, each carrying a full battalion of BattleMechs and support crew, had been making steady progress over the past few weeks. Compliments of a command circuit of Combine JumpShips strung into position across the Draconis Combine, the Fusilier task force had traveled the hundreds of light years from Northwind to the far edge of the Inner Sphere. Where DropShips traveled to and from the surface of planets, JumpShips were the vessels by which humankind traversed the vast distances between stars. Over the past few days the *Claymore* had ridden along the spines of a number of those faster-than-light vessels.

Such a command circuit was a rare enough phenomenon; few but the leaders of the Great Houses of the Inner Sphere had enough starships to spare for such duty. But using a command circuit saved the week to ten days a JumpShip had to wait while recharging the solar batteries that would let it make its next jump through hyperspace. At each new jump point, the Fusilier DropShips would unlock from their docking grapples and shuttle to another ship waiting to take them on the next leg of their long journey.

The trip from Northwind just to its nadir jump point had taken twelve precious days. Loren had made good use of the time, however, spending many hours reviewing the various operational plans, training in the portable simulators they'd brought, and studying the map of Wayside V until it was as familiar as the Highlanders' own beloved world of Northwind.

Gravenhage was almost 500 light years from Northwind, but it couldn't have seemed any further to Loren right now had it been on the other side of the galaxy. Who knew how long before any of them again saw the tall, silent peaks of the Rockspire Mountains or walked the ancient byways of Tara?

As he sat in the small crew mess hall, Loren remembered the pomp and circumstance of their send-off—the elaborate parade, complete with dancers and the wailing of bagpipes. And the many parties, too, which helped the troops burn off some of the tension surrounding the start of any mission. No matter how well this operation went, in their hearts everyone knew that some of the Fusiliers would never return to Northwind.

Loren had remained somewhat detached from the flurry of activity, his mind focused on the mission. He couldn't help remembering the one truth that kept every commander's senses sharp—no plan survives contact with the enemy. He glanced out the *Claymore*'s viewport and contemplated what was to come.

Sitting on the very tip of the Draconis Combine, the

Gravenhage system wasn't just a recharge point for the Fusiliers, but the place where they would rendezvous with their PSL, Major Elden Parkensen, and a company of Combine troops. *Sho-sa,* Loren corrected himself, remembering the Combine word for the rank of major.

The Professional Soldiery Liaison was the branch of the Combine military responsible for coordinating mercenary units with the regular DCMS and making sure a merc unit lived up to its contract. The PSL rep could make recommendations and participate in decision-making, but Loren knew Cat Stirling would never yield ultimate command to anyone else. The mission was a sensitive one and the Fusiliers would be operating with a great deal of independence. No one in the Inner Sphere had tried to do what they were tasked with doing—attack and seize a Clan holding beyond the borders of human-occupied space.

What they knew about the PSL was limited. Early in his career, Parkensen had served with several units during the Clan invasion. He'd been on Tarnby with the Fourth Pesht Regulars in the early days of the invasion when the true origins of the invaders were still unknown. His unit was almost entirely overrun by the Sixth Jaguar Dragoons in the battle of Diver's Grotto, and he was one of only a handful of survivors evacuated.

He returned to Luthien for medical treatment and was still there almost a year later when the Smoke Jaguars and the Nova Cats made their ill-fated attack on the Combine's capital world. Parkensen volunteered to fight again even though he was still not fully healed, but wasn't in the fray more than a few minutes before his patchwork *Grand Dragon* was swarmed and destroyed by the Nova Cats. Honored and promoted by Theodore Kurita himself, Elden Parkensen was given a new posting to the Fourth Alshain Regulars on Rubigen, which was hit by Clan Ghost Bear just weeks after his arrival. Somehow fate managed to preserve Parkensen once more, and he was lifted off planet with some of the last wounded who managed to get out of the system.

Since then he'd been posted to minor defense garrisons along the Clan border but had seen no further action. Studying Parkensen's record, Loren couldn't tell whether the man was an inept MechWarrior who got by on sheer luck or an excellent MechWarrior plagued with being at the wrong place at the wrong time. Perhaps the truth lay somewhere in between. That, at least, was Loren's hope.

Loren was shaken from his reverie by the arrival of Colonel Stirling, her flight jumpsuit marked with the black regalia showing her rank and position as CO of Stirling's Fusiliers. Trailing after her came Majors Craig and Blakadar. The small mess room boasted not much more than a table and two benches of ten seats each. It was cramped, uncomfortable, and positioned over the gently throbbing fusion reactor engines of the *Claymore*. This evening, however, a cloth as well as china and silverware had been laid over the carbon-fiber table top. Meager enough, but the best they could do. "Captain Spillman tells me our guest's shuttle should be docking about now."

"And their JumpShip charge status?"

"Equipped with lithium-fusion batteries, just like ours. Apparently they're carrying enough of a charge to make the jump when we do in a few minutes." From this point forward, the two ships would travel together.

"Theodore Kurita spared no expense on this mission."

Stirling nodded. "I have no doubt the Coordinator takes this seriously. Our PSL's seen a lot of action. He must be pretty good to get assigned this mission."

Loren nodded while checking to make sure his jumpsuit was in order. He did not voice his concerns regarding *Sho-sa* Parkensen. Time would tell. "I've detached an honor guard to escort him here, sir."

"Good, what's the fare?"

"Ground steak, potatoes, and summer corn," Loren replied.

Stirling made a sour face. "We've got to remember to pack more real food next time. And we should make sure that what we do pack is better than this meal."

Loren smiled. "I wanted to bring more, but Mitch Fraser has filled every nook and cranny of this ship with tools and repair parts. Our KP complained today that there were a hundred liters of 'Mech coolant in the food freezer unit."

"That monkey-wrench has been as busy as a drunkard in a brewery," Major Blakadar put in, running a hand through his dark hair. "Fraser's rigged one of those old J-27 ammo haulers into some sort of bastardized mobile repair unit. He's got that monstrosity of his in parts all over the cargo-hold floor reconfiguring it." Blakadar gave a small laugh. "I told him he'd better have that tinker-toy put back together by the time we burn in or I'm using it as a scooter for my 'Mech on the way out the door."

Stirling laughed along with him. "If anything, Mitch *is* creative." There was a knock at the door and both she and Loren rose to a more formal stance. "Well, then, it's time to meet our partner in this endeavor." She motioned to the door and Loren went to open it.

The figure standing there was of medium height and dressed in the tan flight jumpsuit of the Draconis Combine Mustered Soldiery. *Sho-sa* Parkensen's hair was an oily black, his features classically oriental, his expression a polite mask. Stepping into the cramped room, he bowed his head slightly. "Greetings, Officers of Stirling's Fusiliers of the Northwind Highlanders. I am *Sho-sa* Elden Parkensen, your PSL. I bring you a welcome to the Draconis Combine and the heartfelt wish for success from the Coordinator himself." He then bowed to Colonel Stirling.

Stirling returned the bow with one of her own. "*Kon-nichi-wa, Sho-sa* Parkensen-*san*," she said in practiced yet strained Japanese. "I am Colonel Andrea Stirling and these are my officers." One by one she introduced them, and they too exchanged bows, though Loren thought everyone but Parkensen looked a little uncomfortable with the Combine tradition.

Parkensen lowered himself into a chair while the two officers who'd escorted him shut the mess door behind them. The *Sho-sa* was silent for a long pair of minutes as he opened his battered leather case and pulled out some hardcopy. Then he looked back up at the Highlander officers and put his hands on the table. "It is my understanding that we jump within the hour?"

"That's right," Colonel Stirling replied evenly. Parkensen's rank was the equivalent of Loren's, and he could tell that she was setting the tone for her relationship with the PSL as if it were part of some odd ritual mating dance. "Our next hop will take us right into the Periphery."

"Yes, I am keenly aware of that, Colonel," Parkensen replied. "I have brought with me the latest intelligence updates and jump-point data for Clan operations in the area. We have confirmed the pirate-point calculations for our arrival, but have nothing new on the Wayside system itself.

The pirate point we recommend is very close, requiring only a two-day burn insystem."

Jump points were those coordinates in a system where a starship could instantly materialize in space from another point up to thirty light years distant. The two most commonly used points in every system were the zenith and nadir points, above and below the plane of the orbiting planets and their star, and usually days, if not weeks, from the planets themselves. Pirate points were different. They were nonstandard points that permitted JumpShips to arrive much closer to the planet and without as much risk of detection by the planetary defenders. Even the slightest error in the calibrations could result in a misjump, and the various attendant disasters.

"Major Jaffray, perhaps you'd like to show our associate what we've put together?" the Colonel said.

Loren placed a small circular device on the table. It was six centimeters thick, black and roughly the size of a plate, with several obvious control surfaces. He took out a handheld remote control, pointed it at the holographic display unit, and turned it on. Above the projection device a light came into being in front of them, taking the form of Wayside V spinning slowly for the entire room to see. It was not a gridline construction, but appeared just like a very large globe almost a meter in size.

Parkensen stared at the globe and then looked at his notes. "I notice you've given names to the geography." His dry tone made it hard to tell what he thought of that, but it wasn't hard to imagine.

Wayside had three bodies of water, labeled as seas. Loren had given them names his people could easily remember, borrowing the surnames of former Highlander colonels. He'd done the same with the three former continents. The large C-shaped one in the southern hemisphere he'd named Kurita Prime. In the middle of the "C," where the ocean floor had once been, was the intended Fusilier landing zone.

The largest continent, tagged as New Scotland, was mostly in the northern hemisphere and was covered with mountains and petrified forests. It was shaped almost like a hand with four twisted and contorted fingers reaching for the McCormack Sea just west of it. To the east of New Scotland was the Kearny Sea. On its southern shore, in land that had once been kilometers under the long-lost oceans of Wayside V, was the Smoke Jaguar base. Just southwest of that was the aerospace strip that had been under construction at the time the last surveillance was made.

Below the Kearny Sea in the southern hemisphere was the continent Loren had named New Northwind. It looked like a malformed starfish, with seven uneven arms stretching outward. One of the arms reached toward New Scotland, forming a tight corridor he'd named the Isthmus of Bannockburn, commemorating the infamous Scottish battle. The isthmus was a steep and jagged valley, with sharp drop-offs from the airless continents to the rocky terrain below. South of it, between New Northwind and Kurita Prime was all that was left of a once-mighty ocean, now nothing more than a shallow sea. On the Highlander map it was labeled the Marion Sea, commemorating the Highlander Colonel who'd commanded MacLeod's Regiment decades before.

"Colonel Stirling suggested that naming the terrain features would make them easier for our people to identify."

"I assume you do not expect these names to remain after we take the planet from the Jaguars?"

"Not unless you want them to," Stirling said coolly.

Parkensen ignored the comment. "I looked over the preliminary report you transmitted and have a grasp of your proposed plan, but the distance we'll have to move from our LZ to the attack point is considerable."

"That's true," Stirling said, "but if we end up facing anything more than a second-line Clan garrison Cluster, that distance will buy us the time we need to weather their assault.

"During the drop, our ships will deploy a number of satellites with both active and passive sensory gear. The active sats will give us the best picture of what we're facing, but if the Clan garrison has reinforced aerospace elements, the sats will most likely be the first thing taken out. However, just a few minutes after landing, our regimental intelligence boys and girls should be able to paint us an accurate picture of what's down there. We'll also issue a batchall in hopes they'll tell us their defense."

Parkensen shook his head. "You must have misinterpreted some of our data. The Jaguars are no longer responding to batchalls by us. They believe we lack honor and are corrupting their traditions to our own advantage." The batchall was the Clan ritual by which an attacker issued his challenge of combat to an enemy.

Loren thought that made sense. On the Combine planet of Wolcott the Jaguars had lost the planet in an ambush based on deceptive information given them by the Combine force in the course of the batchall.

"The Clans will not respond, but your own intel shows that they respect such challenges from warriors a lot more than from those they consider nothing more than worthless bandits," Loren noted.

He paused the rotating holographic image and pressed another control button. The landing zone in the middle of the massive lagoon of Kurita Prime lit up bright red on the map.

"Our primary plan of attack calls for us to move along the northern shores of the Marion Sea," Colonel Stirling said. A red arrow traced the path the Fusiliers would follow. "This is the tough part because the old ocean bed we'll be traveling over is a jumble of rocks with pits of sand. And don't be deceived by these straits over here. They look wide on the map—maybe some forty or fifty kilometers across—but the only area we can actually maneuver through is a corridor of steep rock formations that's barely two or three kilometers wide.

"The rest of the isthmus is virtually impassible. We can end up pinched in there very quickly, but this is where I hope to engage the Jaguars first. We hit them hard, then circle around them and move up onto New Northwind continent, traverse the peninsula that forms the isthmus, then climb back down into the old seabed again to hit them in their rear and flank. Then we press on to their base and lay seige to it."

Eldensen was shaking his head as he looked at the map. "You would move your regiment up onto the continental surface? According to the data I've seen, the air up there is so thin it's not even breathable. And it's bitter cold. Your vehicles and infantry wouldn't last five minutes."

"Your assessment is correct, *Sho-sa*," Stirling continued. "I'm counting on our vehicles to hold the isthmus on the ground while we cross the peninsula with our BattleMech forces. After that phase, we'll split our forces to strike at the aerodrome and the Jag base."

Loren shut off the image of the globe and replaced it with that of the Smoke Jaguar base. The base sat at the bottom of a massive basin that flowed into the salt waters of the Kearny Sea, which offered it protection from that direction. Surrounding it on its other three sides were steep hills that would be difficult to maneuver. Every time Loren looked at the map he cursed how easy the site was to defend. Anyone who hoped to rush the base would be totally exposed, while the defenders had the advantage of natural defenses. Fortunately, that wasn't the plan.

"We will use primarily a two-pronged approach against the base. The Jags have dug themselves into a hole, more or less, by having their base butt up to the sea. Despite the apparent advantages, that weakens their defenses. The natural fortification offers them protection, but they're literally blind to any activity outside the basin."

"Your plan is full of risks," Parkensen replied.

"That it is, *Sho-sa*. It's the bloody nature of the business we're in," Stirling said.

7

Wildcat Station
Wayside V (Wildcat)
Deep Periphery
2 June 3058

Galaxy Commander Devon Osis stood at the top of the DropShip exit ramp, taking his first look at Wildcat, the planet where Tau Galaxy was currently based. The only things of note in the desolate scene were the sickly green of the sky and how much thinner the air was here than the recycled atmosphere he'd been breathing on the trip to this remote outpost. Standing at attention at the foot of the ramp, framed by the surrounding warehouses and buildings of Wildcat Station, were the officers of the new Galaxy, *his* Galaxy. He felt a rush of pride.

Descending the ramp slowly, he examined the faces and crisp gray dress uniforms of his command staff. A chill breeze buffeted him as he approached the first warrior standing at attention below. As befitting a Jaguar warrior, Devon Osis also wore his gray dress uniform proudly, and held his back straight and head high. The light from the orange sun shimmered hazily on the surface of the nearby sea, reminding him how little he'd learned that was pleasing about this world of Wildcat. From what he knew and could see, the place offered only one advantage—isolation. From here, he could plan the destruction of the Nova Cats once and for all.

And Tau Galaxy was the perfect instrument of that destruction. It consisted of three Clusters of OmniMech forces. Two of those, the 101st Attack Cluster and the 250th Assault Cluster, were full Clusters; the other was the much smaller 25th Strike Cluster. He knew them by their true names: the Bloodied Claws, the Mist Pouncers, and the Deathstrike Cluster.

He knew that they also had enough supplies stored in the warehouses of Wildcat Station to let them operate indefinitely. The OmniMechs assigned to the Galaxy were all new, some of them test models never seen by the other Clans. And as if to reinforce this fierce array, the Galaxy escort was the WarShip *Dark Claw*. Built during the peak of the Star League, the *Essex* Class starship carried enough firepower to destroy a city from orbit.

From what Khan Lincoln Osis had said, the members of Tau Galaxy still did not know the unit's reason for being or current mission. They had been genetically engineered from the legacies of the finest warriors who had participated in the invasion of the Inner Sphere, but very few even knew of the Galaxy's existence. His task was to ready them for what lay ahead—the destruction of the Nova Cats. Once prepared, they were his to lead into battle. *These are the best my Clan has. Combined with my combat experience we will be an unstoppable combination. A few months of honing their skills and familiarizing them with their intended targets, and then we will hit the Nova Cats and destroy them once and for all.*

At the bottom of the ramp he stopped and looked at the female warrior standing before him. She was bald, but on closer inspection he saw that she actually lacked all facial hair—eyebrows, lashes, everything. A dark gray crown-of-thorns pattern was etched thinly around her head and brow like a tattoo, circling her right eye like a gun sight. This of course was no tattoo, but an enhanced-imaging neural implant that freed a warrior of the necessity of wearing a neurohelmet. The surgically implanted circuitry gave a warrior a wireless link with her 'Mech's computer, providing a virtual view of the battlefield that aided in target acquisition, aiming, and piloting. To see such a young warrior with one of these bio-electric "tattoos" revealed the extent of her aggressiveness.

On her collar were the markings of a Star Colonel of the Bloodied Claws, and under one arm she carried the Galaxy Codex baton, which held memory chips recounting the history of the Galaxy. The baton was to the whole unit what the codex bracelet worn around one arm was to each individual warrior. There was also a communications device connected to the insignia the officers wore on their collars. With the baton, a Galaxy Commander could communicate with those under his or her command instantly and directly.

Devon knew this warrior from the briefing given him by Khan Lincoln Osis. She was Star Colonel Roberta, temporary commander of the Galaxy during their trip from the homeworlds here to the planet Wildcat. Now they were his Galaxy, his command. In the past, he had been forced to deal with the failures of others; now he would be the one in charge.

Star Colonel Roberta was a true warrior in the finest Jaguar tradition, and he had studied her codex with great interest. During her Trial of Position for the right to command a Cluster, her 'Mech's fusion reactor had suffered a breach. Rather than eject, she'd overridden the OmniMech's safety systems and continued to fight even as radiation flooded her cockpit. Though she eventually defeated her opponent, only long weeks of treatments by members of the scientist caste saved her life afterward. Roberta had survived, but she still carried some of the effects of her exposure. Devon was impressed with the story, for it showed that the heart of the Jaguar beat in her breast. Others, weaker, would have ejected.

"Galaxy Commander," she said, bowing her head slightly in deference.

"You are Star Colonel Roberta, quiaff?"

"Aff."

Devon held himself even straighter and spoke the words he'd practiced silently a hundred times on the trip to this isolated planet. "By order of Khan Lincoln Osis, Khan of the Smoke Jaguars, the one true Clan and heirs of the Great Kerenskys, I hereby assume command of Tau Galaxy."

Roberta hefted the Galaxy Codex baton and held it in front of her, gripping each end with a hand. "By the rede of our people, command cannot be assumed. Command must be taken and held. Won with honor, sealed in blood." Her words were loud enough for the other warriors standing at attention to hear, and Devon could smell the anticipation in the air.

The ceremony—the change of command ceremony. He smiled. "Command is mine to take."

Roberta took a staged step toward him, still holding the baton before her. "I hold this command you seek."

Devon also spoke so that the gathered warriors could hear him. "Warriors of the Smoke Jaguar, form a circle around us so that the eyes of equals can gaze upon this rede." He paused and mentally gathered himself for what was to come as the officers of Tau Galaxy moved into place. "Nicholas Kerensky, founder of our people, taught us that leadership goes only to the strongest and best of our warrior caste. Behold as I, Devon Osis, Bloodnamed and fully tested, take what is rightfully mine."

The warriors of Tau Galaxy did as he bid, forming a Circle of Equals around them. Roberta licked her lips in anticipation and lowered her stance, ready for the first blow.

The ritual was simple. Devon must take the Galaxy Codex baton from Roberta through a Trial of Possession. Once he had it in his hands, the Jaguars would acknowledge him as their new leader. The fighting would be a mix of true combat and rite. It was customary, but not required, that Devon draw blood from her in the fight. In some cases, the baton was simply handed over after a series of ritual blows, but there were also other instances in which one of the two combatants had died. Watching Roberta warily, Devon wondered which kind this would be.

He bowed his head slowly as if to acknowledge her standing as a true warrior. She returned the gesture. Then he immediately sprang into action. With one hand he reached for the outstretched baton, with the other he swung inward, hitting her left wrist. Realizing quickly what he was trying to do, Roberta snapped backward, pulling the baton from his one-handed grip.

Devon leaped toward her with hands outstretched as if to choke her. Roberta spun slightly to her left as he came down on one side of her, driving one knee into her hip with all his weight and force behind it. From the look on her face, he knew he had hurt her.

She went into a roll, tossing him aside. He let momentum

drop him into a crouch on one hand, ready to pounce. Roberta was prepared, though, sweeping her leg out to either knock his hand away and send him sprawling or strike at his head. At the last moment, he rose, using both hands to grab her foot.

The grapple was good. Before she realized what had happened, Devon had twisted her foot hard around as if it were the crank on a machine. This time Roberta moaned out loud, dropping the baton and using her hands to turn her body in the direction of his twisting. As soon as she was on her stomach, Devon leaped upward, then let himself come down on her back with both knees. The wind knocked out of her, Roberta was unable to respond as Devon snatched the Galaxy baton from the tarmac. With it in his hands, he left her on the ground and stood up. His own breath was ragged, but he managed to speak the words to the circle of warriors around him.

"Command is mine to take and hold," he said, drawing in a gasp of air. "In the tradition of our Bloodnamed, I hold command of Tau Galaxy in the name of Khan Lincoln Osis of the Smoke Jaguars!" In unison, without prompting, the warriors chanted the solemn oath of "Seyla." It was a word of unity and honor, its meaning, but not its sacredness, lost in the mists of time. To Devon Osis, it told him that his warriors would follow him.

At his feet, Roberta pushed herself up, first to her hands, then to sitting, then slowly and awkwardly to her feet. She stood next to Devon, defiantly refusing to wipe the dirt from her face. The white skin of her bald head was bruised, yet somehow otherwise unmarked. On her shoulder, the patch of her unit, the black outstretched paw of the 101st Attack Cluster, had become half-pulled off in the tussle. Devon turned to look at her and met her eyes. No words were spoken, but she seemed to understand.

In a fluid side-step, Devon Osis pivoted and spun hard, swinging the baton into her face. The end of the small device dug deeply into her cheek, and from the crunching sound that reverberated through the rod, Devon knew he had either broken bones or shattered teeth. Roberta was twisted hard and to the side by the blow, but true to her Clan warrior training, she remained standing despite the geyser of pain that must have erupted in her jaw. A stream of crimson blood ran down from the corner of her mouth to her chin. She drew in a breath, and obvious agony shook her like a wave battering a shore. *Blood has been draw in the way of the Jaguar.*

Just as she had refused to wipe away the dirt, she made no effort to wipe the blood clear. It was a mark of honor in the tradition of the finest Smoke Jaguar warriors. Devon understood all too well. It was important to her to have blood drawn in the ways of the rede. Giving up command without such an injury would have shamed her. Devon Osis could read her expression as she looked at him. There was neither anger nor resentment, only admiration and respect. *She and the others now know that in my heart also beats the heart of the Jaguar. They know I will do what is necessary to fulfill our honor.*

Devon turned to the circle of warriors and met their looks and nods of acceptance. Assumption of Galaxy Command meant that he had the honor of naming the unit. "Today on planets throughout explored space, hearts and minds tremble. A new Jaguar Galaxy is born. Nicholas Kerensky, when he founded our Clans, taught us the importance of names in giving spirit to our warriors. From this day forward, this is not just the Tau Galaxy. Our foes will know us by our true name, the Huntress Galaxy."

He paused long enough to draw another deep breath and compose his thoughts. "Huntress is not only the name of one of our home worlds, but it is the spirit of our Galaxy. The female Smoke Jaguar is a fierce huntress who just as fiercely protects and defends her young. Like our namesake, the Huntress Galaxy is dedicated to protect and defend our Clan and to mercilessly hunt down its enemies. Defense of our Clan—by destroying those who would destroy us. Let warriors near and far mark my words. The Smoke Jaguar is now on the prowl."

8

The Highlanders' transporting JumpShip, the Invader Class *Fox's Bane*, materialized at the zenith jump point of the star system with a silent blue flash of light and a pulse of electro-magnetic energy. It was followed by a silent burst of light as its partner ship, the *Magellan* Class *Kobayashi,* carrying the Combine DropShip, appeared beside it.

Though hyperspace jumps were instantaneous, they used so much power that a JumpShip had to spend up to ten days, depending on the star type, recharging its jump drive by gathering solar energy in a special sail that was unfurled for this purpose. The *Fox's Bane* was an exception to the rule. Equipped with a lithium-fusion battery, the *Bane* could store enough energy for two jumps, and it could quickly recharge itself. Colonel Stirling had insisted that the ship hold one jump's worth of power in reserve while traveling toward Wayside. After all, this wasn't the Inner Sphere, with its well-traveled routes and known star systems. They were venturing into the Deep Periphery, the vast reaches beyond explored space.

Loren got up from his bunk and rubbed his eyes. This jump, like the five others before it, had gone smoothly, but it had awakened him before the end of his sleep period. The ringing of the "all clear" tones from the speaker told him they'd arrived intact in the intended system. Recharging would be quicker here because the system star was a white dwarf.

It was morning, or so the lighting level told him. Telling the time of day in deep space was always tricky because of the lack of sunlight as a reference. Captain Spillman of the *Claymore* manipulated the lighting so that when it was night according to Terran Standard, the lights were only running at twenty percent levels. At dusk and dawn, they were at fifty percent. Despite his faith in the Highlander DropShip captain, Loren always double-checked with his chronometer.

After his morning shave and wash, Loren pulled on a fresh jumpsuit uniform and looked at his perscomp. *Briefings.* The bane of being the regiment's executive officer was that he essentially pulled double duty. Not only did he command the Kilsyth Guards Battalion, he was also in charge of coordinating the efforts of the other two battalions. And now they had the Combine PSL Parkensen complaining to both him and Colonel Stirling that the plan was too risky. The PSL wanted to scrap it in favor of dropping directly onto the Jaguar base.

Loren had to attend such a meeting that day, this time with his own First Battalion—his red-capped Guards. They were waiting for him in the *Bane*'s main conference room, which the Fusiliers had turned into a rec room for their trip. As he entered, the dozen or so officers snapped to attention. Loren gestured for them to stand at ease, which they did instantly. He lowered himself into his seat, and the others standing around the conference table, ad hoc poker table, did the same.

"Gentlemen," he began, looking around at the men and women of his command, noting that their faces were visibly excited. He understood that sensation, the anticipation of being close to a battle. Even though the Jaguars were still days away, this meeting seemed to bring them that much closer to the inevitable confrontation. "You've all had a chance to go over the battle plans for this operation. This meeting is to address open issues in the battalion and make any last-minute changes necessary."

"All I want to know, sir," Lieutenant Greg Hector said, a hint of humor in his voice, "is are we done with the vaccinations? One more hit from a needle and I'm going to have to go into battle sitting on an inflatable cushion." There was a general chuckling among the officers because they all knew it was true. Every one of them had undergone extensive vaccinations, and it had become a sort of running joke aboard the Fusilier ships.

"Point well taken," Loren said, content with his pun.

"Major," spoke up a man in the back of the room. Captain Jake Fuller, formerly of MacLeod's Regiment, had transferred to the Kilsyth Guards only a month after Loren had assumed command. "I want to know how we're going to deal with the isthmus. The terrain is tight and confining and it'll pull our forces into a possible bottleneck. And sending our 'Mechs up onto the continent is a pretty risky maneuver, yet the whole operation rides on doing just that."

"Well, Jake," Loren said, "we've all studied the Jaguars inside and out. If I were the Jaguar commander, that isthmus is exactly the place I'd try and pin us down. Those narrows and the rocky terrain would be the perfect spot to grind us up."

"So you agree then?"

Loren shook his head. "Our ground forces and some supporting BattleMechs can stall the Jaguars down there. We'll let them think they've trapped us, while the rest of our force crosses over to the other side of the peninsula and then drops down on their flank. We'll pinch them like a pimple on the face of the planet."

"That's the part I think Jake's questioning," Lieutenant Klavin Amari of Second Company put in. "It'll be like moving and fighting in a vacuum up there. If they hit us on the continent, we won't be able to hang in for very long. Hits under those conditions can pop actuators, and a cockpit hit *will* kill." She emphasized the word "will" rather than "could," and the other officers nodded their heads.

Jake picked up the argument. "How can we be sure the Jaguars won't be there waiting for us?"

"We'll never be sure, Captain Fuller, but from what we know about Clan tactics, they aren't given to taking positions and defensive postures that work to their disadvantage. The Smoke Jaguars are one of the most aggressive of the Clans. They'll come at us by the quickest route, and that is the isthmus." If Loren had learned anything in the past months of studying the Clans, it was that the Jaguars were ruthless enemies.

"We've studied how the Jaguars fight," he went on. "And we know that their losses on Wolcott, Luthien, and Tukayyid have embittered them. Among all the Clans, they're the first to want to rush into a fight. And when they do engage, they want to win and win fast. You've all heard of the custom of bondsmen, where the Clans take captives as slaves—eventually to convert them into their own warriors. Well, the Smoke Jaguars have all but stopped that practice when it comes to Inner Sphere forces. The Jaguars believe in not just beating an enemy, but crushing them totally. *No quarter given.* Even if we outnumber them three to one, I expect to take losses—maybe even significant losses.

"The only thing we've got in our favor is that they're not expecting anyone to have the audacity to hit them on Wayside V. We've trained, learned everything there is about how the Clans fight, and developed ways to counter them. The Smoke Jaguars will think we're not prepared to deal with them, but I say different. The truth of the matter is that they're not prepared to deal with the Northwind Highlanders. We trace our heritage to the Star League and beyond. Tangle with us, and they'll get a taste of what waits for them if they ever cross the truce line." Loren's words seemed to bring the very air of the room to life with anticipation. He saw several of his officers' faces flush with pride.

"You don't have to sell us, sir," Jake Fuller said, crossing his arms. "I've fought alongside you before and I look forward to doing it again."

"Good," Loren replied, wishing everyone in the regiment had the confidence of his own command. "Are there any other open issues then?"

"Is the Colonel going to challenge them with a batchall?" Fuller asked.

Loren nodded. "That's the plan. We don't expect them to pay any heed to it, but it may help us even the odds, given that they bid their forces before entering battle."

"Major, I've been going over the WCS options," said Captain Torri Chandler. "WCS" was the standard lingo for Worse Case Scenario. These were battle plans that commanders drew up but hoped they'd never have to use. If everything fell apart, if the command structure of the regiment was shattered, if a disaster occurred, they would fall back on the WCS options. "With Major Mulvaney bringing in her task force thirty days after our planetfall, is it necessary for us to have a contingency as extreme as you've outlined in Case Alpha?"

Loren and Colonel Stirling had passed long hours debating the plan, and it was the best they'd come up with. Under the Alpha contingency, the unit would pull up out of the habitable areas of the old seas, and dig into position on the continent of New Scotland in the petrified forest dubbed New Sherwood. "Your concerns are similar to those of Captain Fuller then?"

"Yes, sir," she replied. "We could be up there for weeks living in our 'Mechs. Our ground-based forces would have to fall back to the DropShips to have any hope of surviving."

Loren understood her point. "That's correct, Captain. We'd have little choice. Up there we'd have our best chance of holding out until reinforcements arrive."

Captain Jebediah Lewis of the Combined Arms Support Company was obviously irked by the exchange. "Don't worry about us, Chandler. We're more than able to hold our own. Remember, I only have a platoon of standard infantry on this mission. The other two platoons are Infiltrator troops whose battle armor will let them operate up on the continents. And my tanks are all refitted with new tech has well. We won't drop the banner in this fight."

Chandler bowed her head slightly to concede the point as Loren spoke. "I don't want anyone coming into this without knowing the full truth. We're working with very old intelligence. Things on Wayside may have changed dramatically by the time we get there. You've all got to be ready to accept new plans and new orders on the fly.

"Bottom line . . . be prepared for anything."

9

Pirate Jump Point CEXC-0021-A.2122.97
Wayside V (Wildcat)
Deep Periphery
3 July 3058

The *Fox's Bane* and her attached DropShips materialized at the pirate point over Wayside V, sending a ripple of electro-magnetic energy out to mark their arrival. Loren was on the bridge of the *Claymore* as it passed through a state of energy into matter again. As his sense of balance returned, he turned to face Captain Spillman seated in the command chair of the *Overlord* Class ship. The lanky DropShip captain seemed unaffected by the jump, which must have been merely one of thousands he'd made in his career.

Loren looked out the narrow viewport and saw the image of Wayside V below them, a gray-green ball with wisps of greenish clouds surrounding it. As the all-clear signal sounded, he checked his chronometer, then the status board in front of him. Cat Stirling rose from her seat a heartbeat before he did and checked the lights. "We're all green, Captain," she said, shooting a glance back at Spillman.

"I'm aware of that, Colonel. Hold yer horses fer a second." He checked his own control panel built into the armrest of the chair. Despite the tension of the moment, Spillman's cockiness still managed to shine through. Loren had a chance to observe the man during their trip, and his disdain for authority was obvious. In space, when on a military operation, he was in command. His orders could come only from Colonel Stirling, and though he technically reported to her, he never acted like it. "It appears that the *Kobayashi* has jumped successfully as well."

"Initiate drop sequence," she commanded.

Spillman nodded. "This is the *Claymore* to the *Bull Run, Stonewall,* and *Retribution.* We have a go signal. Say again, go signal." There was a distant grinding noise followed by a jarring thud that seemed to reverberate throughout the ship as the docking ring that held the *Claymore* to the spine of the JumpShip released and the vessel started to move toward the planet. Loren felt a slight pitch in the ship as the massive fusion engines roared to life and the ship began to accelerate toward Wayside V.

From his own cramped workstation, he activated one of the communications controls. "XO to Spyglass," he said, using the intelligence officer's call-sign. Captain Colin Lovat was hidden in another of the ship's topside observation suites where sensor data was correlated. Lovat was already on-line, but before he could respond Loren gave him his order. "Give me pictures and stories."

Pictures referred to long-range surveillance cameras mounted on the DropShip. Lovat had preprogrammed them to pick up the key points of interest to the Fusiliers, namely the LZs and the positions known to be held by the Smoke Jaguars. "Stories" was the key phrase for sensor data from the surface of the planet. Together, these data would tell Loren how accurate the Combine intelligence was. The image of Wayside V came into view on Loren's and Stirling's monitors, zooming in on the hot spots.

"No signs of Jaguar activity," came Lovat's voice. "No active sensors in or around the jump point, no sign of aerospace fighter activity."

Loren activated his communications channel, this time contacting the fighter bays. "Wing commanders, this is the XO. Launch CAP lances. Other lances go to alert stand-by." The CAP, or Combat Air Patrol, would make sure that the small fleet of DropShips had its necessary fighter cover. The other lances of four fighters each were to be placed in a ready-to-launch mode—just in case the Jaguars had somehow detected their approach. The other ships would do the same as a cautionary measure. He activated the command link between his screen and Cat Stirling's, and opened direct feeds of Lovat's intelligence information to the other Drop-Ships.

On his own screen Loren saw the image of Wayside V loom even closer as the cameras zoomed in on their intended targets. Given the rotation of the planet and the positioning of the DropShips, the plan had called for them to make two orbital passes over the Jaguar base before landing. At present, the landing zones were in view as the slow rotation of the world below was matched by the speed of the DropShips.

Captain Lovat's voice over the speaker seemed to shatter some of the tension. "Weather over the LZs is currently clear, and there is no sign of any Smoke Jaguar activity there. A storm front is moving in, however, and there's a fifty percent probability it will hit by the time we land."

"Sensors picking up any activity?" Colonel Stirling asked.

"Negative, Colonel," Colin replied. "At this distance we only get cursory information. But I should be able to get a full scan of the area within the next eight hours. We'll get a visual pass over the Jaguar base in the next thirty minutes."

The next few minutes passed by quickly. Loren, through Captain Spillman, had the communications relays between the four DropShips confirmed. Behind them, at the jump point, the two JumpShips were deploying solar sails and using their thrusters to keep pace with the gravity well in which they had materialized.

Wayside V rotated slowly below them until the high mountain spires of New Northwind came into view. Stark gray, they poked up above the clouds that covered the low-lying seas entirely. Captain Lovat kept the focus on the area, and when the thick cloud-cover blocked his view, his thermal cameras began their work, transforming the image of the planet into a series of reddish and black peaks and valleys. Finally he had a report. "Visuals on the Smoke Jaguar base are inconclusive at this time. Weather patterns are blocking direct line-of-sight surveillance. Our thermal sensors show some activity, most likely BattleMech reactor-heat venting. We still won't know what's there until the next orbital pass."

Lovat's words only added to the tension Loren felt. He sat back in his chair and closed his eyes for a moment in thought. This was the part he hated the most—the waiting.

Two hours passed with only idle conversation as the world below them grew larger and more predominant. On this orbital pass the sensors would provide a more detailed picture, but thus far they had not reported anything. As the landing zones came into view, Loren began to relax slightly. *The Jags are nowhere near our LZs, just as we hoped. They're concentrated at their base.* Lovat's voice shattered his train of thought, derailing it hopelessly. "Sensors are picking up fusion-reactor signatures, ten in number, fifty-three kilometers due east of the Red Landing Zone."

Loren sprang to life. "XO here. Confirm message, ten reactors near Red LZ."

"Confirmed, XO. I am feeding the data now through the tactical database. Stand by." Each BattleMech reactor engine provided a unique neutrino signature based on its shape and the placement of the engine. Though there was a wide degree of variance, depending on the damage the 'Mech had taken or special modifications it carried, the signatures could be matched against the database of known sensor readings to provide close matches to the type of 'Mech that was on the surface below.

Captain Lovat's voice was on a higher pitch when it came back. "Two Stars of 'Mechs, slow moving. Reactor signatures match those of *Uller, Cauldron-Born, Mad Cat, Puma,* and *Masakari.* Numbers as follows: First Star painted as Alpha Star is two *Cauldron-Born* and three *Masakari*s. Bravo Star shows as two *Cauldron-Born,* two *Mad Cat*s, and a *Puma.*" The screen shimmered to life with a tactical display of the area where the 'Mechs were. Loren looked at them, then back up to where Stirling stood over her display.

"Those are OmniMechs, Major Jaffray," Colonel Stirling said, stating the obvious.

"Affirmative, sir," he replied. "Spyglass, confirm readings."

"Double-checked already, sir. Probabilities are eighty-five percent."

Cat Stirling's face flushed with anger. "I'm not worried about the fact that they're near the LZs. What bothers me is that those are Omnis, and Omnis are usually reserved for front-line units."

"They must be on a training exercise," Loren returned.

"This isn't good," Stirling said as Captain Lovat's voice came back on, along with a flash of red light from Captain Spillman's station. "Active scan!" he called. As suddenly as the red light came on, it went off. Loren knew the implications—someone, somewhere had scanned the *Claymore* and most likely the rest of what suddenly seemed like a small task force. The lanky Highlander ship captain leaned over his display and studied it. "One thing's fer sure, lassie," he said to Stirling at his side. "Them kitty-cats know we're here."

Loren ignored him, as did Stirling. "Where did that scan come from?" he asked Lovat over the microphone.

"Coming in now, sir . . . got it! South polar region. It looks like our cameras got an image." Loren's screen showed a slight blur at the edge of the horizon near the greenish sky. He was about to call for an enhancement of the image when Lovat sent the computer-enhanced image on the screen.

The "bump" on the horizon had become a crisp, clear image of a ship. Loren saw it and initially thought it was a JumpShip, but one dangerously close to the atmosphere of the planet.

Lovat gave him the answer he didn't want to hear. "Computer tags the scanning ship as an *Essex* Class destroyer. She popped up long enough to take a picture and scan of us, then disappear."

"*An* Essex *Class destroyer?*" Spillman said from his seat. "Spyglass, tell me that yer bloody computer has made a mistake."

Lovat's voice was down. "Sorry, Captain—Colonel. The Star League fielded those babies three centuries ago and we're still carrying the files in the ID system."

Loren walked over to Cat Stirling, unsure what to say at the verification. Spillman turned to the Colonel and lowered his voice so no one else could hear. "Even with fighter support and four DropShips, that WarShip can take us out before we ever get close enough to do damage. One of those babies mounts long-range naval lasers and particle cannons, and their antiship missiles are big enough to pop this tin can wide open. Yer fighters can get in and wreak havoc, but in the end the results would be the same."

"Hellfire," Stirling spat.

"Colonel, the Jaguars are brutal, but most likely won't bid the use of their WarShip, given the size of our force," Loren said, almost whispering. "This is like the Omnis—what's important is the fact that the ship *is* here. A WarShip like that wouldn't be assigned to protect a garrison Cluster. From what we've already seen on the planet, I think it's safe to say we're facing a front-line Clan force."

The look on Stirling's face told him she knew he was right. "Options are at a minimum here, Major. We can continue down, but with that WarShip there, the odds are in their favor."

"Unless we can convince them to keep it out of the bidding," Loren added.

She nodded. "The other option is to abort and return to the JumpShips."

"Colonel," Captain Spillman said, "given our thrust rate and the descent angle and position of the JumpShips, it will take a lot to bring us to a stop, turn around, and head back to the jump point. In the meantime they'd be able to calculate our trajectory, spot the JumpShips, and move in on them. Unless my statistics knowledge is failin' me, that destroyer is more than fast enough to get there at or before the time we do."

"You're suggesting we continue on then?" Stirling asked.

He nodded, albeit reluctantly.

"Hell of a way to enter a fight," she said. Her voice rose so that everyone could hear. "We continue on. Signal the other ships that we have to assume the Jags know we're coming from this point on. Assume a hot drop."

The next four hours passed slowly as Loren poured over

the scant data they'd gathered thus far. The next pass was the most important. With the sensors now within range to get accurate and detailed information, they'd be able to sweep the area in and around the Clan garrison base itself. Then they'd be able to detect any fusion reactors, even those that were shut down, and actually get an idea of what it was they were facing. Though there were no further sightings of the WarShip, he knew it was out there—waiting.

So now we know we aren't facing a mere Provisional Garrison Cluster. These are truebirth warriors in their best equipment. Now we've just got to find out how many there are. "Spyglass, it's almost time," Loren finally said out loud. His words seemed to stir things to life on the bridge. Everyone had been lost to their duty, to their thoughts; now they would get more information, they would know what they were facing.

There was a long pause as Captain Lovat ran the sensor sweeps across the surface of Wayside V. "Data incoming now, Major. Stand by." Another long pause.

There must be something wrong. This is taking far too long. "Captain Lovat, report."

"Still correlating data, Major," came Lovat's tense voice over the small speaker in the control console.

"Captain, we just need a rough count up here," Loren prodded.

Another silence was all that came back at first. "Scans of the area, combined with those of the two Stars at the LZ, show a total force of one hundred and seventy OmniMech reactors in various states of operation. We've also been able to confirm signatures of twenty-five OmniFighters at the aerobase and approximately one hundred Elemental suits."

Loren was stunned. "Say again, Spyglass. One-seven-oh 'Mechs?"

"Affirmative, XO," he replied.

Loren looked over slowly at Colonel Stirling. The full regiment of the Fusiliers, along with *Sho-sa* Parkensen's additional company, amounted to less than a hundred BattleMechs. They had support craft and troops as well, but given the Smoke Jaguars' technological edge, the odds went from fair to horrific. "Colonel Stirling, we're facing a full Galaxy of frontline Smoke Jaguar forces." Loren's mind was racing as he forced his thoughts to how they might revise their plans to meet this totally unexpected situation.

Cat Stirling stood like a statue, as if his words merely bounced off her like rain on stone. She too was obviously weighing the new intelligence and how it would impact her precious regiment. Finally she leaned toward Loren. "Turning back is not an option, Major."

He nodded, knowing what she would do next. The Jaguars might not respond to the formal challenge of the batchall from an Inner Sphere unit, but it might still help define what the Clan commanders actually decided to throw at them.

Colonel Stirling leaned over her console, activating several of the controls. "Communications Officer, link me on a wide beam for transmission to the Clan base as well as the other ships in our task force." It took less than half a minute.

"Clan Smoke Jaguar, this is Colonel Andrea Stirling of Stirling's Fusiliers of the Northwind Highlanders. We have come to take this world from you and bring a regiment of combined arms forces to do so. We trace our heritage to service in the Star League Defense Force and beyond. We offer you an honorable fight. I don't expect you to answer this batchall, but I do expect you to defend yourself accordingly."

10

Wildcat Station
Wayside V (Wildcat)
Deep Periphery
3 July 3058

Galaxy Commander Devon Osis stared into the dim blue and red light of his holographic display for the fifth time, studying the words that hung in the space before him. Colonel Stirling's transmission had been converted to text for him to review as he waited for his Star Colonels to report. The message hovered in the air like the dagger that MacBeth had seen, bloody and threatening.

Only one word ran through his mind: audacity. *How dare*

this freebirth abomination interfere with my plans or those of the Khan?

Star Colonel Roberta arrived first, her face showing the dull purple bruises from her fight with him. She bowed her head slightly as she entered, then stood at attention. On her shoulder patch was the outstretched jaguar paw, its claws dripping red blood, that marked her command of the Bloodied Claws Cluster.

Star Colonel Patricia of the 250th Assault Cluster entered next. As the commanding officer of the Mist Pouncers, she fielded the largest of the Clan units on Wildcat. Her appearance was distinctive, her jet black hair streaked with white like lightning bolts just over her ears. Her olive skin made her seem exotic, almost like the Jaguar namesake of the Clan she served.

Tall, blonde, and blue-eyed, Star Colonel Thibideau Osis was almost her polar opposite. Thibideau's Deathstrike Cluster was small but powerful. He was of the same blood house as Devon, both men sharing the genetic heritage and a Bloodname of the House of Osis. Thibideau Osis was also the only Bloodnamed officer among the Huntress Galaxy commanders.

"At ease," Devon Osis said as he motioned to the seats around his desk. Ever proud, Roberta chose to stand while the other two officers sat. "So, a mercenary regiment is on drop approach as we speak and will be on the surface of this world within seven hours." The message he had received from Colonel Stirling had been sent to the Star Colonels as well.

"These are mercenary soldiers," Thibideau Osis said. "By their very nature they are inferior to us."

Roberta spoke up with a sharp crack of her voice. "They are not worthy foes. Pursuing them would be akin to hunting bandits, and that is a job for a stinking solahma unit, not the Huntress Galaxy. They should not be accorded the respect due only to true warriors. I say we send the *Dark Claw* to destroy them rather than fight them as honorable foes, quiaff?" Life in the Clans was harsh and strict, with most warriors considered beyond their pride in their thirties. Her reference to the bandit caste, the lowest form of Clan life, made it clear what she thought of these Fusiliers. The new Galaxy had no old or retiring warriors, nothing to make up a solahma unit.

She does not understand. She has only heard the rhetoric

bandied on the home worlds. "Neg, Star Colonel. Do not disregard this or any mercenary unit. I have fought such units before and they are not to be dismissed."

A sneer crossed Roberta's face. "Mercenaries are no match for true warriors."

"Do they not sing *The Remembrance* on the homeworlds, Star Colonel? Does the name 'Luthien' not fire your blood as it does mine?" Unlike them, Devon Osis had been there on Luthien where the combined efforts of the Kell Hounds and the accursed Wolf's Dragoons had crushed the Smoke Jaguar assault on the capital of the Draconis Combine.

Thibideau broke the tension. "You mean to fight them, quiaff?"

"Aff. But we shall fight them on our terms. This Colonel Stirling's attempt at a batchall means nothing to me. I might do these money soldiers honor by allowing them to die on their feet rather than destroying them in orbit, but I shall not let her corrupt the honor of the batchall."

Star Colonel Patricia leaned across the table and activated the display again, this time tapping codes into the buttons along the edge of the base. "There seems to be little information regarding these Northwind Highlanders to which the Fusiliers belong. What do we know of them?"

Devon Osis leaned back slightly. "They claim heritage with the Star League army. When General Kerensky took our people away, they stayed behind. That betrayal has forced them into the life of freebirth mercenaries. They fight not for honor, but for money. Clan Steel Viper has fought them; I heard the Khan speak of it at one of the Grand Council meetings."

One of the greatest challenges the Clans faced upon coming to the Inner Sphere was the lack of Clan-equivalent honor among their foes. Among the Clans, a batchall was not an exercise in deception, but an honest exchange of information on the forces that would encounter each other. There was no need to gather intelligence because to win by trickery was the coward's way, not that of a true warrior.

Devon Osis spoke with raw anger. "They have shamed and dishonored that memory by selling their skills as warriors."

Roberta smiled, a newly capped tooth gleaming as she did. "All that remains is the bidding then."

"Aff," Devon Osis said. "The asset of the WarShip is mine to control, all others are yours as the Cluster commanders. In the ways of our people since the time of the great Nicholas Kerensky, I open the bidding for the defense of this world against those forces known as Stirling's Fusiliers of the Northwind Highlanders—freebirth warriors all. Battles are won in blood and death, but can be swayed by the tossing of stars in the bid. May your bids reveal your heart and spirit, and may you bloody your claws and fangs on the foe you are about to face." The words he spoke were almost a chant, the kind of ritualistic speech he had heard hundreds of times before. Now, as the Tau Galaxy Commander, they were *his* words to speak aloud.

Each of the Galaxy Commanders pulled out a small kit pouch and opened it. Inside were sets of deadly throwing stars, made of ferro-carbon and honed to a deadly edge. Each was colored and labeled to represent the forces the commanders had available. Devon pulled out a large round pad with the symbol of the Smoke Jaguar covering it. The pad was marked in many places, like a dart board. There were dark brown spots, old blood, still marking the symbol of the Smoke Jaguar that covered the board.

Bidding for the right to enter combat was done differently by each Clan. The Jaguar tradition called for the deadly throwing stars to be cast by the bidding warrior into a specially designed bidding board. Though to an outsider it might look like a simple game of darts, it was far from it. Nicholas Kerensky had once said that the art of the bid was part mental skill, part warrior prowess—and the Jaguars honored that. The participants involved in the bid held their hands on the bidding board.

Each star represented a Star—five BattleMechs or aerofighters, or twenty-five Elementals. To reduce a bid, the points of the stars would be broken off as well, each representing a single fighter, 'Mech, or five Elemental warriors. The individual points, if necessary, could be jabbed into the pad at the time of the bidding. The colors told their nature. Red represented 'Mech forces, blue for fighters, and gray were the Elemental Points. Each of the Star Colonels' stars was marked in the center with the unit insignia for their individual three Clusters.

Part of the Jaguar ritual was plain, the lowest bid earning the right to take on the Fusiliers. The secondary and unspoken object of the bidding was to attempt to damage or break a previous bid when you threw your stars into the bidding board. Any commander's star shattered in such a way was taken after the bidding as a prize of the bid.

The elements of risk were high. The bidding warrior never faced the board. He or she looked away, taking a martial arts fighting stance in preparation for the throw. To bid, the warrior pivoted quickly and let the stars fly as if being thrown at an advancing foe. If the star tips cut the fingers of any of the other bidders, that entire star was automatically removed from the bid. This forced good aim. But the scars on Thibideau Osis's fingers showed that, on occasion, even the best Jaguar warriors missed. If a deliberate miss was suspected, a Trial of Refusal on the bid could be waged, as was often the case. One of the worst losses of honor was for a warrior to pull his or her hand away from the bidding board. It almost always removed them from the bidding totally.

Thibideau Osis spoke first after pulling out his star tokens. "As the first and only Bloodnamed among my fellow Star Colonels, I evoke my right to pass on this opening bid. I pass to Roberta so that she might show her claws to us now." As the commander of the 25th Strike Cluster, his Deathstrike forces were the smallest cluster in the Galaxy. By passing the bid, he reserved the right to bid again at a later time, perhaps when the bidding was low enough that he could enter with a chance of winning. He and Patricia moved to the board and placed their hands on it, with full confidence and bravado.

Roberta did not answer with words. She walked away, then spun around with blinding speed, casting her bidding stars at the round pad. She had held back just over one of her Stars—breaking off several of the points a second before the throw, mostly Elemental and 'Mech forces. One point from the lethally tossed bidding star hit less than a centimeter from Patricia's hand.

Devon Osis leaned forward and studied her bid. It was neither impressive nor as bold as he had expected. *She has a plan, something only she knows and which is not obvious now. She has left room to lower her bid, but, like Thibideau, is forcing Patricia to now bid the most boldly.*

Patricia worked on her bidding stars silently as she walked to the throwing position while Roberta took her place at the board. Then, like a skilled martial artist she turned and threw the stars at the bidding board. Had she been throwing at a human target, the target would have been felled by the deadly barrage of razor-sharp stars. One of her bidding stars hit but did not damage those thrown by Roberta. She had pared away equal amounts of fighter, 'Mech, and Elemental support, undercutting Roberta's bid by another Star.

"Your bid showed lack of imagination, Roberta," Patricia said. "I have evened the odds, no matter what the venue."

Having noted their respective bids, Devon Osis returned the stars to the two Colonels. He turned then to Thibideau Osis.

"It is time for the Deathstrike Cluster," he said. Thibideau half-jumped, half-leaped into the air as he thrust his stars at the board. He had removed all of his aerospace fighters and most of his Elemental forces, undercutting Patricia's bid by several points of a star. Devon studied the bid carefully. Thibideau apparently planned to fight on the ground only.

Roberta seemed amused by his bid. She manipulated her stars out of sight of the others, facing away as was the tradition. Then, like a samurai of old Terra, she cast the stars at the board with the force of a hurricane. Her aim was good, breaking one of Thibideau's bidding stars in half and narrowly missing Thibideau Osis's hand with one of her 'Mech stars. Devon looked at her bid and was surprised to see that she had removed several Points of her BattleMech forces and a full Star of both 'Mech and Elemental forces. Then he saw her plan. It had risks, but also promised her much glory if she could pull it off. *She is as dangerous as I suspected. She plays this part of her role well.*

Patricia looked at the bid that had been cast, and Devon saw a flicker of concern on her face. Roberta could not let that pass without comment. "Come now, Patricia, surely you can beat my bid? You have so often bragged how superior your forces are to mine. Now you can prove it. If you can beat this bid, I will bow out."

Patricia stared for a moment at the bidding pad, then put her stars back in her pack. "Your bravado is uncalled for and unbecoming of a true Jaguar. I do not believe that you can defeat this foe with the forces you bid for the battle."

"Poorly bargained and done," Thibideau chimed in. "If that is indeed your bid, Roberta, you will perish. Your 'Mech forces are too weak to score a victory against even this free-birth bandit-trash. You are reckless in your bid, and I, like Patricia, will let you pay the price. By the time these

Fusiliers land and square off against your Cluster, you will be beaten and will forfeit your honor."

Roberta laughed out loud, a sinister sound. She reached down to the broken bidding star she had just shattered and held it in front of her by the points. Then she took the broken halves into her hand, squeezing them in her grasp until blood dripped onto the table. She was showing them her power of will.

She continued to smile. "You are weak and do not see why my bid will win. You think this battle will take place on the ground, but I will shatter these Fusiliers before they can land. Whatever is left of them when my fighters are done will be easy to crush."

Devon Osis slammed his fist on the table top to get their attention. "This is not some game between sibkos we are playing," he shouted. "Do not discount this threat. The Tau Galaxy was raised with the sole purpose of ending the blight known as the Nova Cats. Now we are plagued with this raid. We must defeat these mercenary trash, but in the doing we cannot so weaken ourselves that we are unable to fulfill our ultimate mission against the Nova Cats."

The Galaxy Commander turned his gaze to Roberta, whose face had grown somber at his display of anger. "These Fusiliers are a threat to our plans and the will of our Khan. The time for bravado is over, Star Colonel. You have won the bid as you must now win the fight. I want these freebirths destroyed, utterly, do you hear? No survivors."

===== 11 =====

DropShip **Claymore,** *Approach Vector*
Wayside V (Wildcat)
Deep Periphery
3 July 3058

Loren sat in the cockpit of his *Penetrator* and rechecked his 'Mech's diagnostics for the fifth time. The gentle throbbing of the 'Mech's fusion reactor and the blanket of warmth in the cockpit could not take the chill from his thoughts. His communications feeds to the *Claymore*'s bridge were open, but remained oddly quiet. The deadly silence only seemed to add to the tension. As much as he found Captain Spillman's manners and speech irritating and disrespectful, they would have been a lot more welcome than the low hiss of static that filled his neurohelmet. Things had gone seriously wrong from the moment they'd first detected the Jaguars.

A front-line Galaxy of Clan troops! A part of him was angry at having their plan disrupted by the unexpected presence of so large a Clan force. But another part of Loren Jaffray thrilled to the challenge. He was best under pressure and forced to improvise, making up his moves as he went along.

He also knew that the Fusiliers were in serious trouble. The odds were against them, and not many Inner Sphere forces had survived being outnumbered by the Clans. But if they tried to flee now, there might never be another chance for this mission. The Jaguars would know their base had been discovered. Worse, the unexpected presence of this new front-line Galaxy represented a direct and present threat to the Draconis Combine—the Highlanders' new employer.

A voice shattered his thoughts as the ship began to drop toward the low atmosphere of Wayside V. "Satellites deployed. We are under reentry blackout for three minutes." Spillman's voice sounded different, almost totally calm. They were on his playing field, the bridge of his ship. He was in total command now, no matter what Colonel Stirling or the regulations had to say.

Loren looked out of his cockpit viewscreen at the massive deployment door in front of him. The bay was only dimly lit, as was normal during a combat drop. On both sides of him other 'Mech pilots of the Kilsyth Guards were sitting just as tensely in their cockpits, waiting for the ship to land and the DropShip doors to open.

Suddenly the *Claymore* rocked as if batted by the hand of some giant. Loren felt the restraint straps bite into his shoulders despite the foam pads. *This is it!* There was a roar as the turrets of the DropShip rotated and began to fire. Colonel Stirling's voice came over the communications channel. "Report CIC."

Another massive impact rocked the ship as Loren tightened his grip on the throttle and firing joystick to steady himself. "Fighters," Spillman answered. There was a pause, then another lesser impact off in the distance. "We're being hammered by ten of the bastards," he added.

Loren linked up to the *Claymore*'s tactical display and began to get the target feeds from the ship's battle computer to his own BattleMech's secondary display. The fighters were mostly made up of *Sabutai* OmniFighters, with *Bashkir* fighters as escorts. These two classes of fighters made up the core of the Smoke Jaguar aerospace fighter forces. The *Sabutai*s were a mixed bag of configurations, most mounting massive Gauss rifles. The slugs from those powerful weapons would rip terrible holes in the armor of the Drop-Ships. As he tried to get detailed information on one of the fighters, the secondary monitor went blank, then returned to standby mode. He knew what it meant. They'd lost either the ship's battle computers, sensor feeds, or the lines between here and there. Whatever it was, this wasn't a good sign.

After a long, ten-second pause the *Claymore* suddenly rattled under a mighty barrage. Despite its incredible size, the ship seemed to vibrate under the assault of the Jaguar's fighters. Loren felt the adrenaline jolt, then something else kick in within his body and mind. He called it The Sensation, a name his beloved grandfather had given to the mix of emotions and sensations of battle. It came to him as a rush of hot and cold flashes, bringing all of his senses alive. His eyes widened with excitement and his heart raced. A low hum filled his ears, and his mind and body seemed to be working in overdrive, as if he were having some sort of out-of-body experience where his being was working at light speed.

The attack was not like a punch but more like a series of blows that didn't seem to end. He heard the massive *Overlord* Class vessel moan as its internal structure buckled under the damage somewhere beyond his field of vision. The sound was disturbing, and Loren reminded himself, uncomfortably, that they were still kilometers above the planet's surface. Outside of his cockpit the bay went dark as the internal electrical systems apparently were disrupted. His hands were hovering near the deployment controls. The press of one button would allow his *Penetrator* to break free of its restraints and move to the door. He could use his jump jets to land unless the ship was in some sort of violent spin. His survival, however, did not mean that the rest of the regiment would survive.

The steady series of impacts on the ship made the *Claymore* pitch hard to one side. Without warning the upper portion of the deployment door in front of him buckled inward, then seemed to explode. The blast was not so much from explosives, but from a massive rush of explosive decompression. The dark bay suddenly erupted with light, and the *Penetrator* experienced a massive tug forward as the air from the bay rushed out through the two-meter-hole and everything loose in the bay was sucked out into the hold and beyond.

The local chatter on the ship's channels went on for another minute or more. Emergency calls. Problems with bulkhead doors. Fires. Loren heard them all and they told the story of a ship that had taken a lot of damage, though he couldn't see much of it. Captain Spillman, from his high roost on the bridge, coordinated it all, and Loren waited to inquire as to the rest of the regiment.

His patience finally giving way, he activated his own channel. "XO to Spillman. Damage report."

"Just a bloody minute, XO, I'm still sorting out what's still in one piece up here," Spillman's voice returned, filled with frustration and raw anger. "We've had six hull breaches. One of the bays was hit bad. 'Mech damage was light, but they canna drop deploy—we're gonna have to cut them out. Tactical sensor feeds are damaged so I canna send you a picture. We lost two turrets and our engine shielding has been badly torn. We're a goin' down approximately thirty kilometers from our designated LZ."

If things were off that much, Loren knew the damage must have been pretty bad.

"Reports from the other ships?" cut in Colonel Stirling's voice.

"The *Bull Run* is currently engaged. With this turbulence and storm front moving in, we can't provide cover support and our pilots can't spot the Jaguars until they're on top of them." Spillman paused and Loren imagined him looking over the tactical feeds from the other ships.

"Damn. The *Stonewall*'s been hit bad. Engine and maneuver systems are on manual override. Bloody demons—" He was meters away on the bridge, voice filled with shock. "They've been rammed! Communications are marginal—heavy static."

"Will she make it?" Stirling asked over the line.

"Say a prayer and hope that the good Lord's listening, lass," he replied. "We can't raise the *Retribution*, but I show her moving low, possibly for emergency landing. She might be trying to stay low enough to keep those Clanners from pursuit."

"And that destroyer?" The question bonded Stirling, Spillman, and Loren together. If the Smoke Jaguar WarShip entered the fight, there was little hope of survival. It could orbitally bombard the ships as soon as they landed. From the images Loren had seen of the Smoke Jaguar attack on the city of Edo several years before, both the city and the ground it stood on had been melted into a black-gray glass in the bombardment. These Jaguars were dangerous foes, willing to do anything to win.

There was a pause again, one that seemed to last a lifetime. "She's moved to high orbit. Out of range but in position to get us if we try to make a break for the JumpShip."

Not only were the Fusiliers outnumbered, they were now trapped on Wayside. Apparently, though, the Jaguars were not planning to use the WarShip against them, probably as a result of their bidding. The Fusiliers might yet be able to use that to their advantage.

There were several other orders on the line, all from Spillman to the other officers on the bridge. Loren caught only bits and pieces of them. "Message in from the *Bull Run*. They're still holding together with light to moderate damage. The Jaguars have broken off their attack, at least the ones that were left." A string of green lights came on in the *Penetrator*'s cockpit, and the secondary display flashed the words "Landing Sequence Initiated." Spillman issued several more orders. "We're coming down in fifty seconds. All hands brace for landing."

Colonel Stirling's voice came back on line. "XO, I want a tight perimeter-defense deployment."

"Roger, Colonel," Loren replied.

"Captain Spillman, any further word from the *Stonewall*?"

"No sir. Communications down. Wait . . . sensors show them jump-deploying BattleMechs." Jump deployment was risky but often used in "hot drop" situations. The DropShip would open its doors and its BattleMechs would leap out, making manual landings. Hot drops were often employed to put an assault force down rapidly in the middle of the enemy without risking the DropShip. In this case, with the *Stonewall* so badly shot up, it was a desperate gamble to save lives should the ship crash on landing. Loren bit his lower lip.

He opened a channel to the whole battalion aboard the *Claymore*. It was just fifteen seconds to landing, and his mind and heart were racing with excitement. "Major Jaffray to the Kilsyth Guards and regimental command. Deployment Pattern Bravo, say again, Deployment Pattern Bravo. Anyone who cannot deploy or is damaged, signal to your lance commanders."

He rechecked his own systems and idled the power output from the fusion reactor to a higher level, enough to move the *Penetrator* and bring its powerful weapons to bear. Then he activated his sensors, but found them clouded by the bay. *That's expected, but as soon as that door opens, I want a picture of where we are and what's happening out there.*

Though the *Claymore* landed with a jarring impact, it was softer than what Loren had expected. He activated the release, and the myomer straps that held the *Penetrator* in place fell loose, freeing his BattleMech. Just as he was about to fire at the deployment ramp/door, what was left of it popped open.

The bay flooded with light, but the highly polarized cockpit glass blunted its assault. Outside Loren saw red clay covered with low grass or moss. The sky overhead was filled with clouds, black and dark blue, and rain was pelting down everywhere. In the distance, a lightning strike caught his attention as he thought for a moment that it was a PPC burst. The green sky showed through the clouds in several spots, enough to cast an eerie glow over the ground and the 'Mechs of the Fusiliers.

The deployment sequence called for the lance on his flank to go first and they did. Loren followed them out the door, his weapons ready to engage. He opened his communications channel to the battalion commanders. "Fusiliers, deploy!"

=== 12 ===

Despite all the excitement surrounding their arrival and landing, Loren's first impression of Wayside V was one of disappointment. The terrain in and around the LZ was relatively flat and unbroken bright red soil. The plant life consisted of grasses, mosses, and scrawny vines that crawled over what rocks and stones broke the surface. The raging thunderstorm made visibility poor, but when lightning crackled, he could see what appeared to be mountains to the south of the LZ. That, of course, was an illusion. In reality, he and his men were sitting in an old sea bed, and those "mountains" were the tops of the continental shelves bordering what had once been the sea bottom when all of this had been kilometers under water.

"XO to communications platoon. Priority to establishing the regimental communications link."

Captain Jebediah Lewis was on the line in less than a second. "We're on it, XO. The *Claymore*'s communications can't hail the other ships. We don't know if it's the storms, the communications systems, or what, but we'll get up ASAP."

Loren moved his *Penetrator* further away from the Drop-Ship, coming up on top of a small rise to get a slightly better view. All around him was activity as the Fusiliers of the regimental command and First Battalion began the task of setting up defenses and breaking out the array of gear required to take a battalion into battle. He checked his tactical display and saw that they were at least an hour's travel from their intended LZ.

He toggled the regimental channel, a direct laser-burst relay from this 'Mech to the DropShip and then down to the regimental CO. "Colonel, I suggest we use this as our base of operations until we can link up with the rest of the regiment."

"Agreed," her disembodied voice replied. Loren saw from his tactical display that she was nearly a kilometer away, on the outer edge of the defensive perimeter being set up by the Fusiliers. "We're limited to battalion-level communications for a while. That means we'll have to track down the others the old-fashioned way. We need to find them and link up."

"We can use First Company as a recon-in-force. Split them in half and send them to where the *Bull Run* and the *Stonewall* were supposed to land. Once we make contact with them, we can piggy-back the communications signal to them via the 'Mechs."

"What about our PSL?"

"The *Retribution* was supposed to come down in the middle of our triangle LZ pattern. If we find the edges, the center should be easy to spot, assuming any of the ships landed anywhere near their intended targets."

"Understood and approved. Remember there are two Stars' worth of Clan Omnis nearby, and I don't want to give them anything that will help them locate us or know how bad off we are."

"Roger. See you in a few hours sir," Loren returned.

The hours of scouring the rugged and shattered terrain of the LZ had not totally dulled Loren's senses, but it was getting close. The jagged rocks, the low, moss-covered scrub trees, all added an eerie sense of alien presence as he checked everywhere for a sign of the lost ships. Loren studied his display as he approached the *Retribution*'s signal, his force spread out on his flanks. The Clan force he'd detected seemed to be located in a large depression. From the direction of their firing, he could tell that whoever they were fighting was also in the depression. As his ears buzzed with the rush of The Sensation, he knew he was going to have to tie down the Clan force to give his people time to move to a good position. *Hitting their flanks will help us and get the most relief to Parkensen's people.*

He opened a tight-beam comm channel, lasering his message to each of the 'Mechs in a confined beam. "Heads up, this is XO to all 'Mechs. I'm going in alone. Split off of me. Right flank move to the east and take up a position just outside their long sensor range equal to their current position. Same on the left flank."

"There's five of them sir," Lieutenant Glenda Jura said.

"You've got your orders. Hold all communications until my signal. I'm going to buy you time to get into flanking positions."

From the *Penetrator*'s cockpit Loren saw his people begin to deploy, moving to the flanks. Suddenly alone, he began to walk the *Penetrator* forward, directly toward the Clan position. At one hundred meters his sensors picked up magnetic signatures of other BattleMechs. Checking the tactical readout, he saw that he was facing a variety of Clan OmniMechs, from a *Cauldron-Born* to the menacing *Masakari*. Not only was he outnumbered, he was outgunned as well.

Another fifty meters in his sensor sweeps showed the position of a downed DropShip. From all signs it was the Combine DropShip *Retribution*, or what was left of her. His scanners picked up debris readings in a long drag gully that had to be the result of a crash landing. DropShips like the *Fortress* Class were supposed to land on their struts straight down, but this one had obviously slid sideways for a very long distance. Her landing struts were gone, shredded from impact. Her 'Mech bays were ripped wide open.

The battle had apparently been raging for some minutes, Loren's thermal sensors showing errant missile misses and the recognizable images of downed and probably destroyed BattleMechs. The PSL company was beleaguered, with only half their original force operational, hardly a match for the Smoke Jaguars. At the edge of his sensors Loren saw the other Star's worth of Jaguar OmniMechs.

Loren paused and drew in a deep breath before opening his wide-beam frequency, exposing himself to every Clan OmniMech in the field. The only good thing was that it would also tell the PSL's beleagued forces that help had arrived. "This is Major Loren Jaffray of Stirling's Fusiliers of the Northwind Highlanders. Break off your attack. I offer you a Trial of Possession for the DropShip *Retribution*." He paused. This was a gamble—and a fluke if they accepted his challenge—and he knew it. He saw that the Jaguar forces were pulling back, turning their active sensors on him, attempting to determine if it was a trap.

After a long pause, a signal came back from one of the Jaguar 'Mechs. "You are mercenary freebirths unworthy of the honor of engaging us in a batchall."

Good, I got their attention. "Who dares challenge my integrity and honor?" Loren looked again at his long-range sensors and saw that the replying 'Mech was a menacing *Masakari,* a BattleMech the Clans called the *Warhawk.*

Another voice from off his short-range sensors came on line. "Major Jaffray, this is *Sho-sa* Parkensen. I order you to break off this attack. This enemy is mine!" There was grim anger in Parkensen's tone, but from what Loren could see, the PSL's force had little hope.

"With all due respect, *Sho-sa,* I'm trying to save your butt. My orders come from Colonel Stirling. You can argue protocol with her later. For now, cut the chatter and stand by for reinforcement and possible evac." Whatever Parkensen might have replied was lost just then when another voice came over the wide-band channel, cutting him off.

"I am Star Captain Kerndon of the Smoke Jaguars, the true Clan and heir to the legacy of the great Kerenskys and holders of the Star League's heritage. I declare your batchall invalid and further declare that you and your unit are all bandit waste that we will drive into the ground of this forsaken planet."

Star Captain Kerndon apparently thought the taunt wasn't enough. "And if you think otherwise, you swine, come and face me like true warriors. I promise you a death that will strike fear among your filthy freebirth offspring for years to come."

Loren actually smiled as he broke the *Penetrator* into a full charge straight at Kerndon's OmniMech. "You refuse our challenge to an honorable fight?" he asked.

"Aff, you honorless trashborn."

Loren smiled in the tight space of his neurohelmet. "Have it your way . . ." He paused, trying to come up with the biggest insult he could for the Jaguar warrior. Then it hit him, and he shouted a single word—"Bastard!"

The insinuation that a Clan warrior was born to biological

parents and was not the superior product of engineering was the most stunning verbal assault he could launch, and Kerndon's speechlessness made him think the shot had hit its mark. Loren activated his own unit's communications channel to his two deployed forces. "Fusiliers, attack! Have at 'em!"

He broke to the right the instant he came into range of the *Masakari*'s massive extended-range particle projection cannons. The Clan PPCs were deadly and the Omni mounted four of them, enough to take out his 'Mech in a single volley if the shots were good. His break to the right made tracking a little more tricky, sparing him. Kerndon fired with all four of the weapons at once. The incoming blue blasts mixed in with the background lightning and seemed to light up the entire hillside as they reached out for his *Penetrator*.

Two of the bolts missed narrowly, but the static-discharging energy leaped out and scarred the *Penetrator*'s upper right arm. One of the PPC bursts ripped into the armor of his upper-right torso just above his triple pack of Sutel pulse lasers, exploding the armor plating outward and pushing the 'Mech back hard as the second blast hit in the right leg. It was the leg hit that worried him the most, the bolts of energy tearing through the upper thigh of his *Penetrator*'s bird-like leg like a hot knife through butter. Green coolant oozed from the gash and down over the 'Mech's knee, dripping like blood from a wound.

He fired at the same time as the *Masakari*, scoring deep hits on the frontal armor of the OmniMech. Two more bursts of PPC fire and a volley of ten long-range missiles replied, racing and ripping at him. Anticipating the counter-volley, Loren abruptly slammed his *Penetrator* into a hard left turn at the last moment. One of the PPC bolts hit his lower torso, rocking the *Penetrator*; the other fell short, hitting the ground in front of him. The water-soaked clay exploded, throwing rocks and dirt against his legs like shrapnel.

The missiles twisted to follow his sudden darting action, some more tightly than others. Four of the missiles found their mark, splattering against the wet surface of the *Penetrator*'s massive right arm and torso. The explosions caught the *Penetrator* mid-stride, making Loren bite his lower lip, drawing blood. His ears were ringing as he scanned the *Masakari*. *Damnation, that bastard is still running cool. If that were my 'Mech, I'd be roasted alive by now.*

He raised his own extended-range large lasers and fired at the *Masakari* the instant his targeting and tracking system squealed a lock signal in his neurohelmet. The ruby-red streams of laser energy hit the ferro-fibrous armor of the Clan Omni in the torso, frying off armor plates with a barely audible popping sound, but doing no damage internally. *I've got to even the odds and fast. This guy is configured for long-range combat. PPCs and LRMs are ineffective at point-blank range.*

In mid-step Loren ignited his jump jets, lifting the *Penetrator*'s 75 tons up from the muddy clay into the storm-filled skies, heading straight for the *Masakari*. Star Captain Kerndon started to walk his 'Mech backward, opening up again with two of his PPCs and his missiles. The PPCs went wide of their mark, but all ten missiles streaked toward the *Penetrator*.

A steady stream of beeps from Loren's anti-missile system indicated that it was locked onto the warheads, and he engaged it without even thinking. The anti-missile cannon fired off a seeming wall of shot into the path of the incoming missiles. There was a series of explosions, but three missiles still managed to speed through, slamming into the center of his *Penetrator*'s boxy chest.

Loren landed the 'Mech hard, sinking the machine's giant feet into the moist clay, then he fired his large lasers again at the Clan 'Mech. There was a hit and several misses as his foe took several more steps backward. His tactical display showed that the Fusilier force was on the far flanks of Kerndon's position, slugging it out with the other Clan Omnis. *Kerndon's onto my tactics and knows that maintaining distance is his best hope.* With desperate daring, Loren throttled the *Penetrator* forward into a full run, pushing the machine to its absolute maximum and aiming straight at the towering Omni as it fired squarely at him.

Four PPCs and a wave of long-range missiles blasted at Loren, a glowing flash of sheer death and destruction. All the PPCs found their mark, but Loren had no time to assess the damage. The impact of the assault was square and direct and of such force that his arms ached as he fought to keep the massive 'Mech upright. A wave of nausea came over him as feedback from the damage raced into his neurohelmet, further pitching his sense of balance. Bile rose in his throat, and his eyes fluttered as he strained to keep the *Penetrator* charging at his target. He ignored the whistles and beeps of the warning alarms in the cockpit, fighting to stay conscious.

A sick metallic grinding told him the truth of his anti-missile system. *Gone—it's been destroyed!* The enemy missiles slammed into him, spreading damage everywhere to his 'Mech.

He opened up with everything the *Penetrator* had left, his large lasers cutting deeply into the heart of the *Masakari*. The pulse lasers' tiny bursts of red light were like a shotgun blast, burning a half-dozen holes into the arms of the Clan 'Mech. Kerndon stepped back eight more steps, to maintain distance. Loren matched his strides in a full run, fighting his own dizziness and the raging heat of his cockpit.

Suddenly Kerndon stopped. A flash of lightning showed him backed up against the ripped and torn hull of what had been the DropShip *Retribution*. And so close that it was next to impossible for him to use the particle cannons that made up the bulk of his firepower.

Next to impossible . . .

Kerndon's voice came alive in Loren's cockpit like a specter taunting him from beyond the grave. "Your 'Mech is nearly overheated, fool. Freebirth trash, today you die." The Clanner switched off the field inhibitors for his PPCs one at a time. With the field inhibitors off, the PPCs could fire at point-blank range, though doing so risked totally destroying the weapons.

Loren could trigger one of his large lasers, but that was about it—anything else and his 'Mech would shut down from overheating. As testimony to his plight, the sheets of rain slamming at the *Penetrator* began turning into a smoke-like vapor from the heat on his surface armor. But he was sure there had to be a way out. He scanned the DropShip behind Kerndon. The outer hull was holed and pitted in several areas, with many plates ripped open from the sliding on impact. Inside the ship, his sensors picked up a massive reading of thermal insulation, the kind of signature used to house explosives or . . .

The hydrogen tanks! Loren realized suddenly.

During a crash the hydrogen fuel would almost all be jettisoned, leaving just enough for a landing. But the tanks would still be filled with liquid hydrogen and the inert gas that kept oxygen from mixing with the hydrogen and causing an explosion. Loren raised his right large laser and leveled it at the shape just beyond his foe. With an eerie calm he switched the laser to one of his target interlock circuits, then thumbed the trigger.

The laser beam went past Kerndon by a full three meters, digging through the debris of the ship and into the ripped-open cargo bay, where it sliced into the fuel tank. The laser blast lasted three full seconds, and the already unbearable heat in Loren's cockpit seemed to double. He resisted the temptation to cease firing, and kept the beam blazing away.

Kerndon started to laugh out loud, but the sound broke off as the DropShip's hydrogen tank exploded. The blast came from the bowels of the *Retribution*, blowing straight at Loren. The orange-white ball of flame seemed to pop like a balloon where the Clan OmniMech stood. Loren lost sight of it as the blast wave seemed to envelop it and reach out for his own *Penetrator*. His cockpit warning sensors started to scream as he lost control and his 'Mech began to topple.

Suddenly there was an eerie silence all around him. Looking up, Loren saw that a quarter of the Combine DropShip had been ripped away by the explosion. Lying face down on the ground was the *Masakari* and another Clan 'Mech, knocked flat by the explosion from behind them. Its armor was in tatters, but from what Loren could see visually, the pilot was probably still alive. Approaching from his right was a *Cauldron-Born* very much on its feet.

The last one standing wins. . . .

13

Fusiliers LZ, Bay of Kurita Prime
Wayside V (Wildcat)
Deep Periphery
3 July 3058

Loren Jaffray entered the large mobile van, the two sentries letting him pass without delay. He made his way directly to where the Colonel sat in the command control area. The command post was a highly modified mobile headquarters van that Stirling's Fusiliers carried into battle. The unit was part communications hub, part command information network. Cat Stirling usually liked to set up a portable field tent/dome, which put her closer to the troops and the fighting, but for this meeting it did not seem necessary. From this post Stirling could contact any 'Mech in her command, relay sensor data from all units in the field, and paint a macrolevel picture of what her foe was, where he was, and what he was doing.

The center of the van was circular, with a ring of workstations surrounding the Colonel's. From her central seat, she could turn and view numerous screens showing tactical and strategic data for the planet. Weather data, satellite scans, and field sensor information fed to these monitors controlled by the officers on duty here. From one spot, she could coordinate any battle happening on Wayside V.

As Loren moved to the Colonel's side it was obvious she was absorbed in whatever was showing on one of the screens in front of her. Standing next to her was Major Cullen Craig, silent and stern. He nodded in Loren's direction, and Loren responded in kind. After several moments, Cat Stirling looked over at him too, and Loren saluted immediately. Out the corner of his eye, he saw the figure of *Sho-sa* Parkensen fill the van's doorway, but the sentries did not let him pass, asking first to verify his identification.

"Couldn't wait to take on the Jags, eh, Major?" the Colonel said.

"Just doing my duty, sir," Loren said. "I was trying to link up with our PSL, and the Smoke Jaguars were unwilling to comply." Loren glanced over at Parkensen, who had joined the group by now and was scowling as usual.

She nodded. "We've finally made contact with our other two wayward battalions. We should have a full regimental link-up in two hours' time. Ship status is bad. The *Stonewall* is a loss. One of the OmniFighters actually pulled some sort of suicide run. Captain Kirwan was just able to carry out a landing. From what we've been able to tell, the ship is damaged beyond repair."

"The *Bull Run* is hurt but she can still fly," Major Craig put in. "The *Claymore*'s navigable too, but I wouldn't count on it for any kind of prolonged action."

Colonel Stirling leaned forward from her seat. "Corporal Kinross, pull up primary BDA on screen two," she ordered.

The officer's fingers flew over the keyboard, and one of the monitors flickered to life. "Battle Damage Assessment shows that we took out all but two of their fighters. But we lost half of our aerofighters in the process."

"Ground forces?" Loren asked

"Intact except for *Sho-sa* Parkensen's and your own. All the Clan 'Mechs detected prior to landing have been accounted for. It will take them at least two days to get close enough to strike at us in any significant numbers, maybe even four days," Stirling said, reviewing the BDA again. She turned toward Loren, not hiding her concern. "I'm not worried about those few days. The problem occurs after that."

Major Kurt Blakadar walked into the room and saluted. "Sorry I'm late, sir." He cast a quick glance at Loren and the other officers. Captains Lovat and Fraser arrived shortly afterward and joined the circle of officers, sitting on the outer edges of the group.

"This mission has gone sour, gentlemen," Cat Stirling said. "Several of our strategic premises have been compromised. We don't outnumber the enemy, but they outman and outgun us. We're also probably up against a full Galaxy of their forces. And it looks like these aren't the second-line troops we expected to find, but trueborn Clan warriors, the best they put in the field. And their equipment is almost as good as their skills."

The entire mission plan had been based on the idea that the Fusiliers would hold the upper hand in the fight and lure the Jaguars into engaging them. Now that they were outgunned, the Fusiliers were going to have to come up with another plan just to survive at all.

"They've also managed to cripple our ability to retreat off-world, and somewhere up there is a Clan WarShip waiting to take us out if we try and get away." Cat Stirling's voice had a ring of finality in it.

Major Craig wasted no time expressing his opinion. "We're outnumbered, but we've got a few days before the Jaguars show up here. I say we move forward toward the Marion Sea. Those narrows give us an excellent defense zone, and make it even easier to entrench. We dig in, lay traps for the Jags, then whittle them down. If we can hold out long enough, Mulvaney's reinforcements will be here in thirty-six days. With her fresh forces added to our own, we can finish them off."

Loren winced inwardly at the words. If he'd learned anything from studying the Clans it was that taking up supreme defenses against them simply forced them to bid higher to wield enough force to win. They approached such battles like a massive war machine, grinding up their foe, taking the acceptable losses to achieve victory. It was exactly the kind of defense the Smoke Jaguars would want them to take up.

Major Blakadar shook his head. "No way. They outnumber us way beyond what we could hope to handle in a defensive posture. Another option would be to divide up the regiment and spread out—use some of the guerrilla tactics we've been studying up on lately. We can wear them down, make hit-and-run attacks, pincher their supplies, strike at their command and communications structure. We'll take losses, but over the long haul, we can hurt them enough that Mulvaney can get us off of this rock and back home."

"I think we can hold out," Craig returned.

"You're wrong. If they come in force, they'll wipe us out."

"You underestimate us, Blackie. Ever hear of a place called Thermopylae? A mere three hundred Spartans held off ten thousand."

"You've got to remember one thing about that battle, Cullen. Neither side was equipped with BattleMechs. Also, in your analogy the force of ten thousand would be equipped with better, stronger, and faster 'Mechs than the defenders. Remember, the Spartans did eventually fall at Thermopylae.

"Hiding and playing hit and run games is fine, Cullen, but they're sitting on warehouses full of parts and munitions. There are no civilians to help us stay operational and keep our troops fed and hidden. We wouldn't last very long."

"There've been guerrilla operations on some of the conquered worlds for years now," Craig insisted.

"None regimental size," snapped Blakadar. "And none that have ever beaten the Clans in a guerrilla operation."

Captain Colin Lovat, standing off to the side and working feverously with his hand-held computer, cleared his throat to call the attention of the others. "I've run both of your suggestions against the tactical simulation database for probable outcomes, given the known variables of Clan forces and known fighting tactics."

"And?" Colonel Stirling asked.

The Regimental Intelligence Officer shook his head. "Best-case scenario is that we can hold out for forty-five days, after which time both our force *and* our reinforcements are wiped out. That's if we keep the WarShip out of the equation and count on the fact that the Jaguars will bid low because we're mercenary and they're truebirths."

Loren knew the question had to be asked. "What's the worst-case scenario outcome?"

"Forty-eight hours, sir. That factors in orbital bombardment, the Clans releasing the reserve aerospace forces they probably kept out of their initial bid, and them mobilizing everything they've got against us. Don't forget, they may already be on the move. I've been using only our passive satellites for surveillance, and their accuracy is good, but limited. It's a distant possibility that they're coming for us right now and we just haven't detected it yet."

Craig winced. "Figures and numbers. Give me the order, Colonel, and I'll have us in a defensible position that can weather anything even that WarShip can drop on us."

Stirling shook her head as if she wished that everybody would just clear out of the HQ, and Loren thought he understood. Beating the Smoke Jaguars was going to take something so bold, so daring, that it would catch them off guard, destroy their advantage.

Captain Mitchell Fraser spoke up. "I'm a tech, but if you ask me, what we need are reinforcements. Why not just take one of the DropShips and head back to the Inner Sphere? Hell, our brother and sister regiments would come in and mop up this Clan-trash."

"We haven't got the time," replied Captain Lovat. "Getting home would take months. The most we can hope to do is hold out for a matter of weeks—which is plenty long enough."

The Combine PSL spoke up next, only adding to the fray. "All this talk of running or entrenching does not fulfill either your contract objectives or obligations. We have to find a way to destroy the Smoke Jaguars, and do it without destroying ourselves in the process." He leveled an icy stare at Loren. "Your little death-duel with that Star Captain cost me the *Retribution*."

Loren tried not to let the PSL's attitude get to him, but it was hard. The Jaguars would have killed Parkensen a few hours ago if Loren and his Kilsyth Guards hadn't arrived to save him—yet now the man was complaining about what it had taken to do that.

"Have the Smoke Jaguars gone after any of our satellites yet, Captain Lovat?" Loren asked, knowing he mustn't get bogged down in petty grievances.

"No, sir," returned the younger Captain. "We haven't activated the active sats yet, but thus far the Jags haven't paid much attention to the fact that we're watching them."

"Any activity? Troop changes, movement toward us, that sort of thing?" Loren pressed.

"Some," Captain Lovat replied. "They've got a number of fighters sitting at their aerodrome that never even went out after us. I've seen some activity indicating they're getting ready to pursue us, but thus far there's been no major undertaking. Mostly just fast-moving, light 'Mechs."

Loren's mind shuffled through everything he knew about the Clans, especially the Smoke Jaguars. He thought about the star chart he'd seen showing the resupply points for the Nova Cats and the Smoke Jaguars. *We can't leave, and staying means we're dead. There has to be a solution . . .*

Then he had it. A plan, a bold plan, almost impossible. It was a simple concept, but if it could be pulled off, it might offer at least some hope of success.

Colonel Stirling's voice brought him back to where he was. "Folks, we've laid our cards on the table and we're not holding a flush. Major Jaffray, you're my tactical expert when it comes to these Jags. What do you say?"

Loren wasn't sure if he should speak up or not. The plan that was taking form in his mind was audacious, perhaps even mad. "I've got an idea, Colonel, but we've got to go to the field hospital before I can tell you about it."

He hadn't studied the Clans and their ways for nothing. One of their traditions was that of the victors taking bondsmen as the spoils of war. When a warrior was claimed as a bondsman by another Clan, his allegiance to the new master must be total. Of course, only a small handful of Clan warriors had ever been made bondsmen by Inner Sphere units, and usually only those with ties to the Clans, units like Snord's Irregulars or Wolf's Dragoons.

What Loren had been thinking about during this whole long discussion was that he had fought Star Captain Kerndon honorably from a Clan perspective. *If the man is still alive, perhaps I can make him one of us. He was once a Smoke Jaguar, which could make him the key to how to tangle with the Jaguars—and win.*

"The hospital?" Major Craig asked in an irritated tone.

"Yes. There's a bondsman there and I must speak to him. His name is Kerndon."

═══ 14 ═══

Fusiliers LZ, Bay of Kurita Prime
Wayside V (Wildcat)
Deep Periphery
3 July 3058

The guards stood nearby as Loren and the rest of the command staff moved toward the hospital bed. Loren's first impression of the Clansman lying there caught him off guard: Star Captain Kerndon was young, no more than in his early twenties. Where Inner Sphere MechWarriors fought on for decades, the Clans emphasized the vigor of youth in their troops. *He's a boy, yet by Clan tradition and rite he's almost at my rank.*

"He's been sedated to help with the neural feedback he took when you downed him, sir," the Fusilier medic whispered to Loren. "He's bound to be groggy."

"Thank you," Loren said. *Good. The medication may help him see things my way, help him accept a role as my bondsman.* Loren turned to the Clanner, raising his tone to one of authority and dominance. "Star Captain Kerndon, I presume."

"Aff," Kerndon replied.

"I am Major Loren Jaffray, the warrior who defeated you in combat."

Kerndon's eyes flared for a moment, but that was all. Loren understood. The man was sizing him up, taking the measure of his enemy.

"You should have killed me, yet I live," Kerndon said. "When I awoke they told me that you had named me a bondsman, but this is not an obligation you are required to undertake." It was obvious Kerndon hoped Loren would change his mind.

Loren had studied the Clans enough to know that this warrior could not refuse to be his bondsman. "I understand some of your traditions," he said slowly. "Perhaps one day you might make a good member of my—regiment." Loren was tempted to say "clan," but he refrained. "This is Colonel Andrea Stirling, my commander and the leader of Stirling's Fusiliers. I'm afraid that the other warrior we rescued from the battle site died on the trip back."

Star Captain Kerndon showed almost no emotion. "In death she escapes the dishonor of serving a freebirth as her master," he said slowly, then looked up at Loren. "Major Loren, I ask that you grant me the right of bonsref."

Loren shook his head. "I'm not familiar with that custom."

"Bonsref is when a bondsman's master agrees to slay him in one-on-one combat. Tradition dictates that the bondsman does not fight but accepts death at the hands of his would-be master. You would be granted the use of any weapon you desire."

"You prefer death to serving as my bondsman?" Loren asked, though of course he knew the answer.

"Aff. As a bondsman, I would be pitted against my former Clan should you ever ask me to fight in battle. And I could never return to the ranks of the Smoke Jaguars. They would see me as inferior for having fallen to you. I would have to live out my life as a bandit, or worse. The alternative is to fight for you and die, a death without honor. Either path results in a loss of honor I would not willingly suffer."

There was a part of Loren Jaffray that wanted to grant this Kerndon's request. He understood the dictum of honor, especially the honor among MechWarriors. But he also knew what a prize the Clanner represented. This man Kerndon was a window of sorts for him, a way to see into the hearts and minds of his Jaguar foes. But his plan was a bold one, bold enough that perhaps the man might choose to live and take his chances. A chance to live and die with honor. "Kerndon, I refuse this ritual of yours, this bonsref. We're facing the Smoke Jaguars, but I like to think there are other possibilities, other hopes for warriors to prove themselves."

The young warrior did not speak, just continued to stare at Loren.

"We are no ordinary unit, Kerndon. The Northwind Highlanders trace their origins to service under General Aleksandr Kerensky and the Star League Defense Forces. Our background, despite what your Jaguar commanders might have thought and told you, is the same."

"I have no desire to be your bondsman," was all that Kerndon could muster, the drugs still holding him at bay.

"Perhaps that is true, Kerndon. But think on this. I am kin of Star League warriors. When I fought you, I did it on your own Clan terms—one on one. I defeated you fairly, and with honor. If I release you, your Clan will not take you back. You will be—what's the word?—dezgra? Stand at my side as bondsman, and there is a chance that one day you will fight again as a warrior. You will again have a chance to embrace honor in battle."

Kerndon didn't answer immediately, but seemed to think it over long and hard. Loren was sure that being a warrior was everything to him. Perhaps he would accept that he had been bested in honorable combat and on terms no Clansman could argue.

"Major Loren," he said finally. "I will serve you as your bondsman."

"Excellent, Bondsman Kerndon. Tell me, then, what units defend this planet?"

Kerndon closed his eyes, as if not wishing to see what he must do. "You face the Tau Galaxy, the Huntress Galaxy."

Loren looked over at Captain Lovat, who quickly began tapping queries into his noteputer before shaking his head. "We're unfamiliar with this Galaxy. Is it new?"

"Affirmative."

"What is its strength?" Major Craig asked.

Kerndon did not answer but only glared at the Fusilier officer. He slowly turned his head back toward Loren.

"You didn't answer his question," Loren said. "You don't want to betray your former Clan—is that it?" Hadn't he experienced the same conflict over his allegiance to his former unit, the Death Commandos? Letting such feelings go, Loren knew, was not easy.

"Neg," Kerndon responded. "You defeated me fairly in a fight and I survived. Rather than kill·me as you should have, you have decided to keep me alive. By the rede of my people, I am your bondsman—not his. I am not bound to honor him by treating him as a true warrior. Only you and those who are your superior—unless you so dictate."

"I don't have to take this kind of lip from him!" Craig sputtered, moving toward the bed, as though ready to pum-

mel the already wounded Clansman. Major b͟
Captain Lovat held him back, blocking Craig w͟
bodies.

Loren looked down at Kerndon, who did not even tense i͟
response to Craig. "You will tell me then, what is the composition of this Tau Galaxy?"

"The Galaxy consists of two full combat Clusters, the
101st Attack Cluster and the 250th Assault Cluster. There is
a partial cluster assigned to the Galaxy as well, the 25th
Strike."

"Two and a half clusters, eh?" It was a small Galaxy, but
that still gave the Jaguars vast superiority over the Fusiliers.
"The forces that engaged us were the result of bidding, I
assume?"

"Aff," Kerndon replied almost lifelessly.

"What unit won the bid against us and what is their exact
composition?"

"The honor of the bid was awarded to Star Colonel
Roberta of the 101st. My Binary was one of three included in
the bid. Another two partial Trinaries were assigned as
well."

"Do you know what the next step of her plan is?"

"Neg. I was not privy to that. My unit was allowed to engage the survivors of our fighter attack because we were
close to your drop points."

"Where was your Galaxy to be assigned?" Loren pressed.

"Our exact destination was not revealed to us at this time.
The Galaxy Commander is in the process of determining appropriate targets."

"You were going to be used against the Combine then?"
asked *Sho-sa* Parkensen, but Kerndon would not look at him.

"Kerndon, you will answer," Loren commanded.

"We were not going to fight the Draconis Combine, not at
this time. Our target was one that has drained us of our honor
and dignity as a Clan."

The realization hit Loren squarely. "You were going to be
deployed against the Nova Cats?"

Kerndon nodded slowly. "Aff." Loren knew about the
longtime animosity between the Jaguars and the Nova Cats.
It was why he wanted this Smoke Jaguar warrior on his side.
He had a plan that was beyond bold and daring—perhaps not
even feasible. Only Kerndon could tell him whether it had
any hope of success.

"Kerndon, what would happen if we were to travel to the nearest Nova Cat base and tell them the Smoke Jaguars have a Galaxy of troops here who were going to be used against them?"

Kerndon surprised them all by chuckling at the question. "The Nova Cats would open fire on you without hesitation."

"But the Smoke Jaguars pose a great threat to the Nova Cats, especially a Galaxy poised to wage war against them."

"I fought the Nova Cats once while still in the sibko. They are odd people with odd customs, but they are Clan. They have seen how little honor exists among the freebirths of the Inner Sphere. They know that your people do not hesitate to stoop to trickery to win a battle. They would assume that you were attempting to lure them into a trap and would consider such an act a breach of honor. Thus, they would treat you as honorless bandits and destroy you."

"Can you think of any way to get them to listen to what we might have to say, to convince them that we speak the truth?"

Kerndon paused for a moment, pondering the possibilities. "Neg. If I were the Nova Cat commander, I would not trust an Inner Sphere unit telling me such a tale, no matter what evidence you might present to me."

Damn! So much for the easy path. "Is it safe to assume then that the Nova Cats would be *interested* in the Smoke Jaguar presence here?"

Kerndon nodded. "Aff. The Nova Cats would consider our presence here a present danger to their supply line back to the home worlds."

Major Blakadar spoke up, surprised by the premise Loren had posed. "You're not proposing that we show up on the Nova Cats' front porch, are you?"

That and even more, Blackie. Sometimes the message was not as important as how it was delivered. "If this Tau Galaxy were to attack the Nova Cats, what would be their response?"

Kerndon shook his head and shut his eyes as if frustrated by the question. "The question is irrelevant, Major Loren," he replied, making strict use of Loren's first name only. A Bloodname was the highest honor among the Clans, each one a surname that could be traced back to the Clans' Star League origins. "You will not be able to get them to launch an attack on the Nova Cats as long as your Fusiliers are here."

"I will determine what is relevant, Bondsman," Loren said, emphasizing the last word. "You will answer the question to the best of your ability."

Kerndon's eyes flared again, but he suppressed his anger, maintaining his composure. "I misspoke, Major Loren. To answer your question, the Nova Cats would see one attack as a mere raid, nothing to pose a threat to them."

"It would take several attacks to get their attention—to get them to mount a counterstrike?"

"Aff. They are a Clan that is driven by their visions and spirit quests. Where the Smoke Jaguars are sensitive to threats, the Nova Cats display a patience beyond comprehension. It would take more than one attack by the Smoke Jaguars before they responded with a counterattack."

"Do both Clans know the locations of each other's bases?"

"Aff, but they would only have a list of probable targets. It would take more to guide them to our base. Their knowledge of the Smoke Jaguars' bases would help them eliminate which ones could support a Galaxy, but they would be forced to search the Galaxy out."

"Unless a trail was left behind," Loren said softly to himself as his mind worked over the plan he had begun to formulate earlier. He smiled suddenly. "If the Nova Cats were to arrive here and find us and the Smoke Jaguars, which would they attack first?" It was an answer he thought he already knew.

"They would attack the Smoke Jaguars, of course."

"Of course?" Colonel Stirling asked, not understanding. "We would be a common enemy to both Clans. Why wouldn't they simply unite against the Fusiliers?"

Loren answered before his bondsman, his excitement growing. "Colonel, the Clans see us as inferior because we are mercenary. They would attack each other and fight an honorable battle between themselves before they waste time on us."

Stirling pondered his words for a moment, then her own face lit up with understanding. She caught Loren's eye, and he saw that she grasped what he was driving at.

"It's so simple it's brilliant," she said to Loren just loud enough for the others to hear.

Major Craig broke in. "I don't get it. What does any of this have to do with us beating the Jaguars?"

"Everything," Loren replied. "All we have to do is get the Tau Galaxy to attack the Nova Cats at several of their bases. The Cats will mount a reprisal strike force, come here, and fight the Jaguars for us. Whichever side wins, we mop up."

Kerndon shook his head. "Galaxy Commander Devon Osis will launch no strikes against the Nova Cats until the Fusiliers are eliminated."

"That's the beautiful part of this plan," Loren continued. "This Devon Osis won't have to order the Jaguars to strike at the Cats. *We* will be the attack force posing as the Smoke Jaguars."

15

Fusiliers LZ, Bay of Kurita Prime
Wayside V (Wildcat)
Deep Periphery
3 July 3058

"**W**hat?" came the voice of *Sho-sa* Parkensen. "How can your Fusiliers pose as a Smoke Jaguar unit?"

"We've recovered a Binary's worth of Clan OmniMechs," Loren said. "Mitch Fraser and his crews are working on them, and should be able to get most of them up and running. Paint over the repairs, use the transponders and comm channels right, and no one can tell we *aren't* Jaguars."

"I've never repaired any OmniMechs before," Mitch Fraser spoke up.

Loren laughed softly. "Mitch, you can repair *anything* once you put your mind to it."

Major Kurt Blakadar rubbed his chin in thought, looking off into space, then back to the group. "It might just work. If you think about it, we could've told the Jaguars we were the Gray Death Legion and how would they have known otherwise?"

"That's right," Loren said. "We can tell the Nova Cats anything we want when we make the batchall."

Kerndon rubbed his forehead where it was bandaged. "It is not that simple. The Clans track bloodlines and genetic traits as well. If they can see your face during the batchall, they can verify whether or not you are a Jaguar. Based on your traits, they will see that you are not."

"Then we just don't show our faces," Captain Lovat said before Loren could.

Kurt Blakadar rubbed his chin in thought. "There are still a million things that could go wrong with this plan. I'd want to work out the big kinks before having to decide if this is a suicide run or our best shot."

"Fair enough," Loren replied. When push came to shove, Loren knew that Blackie, of his two fellow Majors, would forget petty politics and do whatever was best for the Highlanders. Craig was stubborn enough that he might let his personal resentments cloud his better judgment.

Major Blakadar continued. "Half our DropShips are grounded, thanks to the Clan fighters. Maybe permanently. With that destroyer hanging in high orbit, how would we get our hypothetical Jaguars out to the jump point?"

Colonel Stirling's face tightened. "That's an important question, Major, and one I want to take up with our DropShip captains once we're done here. It's still only a part of our problem, though." She turned to Kerndon. "Tell me, Star Captain, if you were this Devon Osis, what would you expect us to do next?"

"It is not the Galaxy Commander you must concern yourself with. Star Colonel Roberta won the bid to destroy you. Devon Osis will observe and offer comment, but in the end it is her prowess you must test against."

"Okay, then what can you tell us about her?"

"She is unlike any warrior you have ever faced," the Clansman said slowly, his expression flickering between fear and respect.

"We're Northwind Highlanders," retorted Cullen Craig. "That means we're not afraid of anybody."

Kerndon shook his head. "Star Colonel Roberta is pure Smoke Jaguar. I have seen her in combat, Colonel Andrea. You have not." He had turned away from Craig and back to Stirling, still refusing to utter the surnames of those around him. "She will move like a tornado. When she hits, there will be no stopping her. She will drive through your forces no matter what the odds."

"Tough lass, eh?" Stirling said, giving Loren a quick wink. "I look forward to kicking her ass."

"She specializes in headhunter missions," Kerndon said, ignoring Stirling's comment. "Using her light Stars to penetrate an enemy's perimeter and take out their command staff."

Headhunter units. Loren felt a chill at those words. An Inner Sphere commander would attempt to knock out communications and command facilities. But here was Kerndon suggesting that the Smoke Jaguars, particularly this Star Colonel Roberta, would simply go for the jugular by attempting to wipe out the opposing leadership itself.

"If I were Roberta, I would expect you to be entrenching and fortifying your position in preparation for my attack. And I would strike here, hoping to kill you all. Take off the head and you destroy the body. With the rest of your troops either inexperienced or disorganized, I could wipe them out later at a time and place of my own choosing."

Colonel Stirling put her hands on her hips. "You don't know me, Kerndon, but my people don't call me 'The Cat' for nothing. It's not for my fine looks, but for my tenacity. Thanks to you, I hope to give Star Colonel Roberta something to remember me by.

"What if it looked like we were mounting our own attack instead of retrenching. What might she do then?"

"She will come at you swiftly with everything she has rather than let you attack her first. She will strike without fear, and crush your throat with her powerful jaws. There will be no battle lines. Her forces will plow through your ranks and use the confusion to their advantage."

Colonel Stirling weighed his words. "And if we just sit here and wait?"

"It changes nothing. Star Colonel Roberta is a Cluster Commander of the Smoke Jaguars. Though defeating an Inner Sphere foe does not offer great honor, it would still give her the opportunity to prove her skill and prowess to her commanding officer. Destroying you quickly and cleanly would give her an edge in future bidding for the right to participate in the destruction of the Nova Cats."

Stirling looked over at Major Craig, who had favored digging in, then back to her regimental intelligence officer.

"Captain Lovat, how fast could the Jaguars be on top of us if they moved their light 'Mechs at full speed, full throttle?"

The younger officer licked his lower lip as his fingers flew over the noteputer keys. "Their *Koshi*s and *Dasher*s could hit us first. And if they pushed their power plants to maximum, they could be on us in less than forty-eight hours."

"Sir," Captain Fraser cut in, "as chief tech of the regiment, I've got to tell you that even Clan equipment can't just run full bore like that. 'Mechs are tough but have to be maintained. In all honesty, sir, they'd be wearing the bejesus out of those 'Mechs, moving at top speeds like that. Their power-plant linings and gyros would take days to get realigned once the battle was done, not to mention the accelerated wear on the actuators."

Kerndon stared at Mitch Fraser with distaste, apparently annoyed that a mere tech would speak up in the midst of a discussion by warriors. "You do not know the Clan way. Wear and tear are not the concern; victory is what matters. She would push them because she must as a warrior, plain and simple."

Loren looked around at the other officers. "Well, then, we know we've got less than two days before we can expect an attack by the Jaguars. When they do come, they'll be gunning to kill everyone here, trying to knock us out and leave the rest of the regiment easy pickings."

Loren turned to look at Colonel Stirling, locking his eyes to hers. "We know we can't leave Wayside—we simply don't have the capacity to get the entire regiment off planet. But if we stand and fight, we'll be wiped out, no matter how good we are.

"I say our only hope is to outfit a unit of fake Smoke Jaguars and use them to lure the Nova Cats into following us back to Wayside."

"Clan Nova Cat can devour us just as easily," *Sho-sa* Parkensen said.

Colonel Stirling looked over at the PSL. "I understand your apprehension, *Sho-sa*. But I see no other bloody damned alternative. All things being equal, the Jaguars will defeat us no matter what we do. I never thought I'd see the day, but it's true. And it's just a matter of time. Yes, Major Jaffray's plan is risky, to say the least, but at least it offers a chance."

"It will bring death to us in the end," Parkensen said gloomily.

"Maybe so, but one thing is fer sure, laddie," Cat Stirling said, slipping into her Scots burr. "The Smoke Jaguars will rue the day they tangled with the Northwind Highlanders."

16

Fusiliers Mobile Command Post,
Bay of Kurita Prime
Wayside V (Wildcat)
Deep Periphery
4 July 3058

Wayside V seemed even more eerie now than when Loren had known it only from the maps and intel. The regiment had dropped onworld in the middle of a thunderstorm that had finally stopped. With the fog that followed, the twilight of Wayside's twenty-eight-hour day took on the greenish glow of the planet's sky.

Colonel Stirling had moved fifty kilometers to the east of the DropShips, wanting to keep up the illusion that the regiment was on the move. She hoped to protect the DropShips as a fall-back position, in case things went dramatically wrong. The ships' turrets were still operational enough to provide support fire if the Fusiliers were forced into a retreat. Given the odds, Loren thought that was a real possibility.

Standing outside the portable command dome waiting for the unit's three DropShip captains to arrive, Loren wished he had more time to spend with Star Captain Kerndon. Despite all his intense study of the Clans, things the man was telling them showed how much Loren still had to learn. The Clan idea of honor, for instance, still mystified him, though there was something seductive—alluring—to him about the code Kerndon lived by.

As he watched the Bombardier hover vehicle making its way toward the Fusilier command post, he thought about the decisions they still had to make. The Clan WarShip looming in high orbit seemed like an insurmountable obstacle, but Loren wondered if the true threat didn't lie in the heart of their own ranks. Between the two of them, Major Cullen Craig and *Sho-sa* Elden Parkensen seemed inclined to hinder any operation they might hope to pull together.

Chastity Mulvaney's words came back to him as he realized he was facing exactly the kind of situation she'd predicted. Internal politics. Backbiting. Jealousy. It was obvious that Cullen Craig was operating out of personal animosity, and suddenly Loren felt envious of the Clans. *Were I Kerndon, I would simply call for a Circle of Equals and beat some sense into his head.*

Elden Parkensen, the Combine PSL, was just plain stubborn. He had yet to thank Loren for arriving and rescuing his unit from Kerndon back at the *Retribution*'s crash site. Like Kerndon, Parkensen was the product of a society that glorified the warrior tradition. Perhaps he too harbored notions that the only way to prove himself was by death in combat.

Just then the hovercraft pulled up in front of the mobile HQ, interrupting Loren's gloomy thoughts. Climbing out of it were the men who would either dramatically help this operation, or permanently table it. Captains Spillman, McCray, and Kirwan—commanders of the *Claymore,* the *Bull Run,* and the *Stonewall,* respectively—were now walking straight toward Loren and the van. Of the three spacers, Spillman was the last to salute, and looked like he was proud of it. Loren knew that Spillman was a hard case. He hated authority, but Loren was sure the *Claymore*'s captain would put his shoulder to the wheel when the time came. He might complain like all hell, but in the end, he'd do his duty.

Loren saluted back and then followed the three men into the HQ, where the rest of the command staff was huddled around the van's holographic table display. Loren knew what they were looking at: a planetary map of Wayside V. The time had come to bring the DropShip captains in on the planning of this mission that was fraught with pitfalls that could scuttle the operation at any moment. It was the kind of op that was going to require everyone to think on their feet and be ready to respond in an instant.

In other words, it was exactly the kind of mission Loren lived for.

The three captains all saluted Colonel Stirling as they approached the table. She returned the salute, but it was obvious she was less interested in the formalities than in the reason they were there. Notably absent was the Combine PSL.

"Gentlemen, I've called you here for a reason," Stirling said, her voice quiet but firm. "Our ground-based commanders have already considered our situation and how we might deal with it. Now I need to get up you up to speed."

She leaned forward over the holographic display, her face illuminated by the green light of the image of Wayside V under her. After briefly summarizing their status, she cut quickly to the chase. "Our tentative plan is for one of you to take a DropShip filled with captured Smoke Jaguar Omni-Mechs up to the jump point. From there you will jump out and perform a series of strikes against the Nova Cats, provoking them to mount a reprisal strike against this world. Our hope is that they will take out the Smoke Jaguars for us so that all we've got to do is mop up whatever's left."

There was dead silence in the van as she spoke, the expressions of the three DropShip Captains ranging from disquiet to disbelief.

"So, there you have it," Stirling said finally when it was obvious no one intended to speak. "Now's your chance to tell me what you think."

"Colonel, sir, ye can't be serious," Captain Spillman said. "In case you've fergotten, there's a bloody *Essex* Class War-Ship up there waitin' for us. It will move to intercept the instant we take off. Even if we pass it, she's got more thrust in her power plants than any of our ships. It would only be a matter of time."

"And what about the damage we've taken?" asked the shorter and more portly Captain Kirwan of the *Stonewall*. "The *Stonewall* is in no condition for such an operation and neither is the *Claymore*."

The *Bull Run*'s captain, the older and gray-bearded Rory McCray, spoke up next. "The *Bull Run* is in pretty good shape, but we'd be no match for that destroyer. She'd shred us to ribbons before we got anywhere near the jump point."

Colonel Stirling put her hands on her hips and looked at each of the men standing around her. "Let me rephrase this, gentlemen. This is our only chance. I didn't bring you here to tell me we can't do it. I asked you to come because you've all pulled my butt out of some tight spots over the years. You know me pretty damn well and I know you. There's always a way to beat the odds. If anyone can find it here, it's you. I know one thing fer sure, lads, if we stay, we die."

Kirwan stared at the map, which showed the current position of the DropShips and the nearby Fusilier deployment to the east. Hovering over the table by nearly a meter was the projected image of the Smoke Jaguar WarShip in its approximate position.

It was McCray who broke the silence. "Even if you could spare us the fighters, Colonel, that WarShip would eat them alive. No matter what we've got, we couldn't hope to touch her before she closed enough to use her big guns. A DropShip isn't much compared to a vessel like that. I—I just don't see a way."

Spillman rubbed the stubble of his beard reflectively. "Maybe that's the problem, Rory," he said to McCray. "We're lookin' at this all wrong. We don't have to knock that WarShip out. All we've gotta do is keep her off our tail long enough to jump out of system."

"We can't get close enough to even mar her paint job, Colvin," McCray returned. "How in the hell do you distract something like that warbird?"

"The same way you do anyone else," Spillman replied, reaching down to the holographic table, enabling the plotting mode. "It's all sleight of hand." He touched the icon that represented the *Claymore*, and the image seemed to stick to the tip of his finger. He lifted it up just over the table, then moved it toward the icon representing the Jaguar base, slowly, almost calculating.

"Watch this closely, lads and lasses. This is the *Claymore*. I move her straight at the enemy position." Every eye in the room was fixed on Spillman as he leaned further across the table, propping himself up with his other hand as he edged the icon further out, closer to the Jaguars. The holographic table didn't let his hand move fast, but moved the icon at a relative speed to simulate the actual flight of the DropShip. It began slowly, then sped up as the ship moved into the "air" over the table.

"Rory, you play the destroyer," Spillman said. "Show me how you deal with this attempt on my part, eh?"

Rory McCray reached down and pressed several of the table's control buttons as well, enabling him to perform the same action. He reached up and pushed the WarShip image with his fingertip, moving it in the air over the holotable to meet the icon of the *Claymore* held by Spillman. "Like I said, Colvin, you don't stand a chance."

"Think again," Spillman replied. Suddenly everyone's eyes shifted from the hand holding the *Claymore* to the other one, which suddenly moved the *Bull Run* up and into the air.

Colonel Stirling smiled. They'd all been diverted by watching the hand with the Claymore, while Spillman's other hand did something else. "It'd have to be the *Bull Run*," she said. "It's in the best shape."

"The WarShip could still get her," Kirwan said.

"I've got an idea for that too," Spillman returned. "All our ships are equipped with life boats and escape pods. The pods are non-directional, non-controlled-thrust, but they could become perfect little torpedoes once that WarShip is closing. Fill them with petrocycline and blast them directly into the path of the ship as it comes in on an intercept vector. And don't forget the life boats. We can load them with explosives and program them for flight. Speed-wise they're as fast as that destroyer too, so even if she tries to evade we've got her."

"Who's up for the piloting part of this?" Stirling said.

The three men looked at each other and finally Spillman laughed. "You got me if you want me, Colonel."

"Yer mad as a hatter," Kirwan told him.

Spillman shrugged and laughed again. "So's she," he said, jerking a thumb at Cat Stirling.

17

Bay of Kurita Prime
Wayside V (Wildcat)
Deep Periphery
4 July 3058

Loren Jaffray reached the cockpit of his 'Mech and noticed that the *Penetrator*'s repair job had been rushed at best, armor plates patched and not fitted perfectly in place. He didn't care, as long as it worked. *She's battle-ready, and right now that's what counts.* He skipped the safety start-ups and checklist, hot-firing the fusion reactor to get started as quickly as possible. "Black Adder Leader, this is XO. Status report."

"Bad news is that our 'company' is arriving a little early. Unknown numbers, but we're fairly sure they're running some sort of ECM. Casualties unknown."

"Run Case Snipe," he replied.

Headhunters. They would search out the leadership of the Fusiliers and systematically wipe them out. Roberta's key to success was to hit unaware, but thanks to Kerndon, the Fusiliers knew she was coming. And knowing made it possible to mislead her.

The only way the headhunters would know which 'Mechs belonged to the officers was to scan the radio transmissions between the Fusiliers 'Mechs at close range. Command frequencies carried a four-bit transmission protocol that scrambled and coded their messages. Using sweeping scans looking specifically for that four-bit prefix on the transmitted data packets would tell the Clanners which 'Mechs were piloted by the officers.

The Fusilier plan was simple. The regiment would pull back to line-of-sight range and switch to laser transmissions for orders. Unlike the radio signals the Jaguars would be seeking, encapsulated and fragmentation-scrambled laser bursts were nearly impossible to read in the middle of a firefight. The key to the plan was to lure the headhunters into a location where the Fusiliers could wipe them out with little risk.

Loren reached down and pressed several of the controls on his command panel, then inserted a small optical diskette into a slot. As he switched on his laser communications system, the radio began to broadcast a wave of senseless "noise"—all preceded by a four-bit security protocol. Colonel Stirling had personally selected the music, the wailing sound of bagpipes playing *The Braes of Tullymett*—a march Loren found particularly motivating. Going out on wide beam, it would act as a beacon to anything within thirty kilometers of his BattleMech.

He was the bait.

The communications would be sent to all the 'Mechs of the regiment and would be cross-relayed back to him, repeating over and over. To the Jaguars, it would appear like a spider web of transmissions, all leading to the wide gully where Loren and his 75-ton *Penetrator* stood. To get to where Loren was, the Smoke Jaguars would have to enter the trench, where his *Penetrator* was all but hidden from the surface and the risk of long-range shots. Once they moved in, the Kilsyth Guards would do the rest.

Loren had been on dozens of ambush missions in his career, and each time was the same. There was the bizarre silence, the odd rush of his own excitement, The Sensation, the marble block of his own patience being slowly and methodically worn away in his mind. He had learned that the key was to simply wait. Sooner or later, the enemy came to you. What they had on their side was the location, which they controlled. He had chosen this one carefully, a deep but long, dry ravine that wound and twisted in all directions not far from the shores of the Marion Sea. From here, he and about a company of his 'Mechs were visually concealed, allowing his prey to walk into his trap.

From a kilometer away on top of a hill, a laser pulse was relayed to his 'Mech from a platoon of Highlander infantry. The Guards had spotted the Jaguars: two Stars of light Omni-Mechs closing on his position. He switched to short-range sensors but still did not see them. It was only a matter of time . . .

Then his secondary display suddenly showed him what he was looking for. The Jaguar 'Mechs closed rapidly with the gully where he waited, then bounded into it. Loren reached over to shut off the baiting communications signal. Though he was not in line-of-sight of the enemy, it was only a matter of seconds before he was under their guns. The time had come to let them know they'd blundered into a trap.

Almost instantly the movement of the dots on his sensors stopped. He mentally pictured what must be happening with the enemy commanders. They were probably rechecking their communications gear, wondering how unit communications could have gone off line when they were so close to their target. They too now understood the complexity of the hunt, and that the tables might have been turned on them.

Their sensors must have been painting the same thing his own were now doing, showing the approach of an entire battalion's worth of BattleMechs, closing in on all sides of them, boxing them into the gully. Firing out was possible, but not a good option, and the trench made movement difficult at best. The difference between them and other warriors Loren had faced was that they were Clan. Even three-to-one odds wouldn't strike them with fear.

Loren moved his *Penetrator* in a slow, methodical walk down the twisting gully. As he rounded the first bend, he saw them, two abreast, ten pale gray OmniMechs. He opened a wide-beam communications channel to them before any could lock onto him with their weapons.

"I am Major Loren Jaffray of Stirling's Fusiliers of the Northwind Highlanders. In the name of the Draconis Combine, I ask that you surrender. You are surrounded and outnumbered." His fingers were poised over all three of his trigger switches as he drifted his cross hairs over the lead *Koshi*. *Clan tradition won't let them give up, not without a fight. I had to try . . .*

There was no initial response. Again Loren knew what they were doing, what they were thinking. A recheck of their short-range sensors would tell them how many BattleMechs awaited them in the trench—Fuller's Company. And there was also the wall of 'Mechs surrounding the trench, all prepared to rain fire and death down on them.

A voice finally shattered his thoughts, from the lead *Koshi*. "I am Star Captain Marilen of Clan Smoke Jaguar. The odds you threaten us with are unbefitting a true warrior, but you are only a freebirth and such weakness is no surprise." Even surrounded and outnumbered, this Marilen spoke with arrogance and contempt. It was either the act of a brave person, or an insane one. Equally dangerous, to Loren's mind.

"You used dishonorable trickery to lure us here. But I offer you the chance to redeem this shame—I will grant you the honor of one-on-one combat against me. We fight for the right of free passage from this place and the chance for you to regain honor by facing us again on a warrior's field of battle.

"What do you say, Major Loren?"

He stared at her *Koshi* on his primary display and winced. The fangs and white eyes of a Jaguar had been painted around the head/cockpit, adding to the menace the Omni represented.

"Star Captain, your call for one-on-one battle is refused. You yourself are here on a mission of questionable integrity and honor—coming to kill our officers only. Headhunter missions are no less unbefitting a true warrior." He still hoped to reason with them, but it would have to be through their own version of logic. "There is no loss of dignity in admitting that you made a tactical mistake. Surrender and you will have a chance to fight again, another day, and perhaps regain *your* lost honor."

"You do not fully understand the ways of our Clan," Marilen said, even as her *Koshi* opened up with a laser blast from its left arm. Several hot streams ate away at the *Penetrator*'s replacement armor, digging deeply into the 'Mech's center torso as the big machine reeled under the hits, bending at the waist.

"Engage!" he ordered.

He brought the *Penetrator* back upright, intending to return the blast with his large lasers. As he righted himself he felt a massive impact, not from weapons but from a charging OmniMech colliding headlong with him. The collision hurt both 'Mechs, grinding the impact regions to the point that armor plating contorted and ripped away from the superstructures of the deadly war machines. His viewscreen filled with the fearsome Jaguar image, the face of Marilen's own *Koshi* cockpit, only a meter away.

Even more appalling was what was happening all around them. Rather than surrender, the Jaguar warriors had rushed into near-suicidal attacks against the ring of Fusiliers around them. From the high ground over the gully, a wall of missiles and laser fire rained down on them as they charged. Smoke and the bright red and green bursts of laser light filled the air as the Jaguars charged forward, hoping to take as many Fusiliers as possible down with them.

Loren's Kilsyth Guards maintained their calm and did not buckle, though they must have been shocked by the Jaguar response. Instead they concentrated their fire, two or three 'Mechs opening up on a single Clan OmniMech at once. The Clan *Dasher*s reached the crest of the gully first, firing at point-blank range into the ranks of the Guards. They punched, kicked, and rammed the Fusiliers with a fury that Loren had never imagined could possess a fellow Mech-Warrior.

And he was having his own problems. His *Penetrator* took two steps back as he adjusted the weight and stance to compensate for the impact of Marilen's *Koshi*. *Falling over would be the end of it. She'd kill me before I could even think of standing up.*

As he staggered back she opened up with her Streak short-range missiles. All four dug into the mangled torso armor near his *Penetrator*'s right shoulder, some ripping at the already patchworked internal myomer muscles and internal sensors. The *Penetrator* seemed to moan around him as he opened up with his own wave of six pulse lasers.

The lasers stitched across the *Koshi*'s legs and lower torso, flailing armor plating as they dotted burn holes and scars. Marilen was unrelenting. She fired her jump jets, and for a moment Loren thought she might be attempting to flee the gully. He would have. The odds were against the Jaguar warriors. In the distance he saw a *Dasher* explode in a ball of flame under a hail of autocannon rounds. The other Jaguar 'Mechs were near death as well; it was only a matter of time. *She must be trying to escape, it's her only hope at surviving.*

Instead, a second later Loren saw that she was coming straight at him. *Death from above!* She was going to try to crush him by dropping her *Koshi* on top of his *Penetrator* from the air. Despite the differences in their speeds, Loren was more than capable of making her work for the attack. He turned the *Penetrator* and began to move backward into the gully, passing two of Fuller's 'Mechs as they attempted to fire at her in mid-flight. One hit her with a spray of missiles, eating away at more of her leg armor. The other fired wildly, the laser fire bright red against the green sky. Knowing that the next shot would spike his heat, Loren braced for it, and locked his crosshairs onto Marilen's suicidal *Koshi*.

His second volley of pulse lasers hit her three seconds before her drop. Three of the deadly weapons hit her lower torso, one working its way into her already damaged upper right thigh. Another seemed to seek out her hip joint, drilling deep into the armor and internal structure until Loren saw a swirl of blue smoke, indicating that the joint's lubricant was burning away. His other shots missed, but a pair of lasers from one of Fuller's 'Mechs found their marks on her left arm, mangling the long-range missile rack there.

Then she dropped toward him.

The bulk of the battered *Koshi* missed him by mere meters, managing to club him with its blasted armor on the way down. The extended arm dug into his *Penetrator*'s shoulder, crushing armor plating and tossing Loren and his entire 'Mech hard over and downward as she hit. He saw the fractured hip joint on the *Koshi* buckle upon landing, bursting outward like a broken bone breaking skin. He thought she was going to fall at his feet, but somehow, even with her 'Mech's leg hanging limp and broken like a battered doll's, she managed to stay upright. She opened fire with her machine gun, spraying a stream of bullets at his cockpit. They danced off of his cockpit glass, and Loren simply looked at her in amazement. *What tenacity!* Her 'Mech was directly in front of him, its painted-on Jaguar face still leering at him like the face of death. *The time has come to end this . . .*

Fuller's 'Mechs backed off, unwilling to fire at Marilen for fear of hitting Loren accidentally. Loren knew she was concentrating on staying upright. Rather than have to fight another wave of heat, he opted for a more direct approach. Swinging his right leg back, he then kicked it out, hitting the *Koshi*'s other leg just below the knee actuator. The *Penetrator*'s massive foot dug in deeply, crushing armor and severing the myomer muscle bundles that moved the 'Mech. The sudden impact was more than Marilen could handle. Her *Koshi* swayed backward, turning to one side, then crashed down, destroying her right weapons pod on impact.

The smaller *Koshi* attempted to move, but with the loss of a leg and the other damage it had taken, there was little chance of it ever standing on its own power. Like a fish out of water, the 'Mech thrashed on the ground, trying to find some way, any way, to get upright. It was a losing battle. In the distance the other Smoke Jaguars were pressing a fight they could not hope to win either. The *Koshi* ceased its futile efforts to stand and remained silent.

Suddenly Loren saw the side cockpit hatch open. The figure of a small woman emerged from the smoke and debris. She wore a light cooling vest and shorts, standard thin-sole boots, and no neurohelmet. With a slow, almost exhausted movement, she pulled a laser pistol from its holster.

Loren switched to the external speakers on the outside of his 'Mech as he watched her, knowing what she was doing. "Drop the weapon," he commanded.

Unheeding, she held the pistol in front of her in a perfect firing stance and thumbed the trigger. The brilliant beam of green laser energy hit his cockpit square center, but it was not powerful enough to burn through. Instead it seared the cockpit glass, slowly melting a hold on it. *She wants to fight to the death—even if it's her own. She won't stop until I'm forced to kill her.* He slowly locked his weakest weapon, one of the medium pulse lasers, on her form.

He activated the single laser. It flashed a burst of intense red light that hit her right arm, burning it totally from her torso just below the shoulder. A trail of smoke rose from the now-cauterized stump where her arm had been, blackened and burned. Marilen wavered for a moment as if she thought she could somehow overcome the pain, then dropped to the ground, near death. A small cloud of clay dust rose from where her body collapsed on the soil of Wayside V. Only a meter away lay what was left of her severed limb.

The defeat of ten Smoke Jaguars had cost him five of his own 'Mechs and numerous others badly damaged. Loren and his people had totally surrounded and outnumbered a mere ten 'Mechs, and still had taken significant damage. These Jaguars would apparently go to any lengths to win, pay any price to achieve victory—giving their lives without hesitation.

Were he and his people prepared to go as far to survive?

18

Bay of Kurita Prime
Wayside V (Wildcat)
Deep Periphery
5 July 3058

As he walked into the portable command tent, Loren saw the first signs of fatigue on Colonel Stirling's face. In the distance, some five kilometers to the south, smoke still rose from the small number of Jaguar 'Mechs left burning—the unsalvagable remains of Loren's ambush. The tent sat only a scant ten meters from Stirling's own towering *Grand Titan*. He'd taken a short nap, but the combined effects of a full day of argument, preparation, and combat hung on him like a heavy weight.

"According to our esteemed ship captains, the *Claymore* is ready for decoy duty, and the *Bull Run* is ready for her sprint. Our little 'surprises' for that WarShip are also ready as well. And Parkensen has sent a transmission to both JumpShips. They're under our command for this mission."

"That must have taken a hell of a lot of persuasion, sir."

Cat Stirling leaned forward, holding up both ends of her jumpsuit collar, presenting her Colonel's clusters to Loren. "That it did, Major," she said. Loren almost wished he'd been there to witness the discussion. "There's still a little magic in these clusters," she added. "But I've got something else on my mind right now."

"Sir?"

"I'm thinking about you, Major . . . you leading this operation against the Nova Cats. You've more than proven your skills against the Clans, and the others have seen that as well. Look at your victory against those headhunters. They did some damage, but in the end, you prevailed with minimal losses, netting us some more salvagable OmniMechs in the process."

Loren heard the words and in his half-awake daze, his reactions were fuzzy. A part of him was overjoyed to be assigned command of the raid. Another part of him was cautious. The old line, "Be careful what you wish for . . ." came to mind.

"Sir, I accept. But—"

Stirling looked at him, tilting her head slightly. "No buts, Major. Yes, I could also use you here with me, but that won't necessarily get us off this rock. Among all my officers, you've got the best chance of somehow pulling this stunt off."

"The Kilsyth Guards," Loren said. "Who will lead them?"

Stirling grinned that devious smile Loren had learned to both fear and respect. "You're the XO. What's your recommendation?"

He didn't even have to think twice. "Jake Fuller is the best I've got in my battalion. I'd rather take him with me, of course, but he could do more staying here and leading the Guards."

Stirling nodded as though he were merely echoing her own thought. "I'll grant him a field commission of Brevet Major. That should be enough to get everyone to follow his orders." She did not mention names, but Loren knew who she really meant—Blakadar, but to a greater extent, Craig.

"I'll want Kerndon too," Loren added. "I'll need every bit

of his knowledge and expertise if I'm going to impersonate a Smoke Jaguar commander and deal properly with another Clan."

"I assumed as much. What about technical support? You're going to be a long way from our regimental repair facilities."

Loren hesitated slightly before answering. "Captain Fraser is the only one who might actually be able to repair an OmniMech."

"Mitch? You want my Chief Regimental Tech?"

"No matter how well we do, our equipment's going to get damaged. Being able to repair it could make or break the operation."

Stirling had to know he was right, but Loren could see that the idea of giving him her chief tech disturbed her. "He can go, but he's all you get—your only senior tech. You can take a handful of juniors, but that's it."

Stirling spread out a hardcopy map of the area where the Fusiliers were currently deployed. "I've made some minor changes to your Case Granite battle plan, but overall, it will be the basis of my operations here. Those straits are just too perfect a spot not to use them. The decoy DropShip will draw them there."

"If I were the Cluster commander for the Jags right now," Loren said, "I'd be wondering if my headhunter Stars had achieved their mission goals. Perhaps we can exploit that. Fighting the Smoke Jaguars in the isthmus will buy you some time, but the hard part is to keep from having to engage them in force. They favor big confrontations and use that best. Keeping them on the move will stretch their supply lines as much as yours, maybe enough to even the odds."

Cat Stirling ran one hand back through her hair as she looked at him. "I'm going to bloody them, let them know we can fight. The isthmus is the best place for that, because it lets us reduce their mobility and weapons range advantages and gives us some strong defensive terrain. Even if we only beat them temporarily, it should infuriate them enough to make them come after us. As long as they keep their dander up, I can force them to react to what the regiment and I are doing. I'll keep them in reactive mode by running the longest retreat I can, springing a few little ambushes along the way. As good Clan warriors, they'll be obliged to come after me, and I'll taunt them every centimeter of the way just to keep them mad enough to keep following me."

Stirling smiled. "Everything hinges on two things. One is you getting the Nova Cats to come here and deal with the Jaguars for us. The other is me being able to hold out with a functional fighting force long enough that you've got something to come back to. Fortunately, I think I've got the right people on the job—you and I." She spoke with complete confidence and the serenity that only comes with knowing you don't have much choice in a situation. "Now, then, Major, let's get some shut-eye. Tomorrow's going to be a busy day for all of us—you, me, the Guards. Let's hope it's an even busier one for the Smoke Jaguars."

The Fusilier medic bent over and carefully replaced the bandage on Kerndon's forehead. The former Star Captain said nothing as the medic worked. The pain did not matter. The many tests and trials he had endured in the course of his warrior training had hardened him. The pain he felt was of another order entirely.

Not in his wildest dreams could he have imagined the fate that had befallen him. To be claimed as a bondsman to another Clan was one thing, all part of the life of any Clan warrior. But bondsman to a gang of money soldiers? He found not an iota of consolation in the skill these Northwind Highlanders showed as warriors. No, he had lost something he could never replace. His entire existence had been focused on serving the Smoke Jaguars. Now he had been stripped of the reason he'd been born.

And not just him. Lying in the bed next to him was another Jaguar warrior. Thick burn-gel bandages covered her, yet she too refused to show her pain. Kerndon watched as the attendants adjusted her position in bed and hooked up the three intravenous feed bottles that were keeping her alive. He knew her face.

"Star Captain Marilen," he said, showing neither positive or negative emotion.

The woman rolled her head and looked at him with a scowl. "Kerndon, you live."

"Aff, as do you," he returned. Her being there meant that the Smoke Jaguars were continuing to attack the Fusiliers.

"Is it true you have become bondsman to these barbaric freebirths?" Her voice dripped contempt.

Kerndon's face reddened. "Aff, I was defeated in honorable combat by one of their officer warriors. I asked and was refused the rite of bonsref. I remain his bondsman until I am slain."

It was obvious that Marilen was in extreme pain despite the medication and her bravado. She had to be. The burns she'd received, probably from a laser burst, covered most of her upper torso. Half her hair had been singed off too, and her facial scoring and oozing blisters were visible despite the bandages. "You were always weaker. If not for all this, I would have crushed your skull during the next Trial of Position."

"True warriors do not boast idly of battles that will never take place."

A wave of agony rippled across her face. "You see these mercenaries as your master now. I refuse to"—she fought back another burst of pain—"be a part of these Fusilier free-births."

Kerndon understood her defiance. He too had felt the urge to resist, but the chance to fight once more as a warrior was the one thing that was holding him together. "You were defeated in honorable combat, quiaff?"

"They fought like a pack of bandit-caste children, using excess firepower," she spat back. The effort of speech made her move slightly in the bed, and Kerndon saw that her wounds were bleeding through the bandages. "They had to trick us to win."

"Have they claimed you too?"

Marilen made a sound like laughter. "Let them try," she scoffed.

"They plan to fight the starred-cat," Kerndon told her. "It is a chance for us to die in a cockpit fighting." *Like a warrior* . . .

"You are considering this?"

"Aff."

"You can follow your path to honor with these Fusiliers. I will follow my own." Marilen looked over at the guards standing nearby. They were involved in conversation, paying little heed to their injured prisoners. With her free hand, she yanked the IV tubes from the stump of her arm. Her mouth opened to scream, but no noise came out. Her eyes flared wide and her face turned red beyond what Kerndon would have thought possible. Blood poured from where she'd ripped out the needles and tubes. She rolled her head further into the pillow, burying her face to keep any sound from being heard. But Kerndon was sure she would not cry out in pain. It was a sign of weakness she would never show, neither in life or in death.

Kerndon watched and understood. She refused to yield. She had found her own bonsref rather than compromise what she believed to be her honor. By the time the guards noticed anything and rushed to her side, it was too late. Marilen was dead. Her honor had taken her.

"You've landed yer butt in some serious trouble," the guard said when one of them finally realized something had happened, but two medtechs were not far behind and they confirmed her death.

My fate lies elsewhere. Perhaps death at the hands of the Nova Cats can release me in a more honorable way. "You will inform Major Loren that I wish to speak with him," Kerndon said.

"I heard what happened," Loren said.

"Marilen sought death because she could never have accepted life as a bondsman to your people." Kerndon's tone was matter-of-fact, betraying neither regret nor judgment.

"And you?"

"I am your bondsman, though not formally bonded. I would fight by your side as a warrior when you face the age-old foe of the Smoke Jaguars."

Loren nodded. "Colonel Stirling has offered me command of the operation. I take it you wish to go with me?"

Kerndon nodded. "If you will not grant me bonsref, I would seek death in battle. Between then and now I will break the bonds that keep me from dying a warrior. Once the three bonds have been cut, I will fight by your side for your Clan, your Fusiliers. I will meet the Nova Cats and help destroy them before I die.

"Besides," Kerndon added, "you will certainly fail without me. Would you know that our scientist caste samples each fallen warrior in battle, to verify their lineage for our records? None of your people can be left behind dead or alive, for it would tell the Nova Cats that you are not Clan. Those that fall must be burned, all genetic samples charred beyond testing. If someone survives but cannot be removed immediately, you will have to destroy him."

"You mentioned something about three bonds?" Loren said, knowing he would have to think hard about this most recent bit of information Kerndon had given him.

"Smoke Jaguar bondsmen wear their bondcords wrapped three times around the wrist. The loop closest to the wrist is the bond of integrity. Once I have proven my trustworthiness to you and your Clan, you will cut that cord.

"The center cord represents the bond of fidelity. You can sever this cord only when I have showed you my faithfulness.

"The last cord is for prowess. Once you are assured that a warrior's blood runs in my veins, this bondcord is cut.

"When all three cords have been severed, I am no longer your bondsman but am a member of your Clan as a warrior. It is my desire to accompany you because I was born to fight as Jaguar. I wish to test my skills against the Nova Cats in battle."

Loren stared into Kerndon's eyes and understood. "You'll go with me, Kerndon. I'll bind you and mark you as my bondsman as well. Help me, and I will cut those cords so you can fight as a warrior for the Fusiliers. But mark my words, we will come back here and save this regiment—very much alive."

The almost gentle rapping at his door caught Star Colonel Santin West off guard, something that did not happen very often. The hour was late and quiet hung over the Nova Cat Planetary Command Headquarters in the city of New Lorton on Tarnby.

Santin West wondered who was coming here now, knowing that the only people about at this hour were the night guard shift. If not for his nightmares, he too would have been asleep. But this night, as over the past few, he had stayed awake as late as possible. He had also doubled his daily workout routine in hopes that exhaustion might keep the nightmares from occurring.

Thus far it had not worked.

What bothered him perhaps more than the dreams was the fact that he could not remember them in detail. There were images of fighting, of battling an enemy he could not topple. He also remembered feeling an emotion that was almost alien to him, one he had experienced only rarely, one that left him shamed. It was a feeling of fear. A fear so great it awakened him from the nightmare before he could learn who it was he was fighting. It enraged him that it was fear that woke him and kept him from seeing his enemy. And the rage prevented him from falling back asleep.

He rose and opened the door, surprised to see Biccon Winters, Oathmaster of the Nova Cats, standing before him. She wore the usual garb of her office, the flowing black robe and the armored chest plate emblazoned with the image of Clan Nova Cat, the fierce beast with its jaws open, surrounded by a field of stars. Impressed and raised on the body armor, it stood out as if the cat were springing at him.

Other Clans did not place the emphasis on spirit that the Nova Cats did. The role of Oathmaster had been created by the first Nova Cat Khan to ensure that all Clan rituals and other practices were strictly observed, and Biccon Winters served that function with distinction. What struck West odd was the fact that the older warrior was there, in the late night, outside of his door.

"Greetings, Oathmaster," he said, pulling on a shirt to cover his bare chest. "Please come in."

As befit a warrior, his quarters were spare and unadorned. There was a bed, a pair of chairs, and a small dining and work table, which was currently spread with piles of Battle-ROMs and a portable reader. For West, there was little in life but his duty and his work. He was a Clan warrior, single-minded in his dedication to the Clan he served.

Winters closed the door behind her. "I was making a last tour of this garrison before moving out to one of our other units. Before I left, I felt the need to speak with you. I hope that the hour is not too inconvenient, Star Colonel."

"Neg—of course not." He motioned her to one of the room's two chairs. "May I offer you a refreshment of some sort?"

"Would you happen to have any of that Timbiqui beer I have heard so much about? I understand it is quite similar to some of the brews we know at home."

Santin shook his head. "Neg, Oathmaster, I have no alcoholic beverages here. Alcohol dulls the senses, a risk I cannot take when I might be called upon to fight at any time."

Winters nodded approval. "You serve the Nova Cat well, Star Colonel. But there are also times when it is better to let the mind go. Sometimes we must give up control. In disorder, one can sometimes find sanity and order."

"I understand the need, but duty always comes first."

Winters said nothing for a long minute. Remaining seated,

she reached out and picked up one of the BattleROMs, holding it in front of her for study. Even as she spoke, she kept her eyes fixed on the small computer chip. "You have not asked why I came here."

"I assumed you would tell me," he returned, puzzled by her seemingly odd behavior.

"Last night I saw you in my dream," she replied, setting the chip down and looking at him squarely. "You were in your battle armor and were grappling with an enemy in combat, a cat whose colors were gray. The fight was here on Tarnby in Deep Ellum, and its outcome was unusual, to say the least . . ." They spoke for over an hour, and in the end, Santin West understood more of his own vision, and knew that more than one battle was to come.

BOOK II

Honor's Price

In forty hours I shall be in battle, with little information, and on the spur of the moment will have to make most momentous decisions. But I believe that one's spirit enlarges with responsibility and that, with God's help, I shall make them and make them right.

—General George S. Patton

The ordinary man is involved in action, the hero acts. An immense difference.

—Henry Miller

Bay of Kurita Prime
Wayside V (Wildcat)
Deep Periphery
5 July 3058

"**S**o there you have it," Loren said, standing at total parade rest before the assembled ranks of the Kilsyth Guards. At his side was Colonel Stirling, holding herself tall and proud, her mere presence offering support for his words. They stood with their backs to a cluster of what were the equivalent of trees on Wayside, the command van parked in the closest thing to a clearing in this terrain of broken rocks. As always, the greenish sky cast an eerie light over everyone, as if a thunderstorm were about to break despite the lack of clouds.

Loren and Cat Stirling had spent the long night hammering out the plan together. Their minds working well despite fatigue, they gave additional shape and form to the scheme Loren had originally conceived. Much of the mission would be at his discretion in the field, but planning and preparation would provide a solid foundation no matter what happened later.

"I'm looking for ten volunteers who think they can measure up," he told the group looking back at him expectantly. "You'll be piloting Clan OmniMechs you've never handled before, and you'll be working under some tight operational orders. I need people who think they can deal with that."

Stirling walked along the front row, and looked each trooper in the eye as she made her way past. Her dark hair gleamed even in the dull noon sun of Wayside. "Before any of you steps forward, I want you to remember one thing. You won't be doing this for yourselves, you'll be doing it for the regiment. If the mission fails, we'll all go down, one way or the other. Succeed, and you save the Fusiliers, your family."

Lieutenant Trisha McBride stepped forward without hesitation, along with the other three members of her lance. Loren had hoped she'd be one of those willing to face the risks. And it was exactly why he'd decided to ask for volunteers. Pulling this off was going to take special people, the kind who were willing to put their lives on the line for the regiment. "With yer permission, sir," she said proudly. "I and my lance would like to offer our services to this operation, if ye'd have us. Like you say, the fate of the entire regiment is at stake."

Several other individuals stepped out of the rank and file of the Guards, each one known to Loren by name. His Captains Fuller, Lewis, and Chandler did so without any reluctance. In the case of Lewis, of course, the gesture was more symbolic. His infantry was not suited for this operation, but Loren was moved by his show of solidarity.

The action of the command staff was immediately followed by MechWarriors Burke, Killfries, Gilliam, Jura, Miller, and Macallen stepping forward—all strong MechWarriors who Loren had trained personally. Suddenly others also began to come forward—McAnis, Dollson, O'Brian, and others. In less than a heartbeat, every one of the Kilsyth Guards had volunteered. Loren was stunned. He'd expected a strong response, but not all of the Guards. *Damn, these are fine troops . . .*

"Hector, Macallen, Miller, Gilliam, Killfries, Burke, McAnis, Jura, and McBride, welcome to the Smoke Jaguars. 'Mech assignments will be posted once we're on board. I honestly wish I could take all of you, but those who remain behind will report to Jake Fuller, who now ranks as a Major, thanks to his field commission." Fuller's face lit up with embarrassment and a hint of pride.

Stirling spoke up again. "Major Fuller has my complete confidence. Regimental Executive Officer duty will go to Major Blakadar and regimental command will be transferred to his Black Adders."

She smiled at the small group that had been selected.

"Godspeed all of you. The spirit of the Highlanders be with you."

Loren was caught short, suddenly overcome by his emotions. For so long a time he'd wondered when he would know for sure that he was truly part of this unit, not just someone holding rank and position. He would wonder no more.

Major Blakadar spoke first. "Major Craig and I both have concerns, Colonel, but I assure you we will follow your orders exactly."

"Good," Stirling said. She'd brought the two officers to her immediately after the call for volunteers had broken up. "Is your Black Adder force locked and loaded onto the *Claymore*?"

"First and Second Companies are ready for a hot drop, sir. It's our heaviest gear. They should be able to hold the isthmus until the rest of the regiment is in place. Third Company will position to the perimeter just ahead of Major Craig's battalion. They'll form up on our advanced force."

"Major Blakadar, you've prepped your force for near-vacuum operations, correct?" Stirling asked.

"Second and Third Company BattleMech forces have been checked out and sealed by our techs. My biggest worry about them is that a 'Mech might fall and rupture up on the airless continent."

"You'll only have them up there for a little while, if everything goes as planned," Stirling said. She checked her chronometer, then looked back at Blakadar. "Are you ready to assume your duties as XO, Blackie?"

"Yes, sir," the tall man replied.

"Glad to hear it because it's time to move. Order your perimeter forces to start the advance, as planned. Bring the rest of the regiment to standby and await my word for final deployment. Order both the *Claymore* and the *Bull Run* to launch status and to link up to you and me on regimental command channel two. Get with Major Fuller and provide him a full update of our status."

"On it, Colonel," Blakadar said.

"Lads, we've been over this a few times, but let's make it clear. We've got two objectives here and we can't afford to fail on either. One, the *Claymore* has to decoy that destroyer long enough for the *Bull Run* to get free, hopefully dropping the majority of the Black Adders into position on the way.

Second, we're taking the Jags to task. I want those kitty-cats bloodied and bloodied bad; enough to make them back off and rethink their strategy. On this mission, every day counts.

"Execution of start orders is in thirty minutes."

Loren stepped onto the bridge of the *Bull Run* and saw the lanky Captain Spillman seated in his command chair, staring at the doorway as though waiting for him. Loren crossed the bridge to the secondary command seat, and dropped his carrying bag on the deck alongside it. There would be time to secure the bag before launch, but at the moment he was more concerned about a talk he needed to have with the stubborn ship's captain.

"Captain," he said with a nod.

"Major Jaffray, are you secured and loaded yet? I have a lock down order on hold from command."

"My team is aboard, Captain."

Spillman's eyes never left Loren's as he spoke. "Engineering, secure for launch. Communications, signal command we're locked down and ready for take-off." Tilting his head forward slightly, Spillman raised his finger to Loren and made a motion for him to come closer.

Loren complied and Spillman leaned forward, speaking softly enough that no one else could hear. "Major, you and I haven't worked together very much. I just want to make sure we understand each other clearly."

"I thought you might say that." Loren kept his voice equally low.

"If the life of the regiment wasn't at stake, I'd never have volunteered for this mission," Spillman said with a slight Scottish burr. "But I've got to tell you that yer aboard my ship now, and there's something that will make both our lives easier.

"When we're involved in space operations, *I'm* in command. You've got the clusters on yer lapel, but I've got the experience and know what I'm doin'. I'll appreciate yer comments, but dinna be surprised if I don't follow what ye say. I know ma duty and will act accordingly. When we're on the ground, I'll do push-ups if ye say so.

"So, Major Jaffray, do we have an understanding?"

Loren studied the other man's drawn face, aged beyond his years by the experience of combat. Rules and regulations were clear: the ranking officer, in this case Loren Jaffray, could order a ship's captain to do anything. Command and authority lines were well drawn—on paper, in books, far away on Northwind. This, however, was real life, and sometimes the lines of command got blurred in the field, especially in a situation like this one far beyond the borders of explored space.

I need him, as much as he's a stubborn mule when it comes to authority. "Captain Spillman, with all due respect, I am in command of this mission. I also have no intention of contradicting you unless I feel your actions are in direct conflict with my mission objectives. If such a conflict occurs, *Captain,* I'll do more than resist you."

Spillman did not relent. "This flight crew is mine, *Major,* they've crewed with me for ten years. They know whose orders to follow."

Loren lifted his eyebrows slightly. "That may be true. But I served a long time as a Death Commando. Part of my training is in DropShip piloting and gunnery operations. In fact, I'm qualified to pilot this class of ship and I could do a pretty damn good job. If any of your people decide to mutiny, I'll deal with it accordingly." He reached over and patted the laser pistol resting in its holster on his hip.

Spillman broke first with a broad smile. He wrapped one arm around Loren's shoulder in what seemed at first a gesture of camaraderie, then lightning-fast pulled Loren even closer till their faces were only centimeters apart. "I like you, laddie. Anybody who threatens me on my own bridge either has titanium testicles or is bluffing. Either way, you and I will get along just fine. Hell, I pity those Nova Pussy-Cats when the two of us come up against them!"

He let go of Loren and held out his hand for shaking. Loren took the hand and returned the near-crushing grip. Looking around he saw that everyone on the bridge had been watching, half-eavesdropping, half-wondering how the two men would get along. Loren looked into Spillman's eyes and saw the ship's captain for what he was. Part-actor, part-poker player; all leader. *Yes, this is a man I can work with . . . and god help the Clans when they see us coming.*

20

"**G**o signal was just sent to the *Claymore*. We're on flashing green light for launch," the communications officer said from her station just below and in front of Loren's seat aboard the DropShip *Bull Run*. The tension level on the bridge soared by a geometric proportion. He glanced up at Spillman, sitting tall and proud in his command seat. Solid Green Light was the code phrase for take-off. The flashing green light meant that the ship was to be ready for take-off, but was to wait for "special circumstances."

"Send the following message to Captain McCray: 'Best of luck and take care of my ship or I'll keep this one.' "

The comm officer smiled as she tapped in the words. "Message sent. Incoming from Cat One."

"Patch that one direct," Spillman said.

"*Bull Run*, this is Cat One," came the firm tones that Loren had come to know so well. "You are clear for take-off at your discretion. The Bait is up and on the move."

"Acknowledged," Spillman replied. "We're monitoring the destroyer." A shake of the head from the sensors officer told him there was no movement yet. "She's sitting still there."

"Understood. *Bull Run*, call the ball," Stirling said.

Spillman stiffened slightly in his seat as he accepted the

responsibility for everything that was to come. "*Bull Run* has the ball."

Star Colonel Roberta leaned over the shoulder of the sensors officer, her hairless head beaded with sweat as she studied the display in the command bunker of Wildcat Station. The interior of the bunker was dimly lit, the faces of the various officers visible mainly by the glow from their monitors. The air seemed moist, almost sweaty, yet somehow odorless—thanks to the filtration system.

Standing behind her, Galaxy Commander Devon Osis stood silent, observing her every move. Silently, his mind ran through every decision she made, monitoring and measuring her performance.

"Plot the course of that DropShip," Roberta said. The younger trooper's fingers flew over the keyboard, and the conical shape of the flight path appeared on the display. Wildcat Station, the Smoke Jaguar base on Wildcat, was near the center of that cone if the ship should attempt a landing.

"Blood Claw One to Stalker Star," Roberta said into her wrist communicator. "Take your fighters up and destroy that DropShip."

The aerofighters were fast compared to the DropShip, and within seconds they were on it. Devon Osis could hear their combat chatter as the pilots made their passes, then watched as they found not a crippled DropShip, but one repaired and putting up a fight. The battle lasted a full two minutes, and in the end, the fighters Roberta had bid were gone. The damage they had inflicted on the Fusiliers were considerable, but in the end, they failed to stop the ship.

Without a word or other warning, Roberta picked up a chair and hurled it across the length of the control room into a redundant tactical feed system, destroying the display. Her bellow of rage echoed through the nearly soundproof room with such fury that none of the staff dared raise their eyes from their workstations.

Galaxy Commander Devon Oasis continued to watch and wait, saying nothing.

"Freebirth!" she cursed. "Do they not realize who they are facing?"

The communications officer did not react, but Osis knew it was because the man had mastered the discipline of control.

As a true Smoke Jaguar, he was suppressing his emotions, showing nothing that Star Colonel Roberta might exploit. "Our OmniFighter tactical feeds show some damage to the DropShip. More interesting is that our reflective motion-sweep scanning shows that a large contingent of the Fusiliers are on the move, heading east by northeast. They are some sixty kilometers from the isthmus and are closing rapidly."

"Those ignorant surat spawn," Roberta bellowed again as she leaned over the sensors data and activated the command channel to her ground forces. "Forces of the Bloodied Claws, this is Claw One." As she spoke, her fingers tapped at the controls, pulling up the nav points on the tactical map. "All forces proceed to Nav Point Bravo Epsilon Ten. Enemy force engagement begins in thirty hours. Run at yellow alert."

Devon Osis guessed, as Roberta must have, that the enemy command staff had not been wiped out by her headhunter attacks. In fact, enough of them remained that they were mounting an offensive of their own. He too found it infuriating that these freebirths were disrupting the true mission of the Tau Galaxy, which was to destroy the Nova Cats. At least it would be over soon. With the Fusiliers rushing to meet them, victory would be swift and clean.

Finally, he spoke. "First your headhunter mission failed to meet its intended objective, costing you two Stars of your Cluster. Now you have lost your bid-fighters as well, Star Colonel." His matter-of-fact tone was an odd constant to her fury. "The Inner Sphere DropShip is still operational and apparently heading toward our base. Act, or I will. I will not let you place this Galaxy's mission in jeopardy."

Roberta somehow managed to curb the inferno of her anger as she looked at her commander. Her hairless skull was uncommonly red, the light gray neural implant that ringed it like a tattoo standing out oddly by contrast. "I must accept a loss of honor to achieve the goals of the Tau Galaxy, my commander. I ask that you allow me to revoke my previous bid and use the *Dark Claw*. It can easily deal with the DropShip, and I accept this minor loss of honor as a sacrifice for the Clan." She bowed her head at the disgrace.

In the eyes of the Smoke Jaguars, being forced to revoke a bid was nowhere near the shame of losing a battle. Her action was appropriate and told Devon Osis that Roberta understood that the fate of the Galaxy was more important than her personal concerns. The sense of control gave him a warm feeling, one of domination and power.

"I will grant you this in the name of the great Jaguar." He reached over and keyed several of the control studs in the covered tip of the Galaxy Baton. "May your next bid be more accurate."

"Thank you, Galaxy Commander." Roberta turned to the communications officer, her grin almost devilish. "Contact the *Dark Claw*. Order them to close and engage the Fusilier DropShip. Destroy it."

"Shouldn't we launch, Captain?" Loren asked in a low tone.

"Physics, Major," Spillman replied, looking at a larger tactical display on the nearby wall that showed the course and movement of the DropShip. "Wait a minute or two until that birdie has picked up a wee bit more thrust. Once she's in motion, even a warbird like that canna be diverted quickly. I want her committed, then we're out of here."

Loren understood, but he wondered how much of what Captain Spillman was doing was based on gut feeling and how much on hard tactical data. "Any word from the *Claymore*?"

The comm officer nodded and adjusted the ear pieces of her headset. "She's picked up the destroyer and is slowing slightly. The *Claymore* is ten minutes from her drop point. Damage from the OmniFighter attack was moderate."

There was a long pause as everyone on the bridge looked at the larger tactical display on the port wall of the bridge. Captain Spillman did not seem impressed, but squinted his eyes several times, trying to read the small numbers of the tactical sidebars. Indeed, he was so relaxed he took out a pair of reading glasses and cleaned them with a handkerchief. Loren looked over at the comm officer, who only smiled in response. It was obvious that little seemed to shake the *Bull Run*'s new captain, and his crew knew that.

Spillman's order came without any warning, without any change of facial expression. "Load main operations navigation program and initiate course vector. Fire main engines, launch profile Gamma. All hands, general quarters, red alert."

Loren couldn't help but smile himself. *The game's afoot . . .*

* * *

"Message from the *Dark Claw*," the comm officer said loud enough for Star Colonel Roberta to hear. "Infrared sensors have detected the launch of another DropShip. Its flight path is perpendicular to theirs."

"Impossible," Roberta said in disbelief. "It must be a ruse."

A moment passed. "Neg, Star Colonel," the office replied. "Star Captain Chrisholm requests you specify a target."

Roberta looked over her shoulder at Devon Osis, whose face showed concern. "They play me for a fool. Order the *Dark Claw* to fire a single volley at the first DropShip and then go after the second, full flank speed." Her attention was fully on the tactical display now. "I was fooled once by their little games, but not twice. They mean to try and escape with some of their forces in the second DropShip. They seek reinforcements—aff, aid in their fight. But we are a long way from Northwind and their homeland.

"The first ship was intended to lure us away, perhaps even make us deploy some forward troops. We will hurt that ship—cripple it like the lame animal it is, then go after the real prey."

"You could be wrong about how they will use these Drop-Ships, Star Colonel," Devon Osis told her. "What then?"

"Neg, Commander, I am right and you know it too."

"How can you be so sure, Star Colonel?"

She said nothing, but kept her eyes locked with his. "We share the same soul, the heart of the Jaguar."

"Crush this freebirth trash," he said, "Leave no trace of them when you are done." His voice was low, not a whisper, but more throaty—almost sensuous with the lust for battle.

The comm officer interrupted their intense exchange. "The first DropShip has changed course. It is heading for the isthmus between the two continents."

Roberta stared at him.

"The *Dark Claw* reports numerous flash signals, drop pods, and jump jets. It is enemy BattleMech deployment," the comm officer went on.

"They're going to seize those straits," Roberta said, turning back to Osis. "That ship was not just a decoy." Devon Osis saw the rage flare up in her again, burning hotter and brighter, burning like a bonfire.

21

DropShip **Bull Run,** *Outbound*
Wayside V (Wildcat)
Deep Periphery
5 July 3058

"The *Claymore*'s down," the flight officer said, his voice seeming to shatter the tension of the *Bull Run*'s bridge. Loren smiled broadly and looked over at Captain Spillman, who gave him a confident thumbs-up.

Colonel's Stirling's modification to Case Granite was simple yet elegant. The *Claymore* would deploy its two companies of Black Adders in the tight confines of the Isthmus of Bannockburn. It would then feign a crash nearby to further boost the defense of the narrow pass. Should the Jaguars somehow punch through, the Fusiliers could use the ship's powerful turrets as long-range fire support. On their own, the Black Adders should be able to hold back the Smoke Jaguars long enough for the main body of the Fusiliers to arrive.

"Enemy destroyer moving to intercept course," the navigation officer barked out in a deep voice.

"Time until we're in range of their weapons?" Spillman asked, rubbing his jaw in thought.

"Given our current thrust and course and the head start we've got, she'll be in range in approximately twenty-two minutes."

"Not too bad," Loren said. The mechanics of the space battle were straightforward but risky. The *Bull Run* would continue on its direct course to where the JumpShips were stationed at the pirate jump point. The WarShip's best hope was to close in the wake of the outbound Fusilier DropShip. Once the destroyer was in range, the *Bull Run* would initiate its play. "I only hope your little presents do the trick."

"They will, lad," Spillman said. He looked over at the young female gunnery officer. "Lieutenant Rosen, have your team in Bay Three prep for launch." The lieutenant snapped a salute and leaned over the control panel, furiously issuing orders. The minutes passed slowly as if time itself had slowed down.

"Captain, three minutes from interception range on my mark—mark!" the navigation officer suddenly called out.

Spillman turned to Lieutenant Rosen, "Gunnery control, fire the first wave. Second wave to follow twenty seconds later."

"Aye, aye, sir," she replied.

"Short-range sensors indicate that the objects dumped from the DropShip are in our flight vector," the bridge officer of the WarShip *Dark Claw* reported as he studied the information scrolling in front of him. "It is as you said, Star Captain, they are definitely life pods and three of their life boats." The dull hum of the massive subspace drive of the Smoke Jaguar destroyer seemed to throb with energy as everyone on the bridge of the *Dark Claw* swung into action. The massive viewports, their armor shields down now, showed the vast expanse of space in front of the ship. Against the velvet blackness the ship's target looked like little more than a glowing dot of burning fusion energy.

Star Captain Klark Chrisholm, commander of the *Dark Claw*, nodded with some satisfaction that he had been right. "Any sign that the pods are occupied?"

"Neg. They are making no attempt to avoid us. Apparently they are adrift, sir."

"An old ploy but poorly timed on their part. Had we fired on that ship, perhaps we might be deceived into believing they had been hit," Chrisholm said. "I will not waste precious time investigating this ruse."

"Do you wish to change course to avoid them?"

"Neg," Chrisholm said, as though the question were offensive. "A course diversion of even a few degrees at this distance could add hours to our interception. Continue at current heading and speed." He knew that the *Dark Claw*'s massive frontal armor was more than enough to stop any damage the escape craft might try to do. And, judging from the tactical plot, only three of the pods and none of the life boats would pass close enough to present any danger of accidental ramming. "Are our guns in range yet?" he asked.

"Neg," the Gunnery Control Officer replied. "The turrets will be in range in less than a minute. Gunner's Mate Volks and his crew have won the bid for the right to engage first."

"Captain," called the bridge officer. "We are passing their life boats in ten seconds."

Klark Chrisholm sat tall in his chair, ever the proud Smoke Jaguar warrior. These were not prey worthy of a ship's commander such as him. His WarShip was more than a match for the already damaged DropShip.

He looked out the forward viewscreen and saw the outline of one of the escape pods nearly fifty meters away as the *Dark Claw* passed. There was a slight glow, then the pod's boosters suddenly fired, burning brightly with life and energy. It pivoted slightly, then drove straight into the destroyer's hull just in front of the bridge. Within moments the other pods and life boats also plowed into the WarShip, coming to life all at once like mad dogs suddenly awakened.

The instant the pod hit the WarShip's hull, it erupted in a gigantic ball of light. There was no blast sound, but the massive *Essex* Class destroyer seemed to shudder and moan under the impact. There were four more explosions, four in rapid succession, each seeming to shake the ship hard. Chrisholm rose to his feet as the last blast nearly threw him to the floor.

"Damage report," he barked. As he spoke, the tactical display screen flickered for a moment, then shut off totally.

"We were rammed by the life craft," the bridge officer said.

"That much I know, you fool," Chrisholm said.

The officer leaned over the panel, his fingers dancing furiously as he pulled up the data. "We have lost long-range sensors. Our external array took a direct hit. Starboard was hit by three of their life boats and has sustained moderate damage, with a hull breach of Alpha deck. Emergency procedures are in place. And sir, just as we lost sensors we saw another group of those craft being launched in our path."

"They programmed them like our own anti-ship missiles, loaded with explosives," Chrisholm said, almost admiring the gall of the enemy Captain. "How much time until the new wave is in range?"

"Approximately one minute," the bridge officer said. "They are still out of range of our bid turret, sir."

"How many and what composition is this next wave?"

"Data is inaccurate due to our damage, Star Captain, but it appears to consist of three life boats and four more pods."

"That is impossible," Chrisholm retorted. "*Overlord* Class DropShips do not carry that many escape craft. They must have salvaged the other DropShips." The logic was pure, but the implications were staggering. Given the fact that the other three DropShips were still on Wildcat, that meant he could be facing additional waves of these assaults. "Ready all turrets and fire at will."

There was a humming, almost throbbing sound that seemed to shake the bridge as the enormous naval particle projection cannons began to build up their charge to fire. Along with the massive Barracuda anti-ship missiles, the PPCs provided the *Essex* Class destroyer with more than enough firepower to blow the smaller DropShip to smithereens.

The bridge officer spoke up, "With the damage to our sensors, our accuracy will be reduced by fifteen percent."

"Where are those—" Chrisholm's question was cut off as the *Dark Claw* rolled under another deep and thudding explosion as one of the *Bull Run*'s life boats fired its engines and rammed into the ship's starboard side. The blast ate away at its thick armor, and the ship recoiled slightly to port under the impact. That was followed by another pair of smaller explosions as the escape pods collided near the rear engines of the ship. Chrisholm spilled forward slightly under the blasts and realized something was seriously wrong as the lights flickered, then dimmed.

The emergency lighting and station power came on a second later, activating the systems that were critical to ship operations, but leaving many of the stations with only half their control systems lit. The once-bright bridge lights were at twenty-five percent power.

"Engineering, this is the Captain," Chrisholm barked into the microphone in the arm rest of his command chair. "We are on emergency power. Status report."

"We have a small coolant leak, Star Captain, and have had to divert power from the starboard transfer conduit."

"How serious is it?"

"We will have to reduce speed, Captain," the engineer said.

"Neg, you will have to provide me with more thrust," Chrisholm ordered as if his words alone could somehow change the physics of the situation.

"Negative, Captain Chrisholm. If we comply, the engines will automatically shut down in just a few minutes time."

"What are the consequences if I order you to bypass that automatic shutdown, Engineer?"

The question only added to the nearly palpable tension on the bridge. "Captain, you could thrust to the speed you desire, but the engines would overheat within a few minutes. They would burn through their shielding and then rupture the hull as the reactors went uncontrollably critical."

Klark Chrisholm balled his fists in anger, slamming them into the armrests on either side of him. "Alternatives, Engineer."

"Cut the engines temporarily and use one of our access corridors as a bypass coolant vent. It will take an hour to properly seal and make the connections. At that point we could return to seventy-five percent thrust."

In the meantime, my enemy gets away. It was a bitter decision to make, but one that Chrisholm could not avoid. *There is a loss of honor here, but the loss of my vessel would forever impair the mission of the Galaxy.* "Very well, Engineer. Proceed with this bypass. I will signal Commander Osis and inform him of our status."

22

DropShip Bull Run
Pirate Jump Point CEXC-0021-A.2122.97
Deep Periphery
6 July 3058

Loren walked into the cavernous 'Mech bay of the DropShip *Bull Run*, Kerndon following close behind. Gathered here were the troops who would help him lure the Nova Cats from Tarnby to Wayside. He had called them together for one last briefing. As Loren turned to face his people, Kerndon took his place, always a pace behind, as if an invisible rod held him in place.

"Attention, people," Loren called out, and the murmur of voices echoing through the massive bay ceased almost immediately. Usually the dingy, sweat- and lubricant-stained bay was full of the sounds of repair and effort, but now it seemed eerily empty. Even the repair gantries and winches seemed to stop and pay heed to the call for attention. "I called this meeting to let you know what we're up against, and what I expect from you. You all know the importance of this mission to the survival of the rest of the Fusiliers, so I won't bore you with a motivational speech.

"You've all had plenty of time to review known Jaguar tactics. We've left the Jag signals still active on the IFF transponders in the captured Omnis. What you need to remember most about what's coming is that the Nova Cats will come at us with pure Clan tactics. They'll square off in one-on-one battles unless you give them the opportunity to do otherwise. In their minds, they will be fighting the Smoke Jaguars, their long-time enemies.

"From what we've read, they're some kind of mystics or dreamers," said the lean Lieutenant McBride. "Yet the battle reports make them plenty savage in combat. My only question is which are they—dreamers or warriors?"

"For those of you who haven't heard, this man is my bondsman Kerndon." Loren gestured to the muscular man who stood mute behind him. On Kerndon's right wrist was the bondcord, wrapped three times. "Kerndon was a Smoke Jaguar warrior until a few days ago. As my bondsman he is sworn to us, and my trust in him is implicit. He knows all about the Nova Cats."

Kerndon acknowledged Loren with a slight bow of the head as he began to speak. "The Nova Cats believe they have a special insight into the future, and that this future features them predominantly. They perform spiritual quests for visions, attempting to recreate what Nicholas Kerensky did when he formed our—the Clans." Kerndon caught himself as he spoke.

"I have fought them only once, but have studied them deeply. They use their spirituality in combat. It feeds them, gives them a concentration that lets them fight with a frenzy exceeded only by the Jaguar. Because they believe they are chartered by some supernatural providence, they fight without fear of harm or death. This makes them deadly foes." Having spoken all he thought necessary, Kerndon took a step back to indicate he was done.

"As you can see, Kerndon can tell us much that is useful," Loren said. "Now let's get down to business.

"We exit the Wayside system in less than thirty minutes. Our batteries are charged enough to support two jumps, which will bring us to our first objective. We're taking both JumpShips with us, but the *Kobayashi* won't go the whole distance. At one point she'll stop and wait for us, ready to get us back to Wayside fast once we're sure the Nova Cats are coming after us.

"Our first target is star system EC-EY-4170, which is little more than a Clan Nova Cat recharge station. Posing as a Smoke Jaguar Cluster commander, I will initiate a batchall for possession of four of their recharges. We'll use two of those charges to reach our second objective, and the other two on the way back." Loren stressed this last just to remind everyone that there was no question he fully intended to return to Wayside V.

"Excuse me, sir," said Lieutenant Gregory Hector. "But why not just challenge them for the whole recharge station, lock, stock, and barrel?"

"Kerndon can shed some light on that, too," Loren said, gesturing to the bondsman.

"The Nova Cat station is known to be garrisoned by a Star of Elementals and a BattleMech force, plus supporting infantry troops. The Smoke Jaguars have struck the recharge station twice before but have only taken recharges. A Trial of Possession for the entire station would have forced them to commit everything they have to its defense. Such trials would usually involve a different mixture of troops than we're equipped with—primarily Elemental forces." Again, this was something Loren had learned in private discussions with Kerndon. In the void of space, Elementals were favored by the Clans in combat.

"In other words, Greg," he added, "we're posing as Jaguars so we've got to act like Jaguars. Besides, we don't have the forces it would take to garrison or run a base of this size even if we won. Remember, this isn't a war of occupation. We simply want to get the Cats' attention.

"Once we have our charges, we'll proceed on to a small system that both the Explorer Corps files and Kerndon have briefed us on. It's only one jump away, which is good because we're going to need that battery charge for the next hop. The system is known as Boltin, and the Nova Cats have a supply base there. We'll hit them there and hit them hard. The *Kobayashi* will stay and wait for us there, building up enough of a charge that she can get us back to Wayside on the return trip.

"Our next stop is Tarnby, the end of the line. The Nova Cats have two Clusters there, one of them a front-line unit—the 100th Strike Cluster. Our goal will be to take possession of Tarnby's HPG facility, even if just for a short time. If they aren't on our trail after that, I don't know what will get them there."

"Sir?" the burly Sumpter Burke spoke up from the front row. "How are we going to take on all the units you're talking about with only ten OmniMechs of our own?"

"You're thinking too much like an Inner Sphere warrior, Sumpter," Loren said. "Clan bidding will allow us to be very selective about what we commit in the way of forces as long as we choose specific targets. The Nova Cats won't throw an entire Cluster at us if we let them know what we're coming in with and just how small are the targets we want to take."

There was one more sensitive point he still had to address. "We also know that the Clans carefully check the genetic patterns of anyone killed on a battlefield. We can't afford for them to learn that any of us aren't actually Smoke Jaguars. That means no one will be left behind, living or dead. If there's blood in a cockpit, I want it burned totally—without a trace left. If you're unable to recover a dead comrade, we'll have to destroy anything that would allow their scientists to learn our true backgrounds."

"You're asking us to desecrate our dead, Major?" Ralston McAnis asked.

Loren kept his expression neutral. "That's right, Sergeant. And that goes for me too. I expect you or anyone else on this mission to char me beyond any hope of recovery if that becomes necessary."

Before anyone could protest further, Loren pressed on. "Now then," he said looking over the crew, "who here has zero-g experience?" The question was rhetorical, but he asked it anyway. He had gone over the Guards' personnel records several times before leaving Wayside. His choices for mock Smoke Jaguars had not been made casually.

"Sir," Gregory Hector spoke up again. "I had some hands-on experience a few years ago during a raid on the orbital facility on Ballynure." He shrugged. "It's been a while, but I've done it before."

"Excellent. Okay, everyone, get to your jump stations and secure for a leap out of system. Greg, download the specifications for this jump station. Concentrate on the exterior as a possible operations area. Corporal Killfries, I'll need to borrow your *Black Hawk* for this one."

"Yes sir," the tall mustached man replied, unsure why this OmniMech had been singled out.

Loren would explain later, if this plan worked. "Mitch," he called, scanning the group for his technician.

"Sir," Captain Fraser returned.

"Mitch, tell me we've got some of those exterior magnetic foot adapters on board."

The slightly balding Chief Tech nodded.

"Rig them to Lieutenant Hector's *Masakari* and the *Black Hawk*." The time has come to show the Nova Cats what the Smoke Jaguars are capable of . . .

Loren answered the rap on his stateroom door and was surprised to see Kerndon standing there, the man's powerful frame filling the narrow doorway. Usually a DropShip offered staterooms only for officers, but with such a small force on board, Loren and almost all his troops had the luxury of individual rooms.

The former Clansman's expression was unyielding, offering no glimpse of his emotions. Loren motioned for him to sit down, then waited for his bondsman to speak.

"We are recharging for the next jump," Kerndon said. "I came to discuss your batchall to the Nova Cats."

Loren nodded. He too had wanted to speak with Kerndon before the actual transmission of the formal batchall, but there'd been no time until now.

"A Smoke Jaguar batchall is not simply a statement of the intended target or a challenge to a fellow warrior," Kerndon said. "It is a statement of power. This I was taught my entire life." He looked down for a moment at the thrice-wrapped bond cord around his wrist. "With the Inner Sphere, we usually declared our intended target and asked what defense would be mounted. But you have another option, Major Loren, though it was rarely used. You can issue the batchall and tell them what you intend to attack with."

Loren weighed his bondsman's words. "What's the advantage of that?"

"The Nova Cats would cede to you the choice of the battleground."

"Well, that could be handy because I intended to go in with two of our 'Mechs, and I think the station's exterior surface would be the best place for the fight. From the data you've provided us, they rely heavily on Elementals. I don't know anything about Elementals being used in a zero-g environment, but I assume they've been trained for it. Using the exterior of the recharge station would even the odds, because we'd be working in no gravity and no atmosphere."

"Aff," Kerndon said. "But you will have to conceal your face during the transmission. Their scientist caste will attempt to scan your face and compare it with known genetic profiles for the Smoke Jaguars." Between the scannings and the recovery of dead DNA samples for testing, Loren began to understand the importance of the scientist caste among the Clans. Whoever controlled the genes, controlled the Clans— that much was becoming obvious.

Kerndon spoke sternly. "Our batchall must be visual. The Jaguar warrior wants to strike fear in the heart of his intended foe."

"But my face will be covered."

"I must speak to this one you call Mitch. We must create a mask of the Jaguar. The use of such a mask is not uncommon. It is used to show authority."

"Is there anything else I should know before going into this?" Loren asked.

"We will need to practice, Major Loren," Kerndon said flatly. "You must learn to talk like a Smoke Jaguar. You must speak with the fire of battle burning in your veins. You must speak from total superiority. From this time on, you must live as if the heart of the Jaguar beats in your chest."

23

The hyperspace jump to the EC-EY-4170 system included one small element of risk that had nothing to do with the Nova Cats. Jumping between stars was a feat meant to be accomplished slowly and methodically, not rushed the way the Fusiliers were doing.

It took time for the ship's computers to calculate the coordinates of the next jump point exactly, so the ship wouldn't rip apart in a gravity well on arrival. Two jumps in rapid succession carried a risk because on some occasions the delicate drive core could misalign. A prudent and careful commander would wait some time between jumps, making sure the core was in perfect alignment and the calculations verified several times over. A second jump, so short a time after their first, might fail, but the odds were worth it in Loren's mind.

He stood in his stateroom and adjusted the gray cape that had been quickly sewn from one of the shipboard blankets. The mask he wore had been carved from a ball of foam insulation used primarily in emergency repairs on the ship. It was a wide cat's face, with deep-set eyes. Its mouth was open and the fangs were bared.

The mask looked crude, but from what Kerndon told him that would not be unexpected. Intended to show Clan pride and honor, such a mask was more bravado than art. Loren didn't totally understand this business of Clan masks, but he was sure of one thing—Captain Mitchell Fraser should not pursue a career as an artist.

The ship's comm officer had relayed a camera and audio set into the stateroom. Loren had personally painted a large "T" for the Tau Galaxy behind him on the flat gray bulkhead. The illusion was important; in fact, it was all he had to count on.

"Major," came the voice of Captain Spillman over the intercom. "This Nova Cat station is only a thousand kilometers from our current position. Our sensors show they've got active scanners running, so they must know we're here by now. I suggest you do whatever it is yer gonna do before they decide to scramble fighters after us."

Loren was adjusting the mask over his face as Kerndon entered the room, taking up a place beyond where the holocamera would pick up his image. They had practiced this several times, Loren walking through the nuances of the batchall with Kerndon's biting critique. Now the time had come to play the role for real. He activated the intercom to the bridge of the *Bull Run*. "Understood. Comm officer, open a channel with the Nova Cats. If they demand identification, tell them nothing."

The comm officer replied quickly. There was a pause for several beats of Loren's heart before he heard her come back on the line. "You're on in three seconds, Major."

The little green light on top of the holoprojector came on and Loren stood staring at the camera system. The receiving system consisted of a floor-mounted circular disk rimmed with lights to control and maintain the image. The camera system consisted of three tripod-mounted cameras to catch him at a number of angles, as well as a computer-enhancement system in the hand-held control pad that generated elements of the image the cameras didn't capture. With the control pad he was able to control both the receiver and the transmitter, in this case tied into the ship's communications array.

Loren had played many roles in his career—MechWarrior, officer, terrorist, loyal Capellan, spy, saboteur, and Northwind Highlander. This should have been another role, another acting job, something required to fulfill a mission objective. Somehow, it felt different. Before, the stakes had always been for nation. *This is for the survival of the Fusiliers. For the first time ever I have a family. Even if I fail and somehow survive all of this, I will die inside.*

"Nova Cats, I am Star Colonel Loren of the Smoke Jaguars. Hear my batchall and quake with fear in your dens." His voice boomed, as arrogant and proud as he could make it. "I stalk you like my namesake and will toss your fetid carcass into the flames of defeat."

He paused to let the words of his batchall have their effect. "I come in the name of the one true Clan, the Jaguars, to take from you in a Trial of Possession four of your charges. Like a true warrior, I come at you with two of my OmniMechs, knowing that whatever you send at me will be crushed under their feet. This I do in the name of my Clan.

"With what do defend yourself? What warriors do you wish to send to their deaths?" Loren paused, and Kerndon shut off the projector and gave him a nod-like salute.

"They will acknowledge your batchall and bid internally for the right to destroy you."

"Message incoming, sir," the comm officer signaled. "Relaying now." The audio would come through the built-in ceiling speaker tied into the DropShip's communications system.

The holographic camera also acted as a miniature projector. In front of Loren appeared the image of a man dressed in a black uniform with a hooded cape. The image stood facing him, even though it was the size of a child's toy doll. "This is Star Commander Edward of Cat's Eye Command Number Nine of Clan Nova Cat—the true followers of the vision of Nicholas Kerensky. We have received your bid and acknowledge the forces you will deploy. You are rash like the rest of your Clan, Jaguar, and cannot hope for victory. We shall teach you the power of inspired vision. I will contact you within the hour to tell you our defense." The small image disappeared.

"How did I do?" Loren asked, removing the mask and letting the cool ship's air sting at the sweat on his face.

"Major Loren," Kerndon said coolly, "you have potential."

Mitch Fraser stood with his hand-held stress analyzer and ran another sweep of the *Black Hawk* Loren was going to pilot. Loren watched with appreciation the care his tech was taking.

"Am I set for space operations?" he asked.

The *Claymore*'s 'Mech bay, which had been so quiet before, was abuzz as the 'Mech pilots checked and re-checked their BattleMechs to make sure they were operational. The sounds of metallic tools hitting metal echoed in the air, and the smell of sticky-sweet lubricant bit at the back of everyone's throats.

Mitch shut off the analyzer and turned his bloodshot gaze back to his CO. "Yes, sir, as set as anybody can be. The magnetic gear is installed and programmed into your battle computer. If this fight takes place on the surface of the station, you'll be able to walk at .7 gees."

"Good. What about the tether?"

"Every 'Mech we've got is equipped with a tether tie-hook. I've rigged the myomer cable for a slight electrical charge you can control through your comm system. Just enter the code and that cable will snap back from wherever you are." Myomer was the same material that gave BattleMechs their internal "muscles," allowing them to move with almost human precision. When an electrical charge was applied to a segment of myomer, the piece would contract thousands of times smaller.

The use of myomer tether-ties for 'Mech operations in space was common. Fighting in such an environment was not. Even with the special magnetic adapters on its feet, a 'Mech could still easily be knocked free and adrift into space. Despite the durability of the ties, a lucky cockpit hit could cause explosive decompression, instantly killing the MechWarrior. Fighting in the icy and silent cold of space was not something any warrior wanted to do.

"I hope to use it to our advantage," Loren replied, picking up and inspecting a segment of the tether.

"Sir, what was their bid?"

"Two Points of force. I assume they'll use at least one Point of Elementals, maybe more. Kerndon said I could ask for information on the forces we'd be facing, but he also said that a Jaguar would show more audacity by not asking. And since the Nova Cats didn't ask for our make-up, I didn't want to seem cautious."

"So instead, you'll go in blind?"

Loren nodded, understanding the implications even more than his friend. "In this case, yes. I'm fulfilling a role here and don't want to risk the lives of our comrades on Wayside by giving the game away right off the bat."

"If I may ask sir, why you? Why do you have to do this?" Mitch wanted to know.

"I'm in command and have experience with this kind of

combat," Loren said. That was true enough, but it was more than that. *I have to do this, to prove something to myself.*

"If anything happens to you, the entire regiment will die back on Wayside," Mitch said.

Loren put one hand on Mitch's shoulder. "No," he said, "if anything happens to me, you'll have to carry on with the mission."

"Me?" Mitch was flabbergasted.

"Of course you," Loren said. "You're the ranking command officer, Captain. If I die, you'll have to make sure this mission comes off successfully. I've left detailed plans covering the mission in your directory."

"Major Jaffray," Mitch almost wailed. "I'm a technician, not a MechWarrior. I can't accept that kind of responsibility."

"Mitch, you're a Northwind Highlander and a Fusilier—first and foremost. You're as worried as the next man about the Colonel and the others back on Wayside. You won't let them—or me—down. I know—"

His words were cut off by the blare of the ship's intercom. "Major Jaffray, incoming message from Cat's Eye Recharge Station. The Nova Cats demand to respond to your batchall, sir." The voice came from the far-off bridge and the comm officer there.

"I have to go," Mitch Fraser said, his face suddenly pale.

"So do I. Where're you off to?" Loren asked as he turned toward the ladder to the upper deck.

"Well, sir," Mitch Fraser said, "I'm going to go and pray like hell that you live through this."

24

Cat's Eye 009 Recharge Station
System EC-EY-4170
Deep Periphery
8 July 3058

Loren's borrowed *Black Hawk* and Lieutenant Hector's *Masakari* stood on the undersurface of the recharge station as the ship's engineers, working in zero-G gear, finished the necessary attachments of their myomer tethers to the bottom side of the Nova Cat base. Mitch had wired the tethers so they could be electrically charged. They were a lifeline, one that both Loren and Greg Hector would need if they followed the plan he had devised. Hector was worried about it, and Loren didn't blame him.

The Nova Cat recharge station was long, just under a kilometer, and at least three-quarters of that wide. The slight curve to it was hardly noticeable in space, but someone like Loren, using the magnetic adapters on his feet to remain upright, took note of it. His training kicked in almost instantly as he studied the projections along the bottom, some only a meter or two tall, some, like a nearby antenna array, standing twice the size of his OmniMech. *This would provide more than ample cover for the Elementals, making the fight with them all the more difficult. For us, it means the Nova Cat 'Mech will be able to provide long range fire support using the projections and sensors to block some of our shots.*

Loren checked the comm board and saw that no power was currently running to the myomer line. Both he and Hector had enough power to reach the other side of the base, if necessary. Myomer cable, all on its own, was powerful enough to hold a 'Mech, but electrically charged, it was even more so. Loren knew his physics well enough to know the importance of that line. If the magnetic couplings on the *Black Hawk*'s feet got damaged or came off somehow, he would be adrift. Motion, any motion, would become his enemy.

Perfectly on time he saw the arrival of the opposing 'Mech and Elementals at the far end of the station. It was a massive *Gladiator*—or an *Executioner* in Clan nomenclature. Bristling with weapons, it was menacing. The cockpit, shaped like a human head, seemed to look down on them with evil intent as the Clan technicians performed the same sort of attachments Loren and Lieutenant Hector had just finished.

The *Gladiator* out-massed Loren's *Black Hawk* by a full forty-five tons, nearly double his 'Mech's weight. Against Greg Hector's *Masakari* the match would be more even, but Loren had the jump jets. He knew he should be the one to take on that big boy. His sensors told him that a Point of Elementals was next to the 'Mech, though he only caught a glimpse of them visually because of the obstructions on the surface of the station.

No matter what, they must think I'm a trueborn Smoke Jaguar, nothing less. As the technicians cleared the surface of the base, he opened a broad-band broadcast to everyone who could hear. "I am Star Colonel Loren of the Smoke Jaguars. Come forward, Nova Cats, so that I might drink your blood and toast your death at my hands."

"I am Star Commander Otis of the Nova Cats," came the response. "You use words like a freebirth whore, tossing them about like cheap trinkets worn once and cast aside. You have come to fight for JumpShip charges it is my duty to defend. Let us finish this child's play so I can get back to the business of a trueborn warrior." Loren was suddenly amused at this ritual exchange of Clan insults.

He activated the *Black Hawk*'s HUD targeting cross hairs, which settled on the *Gladiator* as his weapons locked on. The 'Mech's array of armaments normally locked squarely onto the center of the enemy, but this time Loren took the autocannon off the normal lock sequence and aimed and targeted it independently. While his large and small lasers were aiming squarely at the fusion-reactor heart of the *Gladiator*, the deadly autocannon was aimed off to the side, at a target that simply could not be pulled up by his battle computer as a viable target.

Star Commander Otis did not falter or react to the weapons lock. Loren triggered the large pulse laser, scoring a hit that silently ripped the ferro-fibrous armor plating away from the *Gladiator*'s torso, sending the pieces spinning off into the blackness of space. Bursts from the small laser and one of the machine guns followed, hitting the 'Mech's shoulder and right arm. Neither hit did much damage, merely peppering the plates.

Loren next thumbed the trigger for the autocannon, one of the *Black Hawk*'s more powerful weapons, sending out a stream of shells that seemed to hit the decking some five meters from where the *Gladiator* began to pivot under the impact of the lasers. Loren was waiting instinctively for the deep rumble of the impacts of the shells exploding, but the vacuum offered none of that. Instead all he saw were the explosions and bright flashes of light as shrapnel riddled the area near the massive OmniMech's feet. To anyone watching, the autocannon shot looked like a clean miss.

The five Elementals nearby lifted slowly on fluttering jets of flame from their ankle jets, gracefully rising and moving toward Hector's *Masakari*. They obviously had one goal in mind, to swarm the sides of his OmniMech and cripple it.

"Now you become one with the stars," Star Commander Otis said, opening up with the *Gladiator*'s heavy firepower, a brilliant flash of ruby red light from its pair of large lasers scathing across Loren's right leg and upper torso like swords of light. The *Black Hawk* only shuddered slightly as Loren moved it three steps forward, wading into the laser light.

There was a flash in front of him as the Gauss rifle slug from Otis's *Gladiator* found its mark in his left torso, burying itself deeply in his armor and internal structure. The upper torso of the *Black Hawk* reeled backward, but the magnetic couplers held Loren upright—just barely. He saw the story he already knew to be true: the armor of his right torso was all but gone. Another hit there would spell the end of the Trial, and possibly his life.

Instead of retreating, he charged forward. Each step was sluggish, the magnetic couplings making him feel like he was running through muck two meters thick, but he charged forward regardless. He maintained his earlier weapon systems locks and fired again. His large pulse laser spit forth a wall of red fire, hitting the upper chest and cockpit of the *Gladiator* just as the Nova Cat 'Mech fired. The *Black Hawk*'s small laser rattled the right leg of the *Gladiator*, with no apparent effect other than pitting the thick armor there.

Loren's autocannon once again seemed destined to completely miss its target, but recoiling from the laser attack, the Nova Cat turned into the fusillade of cannon fire, which riddled its cockpit. A hit to the cockpit, even a pinhole-size breach, would kill a 'Mech pilot in a complete vacuum. Star Commander Otis had fired his weapons just at the moment of the hit, but the sudden pivot made his lasers and Gauss rifle miss their mark. Loren saw a flash of silver as the massive Gauss slug whipped past his cockpit silently, casting itself forever into space.

At a distance of two hundred meters Loren tipped his 'Mech forward, bowing slightly as he ignited his jump jets. In a gravity situation the jets would carry him a distance of only one hundred-fifty meters. Killing the power to his magnetic coupling, he took off like a bullet, unrestrained by the pull of gravity. With no jumping limit, the *Black Hawk* shot forward at an incredible speed, straight at the *Gladiator* still trying to recover from the attack.

Star Commander Otis tried to move out of his flight path, but Loren was able to easily adjust the thrust of the jets to compensate. In mere seconds the image of the massive Clan 'Mech filled his viewscreen and he collided with it.

The impact did moderate damage to both of them, but knocked the *Gladiator* free of the station. As Loren bounced back, drifting slightly away from his target, he saw that his attack had the desired effect. The Nova Cat warrior was no longer standing on the station but was adrift, moving quickly away from the station, as was Loren's own *Black Hawk*. His target image showed that the *Gladiator*'s center torso had taken most of the damage, but it was so thick with ferro-fibrous armor that it would take more.

At point-blank range he opened up with his machine guns, autocannon, and small laser, aiming at the right leg of the Nova Cat 'Mech. The machine-gun fire pushed them even further apart as Otis attempted to determine just how seriously he'd been damaged. While the guns and the small laser did only marginal damage to the limb, the autocannon tore massive gouges in the *Gladiator*'s already mauled right leg. Loren saw gobbets of silvery liquid spilling into space, drifting between them as the two 'Mechs moved further apart under the assault. *The jump jets! I've hit one of his jets!*

Before Otis could react, Loren reached over to the controls Mitch had set up, the ones that would provide power to his myomer tether cable. As he applied a slight charge, the cable tightened, its long slack gone in an instant. It snapped like a rubber band, not hard, but enough to pull him backward—down toward the recharge station.

"Always fast to the fight, my Jaguar friend," taunted the voice of Star Commander Otis. "I too have a tether and a way back," he said as Loren quickly returned to the base, using his jump jets to soften his landing. He stared up and saw the *Gladiator*'s severed and charred tether pass by him, its end shredded and frayed. The burn marks from his autocannon round bursts showed as the tether whizzed past his own *Black Hawk*. There was a long pause, and he imagined Star Commander Otis frantically attempting to send a charge to his tether, only to see it contract toward him with no tie whatsoever to the recharge station.

"The battle is over for you," Loren said. "I am a Smoke

Jaguar and I rarely miss my aim." His autocannon bursts, the ones that seemed to miss their mark, had done just what he wanted.

"Damn you!" Otis cursed, firing his lasers wildly down toward the *Black Hawk*. The 'Mech was hopelessly out of range, though, the distance increasing with each second. A flash comm signal came into Loren's neurohelmet, a voice he identified as Kerndon's. "Star Colonel Loren, your Starmate needs aid," he said, playing his part. Loren immediately pivoted and looked over at Gregory Hector.

As the Lieutenant's *Masakari* came into view, Loren saw the last of the Elementals adjust its flight and join the others on the surface of the 'Mech. All five were using their huge claws to pull off armor plating apparently already damaged by a barrage of short-range missiles from their shoulder packs. The eerie glow from those holes told Loren time was running out for his Lieutenant.

One of the Elementals barely hung on to the swinging right arm of Hector's *Masakari*. The Elemental was missing his power claw, which had apparently been severed by a shot from Hector earlier in the fight. Another of the armored infantry, clinging to the right leg, had burn marks all over him from close hits from lasers. The Nova Cat Elementals, however, were very good and clung tenaciously to Hector's OmniMech.

"I could use some help, sir," Hector said, obviously using everything he had just to keep the Elementals at bay—a losing proposition at best.

"Go with the plan, Lieutenant. They're all over you."

"Sir . . ."

"No talk, just do it," Loren commanded.

"I've always hated physics," Hector muttered. Loren watched as the magnetic couplings on the *Masakari* disengaged, shutting off so the 'Mech could move without being held to the station. The huge knee actuators on the *Masakari* bent way down as it virtually squatted over one of the Elementals who was firing at the armor between the legs of the 'Mech, burning away a wide swath of plate in the process. Then, without warning, the *Masakari* jumped up, snapping the knee actuators as fast as they would go and pushing off with the feet.

The eighty-five-ton *Masakari* took off from the bottom of the recharge station like a rocket. Its mass gave it incredible momentum, and the Elementals were caught off guard by the sudden movement, breaking off their attacks just so they could assess their plight. Loren watched the trip upward in amazement, keeping his eyes on the myomer tether line that was rapidly unwinding as Greg Hector and his unwilling stowaways continued their flight. The line seemed to be intact.

As Hector and his "guests" reached the end of the line, Loren knew that the Elementals would be concentrating on maintaining their hand-holds. The ploy would not be obvious, not until the last moment. Then, as Greg had pointed out, physics would take over. He applied a powerful electrical burst to his myomer tether cable just before the peak of the trip up and outward.

A trickle of power to the myomer tether had brought Loren back to the station at approximately the same distance. The amount of power Lieutenant Hector had applied made the thick myomer cable contract to a hundredth of its length. The sudden contraction violently jerked the *Masakari* back to the base at a faster speed than it had left with.

The result to the Elementals was obvious as well. The outward momentum of the massive *Masakari* was passed to them as it suddenly stopped and began to rapidly return to the recharge station. The jerking motion, while violent for Lieutenant Hector in the cockpit of his 'Mech, was devastating to the Elementals.

The results were instantaneous. Three of the power-suited infantry lost their grips simultaneously, continuing outward into space on the original jump path of the *Masakari*. A fourth's clawlike hand snapped, and a millisecond later he spun wildly into two of his comrades. Spinning madly, it would take hours for them to use their boots to adjust their flight paths enough to even start back to the recharge station. Physics had come through.

Lieutenant Hector's OmniMech raced downward, with one Elemental crawling up the surface of his chest, clinging lest it end up in the same predicament as its comrades. The snapping of the tether had not been clean, and the *Masakari* spun slightly as it plummeted toward the station. Loren saw the legs of the Elemental outstretched as it refused to let go. The *Masakari* hit the exterior hard and bounced slightly upward, a whiff of oxygen or other gas spilling off.

As he stood, Loren saw the remains of the last Elemental,

the Nova Cat that had refused to release its grip. It had been on the *Masakari*'s center torso when Lieutenant Hector collided with the station, sandwiched between the two masses as they crashed together. The Elemental's chest and head were flattened as he drifted away from the *Masakari*. There was a slight stain of blood on the *Masakari*'s mauled armor where the head of the Nova Cat had been. The power-armored trooper's legs were crossed when the impact occurred, and were mashed together like those of a plastic toy soldier that had melted in the hot sun, flattened beyond recognition.

Loren opened his broad communications channel. "Star Commander Edward of the Nova Cats, this is Star Colonel Loren of the Smoke Jaguars. Your forces have been defeated by superior skills and tactics. Once more we have seen who is the true bearer of the Kerensky heritage. Send your free-birth technicians to recover your dead and those who are drifting to their death. Our JumpShip's sails are deployed, and you can begin beaming us the two charges we have won.

"On this day, the Jaguar has beaten you. Remember this and tell the others in your Clan that we have come, stalking those who would stand in the way of our destiny."

Loren knew that one thing remained. He would cut Kerndon's first bondcord. The bondsman had more than proven his loyalty in helping pull this off.

25

Isthmus of Bannockburn
Wayside V (Wildcat)
Deep Periphery
9 July 3058

Cat Stirling looked around the portable command dome and observed the tired, tense expressions of her command staff. They'd reached the Isthmus of Bannockburn, but there still had not been a peep from the Jaguars. Major Craig had dark circles under his eyes. Captain Lovat, her intelligence officer, looked edgy as he tilted his head from side to side to stretch his neck muscles. *Sho-sa* Parkensen stood defiantly cross-armed at the back of the group near the tall form of Major Blakadar. Blackie was leaning against the field dome's shaped carbon rod as if it were a solid wall, not a collapsible tent that could be broken down and stuffed into the back of a cockpit for storage.

Stirling looked around at the ten-meter-diameter gray dome and wondered how many times she had used it on various campaigns—and how many times she would continue to use it. *Too many memories here, and I keep hauling it with me battle after battle.*

Most edgy of all was newly promoted Major Fuller. To him these command-level meetings were all new, and he had no idea what her or anyone else's expectations were.

"We're in position and are holding the straits," Stirling said. "The Jaguars should've been on top of us yesterday. What's the latest scouting report, Intel?"

Lovat spoke up quickly. "Lewis's scouts have spotted them. They seem to be holding position on their side of the isthmus."

"Digging in, I'll bet," Craig put in.

Captain Lovat shook his head. "That isn't their style. If they were using normal Jaguar tactics, they should've rushed in on top of us. For some reason they're holding back."

"Take advantage," *Sho-sa* Parkensen prodded from the back of the field dome. "Drive into their forces now before she can implement an assault against us."

Stirling shook her head. "That may be just what this Star Colonel Roberta wants us to do. Before I jump in, I want to know why she's waiting."

Captain Lovat stepped forward. "Sir, if I may. We still have a number of satellites in orbit that the Jaguars have not yet detected. Our passive information hasn't told us anything. I can use one of our active satellites to get a scan of the entire region."

"But once you turn it on, won't they just take it out?" Major Fuller asked.

Lovat nodded. "Yes, but if we get the data we need, the loss will be acceptable.'

Stirling nodded. "Make it happen, Captain," she ordered. "Reconvene here in two hours. Keep your forces at full alert in the meantime." She walked with them to the dome entrance and looked off into the distance. The steep rock walls of the narrow, canyon-like isthmus loomed off to her right. To the left she saw, in the distance, the shelf of the New Scotland continent edged by a dark green sky as clouds rolled in. To the right, the continent of New Northwind, capped with its own thin layer of clouds. A stiff cool breeze swept the area as she studied the battle site. *Somewhere out there is my enemy. Roberta's up to something. And as soon as I know what it is, I'm going to make her rue the day she ever crawled out of that damn little Clan test tube.*

"We were able to run the satellite for about twenty-five minutes before their destroyer picked it up and knocked it out," Captain Lovat said as the officers gathered around the dome's portable holographic projector. "The good news is that I think I know why our Star Colonel has been holding back for the past two days or so."

He activated the projector system, and the holographic map of the isthmus came to life. The positions of the Fusiliers were shown as blue icons while the 'Mechs and Elementals of the 101st's Bloodied Claws appeared as red images, with only a short rock-strewn distance between them. Colonel Stirling leaned over the projector, studying every centimeter of it. "I'm missing whatever you're seeing, Captain."

The isthmus was some twenty meters wide, essentially a canyon running east and west. The floor of the canyon was strewn with massive rock formations. To the west, the Fusiliers were huddled in behind the jagged rock outcroppings. To the east, the Smoke Jaguars were doing the same. Framing the canyon, the continents rose upward into the nearly airless void.

"Backing out the image now, sir," Lovat said. He pressed the control on the map, and the image shrank, bringing more of the region into view. Each time he pressed it, the map got smaller in size, but made more of Wayside V visible. Suddenly, there was another red image on the map, somewhat southeast of the isthmus.

"There she is," Lovat said, aiming his hand-held pointer at the red dot. As he did, the map zoomed in again, this time showing the icons for 'Mechs and Elementals that made up the red dots of light.

"Well, well," Colonel Stirling said, smiling for the first time in several days. "What have we got here?"

"Assault Omnis, a full Star," Kurt Blakadar said. "And

two Points of Elementals to boot." He turned to Captain Lovat. "What's the accuracy of this data?"

"Ninety-five percent," he returned flatly. "Accurate enough . . ."

"She's sent them around, probably over the continent just like we were planning to do, but further to the east, that's why it took so long," Colonel Stirling said. "Star Colonel Roberta is holding off until they're in position on our southwest flank. This force is coming around to hit us from behind, taking the long way to get there. That's why they're biding time in the isthmus. She's planning to hit us from the north with her main body, and from the south with this little surprise."

"Damn," was all Cullen Craig could muster.

"Damn is right," Stirling said. "Major Blakadar, she knows we scanned the area. What do you think she'll do?"

"I'd assume my plan was blown," the large officer replied. "I'd throw everything I had at you and get this over with."

"Just what I was a-thinkin'," Colonel Stirling returned. "And two can play at that game." She turned to the new leader of the Kilsyth Guards. "Major Fuller, have Captain Lewis and his combined arms folks hunker down here in the rear as we planned. Then take one of your companies and go after Roberta's little surprise group. The rest of your force will assist the Black Adders on the right flank from the isthmus floor."

"Yes, sir," Fuller replied with a salute.

"And you, Blackie," Stirling said. "Get your Black Adders ready and begin moving them up onto New Northwind on the east side of the isthmus, as planned. Major Craig, ready your forces for assault."

Stirling stood looking at her officers for a moment, hands on her hips. "Remember, lads," she said finally, "we're not here to beat them or grind them into pulp. We're here to bloody them and get away. Major Jaffray is bringing us help. We just have to hurt them bad enough to force them to take time to lick their wounds."

"Do not mince words with me, Star Captain," Star Colonel Roberta said sharply into her cockpit microphone. Sitting and waiting for battle was not her strong suit. The cockpit of her 'Mech seemed to get smaller with each breath she took, closing in around her. It frustrated her that the Fusiliers were less than a kilometer from where she stood, digging in and waiting for her to come and get them.

Her plan was sound, the force that she had sent around the continent was slow-moving, but would slam into the Fusiliers' rear at the same time she started her assault. Sandwiched into the straits between the continents, the Fusiliers would be pinned in and destroyed to the last man and woman.

Star Captain Klark Chrisholm answered calmly. "A satellite was detected running active scans of your current area of operations. We have destroyed it and several others that have been detected thus far."

"Were we successfully scanned?"

"Unknown, Star Colonel. I know scanning was done, but I have no way of knowing if it was successful or if the information was relayed to the Fusiliers."

The raging fire that Star Colonel Roberta had managed to suppress until now suddenly began to burn through her heart. An anger beyond raw frustration, a fury born of a lifetime of combat and the genes of warriors dating back two centuries erupted in her cockpit at that moment. Her face seemed to contort with anger. "My plan is ruined!"

"I do not know that for sure, Star Colonel," Klark Chrisholm said.

"I do, you insolent kit," she snapped. She turned and looked out the viewport of her *Executioner* and surveyed the rocky outcroppings that loomed before her. *We have been toying with these Fusiliers long enough. It is time they face the full fury of the Smoke Jaguar.*

26

Isthmus of Bannockburn
Wayside V (Wildcat)
Deep Periphery
10 July 3058

"**C**olonel," came the voice of Captain Lovat over the secure channel, immediately waking Cat Stirling from a slight doze as she sat waiting in the cockpit of her *Grand Titan*. "Perimeter pickets are picking up numerous OmniMechs throttling up their reactors." Like most of the Fusiliers still on Wayside, she'd gotten little real sleep in the past few days as they prepared for the assault on the isthmus.

"Do you think this is it?" she asked, the urgency of his words waking her like a splash of ice cold water. She checked her chronograph and saw that light would not dawn for several hours more. The pitch-dark night would work to everyone's disadvantage.

"I think so," Lovat came back.

"Time to play then." Stirling activated her command channel, which would send her voice to every company and lance commander waiting out there in the night. "This is Colonel Stirling. The Jags are on the move. Battalion commanders, execute Plan Alpha. Black Adders, await my order."

There was a long silence, at least a full five minutes where nothing happened. Cat Stirling surveyed the area, knowing that somewhere out there in the darkness, her faceless enemy, Star Colonel Roberta, was finally coming.

Then it happened. The ground of the central isthmus shook as if a stampede of buffalo were rushing toward them. In the distance where Craig's battalion was holding the front line, the night lit up as several Elementals rose into the air above them, their bright rain of short-range missile fire hitting the Fusilier BattleMechs below. Down on the ground lightning-like blue flashes of PPC fire filled the narrow confines of the rocky outcroppings. Laser light, pulsing red and green, a literal wall of raw energy and pure death, also came pouring at the Fusiliers.

"First and Second Battalions, engage!" Stirling ordered her forces in the isthmus as she walked her *Grand Titan* out from behind its rocky cover. She dropped her targeting cross hairs onto a *Loki*, the first Jaguar 'Mech to emerge into view in the pass, having charged through the heart of the Fusilier defense at a full run. Her long-range missiles raced from their rack, arcing slightly to catch up with their moving target, tearing into the legs and hips of her foe. The missiles were followed by fire from her paired large pulse lasers, which ripped into the *Loki*'s right arm and hit its shoulder-mounted missile rack. The battle was engaged.

Out ahead of the rest of the Fusiliers, Major Cullen Craig's *Victor* was hit so hard in the torso by a slug from a Gauss rifle that his 'Mech was almost knocked off its feet.

The birdlike *Vulture* stalking toward him was responsible. With just the Gauss rifles as weapons, that 'Mech was going to run cold as ice, while Craig would have to deal with ever-building heat.

With cold precision he leveled his own Gauss rifle at the approaching *Vulture*. Apparently guessing his intention, the Jaguar 'Mech pivoted its lower torso, keeping its weapons lock on Craig's *Victor* but moving laterally across his field of fire. Craig compensated with the skill of a great marksman and let go his shot. The Gauss slug hit the *Vulture*'s stubby right arm, ripping it clean off. Sparks flew from the shoulder attachment, followed by smoke.

The Jaguar was unrelenting. Firing with its remaining arm, the injured 'Mech caught the *Victor* just below its left kneecap. As the temperature in Craig's cockpit began to spike, he also felt his 'Mech's balance shift as he struggled to compensate for the hit. Switching to his second target-interlock circuit, he brought his short-range missiles and medium pulse lasers to bear. The instant he heard a lock tone in his neurohelmet earpiece, he punched the trigger button, pumping fire into the torso of the *Vulture*.

The Smoke Jaguar closed in as its remaining Gauss rifle loaded another round. The weapon lifted to track Craig just as another 'Mech appeared nearby in the flickering shadows of the early-morning darkness. Craig yanked on his throttle and began to pull his 'Mech back, maintaining the distance between him and the *Vulture* as he moved his own rifle into firing position.

The newly arrived 'Mech, a Fusilier by its markings, opened up with a barrage of PPC fire squarely into the back of the *Vulture*. There was a brilliant burst of blue light, and for a moment the *Vulture* was silhouetted in the darkness. Craig watched as it stumbled forward one more step before it lost its balance and fell.

The moment it hit the ground, he saw yet another Jaguar rush in to take its place, this time a *Mad Cat*. The Clan 'Mech fired a wall of long-range missiles into the 'Mech that had just saved Craig, and in the lights of the missile warhead going off, he saw the familiar outline of the *Hatamoto-chi*, the BattleMech piloted by *Sho-sa* Elden Parkensen.

Craig throttled his 'Mech forward again just as an Elemental landed on his torso, firing its stubby laser madly into the sidewall of his Victor's cockpit. If he ever made it out of here alive, he would definitely owe Parkensen a big one.

Just below and to the left of his current position, Major Kurt Blakadar watched as the fireworks of the battle erupted. He'd been busy getting his two companies of Black Adders up onto New Northwind, then back down into the isthmus on the other side of the peninsula, facing the rear south flank of the Jaguar's forces. Stealth and extensive use of thermal tarps and light ECM had kept their movement from being detected. It had taken a full day to get his troops into position, and now the payoff would come. Thus far, the Jaguars didn't seem to know they were there—and that's the way he wanted to keep it.

The trip down the rocky outcroppings had been treacherous, with no paths to ease their progress. The battle was two kilometers away, and from what he could see from the lights and bursts of explosives, it was as vicious as any scene from hell.

A part of him wanted to disobey his orders and charge immediately into the flank and rear of the Smoke Jaguars. But he knew better. Those who defied Andrea Stirling rarely lasted long. No, he would wait until the signal was sent.

"Adder Leader," came a harried voice over the commline on the secure command channel. "This is Craig. Get your butt in here and fast. We're getting pasted."

"Negative," Blakadar said, wiping the sweat from his palms onto the shorts he wore to withstand the heat of a 'Mech cockpit. "I'm waiting for Cat One to make that call."

"Damn it, Kurt, we don't even know if she's still alive. Get your ass in here." There was a hint of panic in Craig's voice. A hiss of static cut off the conversation, proof that the Jaguars were using electronic countermeasures to jam the communications channels.

Blakadar didn't even want to think about the possibility that the Colonel was dead. He was the acting Executive Officer. Her death would pass command of the regiment to him. A trapped regiment, pinned down on an unforgiving planet with only scant hope of survival. He revved his 'Mech's fusion reactor up a little higher to prepare to move out. The powerful *Albatross* vibrated as if it too were ready to race into the battle.

Again, he told himself no. If the Colonel were dead,

someone would have communicated it. He would hold until he got word one way or another. With the use of ECM in the area, it was possible Colonel Stirling had been cut off from communications. As much as he wanted to charge his companies into the gap, he resisted the urge. The only question was, how long could he continue to do so?

"Holy crudstunk!" yelled Major Jake Fuller at the sight of the wave of enemy 'Mechs coming at them. "Have at 'em, boys and girls!" he shouted into his neurohelmet microphone. Then he quickly switched his comm channel to the regimental command net. "Cat One, this is Guard One. Enemy engaged."

There was no reply, and no way of knowing if something prevented the Colonel from doing so or if she was just too busy. Either way he had his own problems. His two lances of Kilsyth Guards had encountered the Smoke Jaguar sneak-attack force in the early morning hours. The Jags had charged right past Fuller's encampment, either not detecting the Guards' presence or simply ignoring them in their fury to attack the rear of the Fusiliers' formation. Fuller had powered up and hit their rear flank just as the Jaguars realized what was happening. Now, all hell was breaking loose.

This isn't how I like fighting, alone and without support. We're eighty klicks from the isthmus and if we don't stop them here, the survivors will still manage to pull off their attack. Everyone in Blakadar's command understood the situation, and knew they had to win the battle. "Time to die, kitties," he muttered as he leaped into the fray.

Three Elementals rose up into the night sky ahead of him, firing their shoulder racks of short-range missiles into him with deadly precision. Jake turned his *Cerberus* and broke into a run, blasting the airborne Elementals with his four medium pulse lasers. Then he shifted the twin arm-mounted Gauss rifles to a different target interlock, knowing that the powerful weapons would be useless against the Elementals he was engaging. His laser burst lit up the early morning darkness, and two of them found their mark. One of the Elementals lost its leg to the fire, the other took the hit in his chest. The legless one tumbled to the ground out of control. The second recoiled, knocked back by the armor being blasted from its chest. It flew backward, away from Jake.

Another Elemental rose in front of Jake, firing an arm-mounted laser at his *Cerebus*'s chest, hoping to hit the 'Mech's fusion heart. He saw, in amazement, that it was the Elemental whose leg had been shot off only a few moments before. Rising into the air on a lone jet, fully throttled open, the Elemental was coming in for the kill as if he hadn't been hurt at all.

As the young brevet Major let go with both his Gauss rifles, his only thought was that if anything happened to this unit, Major Jaffray would have his butt in latrine duty for the rest of his natural life.

Major Kurt Blakadar throttled up again for the third time, his *Albatross* now running at full battle level. He listened to the command channel as he had for the past ten minutes, but all that came through was static. Suddenly he heard a voice, clear and crisp, shattering the static as it spoke.

"Cat One to Adder One, engage, engage, engage."

For a moment he wasn't sure if he'd actually heard the voice, or if it was some kind of waking dream. Beads of sweat dripped from his brow inside the neurohelmet, stinging his eyes. He was frozen, but only for a second. In that moment Kurt Blakadar decided that even if it was a dream, his own mind playing tricks on him, he couldn't wait any longer.

"Black Adders . . ." he signaled on his battalion's channel. "Let's roll!"

27

Isthmus of Bannockburn
Wayside V (Wildcat)
Deep Periphery
10 July 3058

Star Colonel Roberta pivoted hard as a lightweight *Wolf Trap* bearing the emblem of a twisting black snake fired its LB X autocannon and long-range missiles at her. The image of the snake burned in her mind as she saw it through her infrared filters. When the 'Mech appeared she'd just been closing on a massive *Hatamoto-chi* with the intention of engaging the magnificent BattleMech in one-on-one combat. Most of the new enemy's incoming missiles streaked past her *Executioner,* missing entirely, but the autocannon hit true, chewing away at her torso armor. She targeted her large lasers at the smaller 'Mech and fired, bathing both arms of the *Trap* in a blaze of red light and fury.

A glance at her tactical display showed her nearly two dozen Fusilier BattleMechs closing in on the isthmus to her left flank and rear, coming at her force from behind. "Gamma Strike Star, pull to the rear flank and lay down a pattern of suppression fire. Attention, Bloodied Claws, the enemy is at our rear. Rally to me and we shall crush them!"

A hit in her side again forced her to turn as a Fusilier *Jenner* raced past her, firing as it ran. Half its medium lasers missed, but the others sliced through her left-arm armor, popping it as they blew. Angry at the insult, Roberta leveled her Gauss rifle at the sprinting 'Mech and fired.

The silvery round passed straight through the *Jenner*'s right torso, bursting out the other side. Its ammunition stores exploded, and despite its cellular storage protection, the small 'Mech exploded in a blinding flash of light. Somehow the *Jenner* pilot had managed to eject at the last possible moment, riding the shock wave of the explosion up into the night. Then the pilot's parasail opened, and she started to drift back down toward the isthmus floor.

Roberta fixed her gaze on the Fusilier MechWarrior. All she saw was an enemy, a foe who had fought well, but a foe nevertheless. She ran the nearly seventy-five meters to where the warrior was coming down.

With full knowledge of her actions, she dropped her targeting sight on the Fusilier warrior and opened up with her machine gun. The first two shots hit, while the others simply shook the Fusilier's dead body, hanging limp in the harness of the chute, with each impact.

Roberta activated the commline to her command officers. "Leave no survivors," she said. "Eat them alive."

Roberta licked her lips and looked at the distant *Hatamoto-chi* with renewed gusto. The tall 'Mech loomed like a giant, calling her to battle, calling her to death.

* * *

Colonel Andrea Stirling moved in on the right flank of her infantry position just as what was left of the Smoke Jaguars reached the same point. The Jaguars who had made it this far had plowed through her Fusiliers, rushing to the rear to wreak havoc. It was quite a feat. Though only a Star in size, the group was formidable in composition—a *Dragonfly,* a *Cauldron-Born,* a *Koshi,* a *Stormcrow,* and a *Hanyu.* They were damaged from running the gauntlet of her troops, but their charge showed there was still fight boiling in their pilots' bellies. It was far from a calming thought.

Captain Jebediah Lewis's regular infantry were dug in on the hard rock floor, opening fire with inferno missiles and manpack PPCs as the Clan Omnis moved into firing position. Stirling drew a lock on one of them, a *Dragonfly,* then opened up at long range with her large lasers and long-range missiles. A familiar wave of heat rose in her cockpit, but she ignored it.

The odd stance of the light *Dragonfly* hurt it during side attacks like the one Cat Stirling had just made. Its weapons pod-arm comprised almost all of the target area. Both lasers hit the limb first, gutting the armor plating and filling Stirling's infrared display with a burst of light as the ferrofibrous plate exploded. Her missiles, aided by their fire-control computer, burrowed in on the limb in quick secession.

Parts of the arm's internal structure exploded off, and the last two missiles passed straight into the torso of the *Dragonfly.* She saw a spray of green coolant in the night as a flame seemed to lick at the Jaguar OmniMech, followed a millisecond later by an ammunition explosion of the short-range missile rounds in the mangled stump of the arm. The CASE doors, too twisted to open, did not release the explosion. Instead the full force of the blast blew the torso armor off the *Dragonfly.* The 'Mech listed under the force of the arm explosion, yet remained standing.

Instead of turning to engage her, the Jaguar pilot leveled his remaining lasers and machine guns at the infantry position and opened fire. In angry horror, Stirling saw her infantry troops riddled with fire and death where they stood. *This Roberta doesn't just want to beat us, she wants to destroy us totally.*

Moving closer in a blaze of anger, Stirling opened up with her short-range missiles. Her lock was true, and the missiles bore in on the squat torso of the oddly shaped *Dragonfly.* The burned right side of the 'Mech was hard to make out except for the hot spots that still glowed in the night. Her missiles changed all that, reaching into the very bowels of the machine and seeming to scoop out its internal organs as they exploded. The *Dragonfly* was dead, its internal superstructure blowing outward from the gaping holes.

Captain Lewis's Infiltrator troops, wearing power armor similar to a Clan Elemental's, with scaled-down equipment and technology, emerged from their hidden positions and opened up on an approaching Clan *Stormcrow.*

Then another 'Mech appeared in the distance, the charred hulk of a Fusilier *Victor,* barely visible in the flickering lights of the battle. It staggered into the area, also firing its Gauss rifle. Cat Stirling recognized the 'Mech and was shocked at how much damage Major Craig had sustained. If he was hurt that bad, just how bad off was the rest of her regiment?

And in the back of her mind, she wondered what had become of her PSL officer . . .

Star Colonel Roberta turned to see where the missiles that had gouged her were coming from just as a voice filled her cockpit, a voice filled with anger and command. "Star Colonel Roberta, I have been monitoring your progress. Your losses are much higher than estimated. To press the fight further at this time would leave the Huntress Galaxy too crippled to ever defeat our Nova Cat foes. I order you to withdraw your remaining forces immediately."

The order was a death-blow for her. She would suffer a severe shame if she withdrew, an action Roberta had never committed in her whole life as a Smoke Jaguar. She had always been victorious, no matter what the odds. Now a strange new emotion overwhelmed her, one almost alien to her—humiliation. Roberta was sure of one thing as a Smoke Jaguar officer, defeat was something she was not prepared to deal with.

Galaxy Commander Osis's voice reached out to her again, crisp and commanding. "You will respond, Star Colonel."

For Roberta, it was as if her body were moving without her control. She switched to the Galaxy communications channel and spoke, but she hardly knew that she did. "Aff, Galaxy Commander. My forces will withdraw." *Such is the will of my Clan, the Clan that I have failed* . . .

She gave the order. The words came from her mouth as

she did what a Jaguar must do—obey the orders of a superior officer. She could speak the words, but that did not mean she could do the deed. It was inconceivable for her to return to the firebase camp in defeat. There was only one way she could deal with the way the battle had swayed—a way consistent with the path of the Smoke Jaguar warrior.

Roberta saw the *Hatamoto-chi* still in the distance. Her infrared filtering system was not functioning perfectly, but she could make out the image of the Inner Sphere BattleMech walking backward as it made its way out of the battle zone. Star Colonel Roberta smiled thinly. *Yes, there is a way to still claim victory in the name of the Jaguar.*

"We engaged the enemy an hour ago," Jake Fuller reported. "We took heavy losses, but none of the Jags got away." There was a long pause. "They fought to the last man and woman."

Fuller's voice was weary and hard to hear as Stirling piloted her *Grand Titan* forward, rounding a rock formation, searching for friend and foe alike.

"Understood. Work your way back to the rendezvous coordinates."

Suddenly a voice came over Stirling's neurohelmet speakers: "I am Star Colonel Roberta of the Smoke Jaguars. Prepare to face me as warriors are meant to, one on one to the death!" The message was not intended for Stirling, but was directed at the nearby *Hatamoto-chi* of Elden Parkensen. Knee-deep in mangled OmniMechs, the *Sho-sa*'s 'Mech was just finishing off a final Elemental. As Stirling's *Grand Titan* continued on, she saw the image of a battle-weary Clan *Gladiator* also slowly making its way forward.

"Come, child, together we will find what we seek," came back the grim voice of *Sho-sa* Parkensen. Both of them were seeking death, Stirling realized. Parkensen for his past, Roberta for her failure here. Regardless of what she thought of the PSL and his constant harping, she needed him and his BattleMech. Everyone mattered from this point on, just as they had from the start. *If he seeks death, there are better ways and times for that still to come.*

She locked her own targeting cross hairs onto the slow-moving *Gladiator,* seeking out the already-damaged areas of the Omni. Setting her sights on the mauled torso, she brought her last salvo of long-range missiles and her large lasers on line.

Her sensors told her that another BattleMech lay at their extreme range, past the *Gladiator*. She triggered her primary target-interlock firing stud and let go with her long-range weapons. At the same moment, the 'Mech in the background also opened fire on the *Gladiator*.

From two sides at once, the *Gladiator* was pummeled by an overwhelming wave of fire and death in the darkness. The fusion reactor's shielding ruptured, and Stirling knew that radiation was at that moment bathing the 'Mech's cockpit. The automatic ejection system should have engaged and shot the pilot out to some other fate. But Roberta must have over-ridden the system, because no warrior sailed free of the destroyed 'Mech. She was surely dead.

"She was to be mine!" *Sho-sa* Parkensen howled over the commline as Stirling and Major Blakadar both closed on his position. "She challenged me to the time-honored tradition of one-on-one combat."

"We saved your life," Blakadar said.

"It was not yours to save," the PSL returned bitterly.

Cat Stirling stared at his *Hatamoto-chi* with disgust and anger, yet the battle had taken its toll on her as well. *"Sho-sa,"* she said wearily, "didn't anyone ever teach you how to say thank you?"

28

Nova Cat Planetary Command, New Lorton
Tarnby
Smoke Jaguar/Nova Cat Occupation Zone
13 July 3058

Star Colonel Santin West was an imposing figure in his Elemental armor as he came off the test range, but he was in a bad mood. He hadn't performed as well as he should have, something that always made him angry. Displayed on his helmet, just over the eyeslot, was the insignia of the Nova

Cats—the open-mouthed cat, the field of stars behind it, all standing out on his ebony black armor. Below it, on his chest, was the insignia of the 179th—his Cluster, his command, the Circle of Power. The bright yellow-white ring circled the blood-red numerals of 179. The unit was named for the circle that Nicholas Kerensky drew around himself during his fast in the mountains of Strana Mechty when he first had his vision of the Clans.

Santin West walked off the range and went down into the ready-room, his battle suit covered with a fine dust from the firing range. With casual ease he lowered himself into a sitting position in the rack while two members of the technician caste stepped up and began to remove the gear. He was trained in putting on and taking off the armored suit, but in most situations it was the work of the lower castes to assist Elementals with the task.

The helmet was removed first, its pressurized seal hissing slightly as the safety bolts were thrown and the two techs removed it. He didn't look them in the eye; he never did. They were but techs after all. It was not their place to speak or be acknowledged. It was their place to perform their duties and do them well, lest they incur his wrath.

Next they removed the suit's frontal chest plate, which was more than just armor. Sophisticated circuitry was interwoven into the array as well as a life support system and a balance system. Power came from the pack he wore on his back. The techs worked quickly as if they could sense his dark mood and did not want to provoke his anger.

A MechWarrior appeared in the doorway, and Santin West locked eyes with the fair-haired woman he had come to know well. Star Captain Jill Lenardon, of the Command Supernova and his second-in-command, leaned against the door frame with an almost casual attitude as she watched him unsuit.

"I bring a message for you," she said. "Silver Claw clearance."

"Silver Claw, you say?" These were the code words he had fed into the communications interface. It was a flag for his attention, an indication that the gigantic strategic database maintained by the Nova Cats contained some information on Smoke Jaguar activity. Santin West's senses seemed to come alive, as he wished they had on the test range earlier.

"Have the command center download it to the terminal in my quarters."

"Affirmative, Star Colonel," Jill Lenardon said, suddenly

taking a more formal stance as she sensed his change to a command tone of voice. He studied her as she brought herself to attention. Her frame was lithe, compact, and muscular, the epitome of a Clan MechWarrior. Her firm breasts, even under the dull gray of her jumpsuit, caught his attention. "And Star Captain, if you so desire, I would couple with you this evening."

"Aff, Star Colonel," she said, staring just as openly at his well-defined chest muscles and powerful thighs. "That would be invigorating."

Santin nodded. Invigorating, yes. And if this message brought good news, the coupling would be even better.

To anyone but Santin West, the message would not have been particularly interesting. It was merely a field report of a Smoke Jaguar DropShip, *Overlord* Class, battling for four jump recharges at a Nova Cat recharge station in the Periphery. Two recharges were taken, with two held in reserve for some future point in time. The verbal and written testimony of Star Commanders Edward and Otis told the cold hard facts of the battle. They did not conceal the truth of the loss of honor at the hands of the Jaguars.

As his eyes roved over the data, pulling up the holographic images from the battle ROMs of the survivors, he found what he was looking for. Their OmniMech paint schemes and markings were those of the Smoke Jaguars. Like many Jaguar units, they displayed the Greek letter for their Galaxy, followed by a much smaller Cluster number, Star number, and position. What struck him most was the fact that the image of the *Battle Hawk* he was looking at bore the mark of the Tau Galaxy.

"The Jaguar has finally emerged from its den," he said softly to himself as he watched the Nova Cat *Executioner* that was the Trial loser. He saw and felt his fellow warrior's shame at losing a battle. He then pulled up the transmission by the Smoke Jaguar Cluster Commander and stared at the mask of the stalking cat that had plagued his Clan for generations. In the background, the faint glimmer of the "T" symbol again.

He stared at Star Colonel Loren long and hard. This was his foe, his enemy. *He hides his face so we cannot even guess at his genetic heritage. When I have crushed him in battle, our scientists can take from him what they need to learn, what the scientist Jaguars have been forging in their iron wombs.*

Then he pulled up the location of the system where the

Cat's Eye 009 recharge station was located. A holographic map of the Deep Periphery flickered in front of him. Next he pulled up the known Smoke Jaguar bases and supply routes and overlaid them on the map as well.

He projected a sphere thirty light years in diameter around the recharge station, the approximate maximum distance that could be covered in a single hyperspace jump. He doubled that sphere again. They had taken two charges, which told him their ships had lithium-fusion batteries. And the fact that they needed two recharges indicated that the ships had traveled at least two jumps before reaching the station—not taking the time to recharge. *Smoke Jaguar mentality; charging into a battle rather than biding their time.*

The known Jaguar supply bases and transport lanes were not near the volume of space the ships had traversed. Two JumpShips, one DropShip, one Cluster commander. The story was partial but was more than he had before. Tau Galaxy had emerged from hiding and was striking at the Nova Cats. They had to have a base, a new and unknown one, somewhere in the Deep Periphery.

They have come to test us, to see if we are ready for them. He activated his personal communicator. "My Khan, this is Star Colonel Santin West. I request a meeting with you."

The voice on the small speaker came back. "You have word of our foe, quiaff?"

"Aff, my Khan. Aff . . ."

===== **29** =====

DropShip **Bull Run,** *Zenith Jump Point*
System EC-EY-4150
Deep Periphery
13 July 3058

The small briefing room in the bowels of the *Bull Run* was cramped and tight as Loren's people attempted to find standing or sitting room there. They had left the Nova Cat recharge station no worse for wear, and Loren couldn't wait until they'd left the system. Each hour there was one more that they might be exposed, their disguises penetrated. Now, they were finally alone at the jump point over a star in a binary system. They would be here for four days rather than risk a misjump. During that time they could recharge while minimizing the risks to the control circuits and the delicate jump-drive core that propelled the ship faster than light across the stars. And here, in the void of space, he would plan his next strike on the Nova Cats.

"We jump again in four days to a system the Clans call Boltin, our next target. The problem is we're working with limited intelligence about the planet, so I thought you all should know what we're potentially up against."

Lieutenant Hector chuckled. "No offense, sir, but nothing can be as bad as bungee jumping a BattleMech, in deep space, covered with Elementals who are trying to kill you." Several of the other Fusiliers laughed in appreciation.

"I don't want to burst your bubble, Greg, but we've got very little information on this planet or its defenders, save what Kerndon can tell us." Loren gestured to his bondsman, who stood at parade rest next to him.

Kerndon nodded at the signal to speak. "My information is limited to briefings I studied during the journey to the Inner Sphere. The subject planet is primarily a desert world with very limited plant life. Temperatures reach peaks that will create overheating problems for 'Mechs fighting there for long periods of time. There are no polar caps and limited cloud formations or weather.

"Its rotation is long, as I recall—nearly sixty-five hours. The Nova Cats have one base on the world, centered on a water-pumping plant and a series of warehouses."

"Sounds like the key word here would be desolate."

"Aff, Major Loren."

"What's stored in the warehouses?" Loren asked.

"I cannot speak as to what is there now. It is known that originally the facilities on the world stored repair parts, munitions, and foodstuffs."

Lieutenant Trisha McBride spoke next from the opposite side of the table. "I take it your former Clan has fought there before."

"Aff," Kerndon said. "The planet was originally one of our holdings. When ilKhan Ulric Kerensky allowed the Nova Cats to share our invasion corridor, we were forced to fight a series of Trials of Possession for supply bases and trade routes leading into the Inner Sphere. Boltin was lost to the Nova Cats during one of those Trials. We attempted to take it back once but failed."

"Where was the Trial of Possession fought?"

"I believe the battle was fought inside the old warehouse complex near the former Jaguar base."

"Old complex?" McBride probed.

"Aff, Lieutenant Trisha," he answered. "The current base is new, built by the Nova Cats. Our original compound was located eight kilometers from the present one. A series of stray shots caused an explosion during the Trial of Possession, and a fire gutted the facility. Due to chemical contaminants and other exposure risks, the new base was built nearby."

The information was useful to Loren. He had fought in desert environments before and knew that heat would play a crucial role. One advantage his mock-Jaguars might enjoy was that they were used to the sweltering cockpits of Inner Sphere 'Mechs, which lacked the extra heat-sink capability of Clan 'Mechs. Of course it wasn't enough to turn the tide of battle. Any garrison force on such a planet would most assuredly be accustomed to such conditions, and if the Clans were anything, they were adaptive.

"That warehouse complex is the only defensible point anywhere in sight. Everything around it is wide open. I'd like to keep the battle there, but how?"

Kerndon stared at Loren for a moment, considering the possibilities. "It may be possible, given the nature of our enemy, to achieve that goal, Major Loren. Inform them that you wish to challenge them to a Trial of Refusal rather than a Trial of Possession. Inform them that your Tau Galaxy comes to refute the loss of the original base."

Loren shook his head. "I don't want to take the whole planet from them, Kerndon. I just want to get their attention. Wouldn't a Trial of Possession for their warehouses full of supplies suffice for that?"

"Affirmative, Major, under normal circumstances. But you must understand the true nature of such Trials. As I explained to you before, they are not just statements of intention, but an expression of power."

"What are you talking about? How will just changing the name of the Trial get us the old complex as a battle site?" asked Lieutenant Leigh Ann Miller.

"The Nova Cats are a superstitious crew. If you challenge

them to a Trial of Refusal for that site, they will certainly select it as the venue for the Trial, as is their right as the de-
fender. In their minds, the site would be auspicious because
they defeated the Smoke Jaguars there the last time. They
will select it because they won there before—such is their
superstitious nature."

"What kind of garrison force are we likely to encounter on
Boltin?"

"At least a Trinary's worth," Kerndon said, "and an element of a Provisional Garrison Cluster or a solahma unit
would also be likely for such a remote and minor duty."

"Just like what we was supposed to be a findin' on Wayside V, it sounds like ta me," the slightly overweight
Sergeant Ralston McAnis muttered.

Loren ignored the remark. "If that's right, then we'll be
facing second-line Clan tech rather than OmniMechs."

"Aff, but your bidding will have to reflect that as well," Kerndon said. "It would be dishonorable to attack in equal numbers."

"I've gone over the intelligence data on these solahma
units," put in the brawny Sumpter Burke from the far end of
the table. "These are some of the Clan's most veteran warriors. You'll be factoring that in too, won't you, sir?"

"You confuse the concept of age in the Clans and experience in the Inner Sphere," Kerndon said. "Among the Clans,
older warriors are considered used up. They have experience, but most have missed the opportunity to die with glory.
They are reassigned to solahma units, so that younger, more
genetically improved warriors get the chance to test their
mettle and develop their skills more quickly."

"That doesn't explain the likes of Natasha Kerensky—the
Black Widow," Burke rebutted.

Kerndon was unmoved. "She was an anomaly. Do not mistake a freak of nature in the former Wolf Clan for the rest of
the Clans."

"I plan to bid like a Smoke Jaguar," Loren said, addressing
Sumpter. "If I don't do it right, it will tip them off."

"Speaking of which," said McBride, "all of this is supposed to stir them up and have them trekking back to Wayside V. How are you planning to do that, sir?"

Loren did have a plan, a simple one, but equally tried and
true. "Don't worry, Trisha. I'm planning to leave behind a
few little clues that will make it easier for the Nova Cats to
find us later."

His smile faded as he looked at each face in the small group. "We have to make sure we're ready for this, people. When we're done on Boltin, Tarnby is next. That means this one has to go off without a hitch. I want everyone to double up on their simulation time and double-check for launch prep."

"Well bargained and done, Star Colonel Patricia," said Galaxy Commander Devon Osis. "We've lost enough time dealing with these mercenaries. I expect that you will prevail better than the one you succeed, quiaff?" Patricia had just beaten Thibideau Osis in the bidding to resume the attack on the mercenaries, and the two of them stood before him in the command bunker of Wildcat Station.

"Aff, Galaxy Commander Osis. I will not disappoint you," she returned.

"See that you do not," Osis said, letting menace edge his words. "Much has already been lost."

"I assure you that I will not fail either the Jaguar or the Huntress Galaxy as my predecessor did. She lacked an understanding of our foe. I have seen them for what they are, dishonorable freebirths. We will crush them like bandits under our heel."

Osis's temper flared at her words. "You will not speak of the honored dead in such a fashion, Star Commander. It is true that Roberta failed in her mission and there is great loss of honor in that failure, but she fought to the end." *As I expect you will if called upon . . .*

30

Fusilier Base Camp, South of New Scotland
Wayside V (Wildcat)
Deep Periphery
13 July 3058

Stirling's Fusiliers were still a functional unit after the battle in the Isthmus of Bannockburn, but they'd taken severe damage. Looking out her portable command dome at what was left of her regiment, Colonel Andrea Stirling thought they were beginning to look more like a refugee camp than one of the Inner Sphere's most elite mercenary units—testimony to the ferocity of their enemy.

The outcome of the fighting in the isthmus was staggering, if all she looked at were the numbers. The Kilsyth Guards, minus Jaffray's special detachment, was running at forty-five percent of its operational size. Captain Lewis's combined arms had taken severe losses and had been driven back to the protective cover fire of the *Claymore* even before the Clans broke off their assault. The Black Adders Battalion had fared somewhat better, with sixty-five percent of its force still able to fight. Their blow to the rear of the Jaguar force had turned the tide of battle, but the fighting had taken its toll. Major Craig's Third Battalion had also taken a beating, though more than half its ranks remained.

The PSL's company of Combine troops been decimated, however, and Parkensen had refused all discussion with Colonel Stirling or her staff since his rescue. That didn't surprise her, though. She'd cheated him of the chance to regain some of his honor by killing Roberta before the two were able to face off in a one-on-one duel. Cat Stirling shrugged. He'd have to snap out of it. The man had skills she still needed.

Despite their losses, Stirling considered the battle a success. A bloody victory, but a battle won nevertheless. The 101st Cluster was hurt bad enough that they hadn't pursued her, but she knew that wouldn't last long. *The question is, how much time have I bought for the price?*

Cat Stirling had studied the Clans almost as much as her Executive Officer. These were an unrelenting people gene-engineered for warfare. She knew that a defeat like they'd suffered in the isthmus would not go unavenged. If the 101st Cluster had failed, their comrades would bid for the right to finish Stirling off, if they hadn't already.

The *Claymore* had taken a number of hits from the Jaguars during the battle, enough to guarantee it would never fly again—not without the kind of extensive dry-docking it would never get here on Wayside V. Sitting on the west end of the isthmus, it still commanded a vital passage, but was an island that simply couldn't be moved. She wanted to reinforce it, protect the DropShip as it had done for her so many times before. But Cat Stirling had to admit that the ship was a loss. Hearing the news, Captain McCray reminded her that the ship was really Captain Spillman's vessel.

He had followed her orders, quickly stripping the ship of all vital supplies and salvageable parts and gear. Most important were the water and food stores, which they transferred to several regimental movers and which were now here at the base camp. The final steps for the *Claymore* were harder, requiring the explosive experts in Captain Lewis's combined arms forces to work their demolitions magic. If all went as Colonel Stirling hoped, the *Claymore* would serve the Fusiliers one last time in her long history—by taking a few more Smoke Jaguars with her to the grave.

Meanwhile the withdrawal from the isthmus would go as planned, taking the regiment some twenty-five kilometers back to the west, away from the site of the battle. There, the terrain was less rocky, which would permit her 'Mechs and vehicles to build some true speed and maintain their distance from the Jaguars. She'd have liked to take her troops even further, but knew they were weary from battle.

She had no doubt the Jaguars would rebid to destroy them. When they came, she would be ready for them, the only way she knew how. In all her years, Cat Stirling had never been one to sit back and wait for the fight to come to her, especially when the odds were against her. She was always much better at taking the battle to her enemies instead. It was very possible the Jaguars thought the Fusiliers were licking their wounds while they prepared to move their forces into position for the coup de grâce.

Cat Stirling had other plans.

Of the entire command staff, Major Craig was the worst for wear as they huddled around the portable field holotable in the center of the command dome. His face was unshaven, his eyes glazed over, and his jumpsuit looked as if it had been dragged through the difficult terrain of Wayside V. Major Kurt Blakadar somehow managed to appear tall and pristine as ever, his expression not sagging with fatigue like some of the others. Jake Fuller looked as if he hadn't slept since the first battle ten days ago, bloodshot eyes and ragged crowsfeet around his eyes telling the story of a man suddenly thrust into the hot seat of command. Captain Lovat's shoulders were slumped in weariness from trying to piece together what had become of their elusive enemy.

"How is our defensive perimeter, Exec?" Cat Stirling said, making her tone crisp and authoritative. *We've been recovering for the past two days. It's time to start acting more like a military unit, and we start that now.*

"The Adders have the watch and all is secure, sir. No sign of the Jags yet, but they've got to be out there," Blakadar replied.

"Damn right," she snapped. "And you can all count on one thing, the Smoke Jaguars are getting ready to hit us again. This time, though, they'll come with fresh troops and they'll come to finish us off."

"Satellite coverage shows no signs of pursuit yet, but what's left of the Bloodied Claws Cluster seems to be heading back toward their main camp," Lovat said, standing straighter under the deliberate tension Colonel Stirling was creating.

"When they do come, you can count on them wanting revenge for what we did to the 101st. Star Colonel Roberta was supposed to kick our butts, and the fact that we're alive and she's not means trouble for us," Stirling said.

Everyone went silent for a moment as *Sho-sa* Parkensen entered the portable command dome. He wore a headband of white and red, and a pall hung over his features. Parkensen said nothing, but instead took a place behind the regimental command staff, standing at parade rest, staring hard at Cat Stirling—a gaze she refused to return or acknowledge.

"That's why we're moving out," Stirling said, continuing as if there'd been no interruption. "If we sit still, they'll catch us. As it is, it will take days for them to get here. I want camp broken in ten hours, though we'll get some rest under our belts first. We'll continue west, but north of the LZs." She activated the holographic projector and showed the path she wanted the regiment to take.

"What about their aerospace fighters, sir?" Lovat asked. "If the Cluster Commanders rebid to take us on, they may bring in some of the fighters they didn't use when the 101st came after us."

"Good question, Captain," she replied. "I've got a simple plan for dealing with that threat. We're going to launch a strike against their aerodrome and take out the fighters and the landing field." Her words hit the room like a bomb.

"Sir, are you sure this is the kind of mission we should be undertaking?" Major Craig asked. "You're moving the main body of our force in the opposite direction of that aerodrome. Whoever goes on that mission will have a hell of a long hike back, if they live through it."

Stirling nodded. "What's your point, Major?"

"Sir, it just sounds like a suicide run." He sounded as if he regretted the words the moment he said them.

"You heard the intelligence officer's report. The 101st is pulling back. That base is a clear and present threat to the Fusiliers. If we don't take it out now, their fighters will blow us back into the Stone Age.

"I don't send people to their death intentionally," Stirling continued. "I suggest that the expedition consist of two lances of 'Mechs. We hit them hard and fast, cripple the air base and its equipment, and the odds get a little more even when their ground forces hit. If they move fast, they should be able to get back through the isthmus before the Jaguars send a pursuit force after the rest of us."

Cat Stirling knew that speed would be the key. If the detachment didn't return fast enough from the raid, the pass would be held by the pursuing Jaguars by the time they got there. Such a small force would never have the firepower to make it through that obstacle.

"Colin, what defense does the air base have?" Major Blakadar asked.

"We have almost no idea, sir. What we do know is that our satellites have shown images of Elementals. I'm guessing that at least some of the 101st will be diverted there."

"Going in there is reckless, sir," Major Craig said bitterly.

Stirling nodded. "Reckless times call for reckless actions, Major. We're short on aerospace support. Hell, we don't have any. I've got enough problems without having to deal with that kind of threat."

"The Colonel's right," Major Blakadar put in. "Taking out that base buys us a few more days, and that may be all Jaffray or Mulvaney needs."

"Jaffray?" Craig snorted. "You don't really think that hare-brained scheme of his will work, do you, Blackie? He's not coming back for us. He managed to get himself a ride off planet. We're left here to die, while he goes back and tells command he tried his best."

"As you were, Major Craig!" snapped Cat Stirling. "You can keep your personal opinions of Major Jaffray to yourself. We've got enough problems right now without having to deal with morale issues spread by an officer with a chip on his shoulder."

Craig bowed his head, refusing to verbally acknowledge the order. Stirling pressed on. "I need someone who can get two lances of our 'Mechs in there and back again and can make sure that the Jag base is rubble when all's said and done. Volunteers?"

An eerie silence wrapped itself around the Fusilier command staff. Jake Fuller broke it first. "I still have about two lances operational and ready for a fight, sir. The Kilsyth Guards volunteer for this mission."

"With Colonel Stirling's permission," *Sho-sa* Parkensen spoke up, catching everyone off guard. "I would like to take part in the mission too."

"*Sho-sa,* this is a two-way trip," she said "I want everyone going to come back—and that would include you."

Parkensen bowed his head once to acknowledge his understanding. "I wish to be there, to face the Jaguars again. You can use my firepower, and my experience."

He's still looking for an honorable death, but he's got a point. Jake Fuller is very good, but this is a push on his expertise. If Fuller can keep Parkensen's emotions in check, the PSL might just be an asset. The fact that he's volunteering for this mission in the first place is a start—a change for him.

Andrea Stirling gave the PSL her very best cat's smile. "Very well, *Sho-sa,* you're on."

31

DropShip **Bull Run,** *Approach Vector*
Boltin (System EC-EY-4189)
Deep Periphry
17 July 3058

Loren Jaffray lay in his bunk and stared up at the plain gray of the stateroom ceiling, his mind wandering among myriad thoughts and fears. As the *Bull Run* began to burn toward

Boltin, he knew that the Nova Cats would be hailing them at any time. It was late night by the ship's reckoning, but sleep continued to evade him.

All his years in the military, his training, his discipline, his experience, all the battles on different planets throughout the Inner Sphere had prepared him for this moment. But prepared or not, he couldn't escape the fact that this was an enemy unlike any other he'd encountered. These were the descendants of the legendary Aleksandr Kerensky and his Star League army, the greatest military commander and force in the whole history of warfare. Their heirs were the finest genetic warrior stock ever conceived—the Star League Defense Force.

Deciding that sleep would never come tonight, Loren got up from his bunk, threw on some clothes, and decided to take a walk. The ship's lighting was dimmed to simulate night, but the sequence of darkness would gradually get shorter and shorter. By the time they landed, his mock-Jaguars would be operating on the same relative daytime hours as the world of Boltin.

Ten minutes later his feet brought him without thinking to the 'Mech bay, where his *Masakari* was carefully secured. In the dimmed lighting, the mighty Clan war machine loomed more menacing than ever.

Standing at the base of the 'Mech, his face turned upward in longing, was Kerndon. It was as if the former Clansman were looking up at an old friend, cherishing faded but lasting memories. *It was his 'Mech before it was mine, and he's attached to it still.*

Loren ran a hand through his hair and let out a small sigh. "I couldn't sleep and decided to try and walk the edge off my nerves. Now I'm more wired than ever."

Kerndon turned sharply at the sound of Loren's voice, but he did not appear startled. "Perhaps you are thinking of the batchall, quiaff? We are close to optimum comm range."

"Yes, er . . . aff," Loren said, attempting to adapt to the Clan speaking style, mostly out of courtesy. "I'm sure that's it. That, and I've been thinking of the Colonel and the rest of the Fusiliers."

Kerndon shrugged. "Colonel Andrea seems to be an able warrior for her age. I am sure she will fight with honor." His words might have offended Loren if he hadn't known this

198 Blaine Lee Pardoe

was simply the way Kerndon had been trained to think. "My thoughts are of the enemy we are to face."

"Nova Cats keeping you awake, Kerndon?"

He nodded. "Aff, Major Loren, I believe they are."

"Tell me what you think of the bidding."

Kerndon craned his neck to stretch his muscles, as if it would help him relax. "Solahma and provisional units that get posted to such duty are dangerous. As a Clansman, I was trained to fight to the death in combat in hopes of winning enough glory that my genetic material would be passed on to future generations. It was a hope for the future. To die, in a glorious battle, with great honor, was the best fate I could ask for.

"Provisional units or freebirths posted to garrisons this far from the Inner Sphere will see themselves as one step closer to being solahma because there is so little opportunity for combat. Their best hope is to die in battle before they are relegated to solahma. That means they will press for a low bid so they might win greater honor by dying on the field."

"Any suggestions as to how I should deal with that in the bidding?"

"Take care not to be lulled into matching their bid too closely. Like the Fusiliers, they are fighting for a cause. For them it is the survival of their genetic heritage—a chance for the future. In that light, you are both fighting for your survival."

"I expect nothing else."

The mask hid the stern mix of Oriental and Highlander blood that formed Loren's face, and only his piercing green eyes showed through. "Hail and tremble, Nova Cat garrison force of Boltin. I am Star Colonel Loren of the Smoke Jaguars. Hear this batchall and quake in your dens at your fate."

Loren paused to give vehemence to his challenge. "I come in the name of the one true Clan, the Jaguars. I come in defiance of your presence on this soil, ground tainted with our blood. I challenge you to a Trial of Refusal for this planet, which is rightfully claimed by my Clan. I come prepared to fight you to the death and restore what is rightfully that of Clan Smoke Jaguar.

"With what do you defend yourself, Nova Cat warriors?" Loren laced his words with arrogance, even contempt, warming to the role. Surprisingly, his batchall was answered quickly. A flicker of holographic light showed a man standing before him, obviously a seasoned MechWarrior. His face was either horribly burned and scarred, or the holographic projector was failing. The man wore the charcoal-gray dress uniform of the Nova Cats, and his menacing cowl and cape made him appear even more threatening.

"I am Star Captain Mandrake of the Nova Cats. The Smoke Jaguars already failed to best us in Trials of Possession a year ago. A Trial of Refusal is voided by such actions, and I refuse to acknowledge such a claim."

Loren saw Kerndon, who stood in the darkness out of view of the holoprojector's lens, shake his head and wave his hands in a signal of refusal.

"Mandrake of the Nova Cats," Loren said, "I can understand that a solahma unit such as yours lacks the will or pride to take on truebirth warriors such as my Cluster. I assure you that once our mission is complete, your Khans will know of your weakness and your fear."

The mangled face of Mandrake showed no emotion, perhaps having lost that capacity long ago. Instead the holo image remained standing there, staring at Loren. Its eyes seeming to hang from their sockets with just the tiniest bit of scarred flesh supporting them, did not blink or yield. "Brave talk, oh Great Smoke Coward who hides behind a mask as if I were some freebirth scum to be intimidated."

"With a face such as yours, Star Captain, a mask would be an improvement," Loren jabbed.

Mandrake's holographic image actually managed a smile, though it was frightening to look at through the burned pink and red flesh and his half-missing lips. "You talk like some stinking bandit-caste filth," he retorted. "I won these burns of honor fighting alongside the Smoke Jaguars on Luthien when your Clan failed to fulfill the vision of the Kerenskys and brought disgrace on both our Clans."

Loren saw from the look on Kerndon's face that pursuit of the insult would be a mistake he could ill afford. "I was not at either Luthien or Tukayyid, but I and my warriors represent the best of that blood brought now to bear. Had I been there, I assure you our Clans would now stand proudly on the Black Pearl of Luthien as victors.

"But I am not here to talk of old men and their scars. I have come to redeem the honor of my Clan. Will you acknowledge this Trial of Refusal, Star Captain Mandrake, or will I be forced to challenge you to a Trial of Possession for what you hold?"

Mandrake paused, obviously thinking over his options. "I am not obligated by the terms of this rede to fight you for more than what your Clan originally lost. When we took this world from your filthy clutches, the fight was merely for the warehouses west of our complex. Since you call for this Trial of Refusal, that is what you shall fight for and nothing more."

"That is all I desire," Loren said back. "I come not to take this world from you but to reclaim honor that has been stolen by your warriors."

"I shall face you personally," Mandrake said. "I and a Star of my best warriors. To make sure that fortune favors us, I exercise my right to choose the place of our battle."

Loren waited a moment before the grotesque figure gave him what he wanted. "We shall meet where your Clan was crushed once before. You will take the field first and the site is yours to hold so that we can take it from you again."

Loren shot a glance through the eyeslits of the mask at Kerndon, who nodded. "Well bargained and done, Star Captain. We land in two days' time. Be prepared then to meet your fate."

32

Abandoned Jaguar Base
Boltin (System EC-EY-4189)
Deep Periphery
17 July 3058

The ripples of heat coming off the yellow sands of Boltin made normal vision waver, but the sensors on Loren's *Masakari* were working fine. Though they didn't tell him everything he needed to know, they revealed the presence of structures burned and gutted from the inside out. The largest one was but a shell with only roof and walls still standing, its interior five stories heaped into a massive debris field. The old Jaguar base was literally in the middle of nowhere, surrounded nearly 350 meters in all directions by flat desert. A wall and power fence had once surrounded the complex. Now wind and sand had created dunes over portions of the broken wall.

The buildings were in the center. A totally ruined circular structure in the middle of the base had most likely been the command bunker. Now it too was filled with windblown sand, gradually swallowed by Boltin's dry winds. The warehouse buildings, including the large one that still stood, surrounded the bunker remains. Most showed signs of having been in a horrific battle, gutted from the inside out and then stripped by the Nova Cats after the fight.

Loren studied the flat terrain, the bleak horizon, and the lone structure rising up from the sands. It was the only defensible position around for kilometers. Every approach was flat, open terrain with no place to hide. He would see his foes coming for kilometers, and it would literally be a gun battle to the end. The *Bull Run* was sitting out there, somewhere to the east at least fifteen kilometers from the base. It had dropped them nearby and then they had marched in. The DropShip was his key asset, and Loren had not wanted it anywhere near the fighting.

As much as he'd wanted this site for the battle, it made no sense that the Nova Cats had wanted it too. They hadn't even really seemed to think it over. And then there was the almost evil grin on the face of the Nova Cat commander, taunting him every time he remembered the batchall. The Nova Cats obviously knew something he didn't.

As he drew closer to the ruined site, his sensors picked up some background radiation, but nothing to worry about. A total of eight buildings made up the abandoned base, a scene of rubble and crumbling walls scarred by laser fire and burned and pitted by missile or cannon rounds. The bunkerlike structure of the former command post had taken the brunt of the damage. If not for the reinforced wall supports still poking up, Loren would never have guessed a building had once stood there. *The Jaguars must have fought to the last man and woman defending this place.*

He opened a secure commline to his "Star" of mock-Jaguars. "Star, establish a perimeter around that central structure and sweep the area for any sign of the Cats." There were a series of "affs" over the command channel, a precaution Loren had ordered in case the Nova Cats had somehow managed to tap into their communications. They couldn't risk exposing themselves, not at this point—not with so much at stake.

He had countered the Nova Cat bid of a Star's worth of defense by bidding one of his own Stars, made up of light to assault 'Mechs. The odds would be fairly even, he assumed, especially if the Cats deployed at least some of their second-line 'Mechs. Kerndon had advised Loren to drop down to four Points—four 'Mechs—in his bid, but Loren had decided against it. Winning here would be important if they were going to get the Cats stirred up enough to follow them back to Wayside V.

Maneuvering his *Masakari* through the massive doorway that led into the building, Loren saw that a path had been bulldozed through the debris field. It was a tight operating environment, but he was able to get the *Masakari* in far enough to see that the path led to a large cleared area in the middle of the building. There, on the floor and running under it, was an impressive piping system all sealed and capped off. The Nova Cats had apparently come here at some point and sealed off the huge, five-meter-diameter pipe.

Studying his surroundings, Loren thought he could probably deploy his forces inside the abandoned building, but only at the cost of maneuverability. The five-story piles of debris would inhibit movement and serve to block line of sight/fire. It would make all combat close range—painfully close.

Almost fifty meters from the piping was an internal storage silo made of ferro-plastic. It was breached in several areas, and the top of the structure had been ripped off. A chalky white powder seeped from the gaps, much of it spilled onto the floor. Loren didn't know what it was, but if these were chemicals, it seemed odd that it had never been cleaned up.

He opened a channel to the *Bull Run*. "Captain Spillman, give me Kerndon," he said.

"Aff, Star Colonel Loren," came the bondsman's voice.

"I'm in the only standing building here and I don't think it was just a warehouse. There's some sort of piping here too."

"That is likely the main well dug when we first set up on the planet. The Smoke Jaguars operated a water-processing plant here as well. The facility was most likely used for both storage and for pumping to conserve space."

"The Nova Cats must have sealed it off after the battle," Loren said, but the existence of the pipe nagged at him as if he were missing something.

Staring at the silo, he decided the only way to be sure was to get out and check the pipe assembly up close and personal.

Leaving his 'Mech idling at fifteen percent power, he popped open the cockpit hatch. He was sweaty from the close quarters of his 'Mech, but the thin dry air of Boltin seemed to eat up every drop of perspiration, leaving him almost chilled despite the heat. He descended the rungs down the side of his 'Mech to the debris-strewn floor.

He carefully climbed over the rubble to what was left of the silo, still wearing his captured Jaguar neurohelmet and coolant vest. He carefully touched a finger to the substance and smelled it. The scent was faint, but he recognized the odor. Flour. He put a dab on the tip of his tongue, careful to spit it out once he'd tasted it. It wasn't a chemical at all, just spoiled flour.

It took a full five minutes to make his way to the massive pipe, which he found cold to the touch. On one side was a small digital gauge that showed the pressure dropping steadily. Descending slowly, the small green numbers on the readout told Loren something was afoot. The Nova Cats were changing the water pressure in the pipe and there had to be a reason. *It isn't just a capped well, it's something more.*

Loren made his way back up to the *Masakari* cockpit, breathing heavily as his lungs tried to take in enough of the thin air of Boltin's atmosphere. There was something about all this that still bothered him, but he couldn't put his finger on it.

Next he turned his attention to the several tons of flour. His Death Commando training had taught him to take advantage of anything at hand, to twist and turn it to his advantage. All around his *Masakari* he saw the powdery flour. He activated the battle computer through the small keypad and scrolled through the personnel records of his volunteer mock-Jaguars. It took only a few seconds to find the key word he was searching for—Demolitions.

Glenda Jura. Looking around the vast building, he knew that the job would be a big one, but that she could handle it.

It would take time, but he thought the building could provide him with a powerful asset should the Nova Cats press him hard enough or if he could lure them into it.

He opened a channel to her *Koshi*. "Glenda, this is Jaffray."

"Sir," her voice came back, obviously a little surprised to hear directly from her CO.

"I need you to fall back to my position. Did you bring any of your explosive charges?"

"Yes, sir," she returned.

"Good." Loren smiled as he spoke. "You've set up DAIs before, haven't you?"

"Dust Air Initiators, yes, sir."

"Good. You're going to have to rig a rather large one here. And time is critical."

The rock formations of the terrain north toward the Jaguar aerodrome cast early evening shadows where what was left of the Kilsyth Guards had parked their 'Mechs. Major Jake Fuller and the two lances under his command quickly climbed down from their machines and spread thermal tarps over the cockpits and upper torsos of their 'Mechs to shield them from any Jaguar aerospace recons. The tarps helped mask the heat readings of the fusion reactors and deadened their magnetic signatures, making them much harder to detect. Thus far, they'd be successful.

In the two days since the battle at the isthmus, Jake's group had traveled almost one hundred forty kilometers from the isthmus, making their way east and north toward the air base. It was now only a scant thirty kilometers to the north. Soon, their mission would be over and they could begin the non-stealthy sprint back to where the rest of the Fusiliers were—putting as much distance as possible between them and the rest of the Jaguars.

Fuller kept half his unit on alert, in their cockpits, ready for action and running with passive sensors so they would be warned if they became the targets of Smoke Jaguar scrutiny. The rest made camp, setting up collapsible command domes among the jagged rocks. This was the first watch, and Jake Fuller, sore from riding in the cramped cockpit of his 'Mech for hours on end, stood and stretched as he surveyed his patched *Cerberus*.

Nearby Elden Parkensen was also climbing down from his

Hatamoto-chi. Till now, Jake had found it hard to guess the age of the Combine officer. But suddenly he noticed that the PSL's tanned skin seemed to hang like a leather garment in some areas, indicating that the *Sho-sa* was much older than he let on.

Why in the name of hell did the Colonel saddle me with him? He's been bucking her and us ever since the start of this mission. Jake had hoped that the PSL's icy exterior might thaw once away from Cat Stirling. Instead, Parkensen had remained as stubborn and aloof as ever.

But Jake knew they had to start talking sooner or later, and now was as good a time as any. He strode up to the *Sho-sa* as he too stood stretching out the kinks in the pale green light of early evening.

"Hello, *Sho-sa* Parkensen," Jake said in as friendly a tone as he could muster.

Parkensen merely nodded in acknowledgment.

Jake tried not to show how much that irked him. "We're two days from the aerodrome. You've had a lot of experience with the Clans. Don't you think we should talk about how we're going to carry out the attack?"

Parkensen surveyed the area, then turned back to Fuller. "Our progress has been slow, Major. I am confident that the Jaguar attack force is already to the south in pursuit of the rest of the Fusiliers."

"That's pretty much what we get from the satellite scans, too." The compressed and scrambled intelligence data from Captain Lovat confirmed what the *Sho-sa* suspected.

"If we complete this mission, there will be no way for us to return to the Fusiliers. You must know that by now."

Yes, Jake knew that. The Smoke Jaguar Cluster pursuing Colonel Stirling and the rest of the regiment would stand between his current position and safety. "That's true, but we've got our orders and they are to take out the enemy aerodrome. Once we've done that we can figure out how we're going to get back."

"I don't think you fully appreciate how much—" Suddenly Parkensen stopped and lifted his face toward the green sky of Wayside V. There was a distant sound, like thunder, except that it did not die away but seemed to get louder.

Jake's wrist communicator went off with a squeal, and he activated it quickly. "Warning, incoming fighters, warning!"

came the voice of Paul Kriter, one of the lance members still on duty.

Jake activated the communicator for general broadcast. "Scramble. Mount up and deploy immediately." Even as he spoke he was moving toward his *Cerberus,* ready to leap for the ladder as soon as he got close enough. But first came a brilliant flash of light that seemed to surround the whole area. He heard nothing, but felt a rush of air that lifted him into the air. The explosion was warm and wet as the sound finally reached his ears, a roar like the entire planet erupting around him.

Jake was thrown into the air, then hit the ground nearly ten meters from where he'd been standing seconds before. The ground scraped at his flesh, ripping at his bare thighs and arms and shredding his coolant vest. He felt dirt and rocks pelting him as they rained down, and a wet, warm, sticky feeling everywhere. Nearby was the fallen form of *Sho-sa* Parkensen, covered in blood.

Jake tried to pull in a gasp of air, but his lungs refused to suck it into his body. The wind had been knocked out of him by the explosion, and he panicked briefly as he struggled to breathe. His lungs finally gave him what he needed, the smell of smoke stinging his nose as he drew in air.

Jake tried to move but couldn't; it was as if his body refused to cooperate with his intentions. His arm was covered with sticky gore, and gobs of dirt stuck to the blood. He ignored the painful ringing in his ears and concentrated on trying to move, if only to prove to himself that he was still alive. The wave of pain was like a huge pressure, like someone piling stones on top of him to crush him slowly to death.

At that moment Jake Fuller understood that he was going to die. His mind filled with an unnameable panic as a ringing sound seemed to wrap itself around him. Then he thought of his mother and wondered how she would take the news of his death. His next thought was an image of Colonel Stirling and Major Jaffray standing over his grave. *Jaffray. If only he had stayed, this never would have happened.* It was his last thought as consciousness fled his crumpled, bloody body.

33

Abandoned Jaguar Base
Boltin (System EC-EY-4189)
Deep Periphery
17 July 3058

"**B**attleMechs on the outer marker," came the warning from Sara Macallen on the open channel. Loren's sensors told him that only three 'Mechs were out there in the yellow desert of Boltin, awaiting their chance to engage him. His own deployment counted on that. He had poised his forces near the center of the complex facing outward. Macallen faced the east, Jura to the west, he and Burke faced north with a view to the east, and McBride faced south.

"Confirm three Nova Cat 'Mechs," Macallen continued. "Configs as follows. Lead 'Mech is a *Warhammer IIC*. Second is a *Rifleman IIC*. Third is a—well, I'll be damned, a *Behemoth*!" Loren checked his sensors and his deployment. Given the layout of the ruined buildings, only McBride was not able to turn and face the Cats. *Good enough for now . . .*

At one hundred tons the *Behemoth* was an awesome killing machine capable of inflicting a lot of damage. Kerndon's disembodied voice came in from his post aboard the *Bull Run*. "The *Behemoth* is a Smoke Jaguar 'Mech. It must have been taken during a Trial of Possession or won as a prize from someone in the battle for this world."

"I thought they were going to come at us with a Star's worth?" That was Lieutenant McBride swinging her *Vulture*

around in the opposite direction of the sensor readings to
cover their rear. All that stood between her and the flat open
space of the desert was the one remaining structure, the
warehouse. Inside it, Loren knew that Glenda Jura was finishing her work.

"The day is still young," Loren replied. "Keep your eyes
on the long-range scanners. The rest of the 'Mechs they bid
could be out there just beyond our reach."

"Nothing so far," Macallen said. "Those Cats are just sitting there."

Loren stayed his hand and held off. He felt the same nag-
ging uneasiness as when seeing the capped-off water main in
the warehouse/pumping facility. He just didn't know why.

"Everyone hold your fire and your ground," he ordered.
"Glenda, what's your status?"

There was a pause followed by the breathy voice of Lieutenant Jura on the commline. "Charges are set in place.
Everything is tied to command channel ten. If you transmit
any digital message of five or higher, you'll trigger the initial blast. I'm guessing the explosion will take place four
seconds later."

"Excellent," he replied. "I don't know what the Nova Cats
are up to, but everyone needs to tie in this conversation," he
said, scrambling his message. "Glenda has rigged us a Dust
Air Implosion trap inside that warehouse with some dried
flour. If the Nova Cats hit us, we fall back and let them get
inside that building for cover, then set off the DAI."

He checked his sensors again and saw that the three Nova
Cats still stood abreast, just beyond weapons range. Then he
looked through his viewpoint across the shimmering sands
of Boltin and saw the black outlines of the same Clan
'Mechs wavering in the ripples of heat coming off the sand.
They stood like statues, or gods long forgotten.

"Why are they just sitting out there?" Macallen asked.

Loren understood her impatience. "Either they want us to
make the first move, or they're getting their forces into position." His check of sensors told him that it was still only
three Nova Cat BattleMechs standing there. Something was
wrong. With the flat open terrain, he should be able to spot
the enemy, even if they were skirting the edges of his sensor
limits.

Suddenly he saw the Nova Cats start to move. "Prepare to
fall back," he said immediately. "Sumpter, Jura, and Macallen,

get out of range or line of sight of their weapons. McBride, provide cover fire. Remember, people, we need to get them in near the warehouse if Glenda's little surprise is going to work."

A flicker caught his eye as a Gauss rifle slug from the slow-moving *Behemoth* dug into the ruined wall next to him, exploding that section of it. A check on his sensors showed that the lumbering giant was in his range, so Loren activated his extended-range PPCs, preheating and charging the four weapons with enough power to wipe out a platoon of conventional tanks. His targeting cross hairs swung across his HUD like a hawk swooping in on unsuspecting prey.

Loren fired, sending a pair of bolts of charged particle energy down-range like a thunderclap, plowing squarely into the *Behemoth*'s squat torso and throwing move than a ton of armor flying up into the dry air of Boltin. Despite the fury and raw power of the assault, the well-armored *Behemoth* was more than protected from the PPC barrage.

The *Rifleman IIC*, the Clan equivalent of the age-old design made more menacing with their advanced technology, opened fire on Macallen's *Ryoken* as she moved away from the approaching Nova Cats. The brilliant red pulses of laser fire from the Clan 'Mech dug deeply into her side armor, and she spun under the damage, armor peeling back from the myomer muscle fibers, leaving them raw and exposed, some crackling with electrical arcs. Smoke rose from the hole in the side, telling a tale of much deeper damage.

Trisha McBride leveled her large lasers at the *Warhammer IIC* and opened up on it at the same time it fired its pair of PPCs at her. The lasers found their mark, burrowing into the right leg of the *Warhammer* just below its hip actuator. One of the PPC hits tore into her *Vulture*'s right torso. The *Vulture* wavered under the attack, reeling behind a mound of rubble.

Loren fired again at the *Behemoth*, hitting it as it made its way into range of the bulk of his weapons. The shots from his *Masakari*'s pair of PPCs hit just below the *Behemoth*'s shoulder actuator like a haymaker punch, twisting the shoulder back with the impact. Loren then unleashed a wave of missiles that snaked inward, striking virtually the same location as the hit only a few seconds before. The ripping blasts of warheads exploding was so strong that the *Behemoth* pivoted even further as if to resist the results of the hit. The Nova Cat warrior just barely managed to maintain control.

Suddenly Loren felt two distinct impacts from behind, a rumble of explosions that he knew were missiles. *From behind? Impossible! Where did those shots come from?* The Nova Cat BattleMechs were in front of him, leveling another barrage of death and destruction at his mock-Jaguar force. But McBride's *Vulture* was also reeling under an attack from the rear—*from the abandoned warehouse.*

His sensors told the story. It came in the form of a flicker on his secondary monitor indicating that an Elemental was present in the warehouse. *How did I miss him? Glenda and I were both in there.* He saw another sensor image, if only for a few seconds as it poked up to fire, another Elemental, then yet another.

Then it dawned on him. The capped water main with no pressure . . . It all made sense. "Jaguar force, pull back from the warehouse! Enemy Elementals in the structure! Pull back to the south and brace for an explosion!" *They've used the pipe to move their Elementals directly into our back pocket, and now we're sandwiched.*

He switched to short-range sensors and saw that his Star was obeying, albeit dodging and exchanging shots with the approaching Nova Cat 'Mechs. Loren moved his *Masakari* behind a mound of rubble that had once been a building, giving him cover from the massive *Behemoth* that was intent on getting him in its sights. It gave him a moment to open the communications channel and ready the detonation.

The move was ingenious on the part of the Nova Cats. Rather than dig another deep well on their own after taking the planet from the Smoke Jaguars, they must have simply run a pipe from the old complex to their own several kilometers away. With the water turned off, the Elementals had used the pipe to sneak into the middle of Loren's defensive position, and were now sniping away at his force, trying to lure them into the warehouse so that they could be swarmed and destroyed. Loren mentally applauded the plan, whose only flaw was that the Nova Cat commander had not thought that Loren would set his own trap in the same place.

Three Elementals rose to an open window in the building and he saw them as their short-range missiles leaped out at him. One pair found its mark while the two others hit the debris pile and sent already-ruined ferrocrete and dirt spraying into the air. Almost unconsciously, he coded in the digital signal for the detonations on channel ten, then transmitted.

Glenda Jura had done her job well. The initial explosions inside the silo were not to cause damage but to throw the fine powder into the air, filling the entire space of the warehouse with a thick haze of the powdery flour. Any spark, laser, or missile would set it off. Sitting in the silo, the powdered substance would never burn. In the air, however, it went off instantly.

The blast was immediate and had the desired effect. The powdered substance in the air burned instantly, and in the process sucked up all of the oxygen in the structure in less than a second. The weakened walls and ceiling of the building collapsed as the DAI's devastating secondary effect took place. The building fell inward, crushing anything and everything inside of it. The rumble shook his *Masakari* as Loren held his position, wondering if, somehow, any of the Nova Cat Elementals inside had survived. If they had, they were buried under tons of debris, doomed to a slow and painful death. Dust Air Initiators were specialized explosives. Loren had used them in the Death Commandos. And Glenda, as an explosives expert, knew her craft well.

"Jaguars," he signaled to his Star, "turn and attack!"

The fight had been furious and fast, but the cost was high. The trio of Nova Cats fared well early on. Trisha McBride's *Vulture* had taken a series of deadly hits and fallen despite Glenda Jura's efforts to draw the enemy fire. Sara Macallen's 'Mech bore the brunt of fire from the *Behemoth* and was so badly mauled it had spun into the desert sands, crippled and mangled. Loren himself had fired at the gargantuan *Behemoth,* shattering its right leg at the knee and sending it crashing forward, immobile and crippled. Suddenly, the battlefield was dead quiet and his forces moved in over their wounded and possibly dead warriors.

A voice crackled over his neurohelmet's speakers. "Star Colonel Loren of the Smoke Jaguars, the battle is yours," came the voice of Star Captain Mandrake, speaking from what was left of his *Behemoth.*

Loren said nothing in response, just glared through his cockpit viewport. *Trisha and Sara are probably dead or near death, and somehow, he lives. All it would take is my thumb on the trigger and justice would be served. I have to keep asking what would a Smoke Jaguar do in this situation?*

"I stand defeated before you," Star Captain Mandrake said. "I ask that you destroy me rather than let me live with this blemish on my codex."

Loren's logical half spoke up in his mind. When he had taken Kerndon as a bondsman, it was full of risk but it had gotten them this far. Now he had a chance to take a Nova Cat warrior as a bondsman, something that would certainly be a help in luring the Cats back to Wayside V.

The logical part of his brain continued to speak to him, guiding his actions. *I am playing the role of a Smoke Jaguar. I must act like one.* Loren thumbed his primary target interlock circuit and let go a barrage of death and destruction into the cockpit of the crippled *Behemoth*. There was little hope of survival for Mandrake—there never had been.

"Sir," Sumpter Burke's voice cut in. "Sara, sir, she's dead. I tried to get her out, but her cockpit—sir, it's crushed."

"Understood. And Trisha?"

Glenda Jura's voice came on the air. "I just got her out, sir. She's banged up from the cockpit breach, but she'll make it."

Kerndon's voice cut in. "Major Loren, you must destroy Sara's body. No trace must remain." The words were like a slap in the face, bringing Loren back from deep thought into reality.

He remembered the necessity, but had not wanted to face it. "Sumpter," Loren said, concentrating on the difficult order he was going to have to issue. "Mount your 'Mech and destroy Sara's remains. Leave nothing that might reveal her genetic origins to the Nova Cats. Glenda, you do the same with Trisha's cockpit once you have her out of the area. Not so much a drop of blood can be left."

"Sir—" Sumpter Burke began.

"You have your orders, mister," Loren said firmly. "Follow them or I will." Too much was at stake for them to let emotions cloud their actions now. There would be time later to mourn their dead.

"Yes, sir," Burke said. Loren thought he heard the short warrior add "you bastard," but wasn't sure if it was reality or his mind playing a trick on him.

He followed Burke a few minutes later, stopping next to the smouldering cockpit. He opened his side hatch and looked down at the fire consuming the remains of his fallen comrade. With an almost casual toss, he threw something into the fire that he did not intend to burn. What fell into the smoking cockpit was a bracelet of sorts, one of white with a small chip mounted on it. It was part of the attire of any Clan warrior, something he or she would never part with. Leaving it would verify the remains as those of a Smoke Jaguar. He had ordered the medics to take it from the body of Star Captain Marilen after her defeat. If anyone was tracking their movements and actions, it would be a powerful clue . . .

34

Temporary Field Headquarters,
South of New Scotland
Wayside V (Wildcat)
Deep Periphery
17 July 3058

Galaxy Commander Devon Osis stepped into the command dome as Star Colonel Patricia studied the tactical display. She had set up the dome as a temporary command post until she was sure the isthmus was secure. They had traveled through the pass where Star Colonel Roberta had fought and perished in battle. The scientists and technicians had been dispatched to recover the battlefield debris, verify the dead, and gather the codices and BattleROMs of warriors who had fallen. Devon Osis had personally taken his OmniMech into the battlefield as the Cluster moved into the area.

"Report," he barked, pulling his uniform taut on his chest.

"The isthmus is secured. We located the DropShip that was used to initially secure this area. I have sent a Star of Elementals to the vessel to inspect and strip it of anything of value," Patricia said coolly.

"Why was I not informed you had found the ship?"

"It did not seem a matter that required your attention, Galaxy Commander. It is merely an abandoned DropShip, far too damaged to fly. Is there a problem?"

"Possibly. Are your forces in the ship now?" he asked, his tone urgent.

"Aff, they have just started their sweeps."

"Get them out of there now, Star Colonel!" he barked.

"I do not understand sir," she said.

"Now, Star Colonel, before it is too late," Osis ordered, taking a step toward the comm system to send the order.

"Aff, Galaxy Commander," she replied, activating her microphone. "Lambda Star, this is Mist Pouncer Command. Pull out immediately. Repeat, withdraw immediately."

"Aff, Star Colonel," came a voice over the command link. Patricia turned to face Devon Osis and her brow wrinkled. "Galaxy Commander, is there something I am unaware of?"

"Aff," Osis said firmly, though much more relaxed. "I have fought Inner Sphere warriors before. If they are anything, they are barbaric. They make use of booby traps and other devious means to achieve even minor victories. That DropShip is surely a trap."

There was a distant rumble that reverberated through the portable dome as Devon Osis finished speaking. He showed no surprise, but waited as Patricia scanned the command channels for further information. In frustration, she initiated contact with Lambda Star.

"Status report," she commanded.

"Star Captain Javin reporting," came the voice of the Elemental nearly two kilometers away. "There was an explosion in the lower decks."

"Losses," she said tersely.

"Two Points were inside the ship when it exploded, Star Colonel. Another Point was just clearing the vessel and is partially damaged."

Devon Osis watched Patricia carefully. Where Roberta had thrown things in anger and frustration, this one showed admirable control. "You lost good warriors, but it could have been worse."

"These Fusiliers," she said through gritted teeth, "they fight with little honor. Such traps are the style of bandit-caste slime, not true warriors."

"You underestimate them, Star Colonel," Devon Osis said calmly. "That was Star Colonel Roberta's mistake, and it cost her her life. Remember, these so-called bandits have managed to hold out against us for some days now. The honor of the Smoke Jaguar demands that we right this wrong—in battle, with the spilling of our enemy's blood."

"How, Galaxy Commander? These freebirths flee before us."

Devon Osis smiled thinly, then gave a low chuckle. "Battles

can be won in the bidding, in the heart, or on the field of honor, Star Colonel. If I do not seem angered, do not mistake my intentions. These Fusiliers also blemished my own honor when they defeated Star Colonel Roberta. They have insulted me by even daring such a strike at my aerodrome." His face darkened as if a tempest were passing across his thoughts. "I will soak the clay of this forsaken planet with their blood, mark my words."

"I still do not understand, Galaxy Commander," Patricia said.

Devon Osis gave her a slightly twisted smile. "That is why I am a Galaxy Commander and you are a Star Colonel," he told her.

As the harassing flight of the strafing Clan *Bashkir* fighters broke off their run and swung away, Colonel Andrea Stirling watched with sinking heart from the cockpit of her *Grand Titan.* Things were going very wrong for her and what was left of her command. The only comfort was that intel was reporting that a fast-moving storm front was moving in. The rain would hinder the movement of her own people, but it would also prevent the Smoke Jaguars from any more such strafing runs.

"Colonel, incoming message for you," came the voice in her neurohelmet's earset speakers. The regimental communications officer was hesitant, and she took note of it. *Perhaps Fuller was finally responding. Or worse, this might be news that he'd been captured.*

"Who is it?"

"Sir, it is Galaxy Commander Devon Osis. He has asked to speak with you personally."

"Personally?"

"Yes, sir."

"Patch me in. Send a view-only signal of the conversation to Majors Blakadar and Craig." Stirling angled her *Grand Titan* to the side and came to a complete stop. In the few seconds it took to establish the communications links, her heart began to pound. Whatever she said to this Clansman could be a life and death matter. She and her people were on the run for their lives, trapped on a planet far beyond human space and facing the worst nightmare ever to hit the Inner Sphere. Jaffray and Mulvaney were still her only hope, but until they got here she had to remember that her number one job was to buy time. Otherwise they might make it back to Wayside, only to find her and the rest of the Kilsyth Guards beyond any hope of rescue.

"Image locked and on-line, sir."

"Engage," she said firmly.

The secondary display flickered once and then she saw the images of a man and a shorter female in gray field uniforms, standing in what appeared to be a tent or command dome. They both looked pristine, fresh, as though posing for a recruiting poster rather than in the midst of a small war.

The man had to be Devon Osis. His face was unremarkable, but his dark eyes had some of the alienness of the animal that gave his Clan its name. The woman was muscular and held herself in a way that proclaimed she was not to be taken lightly.

The man spoke first, and Stirling was struck once again by the strange, almost archaic accents of Clan speech. "I am Galaxy Commander Devon Osis of the Smoke Jaguar Tau Galaxy." He paused for her response.

"I am Colonel Andrea Stirling of the Northwind Highlanders, Stirling's Fusiliers Regiment," she replied coolly and confidently.

"I stoop to this contact with you to inform you that your paltry attempt to attack my aerodrome was crushed." Osis pressed a button on the baton he held in his hands like a scepter; the image disappeared for a second. Then the screen filled with a scene of smoke and death. There were Battle-Mechs, most sprawled out on the ground and ripped apart as if they had been drawn and quartered. Craters filled the area being broadcast to her, a scene of total death and destruction. There was no sign of life, and Stirling told herself that Fuller and his people could never have survived that assault. Then just as quickly the screen returned to that of the Galaxy Commander and the other Smoke Jaguar officer.

"Perhaps you will also be interested to know that we discovered your booby trap of the DropShip before it could do much damage. You have failed, Colonel Andrea."

Stirling was angry, but forced her voice to remain the calm. "Star Colonel Roberta provided us with victory enough, Commander Osis," she said smoothly.

"But one that was only short-lived. Do you fear to face the truth, Colonel? You can run from us, but even if you pretend not to fear the Jaguars, how will you provide for your people on this world whose terrain is murderous and offers so little in the way of vegetation."

"So you contact me, Commander Osis. For what purpose? Do you think I will surrender to you?"

"Surrender is not the way of a warrior. And besides, this planet lacks the facilities to support prisoners of your number. No, I speak to you as one warrior to another. You have proven yourself a worthy foe. Stop your flight. Turn around now and face my Mist Pouncers Cluster head-on. I promise you an honorable contest."

Stirling considered it, for all of three seconds. "A generous offer, Commander Osis, but perhaps you underestimate us. Of course that would not be the first time the Jaguars have made that error. Have your people learned nothing from the beatings you took on Luthien and Tukayyid?" Her Scots burr rose to the occasion.

Devon Osis's body seemed to tense slightly, and the briefest glimpse of fury passed over his rigid expression. "Poorly bargained and done, Colonel," was all he said as he reached out with his baton and tapped the control to break off the connection.

=== **35** ===

North of the Isthmus of Bannockburn
Wayside V (Wildcat)
Deep Periphery
18 July 3058

The stinging pain stirred brevet-Major Jake Fuller from his nightmare and back into consciousness, slowly and reluctantly. When he'd gone unconscious yesterday, he thought he was dying. He was wrong. Instead of the peaceful bliss of death, he'd been trapped in a never-ending nightmare of demons, monsters, fire, and a dull ringing in his ears that did not cease upon awakening.

Even the greenish light of the Wayside evening hurt his eyes. Fuller was disoriented for a second, then realized he was propped up against the familiar leg of his *Cerberus*. Turning his head made his neck muscles ache, but in the distance he saw the hulking form of the *Hatamoto-chi*. And beyond that, the remains of his command. Burned and destroyed wreckage of BattleMechs was strewn about the rocky ground, but if he hadn't already known what it was, he'd never have recognized the pieces as 'Mechs.

"You're alive," a voice said, "if that's what you're wondering." Jake looked over and saw the bandaged form of Elden Parkensen standing near him, one hand extending a canteen. The *Sho-sa* wore his arm in a sling and his head was wrapped with an emergency field med-kit bandage. Jake took the canteen as if it weighed fifty kilos, eventually hefting it up to his lips to gulp down a bit of the warm water inside. Just beyond Parkensen he saw one of the women of his command. Chantilly Hamilton. She waved, apparently in better shape than either he or the *Sho-sa,* though he noted that her thighs were both bandaged.

He moved slightly and it felt as if the skin on his back was on fire, stinging like a thousand needles stabbing him all at once.

"Take it easy, Major," Hamilton said, walking up to him. "You caught a lot of shrapnel in your back and have some nasty burns. The *Sho-sa* had some experience with field surgery, though, and says you'll pull through."

Jake looked over at Parkensen and nodded. "Thanks," he managed to say.

"You'll be fine, but there'll be scarring. I did what was required."

Fuller turned back to Hamilton. "What's our status, or don't I want to know?"

She hesitated in responding. "Apparently the Jags picked us up on their passive sensors. We never had any warning when their fighters hit. They used some kind of bomb that seems to home in on operating fusion reactors—maybe using the neutrino signature as a homing beacon. Only the running 'Mechs got hit. Those that were shut down didn't even suffer a near miss."

"Some sort of new Clan weapons system?" Jake asked wearily.

She shrugged. "If we ever get off of this rock, that little info could be worth some bucks to the intel folks of our employer. We're all that's left of our force, but at least our

'Mechs are operational. There was a return flight of Jaguars to check the area, but they didn't seem to pick us up. I think the rock formations we're parked next to helped, so did the tarps. Since then—nothing."

"Anybody contact the Colonel and let her know?"

Hamilton looked over at the *Sho-Sa,* who responded to the question. "We have not contacted Fusilier Command. Such a transmission might expose us to the Jaguars."

The dull ringing in Jake's ears was subsiding, albeit not fast enough for his tastes. He drew a long breath of the thinned air of Wayside V, but it seemed to take more energy than it gave him in return. "By now the regiment thinks we're dead."

Parkensen nodded. "That's what I would think if I were in your Colonel's position."

"Crudstunk." Jake managed to curse, licking his parched lips again. "We can't just sit here and bake. How are the both of you?"

Hamilton looked at him. "Other than a few cuts, nothing holding me back, sir." She looked over at the *Sho-sa* with a look of concern, but said nothing.

"And you, *Sho-sa?*"

Parkensen's face seemed devoid of emotion, yet it was obvious from his tightened facial muscles that he was in pain of some kind. "Lieutenant Hamilton was forced to perform some minor surgery on me, but nothing that would prohibit my performance in combat, I assure you.

"And my back is a pincushion," he said painfully. "At least that's a start."

"There's more," Hamilton added reluctantly. "The *Sho-sa's* right hand, sir, I—I had to amputate several of his fingers."

Jake looked over at Parkensen, who seemed angered at the revelation. "It is of no consequence. I can still pilot my 'Mech."

"Yes," she snapped, "but with the loss of those fingers, you can only use two of your TICs. If you're not careful, you'll overheat that Combine tin can and shut down when we get into a fight." It was obvious to Jake that they'd already had this argument at least once.

Parkensen drew himself to his full height and looked down at Jake Fuller, his free hand propped defiantly on his hip. "My injuries are my concern. I assure you I am fit to fight the Jaguars again—if that is the plan still. Just what are your intentions, Major Fuller?"

Jake's mind was awash with what had happened. His command had been decimated for the second time since he'd assumed the leadership of the Kilsyth Guards. The mission for which he'd volunteered was critical to the success of the regiment; that much had not changed, despite the losses he'd taken. As long as that aerodrome operated, it posed a threat to the Fusiliers.

"The logical thing for us to do would be to turn tail and head back to the regiment—wherever they are. Everybody, including the Jags, thinks we're dead. That's our advantage. But that's not what I want to do. I say we continue on and complete the mission we started."

"Now then, Mitch, tell me we're still operational," Loren said as he leaned against the repair gantry in the 'Mech bay. The *Bull Run* was on its way to the nadir jump point to leave Boltin, and the bay was once again buzz with personnel working on their 'Mechs. Loren even saw a handful of off-duty engineers lending a hand.

"We are, but we're short a 'Mech," the regimental tech replied. "With everybody helping out, we've made a lot of headway on repairs. I've got Trisha's *Vulture* working, but had to remove one of the weapons pods. I was able to make use of some of the spare parts recovered from the *Warhammer* and the *Behemoth* to get something mounted there. She's going to run a little lopsided, but it's better than nothing at all."

"Understood, and the others?"

"Internal repairs are slow, but we won't be jumping for a little while. I think we'll be operational by the time we reach the next target." Loren heard the hesitation in Mitch's voice, but he knew that somehow the tech would get the Omni-Mechs up and running.

"Good work," he said and Mitch Fraser quickly went back to business.

Once Mitch was gone, Kerndon spoke up quietly. "I watched you from the *Bull Run*. You stopped at the wreckage of your fallen warrior and discarded something. I am curious as to what it was."

"Remember the Jaguar warrior who died in the hospital?"

"Aff, Marilen."

"It was her codex bracelet. Finding it would definitely

convince the Nova Cats that they'd found a true Smoke Jaguar warrior, wouldn't it?"

Kerndon pondered for a moment. "That was intelligent, but I am surprised you did not consult me first. Do you not trust me?"

Loren shook his head. "That's not it. Frankly, I wasn't sure about Clan customs regarding desecration of their dead. I also wasn't sure what your people do with the codex when a warrior dies. I didn't want to place you in any moral dilemmas."

"There is no conflict of interest, Major Loren. The Clans do not view death the way your people do. We long for honorable death in combat, we embrace it. If that warrior of yours had been a Smoke Jaguar, it would have been a chance for her genetic heritage to pass on to another generation of warriors. It is a rebirth, not an end."

Loren looked at Kerndon, then reached out for the arm wearing the bondcard. He severed the second cord, leaving only one. "You reminded me of my duty in destroying Sara's remains. As I recall, the second bond was that of fidelity, and thus far you have shown yourself true to me."

Kerndon rubbed his wrist and pulled at the one remaining cord there. "Now I must prove to you my prowess in battle. Once we get to Tarnby we will meet the Nova Cats on the field and there will be time enough to show you that."

36

Nova Cat Planetary Command, New Lorton
Tarnby
Smoke Jaguar/Nova Cat Occupation Zone
19 July 3058

Khan Severen Leroux of the Nova Cats sat at the head of the table, the portrait of Clan leadership. His three Cluster commanders were points around him. Star Colonel Ajax Drummond of the 100th Strike Cluster was visibly irritated, having just come off field exercises for the meeting. Star

Colonel Angelique of the 153rd Garrison Cluster was, as always, sitting with an introspective gaze.

Star Colonel Santin West sat opposite the Khan. "It is my belief that the Smoke Jaguars have mobilized their long-awaited Tau Galaxy," he was saying. "Elements of that unit are being deployed along our supply corridor and are currently testing our defenses and resolve to defend these positions."

"What makes you think it is the Tau Galaxy?" Ajax Drummond asked.

West shook his head. "I have reviewed the reports from Boltin. They recovered a codex from one of the warriors. Though it does not provide us with the location of the Jaguar base, it does tell us about the exploits of this dead warrior. She was part of the Tau Galaxy, and according to her destination orders and assignments, I was able to determine a great deal about this enemy."

"Such as?" Ajax probed.

"I have correlated data from the Cat's Eye Recharge Station, which apparently engaged in combat with the same unit. They won a Trial of Possession for JumpShip recharges there, which helps to narrow down which system they may be using. Cross-referencing the data available, we have identified eight possible systems where the Tau Galaxy might be stationed."

"What do you suggest?" Angelique asked. "Strike at them before they strike at us?"

"Aff," West said. "They are probing us for a full-scale assault. That much is obvious." Nights of either sleeplessness or fighting his nightmares had left him raw. The sooner this was over, the better.

"We only need a few more data and then we can determine their base's location," West continued. "Boltin is only two jumps from here. If I am correct, they will come here next, to Tarnby."

Drummond was shocked by the statement. "You believe they would dare come here?"

"Aff, Star Colonel." *I know because of my vision and the dream that came to the Oathmaster. They will come and I will fight them here.*

Khan Severen Leroux finally spoke up from the end of the table. "Star Colonels Drummond and Angelique, you will find that Star Colonel West may know some things the rest of us do not, which is why I brought his Cluster here in the first place. He has had a vision, one involving the Smoke Jaguar in battle. I have trusted this vision, and behold, the Jaguar comes at us just as the vision foretold. It is on my orders that he is here, ready to face them now that they come to our very door."

Santin West surveyed the faces in the room and saw that Drummond and Angelique were looking at him with a mixture of admiration and respect.

"You have had a vision? One that involves the Jaguars?" Ajax Drummond asked.

"Aff. In my vision I fought two cats, one a Smoke Jaguar, and another one I have never seen. Oathmaster Winters also had a dream, and in it she saw me fighting a Jaguar to a standoff in Deep Ellum, here on Tarnby." Even Khan Leroux seemed affected by his words, as the atmosphere in the room deepened, became more solemn.

"The Oathmaster has not mentioned this dream to me," Leroux said, his tone betraying irritation that he had not heard of this previously.

"To that I cannot speak, my Khan," Santin West returned. "She did not tell me the specifics, only that she saw me fighting a Jaguar in the city, fighting to a draw."

The Nova Cat Khan nodded slowly. "What is it you desire?"

"To go after them." West spoke with fire in his eyes.

Leroux smiled, chuckling slightly. "Your wish to go after these Jaguar is admirable. Worthy of the Nova Cat blood that feeds your heart and your spirit."

"I only seek to preserve our Clan, my Khan," West said, lowering his gaze out of respect.

"We will wait, the enemy will come here. And when they do, we will rip them with our claws, gouge them with our sharp teeth. Fight them with such fury that Lincoln Osis will see the madness of his undertaking."

Ajax Drummond stood up. "Khan Leroux, we place great weight on our warriors' visions. Santin West has proven himself time and time again as a true warrior of the Nova Cat. He bears a Bloodname and a great command worthy of a bloodkin of the Cat. As such I withdraw my 100th Cluster from any bidding to fight the Tau Galaxy of the Smoke Jaguars when they come to Tarnby."

Star Colonel Angelique also stood. "I too would withdraw my Cluster from the bidding, my Khan."

Santin West was stunned by their actions, yet he knew that in the same circumstances he would do the same. He bowed his large head in respect for his fellow offices. "I thank you both. I will not fail you or our Clan."

"Bleed them, but do not kill them," Leroux said firmly. "Let them lead us to the rest of their litter."

"As you wish, my Khan," Santin West replied, still holding his head low.

Leroux's ebony skin shimmered and gleamed in the light as he spoke. "Very well, thus is the bidding to destroy this Tau Galaxy complete. Well bargained and done."

37

South of New Scotland
Wayside V (Wildcat)
Deep Periphery
22 July 3058

Major Cullen Craig was more than nervous as he approached the campfire where Colonel Stirling sat. The nervousness came from knowing that no matter what he said, it would seem like he was still waging his little personal war against Loren Jaffray. But that wasn't the main part of it. For the first time in his military career, he was considering the unthinkable, ending a fight.

Colonel Stirling had placed the survival of the regiment in the hands of her Executive Officer, Major Loren Jaffray. Just thinking about him made Craig angry. *Jaffray.* A year ago no one had heard of him, then the next thing you knew he was XO, running his programs and training on the rank and file of the Fusiliers, and when all was said and done, there'd been no change. Nothing had prepared them for the Smoke Jaguars.

What angered and appalled him even more was that everyone still believed that Jaffray and his team might actually return. Craig knew the truth. Loren Jaffray had taken off to save himself. *He was not a true Highlander, not like me, or Blackie, or the Colonel. He's always been an outsider, and always will be.*

And though Craig and Kurt Blakadar had been friends for years, Craig suddenly saw Blakadar as almost as bad as Jaffray. In the fighting in the isthmus, Blackie had very nearly left Craig and his battalion to die while awaiting an order from Stirling. *Blackie's changed since he took over as XO, that's what it is. And the Colonel is the one who's made all this happen.*

He stepped into the light of the campfire and Colonel Stirling looked up at him. For the first time ever he saw her age seep through her expression, if only for a moment.

"Something on your mind, Major?"

"Yes, sir," he said as the flames flickered up into the night. "Colonel, I must speak my mind and tell you that I don't feel good about how we're dealing with the Smoke Jaguars." He dared not make eye contact with her, fearing her sharp gaze.

"Oh?" she replied coolly.

"This sprinting across the planet is taking its toll. It's wearing us out, weakening our men and equipment. And the Jaguars are gaining on us."

"I'm aware of the situation. Even at our present rate of movement, the Smoke Jaguar Cluster will be on our butts in five days' time." The Fusiliers were moving and so were the Jaguars, but the Clanners weren't encumbered by vehicles. That was what was slowing the Fusiliers down enough that the enemy was starting to gain on them.

"Chafing under my current strategy, Major?" Stirling asked. Cullen Craig didn't answer. His mouth opened, but no words came out.

"Speak freely, Major."

He blinked, then finally looked her in the face. "The Fusiliers are stretched to their limit. In my opinion, sir, now is the time to turn around and let them have it."

"In some ways you're right, Major. The whole point of the retreat was to buy us some time, but we can only keep it up for so long. We've been moving west for more than four hundred kilometers, putting us halfway between the isthmus and the Takashi Straits.

"We've been buying time, but you and I both know we'll end up dead if we press it much further. I've got a plan, though, a variation on our old WCS. We're going to try to take most of the regiment up onto New Scotland continent. A rear-guard force will remain to slug it out with the Jaguars when they show up—primarily our remaining ground armor, infantry, and those 'Mechs not operational enough to make the trek up."

"That rear-guard force won't stand a chance against the Smoke Jaguars, sir."

Stirling nodded. "Their goal isn't to beat the Jags, just to survive and buy us time. Hopefully enough for Jaffray and Mulvaney to get here."

"You'll be ordering those men and women to their deaths," Craig said quietly.

"Many may die, but some will survive. That's part of commanding a regiment. Sometimes you have to order men and women to their deaths. And the only reason I'll do it is because it could save more lives in the end. Those troops won't be ordered to fight to the bitter end. Just to survive and buy time—period."

Cullen Craig had also ordered people to their deaths more than once in his career. "Running the remaining BattleMechs up on the continent will be too risky. The air is so thin it's nearly a vacuum. The nights are bitter cold, and by day the sun will bake you alive."

"Our 'Mech recycling systems should be able to keep us going for several weeks up there, though it won't be easy. The hardest part will be food supplies. Even with the rationing we've started, we're low and it's going to get worse."

"Do you really believe Jaffray will return?" Craig asked. "Major Mulvaney's another story. She'll get here no matter what, but we can't be sure about Jaffray."

Stirling stared at him, her gaze chilling despite the heat of the fire. "You don't trust him, but as far as I know you have no reason not to."

"He's a Highlander in name only," Craig finally said. "You and the rest of the staff treat him as if he's one of us, but his family turned their backs on the Highlanders decades ago when most of the regiment returned to Northwind. I know Jaffray helped us beat off the Davions last year, but he's more Capellan than Highlander. And now he's deserted us."

Stirling shook her head furiously. "There's more to it than that. It's the fact he was made the Executive Officer, isn't it?"

Craig couldn't help himself this time. "That position was *mine*! I *earned* it. I served under you and Major MacFranklin for six years. I climbed the ladder of rank from the bottom up. I gave my all to the Fusiliers, and in payment you made *him* your exec. First that traitor, and now Blakadar."

Stirling looked at him first with an expression of shock, then her look changed to pity. "That's been it all along, hasn't it? You've been harboring this for months. You're jealous of Major Jaffray."

He opened his mouth to speak, to refute her statement, but apparently changed his mind about what he wanted to say. "Colonel," he said finally, perhaps ashamed at his loss of control, "if you're planning to leave any forces behind, I'd like to command them."

"Major—Cullen," she began, "you don't have to prove anything to me. I know your merits, but I also knew you weren't ready for that promotion. You've been blaming Major Jaffray, but in reality, it was *my* decision."

Cullen Craig seemed to look through her, as if something in his mind had given way. The pressure of the past few weeks had finally broken through, finally taken form.

Cat Stirling and her Executive Officer stood by a small and hasty campfire, a stopping point just long enough for the troops to gather their strength and eat some rations before going back on the run again. Despite the fire, Stirling rubbed her arms for warmth in the chill of the night air.

"So what you're telling me is that Craig's cracked under the pressure?" Kurt Blakadar said, rubbing his forehead at the idea.

Colonel Stirling shook her head. "No, I'm saying it's *possible*. There's a big difference, Blackie, and you know that."

"Sir, I've known him for years. He always has a chip on his shoulder about something, he's that kind of guy."

"Be that as it may, we have to decide whether to leave him in charge of our back door while we make a break for it."

"Hell of a decision, sir," Kurt said. "If he loses it while commanding the rear guard, we get fried. If he pops his cork while he's with us, we're in the same boat."

Stirling nodded. "If you want, I'll make the call on this one, Major."

Kurt Blakadar considered that only for a second. "No, sir, the task's mine. I'll go and tell the good Major that he's in charge of our rear-defense." He started to walk away, then turned to Stirling as though he'd forgotten one last thing.

"And God help us all," he said softly.

═══ 38 ═══

Nova Cat Planetary Command
New Lorton, Tarnby
Smoke Jaguar/Nova Cat Occupation Zone
25 July 3058

The massive bonfire raged like a piece of hell brought to the surface of Tarnby. At one end of it, a circular platform was suspended on a pedestal nearly ten meters over the roaring fire. Far from the prying eyes of the lower castes, this ritual was taking place in the heart of the Nova Cat command base in New Lorton, just off of the parade grounds near a small cluster of trees.

The Nova Cat warriors, clad in their ceremonial leathers, encircled the great fire. Their garb consisted of little more than black vests and shorts. Many wore laced leggings and boots, while others stood barefoot, especially the massive Elemental warriors. There was food and drink, though that was not the reason for the gathering.

This was the Nova Cat ritual known as the Chronicle of Battles. Once a month the warriors of Clan Nova Cat gathered under the stars and before each other, reading from *The Remembrance* and telling tales of glory. It was a bonding rite, one that brought the warriors of the Clan together and made them one. Tonight's Chronicle was different, though. This night the 179th was preparing for battle. This night, gathered around the sacred bonfire, the Nova Cats spoke not just of past triumphs, but also of a battle to come—a battle against the Smoke Jaguars.

Santin West stood at the fringe of the crowd of warriors, his Elemental height making him taller than most. He watched the sea of warriors, men and women of the three Clusters stationed on Tarnby, as if he were disembodied. His mind was elsewhere, thinking ahead to the foe he was sure was coming. They had invaded his dreams, turned them into nightmares.

He wanted an end to those nightmares, but he also sensed that matters would not end here on Tarnby. Something told him the real fight lay elsewhere. Here they could face at most a single Cluster of the Tau Galaxy. There would surely be more of them, and they were out there stalking his Clan.

A hand reached up from the crowd and placed itself on his shoulder. West looked down and saw Ajax Drummond, his fellow Star Colonel, at his side. "Greetings," he said. "It is a good night for us to praise the glory of the Nova Cat."

"Many are speaking of your vision, Santin West," Drummond said.

"How is that possible?"

"Word has leaked, most likely from Angelique, but it has leaked nevertheless. It has been some time since anyone in our Clan has known such a vision, and in such detail. Look around you, Santin West. Do you not see how these warriors regard you? They have come to hear your words, to partake in your vision. Do you not see, quineg?"

West let his eyes travel over the gathering and saw that many indeed seemed to be watching him. "They would not wish it. The nightmare plagues my sleep, then I lie awake the long night. They should not look to me for such leadership. I am merely a warrior of the Nova Cat."

"Neg," Drummond rebutted. "You have been touched by the unseen. The hand of Kerensky has reached out and revealed to you the threat of the Smoke Jaguar. This will be a rallying point for our warriors. You are a nexus, a pivot point. Our warriors need to hear your voice."

"They need to prepare to face the Jaguar when he comes," Santin West said.

A drum began to pound, sounding twenty times, once for each of the original Clans formed by Nicholas Kerensky. The deep bass vibration seemed to stir the crowd, touching not only their hearts and minds but something even deeper. It was the signal, the start of the ceremony. The Chronicle of Battles began with each of the highest-ranking officers of the Nova Cats ascending the platform over the roaring flames.

"Seyla," the warriors chanted in unison.

Star Colonel Angelique emerged from the crowd, garbed in her black leathers. She stood by Drummond, and the two of them motioned Santin West to the ramp leading to the platform over the flames. They were granting him the honor of speaking first, paying hommage to his vision.

"Santin West," the warriors of the Nova Cats chanted. "Seyla!" they called out, speaking as one. Feeling all eyes upon him, Santin West began to ascend the ramp to the platform hovering just above the tips of the flames. From there, he would speak to the gathered warriors of the Clan.

He opened his mouth to speak, but his words were cut off by a fearsome sound from below. When he looked down, he saw the crowd part as the Nova Cat, the living, breathing embodiment of the Clan, roared into the night. Its growls were deep and powerful, reaching into the very heart and souls of those gathered. The Nova Cat was looking squarely at him. Then, as if on cue, the mighty beast dropped his front haunches, almost as though bowing to Santin West as he stood there. A murmur rose from the warriors gathered around.

It was time to speak. "Warriors of the Nova Cat, I am Star Colonel Santin West and I lead the Circle of Power Cluster—no finer warriors have been bred in the name of our Clan. Though I am bound to speak of battles past during this Chronicle, tonight I also speak of battles to come.

"I have had a vision. One that spoke to me of our age-old foe, the Smoke Jaguar. I have seen us fighting not only this enemy, but another great warrior cat in battle."

"Seyla," the warriors of Clan Nova Cat chanted, the word echoing in the night against the beating of the drum and the roaring of the Clan's namesake. In the midst of all this a young female tech had begun trying to edge her way into the circle from its outer edge. At first the thick ring of Clan warriors did not let her pass, but then they gradually parted, leaving a path to the ramp leading to the platform. She carried a portable holographic projector as she moved quickly forward, then began to ascend the ramp with a reverence that was obvious. Just short of the top, she stopped and gave a slight bow, hesitating to continue forward.

"This is a ritual for warriors and warriors alone," Santin West said.

"I beg pardon, Star Colonel, but your standing orders indicated that we were to interrupt you at any time for this. A batchall has been issued from a ship that recently entered the system via a pirate jump point. A Star Commander named Gregory of the Smoke Jaguars," the technician said, her voice wavering.

"Tie me in," he said. "Show all gathered here what has come—and how I will reply."

"Incoming response from the city of New Lorton below," the *Bull Run*'s comm officer told Loren.

"Transfer signal now," Loren replied, activating his own holographic projection system.

This far he and he alone had handled the batchalls with the Nova Cats. However, Loren's knowledge of how military intelligence worked told him that sooner or later the Cats might figure out that they were only facing two Stars worth of warriors. To create the illusion of more forces, he would have Greg Hector issue the next batchall to make the Cats think his force was larger than it was.

He turned to Lieutenant Hector, who drew himself up firmly as the projector came on. The holo image of the man standing before them was that of a giant, standing nearly a half meter taller than a normal human being—obviously an Elemental. He wore a black leather jerkin, studded collar, and black finger gloves on his big hands. His expression showed power, resolve, and anger, all somehow controlled. At the edges of the projector's image display were flames, reaching up and around him.

"I am Star Colonel Santin West of the 179th Striker Cluster of the Clan that will crush and defeat you," he said. "Tell me, Jaguar Gregory, has your Star Colonel, the one called Loren, been killed by our forces on Boltin, or is he too fearful to stand before a true warrior, quiaff?"

"Neg," Greg Hector replied from behind his Jaguar mask. "Star Colonel Loren does not see this as a battle worthy of his attention and has designated me as the issuer of the challenge."

"Your insult and insolence are noted and are unbecoming a warrior—even a Smoke Jaguar."

"Words," Hector said firmly, "have little sting. Tell me, with what forces will you defend your HPG?"

Santin West stood proudly and unshaken by their verbal sparring. "I refuse your Trial of Possession. If you wish to use our HPG, then do so. What I come to say is that I challenge you and your Tau Galaxy to a Trial of Grievance. You insult us with your raids."

Greg Hector's eyes darted to Kerndon. The bondsman nodded slowly, indicating that the challenge should be accepted. "We accept your challenge and will defend our honor with . . ." Loren held up nine fingers, one for each of his remaining OmniMechs.

"With nine Points worth of force," Hector said.

The Nova Cat Elemental standing in the firelit scene laughed out loud, and he was still laughing when the transmission cut off abruptly.

$$=== \textbf{39} ===$$

South of New Scotland
Wayside V (Wildcat)
Deep Periphery
25 July 3058

Cullen Craig walked over to where Kurt Blakadar and Colonel Stirling stood waiting for him in the makeshift campsite. In the distance the ground seemed to rise up like a hill that never ended. The green sky of Wayside had taken on a darker tone as storm clouds rolled in, blotting out the bright sunlight. The entire regiment had pivoted hard to the north, ninety degrees from their previous westbound drive. Now they were heading upland, toward the continental surface.

Somewhere out there, only a few hours distant, was the vanguard of the Smoke Jaguars, or so the sensor picket devices they had left in their wake told them. Relentless, the Jaguar forces refused to give up their pursuit.

"You and the Colonel are worried I can't handle the pressure. That's it, isn't it?" Cullen Craig demanded. "Well I'm *not* cracking," he said, shooting an angry glance at Stirling, who stood to one side, arms crossed over her chest. "I just don't have confidence in Jaffray, but this isn't the first time you've heard that. You and I have talked about it a hundred times, Blackie. He's no friend of yours, either, as I recall."

"That's not the point, Cullen," Kurt Blakadar said. "I just

need to know you won't let your feelings interfere with your duty in the next part of our operation."

Craig rubbed his temple, as if he were pressing down a massive headache. "I just need a little rest, Blackie. Hell, we all do at this point."

"While you hold those Jags in place, the rest of us are going to continue north, then back to the east," Kurt said. "There's a petrified forest up there on New Scotland. It's going to be a stretch without our techs, but we can do it."

Stirling finally spoke up. "The *Stonewall Jackson* is back at the LZ. It's ruined for flight, but it would provide you adequate shelter until our relief force arrives."

Craig looked at her in disbelief, then back at Kurt Blakadar. "And what about my battalion?"

"They'll be attached to me until we manage to link up again," Blakadar said. "You'll command a heavily reinforced company—all our remaining infantry, techs, vehicles, and all the BattleMechs too damaged that they wouldn't last up on the continent. It's not a weak force, but one not suited for that environment. Hit the Jaguars, get their attention, then get out of there. The LZ is a ways off, but go straight there. We'll rendezvous with you once Jaffray and his team have returned, or once we get relieved by Mulvaney's battalion."

"You don't really think Jaffray's coming back, do you, Blackie?" Craig asked, not hiding his bitterness even though Colonel Stirling was present. "Once our force splits up, we'll never see each other again and you know it."

Seated in the cockpit of her *Timber Wolf,* Star Colonel Patricia had analyzed the situation again and again, always arriving at the same conclusion. *They are trapped. They have grown weary of the chase and now they are ours.* In her mind she could see the freebirth Stirling turning her ragtag regiment around to face the Smoke Jaguars, and then the whole battle played itself out in her mind. She could see the enemy charging into her pristine Cluster in their old-tech BattleMechs, then a fight so brutally one-sided that it ended with her standing over the body of Andrea Stirling, her boot driving into her enemy's chest.

The commline squealed slightly and she activated it on her secondary monitor—seeing the face of Galaxy Commander Devon Osis looking back at her. "Star Colonel Patricia, have you reviewed the recon flight data?"

"Affirmative, Galaxy Commander," she replied.

"Then you have reached the same conclusion as I," he said coldly.

"Indeed. The Fusiliers will cease their flight and turn to face us," she said, a hint of joy in her voice.

"That is what you think?"

"Aff, Galaxy Commander. Why else would they enter such confining terrain?"

"You are a trueborn Smoke Jaguar, but you lack experience in battle. These Inner Spherers are tenacious, if nothing else. Colonel Stirling takes her force to the north, not to fight us, but to move up onto the continent."

Patricia heard his words but her mind failed to grasp the concept. Such an action was illogical, given the terrain of Wildcat, yet Devon Osis spoke with utter certainty. "It is not possible that she is planning to turn and engage us?"

"Neg, Patricia, neg. If she wanted to turn and fight, she would have accepted my earlier challenge. Neg, she hopes to flee to the uplands."

Patricia was shocked at the thought, knowing the atmosphere on Wildcat's continental masses. "How would you have me proceed, Galaxy Commander?"

"Speed up our pursuit. I want to be on them soon. Then, as they try to make a break for the surface of the continent, our aerospace fighters will bomb them into dust. I do not want to leave even a shred of their genetic material behind."

"It shall be done as you command," Patricia said. In less than two days, there would be nothing left of Stirling's Fusiliers, and the honor lost by Star Colonel Roberta would fall upon her shoulders and become part of her codex. Patricia smiled thinly, thinking of the destruction she would have the honor of wreaking . . .

Jake Fuller studied his long-range sensors and saw the faint images of a pair of enemy *Thor* OmniMechs standing at the end of the runway. These were his targets, as well as the Elementals. "*Sho-sa*, are you in position?"

It had taken several nights of slow and careful movement to reach the Jaguar aerospace complex. Moving only at night, by day he and his two companions had concealed their 'Mechs in the rocks and brush, draping them with thermal tarps and whatever plant life they could muster. Now they were several days' travel from the isthmus, and by now the Jaguars would surely be holding the straits.

The base was on a flat rock of terrain, surrounded by high dune-like hills of sand common to this region. The runway ran north and south. At the north end were a series of buildings—a hangar, communications center, and a barracks. It was wide open, while from his position in the hills, he had the perfect hiding place—for now.

They had scouted the area on foot to avoid detection by the defenders of the fighter base. Jake's plan was simple enough, but had plenty of risk. He would charge to the end of the runway, drawing them into the hills once he got their attention. Parkensen would then strike at their communications facility and hangar, taking out the OmniFighters and the base's ability to call in reinforcements. Chantilly Hamilton was hiding in the dunes, running at low power. While Jake was drawing the enemy Elementals and *Thor*s further away from their base, she would power up and hit them on the flank. Parkensen would come down the runway and hit their rear. Boxed in, the Jaguar defenders would not survive.

"Major Fuller," came the uniquely calm voice of Elden Parkensen, "I stand ready and await your word."

These sleazy bastards blew up my command. They bombed my Kilsyth Guards, and my people never even knew what hit them. Now, it's payback time.

"For our dead and those still alive, let's let them have it. See you all on the tarmac!" Jake Fuller said, throttling his *Cerberus* forward toward the unsuspecting Clan 'Mechs.

40

Deep Ellum, New Lorton
Tarnby
Smoke Jaguar/Nova Cat Occupation Zone
25 July 3058

The city of New Lorton butted up against the Blacklick River, which ran east and west. The river bank was, in essence, a massive cliff rising nearly twenty meters up from the wide, fast-moving river. Even the power of a BattleMech could not make it across the waters. It was a perfect barrier. To the north of the city, past the river, was a massive swamp. A methene-processing facility had once stood there, providing power for half the planet during the Star League era. Now the site was nothing but ruins and swamp. Again, inhospitable terrain for even the best of BattleMechs.

The city was divided into different sectors. The Nova Cat planetary command base had been built to the south, in the wide green and open flatlands running down and away from the cliffs. Deep Ellum was the old section of the city, climbing all the way up to the cliff overlooking the river. The buildings on the cliff were old, dating back to the time when Tarnby was the furthest extent of the mighty Star League. They were well-kept, lined up along tight streets that even light BattleMechs would not be able to maneuver.

The HPG transmitter, where messages were sent out via the same technology that let JumpShips leap between the stars, was located literally at the edge of the cliff. It had been built by ComStar centuries before the return of Kerensky's children, and was Tarnby's one link to the rest of the universe. Like many of the older ComStar stations, it boasted a vast park that extended into the city proper—a perfect makeshift LZ for a DropShip because it offered some maneuvering distance away from the tight streets of Deep Ellum.

Loren was here to send an HPG message, a false one, outward to Wayside V. The message itself was nothing, gibberish. What mattered was that he was sending it to the planet's coordinates, and those coordinates would be left behind for the Nova Cats to find. He was literally giving them everything they needed to find the Smoke Jaguar base of Wayside.

As the *Bull Run,* under Spillman's command, touched down in the HPG park, Loren entered the 'Mech bay and saw Lieutenant McBride. At first glance she looked like the epitome of a Fusilier MechWarrior, ready to jump into battle. As he drew closer, however, Loren saw that impression was totally false. Her skin was a chalky white and her eyes seriously bloodshot. Her wounds were bandaged, but blood had managed to seep through despite the thick gauze pads.

Loren tried to hide his concern with a light tone. "I hate to say it, Lieutenant, but you look like death warmed over."

"Ready to fight, sir," she said, but her expression looked like she might suddenly vomit at any moment.

"Right," Loren said. "And I'm the new First Lord of the Star League."

McBride spoke slowly, adjusting her stance as if to control her dizziness. "You need me. You bid all our 'Mechs for this fight."

"Yes, we said we'd come with everything we had, but if you go out in your condition, it's a one-way trip. You can have a seat in the sit-rep room and do me a bigger favor feeding us tactical data."

"Who'll pilot my 'Mech?" she asked.

"Don't worry about that. It'll be my problem. Now go get something for the pain and nausea so you'll be able to feed me data on where the Nova Cats are."

"McBride isn't in any shape to be part of this fight," Loren said, standing in the doorway to Kerndon's quarters. "She wouldn't last ten minutes in the field. I've ordered her to handle tactical coordination from the ship instead. That means you're going to have to pilot her *Vulture*."

"Mad Dog," Kerndon corrected, insisting on the Clan name for the OmniMech rather than its Inner Sphere name.

"Vulture," Loren countered firmly. "Things have just changed between us, Kerndon. This is no longer a matter of you helping us impersonate Smoke Jaguars. This is about you being part of us—part of our clan, as it were. And you're going to have to drop that 'Major Loren' stuff right now. If you're going to pilot that *Vulture* in battle, you'll do it not for yourself or for your Clan. You'll do it for Stirling's Fusiliers of the Northwind Highlanders."

Kerdon looked at Loren, his dark eyes narrowing slightly. "That is a high price you ask of me."

"You are my bondsman, Kerndon. I could simply order you to do this, but I want you to do it willingly." Loren stood looking at the other man for a moment. "Decide right here and right now—are you part of the Fusiliers or not?"

Kerndon weighed the options. He tugged at the one remaining bond cord, the one of prowess, still circling his wrist. It was a reminder of who he was and what still stood between him and the right to again call himself a true warrior. "Very well, I am yours to command—Major Loren Jaffray."

* * *

Star Colonel Santin West uttered the word "screen" into the voice-command activation system of his Elemental suit and saw the small tactical display relayed from Star Captain Delaportas's sensors. The Smoke Jaguar force had moved away from the HPG compound and had taken up position less than a kilometer away.

Though his force could not visually contact all the Jaguar BattleMechs at any given time, thanks to the protective cover of the buildings, he saw that they had moved into the city, nearly a kilometer from the park and their ship. They were deployed between his own forces and their Drop-Ship, their line running northwest to the cliff area. It was a precarious position, the DropShip offering their only hope of retreat since they would be fighting with their backs to the wall. If unable to make it to their ship, they could be driven over the cliffs and into the river. Walking slowly, he continued to study the tiny display out of the corner of his eye.

"Battle Binary, split and deploy. Charlie Battle Star, sweep to the far west flank along Lucas Street and the cliffs. Hold that flank firm, you are the anchor. Alpha Battle, we will assume a perimeter from Schultz Street running east to the edge of the compound." His own counter-deployment was to engage the Jaguars at the cliff, where he would swing, like a giant door, parallel with their battle line.

"Aff," came joint replies from Star Captains Delaportas and Nina. Ithon Delaportas came back on line in less than five seconds. "Awaiting your attack orders."

Star Colonel West looked at the display one last time before uttering the command word "tactical," which brought up his heads up display inside the helmet/viewing screen of his Elemental armor. *I have the Jaguars where I want them. I must hurt them, spill their blood, but not kill them. Let the wounded cat lead me to his den.*

"Charlie Star, advance two blocks, then hold there. Binary, slow advance from west to east, one block at a time. We want to wound the beast and kill some of its cubs. But we need some of these Jaguars to survive. Other than that, you may engage at will."

"Incoming 'Mechs at two point two one," came a call from Glenda Jura as a wave of long-range missiles streaked at her

Koshi and into a cluster of old storefront buildings, setting off explosions of smoke and orange flames.

Loren saw a number of Nova Cat OmniMechs light up on his secondary display. "Hector, your Star is the anchor. Keep our path open to the *Bull Run* no matter what."

"On it," Greg Hector replied as a hail of static came over the line. "Engagement; two *Huntsman* and one *Mad Cat*."

Loren suddenly saw a faint image down-range of his *Masakari*. He powered his deadly array of extended-range PPCs and braced himself for the battle. The rush that came over him, The Sensation, swept his whole body. His fingers tingled with excitement as a voice he recognized as Trisha McBride's came over the commline. "Smoke Jaguar force, the Nova Cats are concentrating on the center of your positions. Recommend that you pull back your far right flank two blocks."

Loren checked his sensor sweep and saw that Trisha was right. "Confirmed tactical. Greg, pull your forces back, synchronized stagger block by block."

The ugly Nova Cat *Man O'War* emerged from behind a building at the same time Loren saw several jets from Elemental boots light up and dart behind the same structure. The *Man O'War* squeezed off a pair of shots from its autocannons, spraying a stream of shells into the legs of his *Masakari*. Armor flew where the shells erupted, but nothing else was hit. Loren locked onto the enemy, which was behind a building now, as though waiting for Loren to come to him.

Loren locked his quad PPCs onto the target, a target hidden by the building itself, and opened fire. At the instant he fired, the *Man O'War* sidestepped out of the cover of the structure. The bright blue PPC streams struck the building with a stunning force, blasting through the second floor of the structure. Fires broke out instantly, the blast consuming the building's interior like a fire-breathing dragon. There was an explosion, most likely from a gas main, then the building itself blew apart onto the street below.

Santin West had moved behind Star Captain Delaportas's *Gargoyle* as it opened fire on the Smoke Jaguar *Warhawk*. Suddenly he saw the building only a few meters from him erupt in a massive explosion. Knowing he had to get out of the way, he fired his jets and leaned backward even as the wall of debris began to rain on him.

The shattering walls hit him in mid-leap, knocking him backward, and something seemed to hold his legs. He gritted his teeth as he was thrown back and then abruptly stopped, his thighs and lower back straining. Looking down, Santin West saw that he was buried in debris up to the waist. He reached down with his mechanical claw and began to dig furiously, pulling away pieces of the metal and wiring that seemed to be holding him.

He could see that the *Gargoyle* had also taken some damage from the blast that had devoured the building. It lumbered out into the street, firing at the *Warhawk*.

But Santin West was going nowhere. Not until he could dig himself out of this pile of scrap. This wasn't the way it was supposed to end.

"I'm hit," called Leigh Ann Miller as her *Uller* was bathed in a volley of light from a Nova Cat *Huntsman,* the Clan 'Mech's pulse lasers and autocannon shredding away much of her arm. She pivoted and fired her Gauss rifle at what seemed an impossibly close range. The squat-headed *Huntsman* took the shot squarely in the chest, reeling back for only a second.

As Loren took another serious hit in the hip from the *Man O'War,* he saw out of the corner of his eye the *Huntsman* moving in for the kill on Leigh Ann's *Uller*. The Clan 'Mech fired one of its large lasers into the *Uller*'s already mangled leg, hitting the hip actuator, which exploded in a blast of black smoke. The *Uller* rocked and began to fall, just in time for the *Huntsman* to drive a kick into it as it dropped. Armor and internal structure caved in as the Nova Cat battered it with a series of pile-driving kicks.

Loren was having his own problems and couldn't help out. As he and the *Man O'War* exchanged another salvo, his *Masakari* buckled under the impact of several hits. But the Nova Cat 'Mech took most of the hurt. Its already damaged arm erupted as the warheads and missiles inside it went off. The arm went flying backward into the street, leaving only a stump and a few control wires and myomer strands to indicate that anything had ever been attached there.

On his flank he saw the *Huntsman* that had crushed Leigh Ann Miller's *Uller* still standing over her fallen 'Mech. As the Clan 'Mech lifted its foot, Loren watched in horror as he realized it was going to smash her cockpit! He began to turn the *Masakari* to do something about it when he saw a *Vulture* suddenly appear, blazing away at the *Huntsman* with every bit of its firepower. Kerndon!

"Prepare to die, Smoke Cat," came a female voice over his speakers. It was the *Man O'War* pilot, taunting Loren as her autocannons shredded his right arm and leg armor.

Responding instantly, Loren fired his missiles at their minimum range, sending a spread of the deadly warheads straight into the *Man O'War*'s already battered chest. Many ripped away at the ferro-fibrous armor while others dug deeper before going off, mangling the internal structure of the 'Mech and ripping away at the myomer muscles. Pieces of sensors, heat sinks, and other internal components were pulled free by the blast and rained down on the street. Smoke billowed from the hole, and a slight flicker of burning components showed inside.

Loren fired one of his PPCs, the shot lancing outward like a bolt of lightning squarely into the smoldering hole from his previous hits. It dug so deeply that it burst out the back of the *Man O'War*, blasting away the rear armor. The missile and autocannon ammunition there erupted in a blast of incredible fury, further tearing at the internal structure of the Nova Cat 'Mech and spraying out through the CASE doors.

The damage was so devastating that the already battered *Man O'War* dropped to its knees. Loren was about to pivot, to see if he could aid Kerndon or one of the others. Suddenly a pair of short-range missiles reached out at him from behind the kneeling Nova Cat 'Mech. Loren looked up and saw an Elemental, jet black in color, rising on its jump jets and firing.

Instinctively Loren reversed the throttle of the *Masakari* and pulled back, moving behind a building to block the approaching enemy's fire. Checking the tactical display for the status of his forces, he was dismayed by what he saw. The Nova Cats were pressing his perimeter, which was caving in. Several of his 'Mechs were showing as down or missing.

They were losing this fight. The Nova Cats had also been hurt pretty bad, but not enough to stop them from shredding him and his people like a meat-grinder.

Smoke Jaguar Aerodrome
Wayside V (Wildcat)
Deep Periphery
25 July 3058

Jake Fuller's *Cerberus* came over the small rise overlooking the Smoke Jaguar aerodrome, firing away with both its Gauss rifles. The weapons streaked out their deadly, sluglike balls straight at the leading *Thor*. His shots were low, but both found their mark, hitting the legs of the Jaguar 'Mech with such force that the 'Mech fell forward as if it had been clubbed in the shins.

As Jake had hoped, they'd caught the Smoke Jaguars totally off guard. Using the steep sand dunes and rock formations for cover and moving mostly at night, he had poised his small team perfectly. He was striking from the south, hitting the end of the runway. Meanwhile, Parkensen had made his way to the north and would be driving toward him, hopefully taking out the airbase command center in the process. Chantilly would sweep in on his flank. It was a good plan, as long as the Jaguars played along.

But the second *Thor* reacted quickly, beginning to move toward them. Jake swung his weapons at the second Jaguar even as it began to fire its ER PPC and long-range missiles. The deadly blue bolt of the PPC lashed into Jake's *Cerberus*, hitting its left chest, twisting and contorting the Aldis heavy ferro-fibrous armor like wax under a hot flame.

Jake switched on his McArthur anti-missile system just as

he heard the tone of the missile lock squeal inside his neuro-helmet. The small fire door popped open on his 'Mech's chest, spraying out a wall of fire as the *Thor's* long-range missiles came arcing in toward him. There were a series of flashes as some of the missiles exploded before they could hit, but one pair of warheads did get through, digging into his right leg.

In the distance he heard a deep rumble followed by a massive fireball rising into the air above the aerodrome's buildings. A communications signal came on as Jake dodged his *Cerberus* to the right, breaking into a full run. "Communications building destroyed," came the voice of *Sho-sa* Parkensen from the other end of the tarmac.

Both of his Gauss rifles signaled as fully loaded and charged. Locking onto the second *Thor,* Jake saw the first one getting to its feet again. Things were going to get hot very quickly. "I could use some help here, Parkensen," he muttered into the microphone of his neurohelmet.

Locking his cross hairs onto the second *Thor* again, he opened fire. The pair of Gauss slugs raced out and streaked into the Jaguar 'Mech's right leg, one hitting high, the other hitting at the knee actuator, severing the joint cleanly as it passed through the leg. It was the second *Thor's* turn to fall forward, while the first was now standing and ready for a fight despite its damaged legs.

Then, a Point of Elementals rose into the air over the fallen *Thor.* Painted tan with gray streaks, their camouflage blended in with the bleak clay soil of Wayside. They were still far enough away for Jake to keep concentrating on the first *Thor,* but they were a threat nevertheless.

He kept an eye on his Gauss rifle indicators as the weapons slowly loaded and built up the necessary charge to fire. The first *Thor,* now rising like a phoenix, let go a wave of missiles that went just wide of his position. Jake pivoted his torso and locked his weapons the moment his Gauss rifle came on line. He aimed low, locking his targeting cross hairs onto the legs, which he'd hit in his initial attack.

The diehard *Thor* opened up with both its large and medium lasers just as Jake fired his rifles. The lasers found their mark first, slashing at him like ruby-red sabers, slicing massive pieces of armor off his legs and torso. The damage was minimal, but it was still damage. His own Gauss rifles raced down-range, one slamming into the *Thor's* leg while the other shot missed altogether, creating a massive crater just behind the Jaguar. The Elementals rose alongside and began to provide supporting fire, their missiles twisting at him.

Sweat rolled down Jake's brow as he prepared to exchange another salvo with the stubborn *Thor*. Just once, he wished something would go right on this planet.

Santin West cursed to himself as the Jaguar *Warhawk* moved backward out of his reach in the streets of Deep Ellum. The communications signal had indicated that it was from the Smoke Jaguar Star Colonel, Loren, and it was his *Warhawk* that had opened up a barrage that kept him pinned for what seemed like hours, but in reality had been less than a minute. He looked at the tactical display in the helmet of his Elemental suit and saw the damage taken by both sides. His Binary had inflicted significant damage on the Jaguars, but had taken almost as many losses themselves.

A part of him wanted to press on with the battle. This was, after all, a Trial of Grievance. The thin line of Jaguar 'Mechs still stretched from their DropShip in the HPG park to a point near the cliffs overlooking the oddly serene Backlick River. His assault had not broken their line running through the narrow city streets. Instead, the entire line had moved back, recoiling from his assault and inflicting damage of its own. He knew he could crush them with a simple order, but the price of that order would be his own life and the lives of his command. The gains would not be worth the losses. Memories of his vision taunted him. He had not yet held the throat of the Smoke Jaguar in his power claw, crushing it.

Seeing the *Warhawk* as he came around the corner, Santin West opened fire with his short-range missiles again, splattering armor and shooting black smoke and flames into the air as the pair of SRMs struck firmly into the heart of the Jaguar Omni. The *Warhawk* began to move away, firing one of its PPCs as it went. The shot missed, but one of the trailing arcs of charged particles danced over and into his leg. Santin felt every hair on his massive body stand on end as the huge electrostatic discharge burnt a hole in his armor. His flesh had been spared, and the suit's self-sealing protection system covered the opening with a quick-drying plastic coating.

The time had come. Biccon Winters had told him that the

fight in Deep Ellum would be a stand-off—it was part of her dream. Now he would fulfill her vision, and be one step closer to realizing his own.

"I'm on fire here," squealed the voice of Sergeant Ralston McAnis over the unsecured wide-beam frequency in the ears of each of the mock-Jaguars.

"Eject—damn it! Punch out," shouted Sumpter Burke. McAnis was farthest from the DropShip, and Burke was responsible for covering him in case of trouble.

"Oh God . . ." came Glenda Jura's call, followed by an explosion in the distance that seemed to shake the streets and buildings of Deep Ellum.

Loren read the data being fed to him from his own sensors and from Trisha McBride aboard the *Bull Run*. Half of his force was either dead or near death. The rest were falling back, retreating toward his position, fighting for each meter of terrain. He only wanted to hold until he heard back from Mitch, to make sure that the clue had been planted, the HPG transmission sent.

He was considering ordering retreat, conceding the battlefield and giving the Nova Cats the victory. It didn't matter now. The voice of Captain Mitchell Fraser came on line: "The Nova Cat techs were a lot more cooperative than the warriors you're facing. Our message was sent to Wayside V's coordinates as planned."

Loren swung his right arm into firing position and opened up with one of his PPCs at an approaching Elemental. The burst missed by five meters, but the arcing particle beams leaped out and scarred the glossy black armor of the Elemental. In the distance he saw several other dark blue Elementals rising to join Loren's attacker, who was firing his small laser into Loren's chest just below the cockpit canopy.

He pivoted his torso as he moved the *Masakari* further down the street to remain facing his foe as he prepared to concede defeat. Suddenly, he heard a deep and menacing voice over his neurohelmet speakers.

"Star Colonel Loren of the Smoke Jaguars, have you come today to die with your warriors, or do you hide aboard your ship watching them die?"

West. Loren activated his commline. "I am Loren of the Jaguars. I assume this is the esteemed Star Colonel Santin." His tone was openly sarcastic.

"To continue this fight would leave us both dead, with our hands wrapped around each other's throats," West said, sounding weary. "You have fought well enough even for mere Smoke Jaguars, spawn of a gene pool laden with weaklings and surat blood."

Loren gave a short laugh. "You too have fought well, for old warriors and bandits. Perhaps you will one day learn the meaning of honor, or at least how to spell the word, quiaff?" he said, checking his short-range sensors. He found the source of the transmission, the lone jet black Elemental who had fired at him. "Words are of little value with warriors. Is there a point to this banter?"

"Aff," replied Santin West. "Waste is not the way of our Clans. I wish to declare, with you, this Trial void. Let no more warriors die needlessly. We shall settle this trial again, at another time, in another place."

He wants to postpone the fight, leave the Trial open. What choice do I have? I'm not here to wipe out the Nova Cats. "This is not how such battles should end. I accept your offer, on the condition that you and I will face each other again."

"I assure you that I shall hunt you and find you, Star Colonel Loren of the Jaguars," Santin West said. "And the next time we meet, all I will leave behind are your ashes."

BOOK III

Crucible

One more such victory and we are undone.

—Pyrrhus of Epirus

They've got us surrounded again, the poor bastards.

—General Creighton W. Abrams

This man Wellington is so stupid he does not know when he is beaten and goes on fighting.

—Napoleon Bonaparte

42

South of New Scotland
Wayside V (Wildcat)
Deep Periphery
25 July 3058

Major Cullen Craig's *Victor* towered over the array of 'Mechs and equipment the Fusiliers could not carry with them up onto the continent of New Scotland. In addition to his *Victor,* there were four other BattleMechs that could not make the trek due to damage they'd taken in the earlier fighting. In the dim green twilight, they appeared like emerald giants, misting as their heat vents channeled out the heat from their internal structure. The mists hung at their feet, giving the BattleMechs an almost mythical appearance, like titans or giants of ages past.

There was a reinforced lance of tanks as well, heavy ground armor support that the Fusiliers had planned to use in attacking the Jaguar command base—an attack Craig knew would never take place. Even the arrival of Mulvaney's reinforcements would only prolong the Fusiliers' death agony. Captain Lewis's infantry platoons and deadly Infiltrator power armor were set up in concealed positions near the route that the Smoke Jaguars would take.

That route had been easy to predict. The old sea bed rose upward, with rolling hills, and the only relatively clear area was the kilometer-wide pass where Craig and his people now waited for them to come. The thin yellow grass and moss showed scars of the passage of the rest of the Fusiliers two hours earlier—a steady stream of 'Mech tracks running to the north. As he faced south, the direction from which the Jaguars were approaching, Craig knew that nearly seventy kilometers away, in the much higher and thinner air, Colonel Stirling must have reached the edge of what had been a continent eons ago.

The regimental vehicles for communications and control were concealed nearby, ready to make their escape toward the landing zones where the Fusiliers had first touched down. His mission was simple; slow the Smoke Jaguars and then try to get away to safety. Moving along the rugged hillsides, the survivors of his small holding action would head to the southwest, hopefully making their way to the wreck of the *Stonewall Jackson*. That was easier said then done, Craig knew. He'd seen how the Jaguars fought back in the Isthmus of Bannockburn. They didn't stop coming in battle, even when they were losing.

The infantry scouts were the first to signal and relay the information about the Smoke Jaguar forces. The leading elements consisted of a Binary of mixed 'Mechs. The information being relayed from the scouts was feeding into his secondary display as if his own short-range scanners were picking up the information. Cullen Craig braced himself for the onslaught and stared at the communications controls inside his cockpit. *At least we haven't seen their fighters. That would be the end of this quick enough.*

The jamming from his regimental comm vehicle seemed to alert and breathe life into the Jaguar Binary. They rushed forward into the open pass where Craig and his *Victor* stood ready. The leading two Omnis were a *Dasher* and a *Koshi*, moving so fast it was impossible to get a lock on them. The next 'Mech, a stark gray *Vulture,* was a much more viable target. Craig locked his targeting cross hairs onto it at the same time that one of the other Fusilier 'Mechs, a poorly patched *Rifleman,* also opened fire on it.

The *Vulture's* right side took a scarring cut from Craig's lasers while the *Rifleman's* Ultra autocannons peppered it with shells. The impact of the weapons didn't even seem to slow the movement of the 60-ton Clan war machine. Instead it pivoted its torso and opened up with its long-range missile racks, spraying the *Rifleman* with a full barrage at its minimum range. Almost all the missiles found their mark, rattling the already battered *Rifleman* and sending the replacement armor patches scattering among the rocks and clay soil. The warheads that missed dug into the rocks behind the Battle-Mech and sprayed them down on the Fusilier.

Craig fired his Gauss rifle and medium pulse lasers, ignoring the sudden rise in his cockpit's heat. The impact from the rifle slug slammed into the lightly damaged right torso of the *Vulture*. The slug sent armor into the air as it plowed into the 'Mech's internal structure, lodging inside. The right missile rack dropped halfway and jammed in place, rendering the weapon useless. Craig's medium lasers tattered the chest of the *Vulture* as another Highlander 'Mech, a *Grim Reaper,* rose and opened up with its lasers and short-range missiles on the same target.

Cullen Craig broke position, racing past a Fusilier Demolisher tank that was entangled with a pair of *Koshi*s at devastating range. A pair of missiles hit his 'Mech, but from where they came Craig didn't know. *It's falling apart all around me.* "Rear guard, break for cover. Disperse immediately." It was every man and woman for him- or herself. *I've got to get up on the highest of these hills so I can get some better range or I'm as dead as the rest.*

"Message from Star Captain Klark on priority channel," came the voice of the Cluster communications officer in Devon Osis's neurohelmet. He slowed the pace of his 'Mech and broke from the ranks of the Star that held the rear of the Jaguar formation. The path left by the Fusiliers had made tracking all too easy for Star Colonel Patricia and her officers. Devon Osis had remained with the reserve unit, pulling up the rear as Patricia and her forces rushed forward, hoping to nip at Stirling's own rear guard.

"Put him through," Osis commanded.

"I have completed a scan of our aerodrome, Galaxy Commander," the Captain of the *Dark Claw* began. "The complex, the defending troops, and from what we can tell, most, if not all, of our aerospace fighters are destroyed."

A wave of fury swept over Devon Osis as he moved his 'Mech forward. "Impossible. You must have made a mistake, quiaff?"

"Negative, Galaxy Commander. We have verified it with a low-altitude pass as well. Some of the complex is intact, but the communications array and the fighters are destroyed."

"Any sign of who committed this dishonorable act?"

"We have seen no one in the vicinity, Galaxy Commander. It is possible that they are in the buildings themselves, or have moved on and were not in the area that we scanned."

Star Colonel Patricia's voice came on line from her position at the head of the formation, nearly three kilometers further north. "Status report, Galaxy Commander. We are encountering only a small BattleMech force. The rest are ground armor and infantry forces. The bulk of the Fusiliers have apparently moved to the high ground of the continental surface. We have captured a number of their technicians and support staff."

Devon Osis smiled, his mouth a cruel slash. "The ones you have captured, do not waste our resources on them."

"What would you have me do with them, Galaxy Commander, release them?"

"Kill them all," Osis said casually. "Shot them or crush them as you please."

From her cockpit, Cat Stirling saw the last hill she'd climbed give onto the rise of what had once been a continent on Wayside V. It was void of life, almost as airless as an asteroid, yet this was her last sanctuary on this uncharted world. This place was her last desperate chance to save her command and troops.

Andrea Stirling's headset came to life with a voice she had heard before, that of her enemy—Devon Osis, Galaxy Commander of the Smoke Jaguars. "You are only prolonging the inevitable, Colonel Andrea of the Fusiliers. Your vain attempt to slow us has cost us nothing but a few minutes, easily made up as we chase you."

Hopefully Craig and some of the others managed to escape. "You still have not beaten me, Devon Osis. Only those we were forced to leave behind."

"You speak boastfully for one fleeing like a coward," he returned. "But so that you realize what the heart of the Jaguar is, I show you this." The secondary display inside the cockpit of Stirling's *Grand Titan* flickered, showing a battlefield camera projection. She saw the ripped and torn image of a Demolisher tank with several of her ground forces standing on top of its mangled hull, holding their hands up.

The combat camera, which must have been attached to a 'Mech, swept past the surrendering Fusiliers. There was a flash, the sparks of a machine gun rattling the ground and the surface of the tank. The Fusilier troopers attempted to bolt, but only one made it away; two of the others were mowed down in a hail of gunfire. Colonel Stirling saw their blood splatter as the machine gun cut a swath through them.

The message was all too clear. The Smoke Jaguars were

simply killing her people rather than taking prisoners. These troops had already surrendered. But apparently the Smoke Jaguars did not acknowledge any moral obligation in the case of surrender. She bit her lower lip at the terrible sight, then shut off the secondary monitor.

"You bastard," she said into her neurohelmet's microphone. "They were surrendering."

"A curse like that from a freebirth is not the insult you might think. Such filth from your mouth is to be expected. As I told you before, we do not have the facilities to play Inner Sphere games of taking captives. True warriors fight to the death. Those who surrender are a burden on my Clan and one I will not undertake.

"You have hurt me too much already. Do not think your victory at our aerodrome changes anything. It will not be long before I can paint my face with your blood."

The communications signal shut off. Stirling fought back the frustrating tears that welled up suddenly. She clung to one bit of information, something vital, something Devon Osis had given her that still held out a shred of hope. The Jaguar aerodrome was destroyed. That meant Jake Fuller was still alive out there, somewhere. It was a small victory, but the only one she had.

43

DropShip **Bull Run**
Pirate Jump Point, Tarnby System
Smoke Jaguar/Nova Cat Occupation Zone
25 July 3058

"**D**amn it, Jura. Pull this bloody thing to the left," Mitch Fraser snapped as he and Glenda Jura attempted for the third time to move the makeshift replacement armor onto what was left of her *Koshi*. Hovering in the zero-G of the *Bull Run*'s 'Mech bay, both wore straps that kept them strung to the 'Mech so that they didn't drift too far from their work. Both were also covered with coolant, grease, and sweat, and the two glared at each other as Mitch worked the pulley to get the armor in place. Similar sounds of work, strain, and frustration filled the rest of the bay as Loren's force attempted to rebuild what was left of their OmniMechs. Glenda moved the armor forward slightly, but off target, pinching Mitch's fingers in the process.

"Damnation," he hissed and pulled his fingers back. "I said to the bloody left, Glenda." He stepped onto the gantry and squeezed the hand that was in pain into a fist.

"Don't get mad at me, *sir,*" she replied. "I'm a MechWarrior, not a frigging technician."

"On this ship you're both," Mitch Fraser shot back. All across the *Bull Run*'s bay, MechWarriors-turned-techs stopped to watch the confrontation. Tensions had been running high, finally reaching a boiling point with Glenda and Mitch.

Glenda took the heavy armor welder and slammed it down onto the gantry. "Fine, then I quit. If you want this armor in place, you can do it by yourself—sir." She started for the gantry ladder when suddenly she saw the figure of Loren Jaffray starting to move toward her in a slow drift.

"Attention!" he barked angrily, giving first Glenda, then Mitchell, a hard look. Both of them snapped to attention. The remaining MechWarriors also stood at attention.

"Lieutenant Jura, Captain Mitchell Fraser is a superior officer and you will address him as such, do you understand?"

"Yes, sir," she said, giving Mitch an icy glance.

Loren looked around at the vast BattleMech bay where his people, dripping with sweat, were working on their own 'Mech repairs. He understood how they felt, but the time had come to remind them of who they were, and why they were here.

"I know you're all upset about our losses. So am I. Sergeant McAnis was a good MechWarrior, so were Macallen, Killfries, and Miller. But we've come too far to start going for each other's throats." In his mind he remembered the attempted recovery of the bodies. Killfries and Miller and Macallen's remains had been recoverable. From what he had seen, McAnis had burned alive in his cockpit because his CASE doors were blocked when his ammunition exploded. Only his carbonized form remained.

Gilliam had managed to eject, but his landing had been less than smooth, and he had broken his leg in two places. Trisha McBride was better off, but her 'Mech had been badly battered under Kerndon's piloting. In the end all that was left was Jura's *Koshi,* his and Hector's *Masakari*s, and McBride's *Vulture.* Burke's *Dasher* was functional, but was more broken parts than BattleMech. Considering the beating his small team had taken, Loren was forced to count the *Dasher* in. They had recovered Killfries's *Black Hawk,* but Mitch thought the repairs would take the entire trip home, and even then it was iffy whether the Omni would be even marginally operational by the time they reached Wayside V.

"In a few minutes we jump out of system. Another jump and we link up with the *Kobayashi* and return with it to Wayside. We've stirred up the Nova Cats, and they're bound to follow us after what we've done here. Mitch was able to leave them a trail, and they'll follow it back to Wayside. We're some two weeks from rejoining the regiment. And about the time we get there, Major Mulvaney and her force should also be arriving. They'll need us."

"Sir," came back the voice of Captain Mitch Fraser. "We're more replacement and combination parts than anything else. What kind of help do you think we'll be?"

Loren smiled and opened his arms to take in the scene around him. "These OmniMechs are all outfitted with Smoke Jaguar IFF transponders, aren't they?"

Mitch nodded, then a slow smile began to break over his face as he understood the hidden meaning of Loren's question. "I had no reason to change them out. After all, you wanted us to show up as Smoke Jaguars on their sensors." The Identity Friend or Foe transponders were devices used so that the targeting and tracking systems of the BattleMechs could identify who was who on the battlefield. In the confusion of battle, the IFF systems sent out a signal that told enemy and friendly 'Mechs alike which side you were fighting for. The fact that the transponders were still identifying the OmniMechs in his command as Smoke Jaguar 'Mechs was important. It meant that he could wade into battle and impersonate a Smoke Jaguar, even to the Jaguars' own sensors.

"All right then, people, let's get these repairs done and over with. Once we're set, we can start the trek home."

"Major?" Greg Hector said.

"Yes, Lieutenant."

"It might go a little faster if Kerndon came down here and helped. We haven't gotten to his and Trisha's 'Mech yet, and it's a mess. Not to mention that thing we're all loosely calling a *Black Hawk.*"

* * *

Loren Jaffray hung onto a handhold in the small cabin Kerndon shared with several other Fusiliers. It was tucked into the bowels of the *Bull Run,* and seemed to throb with the pulsations of the massive fusion drive idling only a few meters from where they were. Sensing Loren's presece, Kerndon unbuckled himself from his bunk and floated out over the decking to grab a nearby handhold.

"You were looking for me, aff?" Kerndon asked.

"Yes, your help is needed in the 'Mech bays with repairs. See Mitch for your assignment."

Kerndon nodded. "I'll go now," he said.

Loren held up a hand for him to wait. "There's one other matter between us before you go." Then he reached into his pocket with his free hand and drew out a knife. Letting himself float closer to Kerndon, he grabbed a handhold with one hand and severed the last of the bondcords wrapped around Kerndon's wrist with the other. The rope fell unceremoniously and almost silently to the deck. Kerndon stood there looking at it, rubbing his wrist where the cord had been. "You are releasing me, quiaff?"

"Affirmative," Loren replied. "The last cord was the one of prowess, and on Tarnby you showed me that."

"I am a warrior again." Kerndon spoke softly, as though not daring to believe it.

"Yes, you're a warrior again," Loren said, "and I'm going to need you more than ever in the fight still to come."

44

Surface of New Scotland
Wayside V (Wildcat)
Deep Periphery
29 July 3058

Up above the breathable atmosphere of the planet, the days were much brighter and brilliant than Colonel Cat Stirling would have thought possible. She was equally unprepared for the clouds—thin, wispy condensations that gathered around the feet of the Fusilier BattleMechs. Only visible during the hours of light, the clouds disappeared as the day wore on, transforming into frost and ice on the 'Mechs' legs. It was enough to remind her that there actually was some atmosphere up here, but so thin that survival was measured in mere seconds.

As she sat in the cockpit of her *Grand Titan* a warning light showed on her communications system. She reached over to put on her neurohelmet, and found the commline abuzz with voices and activity. Several officers were all talking at once, something about sensor readings and approaching 'Mechs.

"This is Cat One. Clear the channel and give me the story here."

"Black Adder Recon Three," a voice crisp and sounding so young that it tugged at her heart came on line. "We've picked up what appear to be several fusion-reactor signatures at extreme range. They've picked us up as well and have drifted off."

So soon? She had hoped to reach the petrified forests they'd named New Sherwood before the Jaguars caught up with them. Now, for a fleeting moment, those hopes were smashed. The terrain they were currently crossing was flat and offered nothing in the way of cover. *This is the worst possible place for us to try and slug it out. Perhaps the Smoke Jaguars aren't ready to press a full assault yet.* Her mind raced through the various options as her voice, seeming to act on its own, barked out the commands.

"Bring the regiment to yellow alert. Move our forces north except for Adder Recon Lance. Have them run the flanks of these readings. I want to know numbers and types of what we're facing." Stirling pulled up her own long-range sensor readings and studied them.

"Colonel," Kurt Blakadar said from his *Albatross* nearly two kilometers away. "I can deploy an assault lance as well for fire support."

"No, Major. Move the regiment out to our destination. I don't want to fight the Jaguars now. I just want to know what we're facing."

"This is Adder Recon Two," came a voice over her speakers. "Confirm MAD signatures. Three bogies moving at forty-six kph on a bearing straight at us. IFF signals coming in.

We're showing these as two Fusilier 'Mechs, Kilsyth Guards by designation. One is showing as neutral on my sensor."

Stirling lit up. She opened a direct laser communications beam, enough to reach out through the Wayside night to the targets. "This is Colonel Stirling, incoming 'Mechs, identify yourselves."

A voice crackled, the communications system obviously damaged. "Major Jake Fuller reporting, sir. Mission accomplished." An audible sigh of relief followed as if all the tension he'd been feeling had finally dropped from his shoulders.

"Is that *Sho-sa* Parkensen with you?" she asked.

"Yes, sir, but all of us are having comm system problems. His range is less than a hundred meters. If he was on line, I'm sure he'd be sending his congrats."

"Excellent job, Major Fuller," she said. "Regiment, stand down. Major Fuller, form up in ranks and tell me what happened out there . . ."

Cullen Craig stared up into the black but starlit night and tried once again to flush the images of death from his mind. He'd lost track of the battle after his *Victor* was knocked down by a hit from a Gauss rifle. But the memory was blurred. When he'd regained consciousness the fight was over. The Smoke Jaguars hadn't even stopped to see whether he was alive or dead.

But he'd gotten a good look at what was left of the rear guard. There must have been some survivors. The missing repair vehicles seemed to say that the techs had either managed to escape or been captured and sent back as booty to the Jaguar base. But the bodies of others who had not been so fortunate were all around him, bloated, the skin a sickening bluish-white. He could still see them where they'd fallen and the memory woke him screaming in the night. *I should be dead with them.* Guilt over his failure weighed heavily on him.

Since then he'd been running, fleeing the images of the dead and trying to find those responsible. In his mind it was as much Stirling and Blakadar who had killed his people as the Smoke Jaguars. *If she had only put me in command, everything would've been different. So many wouldn't have died so needlessly there.*

He had charged up the hills leading up from the old seabed

and eventually reached the nearly airless void of the continent of New Scotland. One thought consumed him. He had to see this to the end, even if it was his own.

The audible alarm got both Loren's and Spillman's attention. "Report contact," the DropShip captain demanded. The sensors officer responded crisply. "EMPs multiple, twelve thousand kilometers off of our current settings. Size indicates three large JumpShips." The *Bull Run* had reached the nadir jump point of the Boltin system, and had shuttled over from the *Fox's Bane* to the *Kobayashi*, waiting to jump across the stars through the energy field known as hyperspace.

Loren stood up for a moment, staring at the viewscreen as if he could see the ships so far away. "Class of vessels," Spillman requested firmly.

"Two bear the outline of Clan *Star Lord* JumpShips. The other—" The flight officer checked the screen. "Computer IDs it as a destroyer vessel . . . most likely a *Lola III* Class WarShip."

Spillman stared off into the stars for a moment, then turned to Loren. "Well, laddie, I'd say the trip was worth it so far. It looks like the Nova Cats are a'followin' us back."

Loren nodded. "Contact the Captain of the *Kobayashi*, Captain Spillman, and tell him to jump us out of here ASAP."

"Yes, sir, but you do realize that if we don't take enough time recharging for our next jump there's a chance of a misjump or just melting away the JumpShip's core? The longer we take the better, that's the key."

Loren shook his head. "Unfortunately I *do* understand the mechanics of JumpShip ops. But as we speak, Major Mulvaney is racing to Wayside while Colonel Stirling and the others are fighting for their lives. We've got to take some risks and push the safety margin to the yellow zone if we're going to arrive in time to help out. Besides, I want to get back before those kitties all show up."

45

Dropship **Bonnie Prince Charles**
Pirate Jump Point CEXC-0021-A.2122.97
Wayside V (Wildcat)
Deep Periphery
6 August 3058

Something was wrong, deadly wrong. "Position and numbers of Smoke Jaguar forces one more time," Major Chastity Mulvaney asked the sensors officer as the bridge crew of the *Bonnie Prince Charles* suddenly snapped to with excitement over the initial readings that had come from the planet. In the zero-G of the bridge, she held herself in position with the handholds near the control panel.

The sensors operator studied the readings carefully. "I'm picking up just under a hundred BattleMech-reactor neutrino signatures, concentrated in two locations. Some are obvious repairs and most likely inoperative, but this gives you a worst-case scenario. Concentration one is the Jaguar base, the others are on one of the continental masses. Lots of broadcast traffic down there. I checked their aerospace fighter base and show it to be inactive—no functioning reactors, no sign of defenders."

"Hellfire!" Mulvaney burst out. "A hundred 'Mechs! That's at least two of their Clusters. No—more like a Galaxy." Her mind raced over the figures as she tried to comprehend the hundreds of things that must have gone wrong on the mission.

"Where are the Fusiliers?" She couldn't—wouldn't—let

herself think that her sister regiment had not survived their landing.

"On it," the sensors officer said. "Here we go. I show them fifty-five klicks northeast of the Jaguar force. According to the maps we got from the satellite dumps, they're just about at the petrified forest on the continent we named New Scotland."

Chastity Mulvaney knew that things must have gone wrong—very wrong. In the airless void of Wayside's old continental surfaces, both MechWarrior and BattleMech would be pushed to their limits and beyond. To move such a large force up onto a continent with the enemy so close behind was too risky for the situation to be anything but grim.

"Can we contact Colonel Stirling? Is their regimental net up?"

"No, sir. From what we can detect, she's running with a battalion-level net."

"Here's another signal—one that hasn't picked us up yet," came the sensors officer, his voice more tense now. "It's a JumpShip—no, its thrust is too—oh god, Major, I'm picking up a Clan WarShip. Destroyer, *Essex* Class!"

"A destroyer?" Mulvaney was as shocked as the young officer sounded, but all she could think was, where the hell was Jaffray? Thanks to this pirate point, they were only two days' burn from landing, but was that going to be enough?

"There's more, sir. I'm picking up the remains of three Fusilier DropShips. All inoperative."

"What about the fourth ship?"

The sensors officer shook his head. "No trace, Major. Either it's out of range of our sensors on the other side of the planet or it was taken out by that Warship." This was bad news indeed. The loss of even one of Stirling's DropShips could mean the loss of upwards of a third of the Fusiliers.

Mulvaney stared out the viewpoint and tried to maintain her composure as she watched the green, blue, and white ball spinning below her. Its mountains of gray and brown poked up into the stark darkness of space, far above the atmosphere.

Chastity reached out and activated the communications channel. "All right, people, our mission has just changed to rescue and extraction. All senior officers report to the ready room in five minutes to begin planning. All hands, yellow alert."

She nodded to DropShip Captain Andrew Defoe, and he immediately activated the warning alarm, which echoed throughout the ship. "We are at general quarters until this is over with."

"Sir," the sensors officer said, staring at his screen in disbelief. "I just picked up an EMP at very close range—approximately four hundred kilometers off our starboard bow."

"JumpShip," Captain Defoe said calmly. "Suggest we scramble out fighter support."

"Captain, Major," the sensors officer said, "that ship is leaking massive amounts of helium. It looks like a misjump, probably lost the entire jump core."

"A misjump into a pirate point that only we know about?" Mulvaney said, almost to herself. "Sensors, run an ID on that ship."

"Ship is the *Kobayashi*," the sensors officer said with obvious relief. "It's one of the Fusilier ships." He paused and checked his readout again. "Carrying a lone DropShip . . . it matches the IFF transponder of the *Bull Run*." It was as though a silent cheer went up from the bridge crew.

Suddenly the commline crackled to life on the bridge of the *Bonnie Prince Charles*. Hearing the voice, Mulvaney was relieved, but somehow not surprised. "Attention, First Battalion of MacLeod's Regiment, this is Major Loren Jaffray of Stirling's Fusiliers."

Suppressing a smile, she activated the microphone in the comm panel next to her station. "This is the *Bonnie Prince Charles* to the *Bull Run*. Major Jaffray, do you mind telling me what in the name of hell is going on here?"

"I'd love to, Major Mulvaney," he replied, "I toasted our JumpShip trying to get here. I only hope I'm not too late for the party."

"What party?"

"In case you haven't heard," Loren said, "I've invited company to dinner. In fact, they've probably already jumped into another point in the system."

Mulvaney activated the internal intercom. "Attention all senior officers. That meeting we had in five minutes, make it fifteen. And drinks are on the Kilsyth Guards."

46

"**I** want you all to know you've done an outstanding job," Colonel Andrea Stirling broadcast from the cockpit of her *Grand Titan*. Her ragtag force was down to just over a battalion, gathered now at the edge of what had once been a mighty forest when life still existed on this continent they'd named New Scotland. South of her position by nearly ten kilometers were the forces of the Smoke Jaguars.

The petrified rock trees were massive, often as much as six meters in diameter. Many had fallen, forming natural corridors and alleys of fire and movement. The terrain surrounding the forest was flat broad plains. The ages-old forest offered the only real protection for kilometers.

"The Jags have been sitting out there for over a day, sir, just sitting and watching us. What in the name of Hades are they up to?" Major Blakadar called in from his 'Mech.

"If I was Devon Osis, I'd be studying the terrain," Stirling said. "Running recons along the perimeter, learning everything I could about this forest before I committed my troops. Trust me, he's not sitting out there trembling. He's a Smoke Jaguar warrior—our worst nightmare.

"But we've got a few things going for us. One, this terrain is just as deadly to them as it is to us. They may not know it any better than we do, which should be an advantage. Also, there's something they haven't counted on, something all their blasted Clan warrior training never prepared them for—the fact that they're facing Northwind Highlanders." A momentary cheer went up.

"We're trying to buy us some time, folks," Kurt Blakadar said. "Stick to our plan. Fire either from the forest out at them, or lure them in. Make them pay for this fight, pay with their blood and their lives for every meter they take. Remember, Mulvaney and her people must have arrived by now. All we've got to do is give them lights to find us by."

"The Kilsyth Guards stand ready, sirs," Jake Fuller reported. The Guards now consisted of only five 'Mechs, the three used in the aerodrome attack, and two more, Lieutenants Uther and Amari.

"Black Adder Recon Three," came another voice over the speakers of the gathered Highlanders, sending a ripple of unseen tension into the air. "Jags on the prowl. Moving this way. It looks like they're coming in force. Confirm, all Stars on the move."

Stirling smiled inside her neurohelmet. "Lads and lasses, break into your fire groups and brace for them. No matter what else happens, today we're going to send them all to hell . . ." She pivoted her *Grand Titan* and moved into the forest next to a gigantic tree of rock.

"We will be on them in a matter of seconds," Star Colonel Patricia reported from the cockpit of her *Timber Wolf,* the thrill of combat in her voice. She had began the rush forward with her three Binaries of OmniMechs in perfect formation, heading straight at the stone forest. The hope had been to wait out the Highlanders, let them come out at her force. When that did not happen, she had opted for a direct and one-shot approach.

"Flame Claw Binary is on the far right eastern flank, still outside their scanners. We will hit them from the front, then Flame Claw will sweep in and wipe them out." Her own Alpha Veiled Death Binary was in the center formation, with Devon Osis in position in the front ranks. On her left western flank was the Beta Stabber Strike Binary. The Stabbers and Veiled Death were racing forward, while Flame Claw was moving to the far east to sweep in on the side of the Fusiliers, taking their fight to deadly close range.

"Leave nothing to chance. And leave not a shred of these

Fusiliers behind," Devon Osis said angrily from the cockpit of his *Dire Wolf.* "Our mission is to destroy the cursed Nova Cats, not go chasing around after filthy freebirth mercenaries. We've already wasted too much time on them." Osis did not mention the loss of his aerofighter forces or how much more time they would lose rebuilding the 101st Cluster.

"They will pay dearly for their insolence, Galaxy Commander. Of that I assure you," Patricia said.

As the Huntress Galaxy warriors began their charge, Devon Osis saw the flicker and flash of lasers burning lightly in the thin atmosphere as they lanced toward the Fusiliers hiding like children behind their rock-fortified positions. PPC barrages and the flame tongues of missiles also lashed out from the advancing line of Smoke Jaguar OmniMechs, shredding the terrain before hitting their targets. The Fusiliers' return fire, though hardly as ferocious, slowed some of the momentum of the charge as several Jaguar 'Mechs took hits.

Devon Osis preheated his weapons pod as he searched for an undeclared target. He watched with glee as a Fusilier *Wyvern,* rising up and backward on its jump jets, came under a volley of deadly fire from one of his lead unit's PPCs. The shot hit the *Wyvern*'s leg and spun the skinny-framed 'Mech as it fired its lasers and short-range missiles in a wild volley that rocked a trio of Jaguar 'Mechs. Freed from their bonds of honor, all three Jaguars opened fire on the *Wyvern* as it attempted a sprawled landing. Their barrage consumed the 'Mech in a laser inferno.

As he and his warriors came to the edge of the petrified forest, Devon Osis opened a commline to his warriors. "Huntress Galaxy, they are falling back. Rip their hearts out. Show them the fury of the Smoke Jaguar!" Missile and laser fire, the rage and roar and fury of battle erupted all around him.

Suddenly his open commline squealed with a noise, a mournful bellowing that sent a cold chill through him. What was that? Music? The lament of bagpipes? The tactic was primitive but useful, the enemy jamming communications with background noise. His Star Commanders were attempting to communicate with him, but their voices were blurred by the wail of the pipes over the commline.

Just then something rocked Devon Osis's *Dire Wolf* from behind with a force so mighty it tore off pieces of his aft armor and sent them spraying over his head and cockpit. *From behind? Impossible!* Osis spun his massive OmniMech and saw a DropShip sweep past, dropping BattleMechs from its open bay. The newly fielded 'Mechs were firing at his Jaguars, hitting them on their right flank, cutting them off from the Flame Claw Binary being held in reserve.

"This is Major Chastity Mulvaney of MacLeod's Regiment of the Northwind Highlanders," bellowed a voice over the comm. "Surrender your forces or we'll pound you to snail snot."

"It's Mulvaney!" Kurt Blakadar called out over the lower band used whenever the Highlanders were jamming enemy communications.

"Right flank hold," ordered Cat Stirling. "Left flank Guards advance to your forward firing positions and hold there." Her hands flicked quickly over the comm channel as she contacted her sister forces. "Nice of you to drop in, Major Mulvaney."

Stirling then fired a wave of short-range missiles, but knew her ammo was starting to run low. In the distance, a Jaguar *Uller* took half the wave of missiles, the 'Mech's armor shredding away as it ran past.

"Some duty," Mulvaney returned. "I'm pushing through their lines to link up with you."

"Right," Stirling said. Though surprise had given Mulvaney's force a momentary advantage, it would not protect them against the fury of the Jaguar Cluster. She lifted her head just as a laser shot raked its way across her 'Mech's torso from somewhere across the battlefield. Suddenly torn open, the chest of her *Grant Titan* spilled out a rush of air, the blasted armor peeling back from the inside out.

"Push forward, Black Adders. We've got to get our relief force in here with us before they get toasted. Open up, Fire Corridor Bravo." Despite the heavy firepower and deadly aim of the Clan warriors, her people were giving back as good as they got.

"Major Jaffray sends his greetings," Chastity Mulvaney said, even as she was firing.

"He's back?" Cat Stirling felt a wave of relief and satisfaction.

"Can't talk now, Colonel. Suffice it to say he's got a plan."

* * *

Loren Jaffray's battered OmniMech force moved in on the right flank of the Jaguar force almost casually. The orders he'd given were clear and simple—no communications with any of the Smoke Jaguars. Fire when the Clan units around them were engaged by the Fusiliers or Mulvaney's forces, but shoot to miss.

Taking advantage of the confusion set off by Chastity Mulvaney's drop and using the IFF transponders that identified them as Smoke Jaguars, he'd been able to infiltrate his small force into the midst of the battle. Captain Spillman had dropped them nearly five kilometers from the battle site, reluctantly accepting orders to hold his position there in case Loren's force needed extraction in the middle of the battle.

They were more spare parts than anything else. McBride's *Vulture* had more patch armor than original, and the pair of *Masakaris*—Loren's and Lieutenant Hector's—were missing armor plates where replacements could not be fitted. Kerndon, with help from the rest of the unit, had somehow managed to get the *Black Hawk* operational enough to at least pose some sort of threat in battle.

Sumpter Burke's *Dasher* was present even if its pilot wasn't. Burke had come down with a bad fever that had quickly turned into pneumonia. Loren needed the 'Mech, even if just for the sake of having another body. In the end he'd been forced to draft a MechWarrior into service in the guise of one Captain Mitchell Fraser. As a tech, Fraser was fully qualified in piloting, but his gunnery skills were questionable. Loren remembered Fraser's delicate phrasing after he'd finally "volunteered" for the mission: "Major, I couldn't hit the broadside of a barn if I was *in* it!"

Loren looked up into the star-speckled night sky of Wayside and knew that the Nova Cats were, at that very minute, arriving at their jump point, their DropShips ready to begin blazing their way straight here. *They'll scan the planet, recognize the Smoke Jaguars and the Fusiliers. The Cats won't give a damn about us. They come to fight the Jaguar and that is what they will do.*

Over the commline came the sound of a new voice above the din of battle. Loren recognized it instantly.

"Attention, Tau Galaxy of Clan Smoke Jaguar. I am Star Colonel Santin West of Clan Nova Cat. May your hackles rise in fear, the Nova Cat now enters the fray. With what forces do you defend this planet?"

47

New Sherwood Forest
New Scotland, Wayside V (Wildcat)
Deep Periphery
8 August 3058

"**T**hey're pulling back," Chastity Mulvaney said to Cat Stirling over the commline, stunned to see the Jaguar force break into full-scale withdrawal to just beyond range of the Fusiliers' weapons. She held a forward position overlooking the flat open ground extending from the fallen rock-tree that provided cover for the lower portion of her *Marauder II*. Only two dozen meters from her position, the forest came to an abrupt end, opening onto the no-man's land across which she had rushed her forces a few minutes before.

"Why would they pull back now, Colonel? The Nova Cats won't be landing for a while."

"They see us as small change," Cat Stirling said. "To them, the Nova Cats are the real threat. There's no honor in facing us—a bunch of mercenaries." She brought her *Grand Titan* alongside Mulvaney's *Marauder II*. "This buys us some time to get our injured out. Your DropShip is now at our rear. We'll get some of these 'Mechs out of here. One lance at a time, rotational, if only to give them a chance to clean their filters and recyclers."

"Understood," Mulvaney said, then issued the necessary orders.

"Now then, where's my Executive Officer?" Stirling asked sternly.

"He and his men are in the middle of the Smoke Jaguar force, Colonel. Posing as Jaguar warriors to hit them from the inside—when the time is right."

"Once the Nova Cats land, that battleground's going to turn into a graveyard," Stirling said. "I sure as hell hope he knows what he's doing."

"It is impossible that they come here, now," Devon Osis said to himself. "This is madness, sheer madness." His Omni-Mech idled at the forefront of the Jaguar position, still facing the Highlanders in the distance—yet out of range of their weapons. He was enraged, but another part of him felt a stab of fear—fear of facing Khan Lincoln Osis and reporting what had happened.

Devon Osis opened a communications channel to the Nova Cat Star Colonel. "Your seers and oracles cannot help you now, Santin West.

"In the name of Khan Lincoln Osis of Clan Smoke Jaguar, I, Devon Osis, Commander of the Tau Galaxy, will defend this planet with everything I have—two and a half Clusters of the best warriors of Clan Smoke Jaguar—trueborn all. We are ready when you are, but first you had better make your odd little prayers and prepare for death."

Santin West laughed harshly. "I will crush you, here, now, with the fierceness that only my Clan can carry into battle. And you will know the price of anyone who dares anger the Nova Cat. You have called your own death down upon your head."

Osis did not answer immediately, puzzled by the Nova Cat's words. "It is you who brings this fight upon yourself. And I will defend the Tau Galaxy and this planet with everything I have, two reinforced Clusters of the best warriors Clan Smoke Jaguar has ever produced—trueborn all. A Cluster stands with me now while my remaining force sits waiting for you to die at our base seven hundred kilometers from here. If you have courage, face me now and put your boasts to the test."

"We have detected another unit near your position. Are they to be part of your defense bid?" asked Santin West.

"Neg, they are of no concern to you. Those are Inner Sphere mercenaries. When I am done with you, they will be mine to crush."

"Will they not interfere?"

"Forget them, Santin West. Their deaths are foregone. Come quickly. I promise the end will be quick."

"Do I assume you choose as the field of combat the site where your forces are now deployed?"

"Affirmative," Osis said with contempt in his voice, thinking that a Star Colonel like West would command no more than a single Cluster, hardly a match for an entire Galaxy.

"Galaxy Commander Devon Osis of the Jaguars," returned the voice of Santin West over the speakers. "You boast and bid like a freebirth, hoping to taint me with your own dishonor. I fear you not and accept your bid."

"Well bargained and done," Devon Osis replied, already savoring the defeat of the Nova Cat Cluster.

"Neg," cut in West. "What you do not know is that I have been given temporary command over an additional Cluster. If you think you outnumber me, Devon Osis, you are wrong."

Santin West laughed that same harsh laugh again. "Poorly bargained and done."

"When do we attack, sir?" Mitchell Fraser whispered to Loren over the lower band commline from his 'Mech.

"I'm not sure yet, but we'll know when the time is right. If the Colonel does her job, she'll play the two sides off against each other and then we can mop up the survivors."

"I didn't ask this before," Mitch said, "but just how are our own troops going to tell us apart from the real Smoke Jaguars? We look just like them to their sensors."

"They won't," Loren replied. "That's the part that requires us to be very careful, Mitch."

The Nova Cat DropShips had deployed a kilometer west of the battle site and moved their 'Mechs forward like a legion of Romans until they were at point-blank range with the Smoke Jaguars. It began like a summer thunderstorm on Northwind, light years and a full season away. It was impossible to tell who fired first, but it didn't seem to matter. Both sides immediately opened up a wave of fire—autocannons, lasers, PPCs, Gauss rifles, and missiles. It was a stunning sweep of light, stark against the darkness falling over the terrain as the battle began. Loren and the others dropped back slightly in the ranks. Their time would come.

"Holy crudstunk!" Jake Fuller cursed out loud as he watched the holocaust-like confrontation as it unfolded several kilometers away across the bleak dusty ground of the open terrain. The blue arcing discharge of PPCs and the red and green flash of laser lights created an eerie aura around the battle, a glow of death and destruction. From his position nearly fifty meters back from the forest's edge, the display of sheer firepower was as awesome as it was brilliant.

Colonel Stirling came on line quickly. "Major Fuller, check your long-range tactical display. I want you and Captain Lovat to keep track of which side is winning and when. Our job is to keep the odds even for as long as possible, until they've clubbed each other back into the ice age. We'll play them against each other. When one side gets the upper hand, we'll pepper them from long range—wear them down just until the other side can rally."

"Yes, sir," Fuller said quickly.

"Major Mulvaney, are you picking up what I'm seeing here?" Stirling asked.

"It looks like the Nova Cats are punching through the Jaguar line and sweeping past with their flanks and butts to us."

"That's what I see too," Fuller said. "Cat One, this is Guard One, the Nova Cats are getting the upper hand."

"Then it's time to move," she said. Signaling the combined force of Northwind Highlanders, she charged forward, bringing both of the fighting Clans into the reach of their weapons. "Concentrate your firepower on the Nova Cats until you hear otherwise." Long-range missiles, PPCs, and Gauss rifles raked away, slamming into the flank of the Nova Cat's 179th Cluster, popping off armor and forcing the Cats to recoil.

"Major!" came a panicked call from Mitch Fraser in his *Dasher,* skirting the edge of the battlefield with a Nova Cat *Ice Ferret* attempting in vain to fire its way through the last shreds of his rear armor. The roar of the battle was weaker in the thin atmosphere, but the light show from the firefight was stunning. The Nova Cat forces had poured into the middle of the Smoke Jaguar position where Loren and his small contingent were concealed. The attackers had flowed around the other Jaguar 'Mechs, placing Mitch and the others in peril.

Loren couldn't respond fast enough, but Greg Hector could. The Lieutenant fired two of his PPCs in unison, both hitting the legs of the *Ice Ferret.* One shot merely mauled

armor, but the other exploded the leg at the hip, sending the
Nova Cat 'Mech flying forward.

Out the corner of his eye, Loren saw Kerndon's *Black
Hawk* suddenly appear and begin a punching match with a
Thor. The stout *Black Hawk*'s punches were low, by nature
of its design, and between each hit, Kerndon's lasers blazed
away at the holes they were ripping. The two Clan forces
mixed it up at point-blank range, the air alive with fire.
Loren had always wondered what a Clan Grand Melee
looked like, and now he knew.

From her 'Mech's position at the edge of New Sherwood,
Cat Stirling intently studied the battle that was occurring just
at the edge of her weapons range. Events shifted suddenly
and swiftly as the Jaguars seemed to rally. Moving her
Grand Titan in closer, she opened fire with her large pulse
lasers as Jake Fuller informed her that the tide was turning.
She knew that if one side achieved a sure and total victory
too soon, they might end up coming to her people instead.

"Cat One to the Fusiliers, turn your attack on the Jaguars
now," Stirling said over the commline, then added quickly,
"Major Mulvaney, stand by." Stirling had moved forward,
but Mulvaney was still slightly behind.

A Jaguar *Vulture* stopped its bird-like gait and fired at her
with a pair of long-range missile salvos that wracked her
Grand Titan, punching several deep and deadly holes in
her armor. She heard a thudding sound as her right arm de-
compressed, spewing forth a cloud of air from the inside.
The weapons lights on her armaments there flickered to yellow, then to red, indicating that they had been lost in the
assault.

"Hellfire . . ." she muttered, savagely returning fire at the
Jaguar that had ravaged her.

A low cloud of smoke roiled across his cockpit viewscreen
as Loren gave his secondary display two quick glances and
saw what Colonel Stirling was doing. Playing both sides off
each other, she was injuring both. With Mulvaney in reserve,
she could make sure that neither side had the upper hand
when they were done with each other.

He watched as a swarm of Elementals came in toward his
flank, hitting four of the Jaguar 'Mechs with their deadly
missiles. The armored infantry scaled the Jaguar machines

and immediately went to work attempting to breach the cockpits. Two of the Jags managed to shake them free, killing several in a hail of laser fire at point-blank range as they tried to regroup and counterattack. Loren saw the explosive escape of air from one of the other cockpits and then the lights inside went out. The warrior never stood a chance.

A jet Black Elemental, its armor glossy and almost evil-looking, rose into the air nearby. Santin West, Loren told himself. It had to be. West was the only black-armored Elemental he'd ever seen since encountering the Nova Cats. He watched as the Elemental jetted to a perch on top of a fallen *Mad Cat,* standing on its missile rack as he searched for a target.

Loren was pivoting his torso to face the Nova Cat, when suddenly another 'Mech moved between them. It was one of the largest OmniMechs ever built—the 100-ton *Dire Wolf,* its incredible bulk pitted and scarred from the fighting. Three nearby Elementals opened fire on the *Dire Wolf,* but only seemed to anger it as their missiles tore hopelessly at its thick armor hide. While continuing to face Santin West's position, it moved its arm to the side and fired a blast at the Nova Cat Elementals—driving them to their death or cover.

A voice came over the speakers. "Santin West, I am Devon Osis," the *Dire Wolf* signaled. "Prepare to meet the Kerenskys."

48

Outskirts of New Sherwood Forest
New Scotland, Wayside V (Wildcat)
Deep Periphery
8 August 3058

Loren wasted no time giving orders as he saw Santin West's ebony battle armor about to be blasted in the midst of the close-quarters fighting between the two Clans. "Jaffray to Guards, open up on the Jaguars. Get behind the biggest ones you can find and send them to hell!"

He brought his *Masakari*'s PPCs on line as Santin West
opened up with a volley of short-range missiles and hit the
gargantuan *Dire Wolf.* Loren then saw him leap down from
his perch on the fallen *Mad Cat* and attempt to maneuver
away. At the same time Devon Osis moved his huge machine
forward, aiming its deadly array of firepower at the tiny Elemental. Seeing West helpless against the 'Mech, Loren targeted the thin rear armor of the *Dire Wolf,* opening up with
everything his PPCs could do. Devon Osis's 'Mech, easily
identified by its "T" symbol topped with three red stars,
stepped forward, bringing his fearsome firepower to bear on
Santin West.

Loren and Devon Osis fired at the same time. Two of
Loren's PPCs penetrated the weaker rear armor of the *Dire
Wolf,* punching through to the fusion-reactor heart of the
OmniMech. The powerful static discharge from the impacts
danced into the gyro housing, a heat sink, and then the en-
gine itself.

The remaining PPC hit the *Dire Wolf* in the head from behind while the impact of Loren's shots must have thrown the
'Mech's targeting system off. Just then Devon Osis's death
shot discharged. The hurricane of firepower intended for
Santin West tore into the ground ten meters away, ripping a
huge crater in the parched soil of Wayside.

"Star Colonel Loren," West transmitted, his voice reveal-
ing shock at what he had just seen, a Smoke Jaguar firing on
another of his Clan.

"No," Loren replied, turning and firing his last rack of
long-range missiles at a Jaguar *Ice Ferret* just running past.
"Actually, it's Major Loren Jaffray of Stirling's Fusiliers."
Suddenly a pair of Jaguar 'Mechs emerged between him and
West, one firing at each of them. The time for talk had
ended. Both warriors broke contact and moved to defend
themselves.

Killing the Galaxy Commander of the Jaguars had exposed Loren's ruse, as did the actions of his fellow mock-
Jaguars as they leaped into battle against the Jaguars they'd
been impersonating. Suddenly both sides of the melee saw
Loren and his men as targets of opportunity.

"This is Jaffray to everyone," he called. "Move to the east
as fast as you can. Pull your transponders out! Fusiliers, let's
get out of here!"

* * *

"Major Mulvaney, get a company up here and fast," Cat Stirling called over the commline as she moved her *Grand Titan* out from the protective edge of the forest, moving south toward the melee where the Clans fought. From what she saw, the two Clans had gone wild, their warriors literally beginning to pile into a small area of the battle zone. Punches and kicks reigned as did fire from shorter-range weapons. It was a melee of BattleMechs unlike anything she had ever seen. She closed her assault 'Mech to fifty meters more, only to be slammed hard with a Gauss rifle slug to the left shin, caving in the armor there and almost making her lose her footing. The battle was a malignant blemish on the face of the world, an orgy of death and carnage.

And Loren Jaffray was somewhere in the middle of it.

As Mulvaney's company of BattleMechs charged out of New Sherwood Forest, they were met with a combined hail of fire from both the Smoke Jaguars and the Nova Cats. Within seconds a lance of light Highlander 'Mechs was either destroyed or stopped dead in their tracks, unable to advance for fear of instant destruction. The rest of the company Mulvaney had sent out found some sort of defensible terrain and added to the conflagration by showering the area with missiles and PPC fire.

"No good, sir," Mulvaney said over the commline. "We can't get close enough to make a dent. The Jaguars are throwing out enough suppression fire to hold us back here." Frustration and anger edged her voice as her *Marauder II* laid down a barrage of PPC fire into the melee. Two of her reinforcement 'Mechs, a *Catapult* and a *Cyclops,* twisted and crumpled under a rain of Gauss rifle and extended-range PPC fire.

"We've got to find a way to get Jaffray and his people out of there," Stirling said.

Loren Jaffray brought his *Masakari* over on top of Mitch Fraser's *Dasher,* which had fallen, and fired his PPCs on the Jaguar *Uller* that had knocked Mitch down. Loren and his team had been slowly making their way toward the new Nova Cat assault on the far eastern edge of the battle zone, fighting for each meter of ground. Two of the Nova Cats had been felled, but in the process, Mitch's 'Mech had been knocked to the ground, spewing forth coolant as it stirred dust and dirt in the thin air.

At point-blank range, the shot overloaded his weapon, fusing it into a solid piece of worthless metal. However, his aim had been true, striking the *Uller* under its stubby armpit as Greg Hector's *Masakari* passed. The Nova Cat 'Mech ripped open, then collapsed like a lifeless doll as Mitch struggled his mangled OmniMech back to a standing position.

Suddenly Loren felt his *Masakari* lurch hard under a horrific blast. He fell forward, colliding with the ground so hard that it felt as if the 'Mech was going to come apart around him. His ears rang with a low buzz and his vision began to tunnel as he tried to concentrate on the controls. Blood burst from his nose, splattering the inside of his neurohelmet. Warning lights, bursts of red, everything seemed to be coming apart on his 'Mech. There was an explosion in front of him in the cockpit, but he didn't move even as the arc of electricity stung at his arm and hand. He couldn't move. Instead he let the tunnel of his vision get tighter and tighter until he was unable to resist it any longer. Just as everything was going black, he heard Mitch's voice calling his name.

The light in the distance got closer as Major Cullen Craig broke his *Victor* into a trot across the powdered dust of the surface of New Scotland. He was heading north, following the tracks the Highlanders and their Jaguar pursuers had laid before him. He reached a small rise and came to a stop, staring at the battle raging in front of him. It was awesome, an almost diabolic sight.

He scanned the 'Mechs from a distance of nearly two kilometers away. A *Cauldron-Born*—the Smoke Jaguars. Then his sensors picked up a *Supernova*. His first reaction was that that was impossible—the *Supernova* was a Nova Cat 'Mech. Then the truth hit him like a hard slap.

Loren Jaffray had made it back. His plan *had* worked. In the cockpit of his *Victor,* Cullen Craig sat mute, immobile, unable to move his 'Mech. Part of him was glad he had survived the ordeal of his failed rear-guard action and that the Fusiliers might still be saved by evacuation from Wayside V. Another part of him was on fire, sick and twisted in the gut at the knowledge that he had been wrong about Loren Jaffray.

"Greg, you and Kerndon get over there to provide cover!" Mitch Fraser commanded in a tone he rarely used. What was left of Trisha McBride's *Vulture* emerged from the battle and stood near Jaffray's fallen *Masakari*. Fraser leveled his weapons and opened up a burst as Kerndon and Hector moved in on Loren's flanks to give his fallen 'Mech cover.

"Cat One," Mitchell barked over the emergency channel so that everyone could hear. "We need immediate extraction. Major Jaffray's down."

"Cat One, say again. We need help . . ."

Suddenly a shadow crossed the battlefield and fell over Mitch Fraser and his comrades. Lifting his eyes hesitantly, Mitch was terrified that what he would see was the destroyer looming over them.

Instead he saw the smooth, egg-like shape of the *Bull Run*. Its turrets strafed both the Nova Cats and the Smoke Jaguars as the ship touched down smoothly, its fusion engines scouring out a crater and spewing dirt and rocks as it did. Its ramps were already open and ready, and Mitch didn't need any prodding.

"Highlanders!" he bellowed into the neurohelmet microphone. "We're out of here!" Kerndon and Hector grappled with Loren's fallen *Masakari* and literally dragged it to the ship under a hail of fire.

Colonel Andrea Stirling watched in awe as the *Bull Run* descended into the battle zone. It towered over the raging fight between the Cats and the Jaguars, a wide-open target as both sides attacked it freely. Opening a channel to the ship, she was surprised to get Captain Spillman directly.

"Captain Spillman, what are you doing?"

"What you can't, rescuing these lads and lasses," he replied.

"Get out of there—that's an order," Stirling barked. She needed the ship. Too much had been lost already in this fight.

"An order?" Spillman said. "'Tis been a while since I ignored one of those." Less than two minutes later, as elegantly as it had descended, the *Bull Run* fired it fusion drive and swung around free of the battle.

The battle lasted another twenty-five minutes, with both Clans putting up a horrific fight. Dug in at the edges of the petrified forest, Colonel Stirling held her forces back, awaiting the final outcome. Her earlier efforts to keep the fight balanced paid off. Only about fifteen OmniMechs and fewer Elementals remained. Those that did were horribly mauled and mangled, a tribute to the fight they'd put up. It was hard to make out much in the haze of battle, but her long-range sensors told her that the victors were the Nova Cats. There was no sign of survivors among the Smoke Jaguars. They had fought to the death.

Despite the exhausting battle they'd just undergone, the Cats now began to deploy quickly along a line in readiness to advance into New Sherwood, if the order were given. Stirling watched them, impressed with their sheer grit. She had come to respect the Clans for that. As far as she was concerned, the same tenacity was what made her and her people Highlanders.

The voice of the Nova Cat Cluster Commander came over her speakers loud and clear. "I am Star Colonel Santin West of the Circle of Power, of the Sigma Galaxy of the Nova Cats." He paused for a moment, as if to gather himself or regain his composure, the words obviously coming hard for him. "I wish to speak to the one called Loren Jaffray."

"This is Colonel Stirling of the Northwind Highlanders," Cat Stirling replied stiffly. "I cannot comply with your request. Major Jaffray has been injured."

Santin West paused again. "We have beaten the Jaguar at his own game. The Jaguar base has fallen to the Cluster I dropped there as part of my bid against them. Our WarShips have battled too, and despite losses, we have destroyed their vessel. On this day, on this world, the Nova Cat howls in victory over the dead."

Stirling wasn't sure what to make of this proclamation, but she feared it might be a prelude of things to come . . . another battle to be fought.

"Your Jaffray, he deliberately lured us here, quiaff?"

"Yes, I sent him to find you and draw you here to fight the Jaguars. It was the only way to save our regiment."

"Major Jaffray's actions violate our code of honor. Deceit is not one of the weapons a true warrior carries into battle."

"Would you say he fought courageously, Star Colonel?"

"Affirmative. I never suspected I was fighting anything but a true Smoke Jaguar."

"Then there is no loss of honor to you."

West did not reply at first, and Cat Stirling wondered if she'd provoked him. "And you, Colonel," he said finally, "you fearlessly proclaim your actions—the mark of a true warrior. I did not expect this from you."

"So where does that leave us?" Stirling asked, staring off at the arrayed line of Nova Cat 'Mechs.

"The victory that I have won here is tainted by your actions, Colonel," West replied calmly. "And that places me in the position of being forced to consider your destruction, which would also probably be my own. Your sensors no doubt have shown what severe losses we have suffered here. I am backed into a corner, forced between allowing you passage or perishing in a last fight with you."

Stirling smiled. "They don't call me 'The Cat' for nothing, Star Colonel," she said.

This time the silence that followed was even longer than the previous one. Andrea Stirling wondered again if she'd angered the Nova Cat commander, or if this whole dialogue had been just a ruse to distract her attention. She checked her short-range sensors just to make sure the Nova Cats weren't redeploying their forces. Finally she broke the silence.

"So, Star Colonel. Have you arrived at a decision?"

"You are called 'the Cat,' quiaff?" he asked.

"Yes, I am," she returned.

"Your Major Jaffray saved my life, Colonel Stirling. As a Nova Cat warrior, I place a high regard on such actions. It is said that when one warrior saves another, our souls become bound—even between a freebirth and trueborn. To defeat you, I would be forced to destroy him. In doing so, I would risk my own soul as well.

"As such, I have no desire to continue this fight now. No bid was ever made against your Fusiliers, and such a battle would only produce waste—something I find intolerable. This matter is closed."

"So that's it?"

"Aff. I will withdraw my forces—for now. Remember that the spirit of the Nova Cat knows of this place and its significance. At the moment I see no reason to hold on to this barren rock. Should that change, be assured that I will not hesitate to return to this world and take it from you, no matter what the cost."

"Of that, Star Colonel," returned Cat Stirling, "I feel assured."

"Well bargained and done," said Star Colonel Santin West, and then the speakers went dead.

Epilogue

DCMS Planetary Command
Wayside V
Deep Periphery
9 September 3058

Sho-sa Elden Parkensen watched with pride as the red banner was raised high in the air, catching the light breeze over the Draconis Combine command post on Wayside. The banner fluttered open, displaying the coiled black dragon, emblem of the Draconis Combine. At his side, Colonel Andrea Stirling also saluted, though he was sure it was more for the smaller banner of Stirling's Fusiliers that flew under the Combine's colors.

Cat Stirling had remained behind with a small garrison force drawn from both Mulvaney's and her own troops, waiting until the permanent Combine garrison had arrived. The work of rebuilding the former Smoke Jaguar base had already begun. Some of the structures had taken severe damage before the Nova Cats finally took the base from the Jaguar defenders, but a larger number were still intact and of value.

Parkensen walked over and gave her a firm salute. "Colonel Stirling, this brings to an end our contract and our working together," he said with an emotion that surprised her. "I never thought to see this day. I am very proud to have been a part of it. My entire command was lost again, as it has been every time I have served the Dragon. But this time I fought to the end, and in that end, there was a victory.

"The Combine has its moral victory—we have taken back a world from the Clans—something that has not been done before. And add to that, a planet that was virgin to war, one never invaded, never fully colonized. Together, Andrea Stirling, we have made history. A glorious history for the Kurita Dragon."

"It is one planet," Stirling was quick to point out. "One planet, barren and isolated in the Periphery."

"The longest journey begins with one step," Parkensen said, looking up again at the flags fluttering over their heads, then back to the dark-haired Highlander officer. "One day we will take the fight to the Clans themselves. This world, Wayside, is but one brick in the Exodus Road—the way back to the Clan homeworlds.

"I will not forget—no one will—the sacrifices you and your people made here. The honored dead will be remembered. I have sent a message via JumpShip to the Coordinator. The names you and Loren Jaffray have given to the places of this world, they will remain."

Cat Stirling understood the significance of the gesture. She followed the handshake with a salute, which the Combine officer returned. With perfect military precision, she then did an about-face and started toward the hover car that would take her to the waiting DropShip and the long ride home.

The command chamber of the Nova Cats was deeply quiet. Even the heavy leather chairs around the oak meeting table did not creak. Through the wall of blast-proof glass a small slice of the twinkling lights of New Lorton could be seen.

"Santin West," said Khan Severen Leroux, "you have served your Clan and your vision well. Your forces fought with skill and bravery. You defeated an age-old enemy in the Smoke Jaguars, and removed a threat to our Clan. The Keshik is pleased and you have brought great honor to the Nova Cat." The small gathering was highly prestigious. SaKhan Lucian Carns, his ebony skin and head gleaming under the lights, nodded agreement, as did Oathmaster Biccon Winters, who stood at the back of the room, her hooded robes, as always, concealing her facial expression.

"Thank you, my Khans," Santin West replied, bowing his head deeply. "I fulfilled my vision," he said proudly. "And served my Clan with all that I had."

Leroux nodded. "Your actions are to be commended. Who

would have thought the Cat you saw in your vision was a warrior of the Inner Sphere? Others have heard of your vision quest, and of the mission you led against the Jaguars. You are a leader among warriors, more so than ever before, Santin West," the Khan said. "Such a ristar is to be nurtured and given a command of his own, one of greater authority."

"There is the matter of Wildcat Station," Lucian Carns added. "I assume you wish I commence bidding to retake the world, Khan Leroux?"

"Negative," the older Khan replied firmly.

Cairns raised his brows in surprise. "Having an Inner Sphere holding in the Periphery is unprecedented."

Leroux was unmoved. "The world taken was not one of ours but one claimed by Clan Smoke Jaguar. Losing it endangers their supply route, not ours. If the Combine or these Highlanders use the world to stage raids against us, then I will pursue its destruction. For now, it serves a greater purpose—a thorn in the side of the enemy who sought to crush us. The Jaguars will bear the shame of the loss, further serving our Clan in their disgrace."

"Major Craig," cautioned Colonel Edward Senn. "It is inappropriate for you to address this Assembly on a matter that is purely internal to your regiment. Your CO will be back on Northwind in less than two months' time. Until then, you remain off duty, per her orders."

"Don't you see?" Cullen Craig demanded bitterly. "He's corrupted her just like everyone else." His arguments regarding the evils of Loren Jaffray had already taken up more than thirty minutes of the Assembly's time, and their patience was running out.

"Lad, you need some time to cool off," Colonel MacLeod said, hoping to defuse some of Craig's anger.

"No!" Craig shouted, ripping the clusters from his uniform. "I resign my commission. I'm going to find a unit that's willing to take a stand against this kind of treason. Next time I face you, it'll be from the cockpit of a 'Mech . . ." Before anyone could say more, he had stormed out of the venerable old Hall of Warriors of the Northwind Highlanders.

Loren Jaffray got up from his bed and made his way across the room slowly. His arms and legs still ached, a result of suffering the slow decompression of his cockpit and then two weeks spent battling the results of the bends. His arm still bore a long scar from the electric shock he'd received in the destruction of his *Masakari*. Looking out of the window he saw the government buildings and the inner walls of The Fort in the distance. His apartment had become a prison during his recovery, and he looked forward to the day he could return to duty.

A rap at the door disturbed his reverie, and the next moment Chastity Mulvaney was standing there, in her formal uniform.

"Damnation, it's good to see you." Loren reached out for her and pulled her close, an embrace he dropped quickly when he saw she was not alone. Just outside the door to his apartment were Mitch Fraser and Kurt Blakadar. With a slight twinge of embarrassment, he released Chastity and shook hands with each of the men as they entered the apartment.

"We thought we'd pay you a visit," Chastity said, exchanging quick glances with the other two officers.

"Thank Kerensky you did," Loren exclaimed. "I've been going stir crazy. The doctors won't release me to duty."

"Have you heard about Craig?" Mulvaney asked.

Loren shook his head as she continued. "He's resigned. Not surprising. He tried to drag you through the mud, but it was a wasted effort. You'll have to watch your back with him from now on. He's on his way to Outreach, if you believe the rumors."

"How's the rebuilding going?" Loren was hungry for news of the regiment.

Blakadar and Fraser exchanged quick glances. "Those OmniMechs and parts we recovered after the Nova Cats picked up their dead were a virtual goldmine. We're probably going to be right up there with the Kell Hounds and the Dragoons for Clan tech after this."

"Machines are important," Loren said. "But what about our warriors?"

Chastity fielded the question. "The Fusiliers are running at about thirty percent their total numbers once your injured get better. It's going to take a lot of recruiting to get them back up to speed."

"Don't worry," Kurt added. "I'm on top of it already."

"Don't get too settled in, Blackie," Loren said. "I'm going to be back on duty in a week or so."

A quiet fell over the room. "You haven't heard then?" Chastity asked.

Loren felt his heart race. "Heard what?" he demanded.

Chastity pulled out an official command order and a small box from her dress uniform sash. "By order of the Assembly of Warriors, the Northwind Highlanders, Major Kurt Blakadar is granted commission as the new Executive Officer of Stirling's Fusiliers."

Loren felt his heart drop. The words hit him like an unexpected splash of ice cold water, leaving him numb. "I don't understand," he said, stunned by the loss of his command. "Why?"

"Oh," Chastity said, "there's more." She looked down at the order, reading on. "And for his action above and beyond the call of duty, and his efforts against the Clans, Loren Jaffray is hereby promoted to the rank of Lieutenant Colonel." She handed him the small box. Inside was the bird insignia that signified his new rank.

"Lieutenant Colonel?" Loren said, still dazed even as he suddenly realized the news was not all bad. "Under what command?"

"Loren," Mitch Fraser said excitedly. "You're going to love this. The Assembly of Warriors decided that your ideas about studying the Clans and their fighting tactics should become part of the Highlander regiment—that we're going to have to fight them again sooner or later. They're forming a new unit with you as the CO."

"What?"

"You're in command of the Northwind Hussars."

Loren drank in the words. "The Northwind Hussars?" *My own unit, my own command. I've worked my whole life for this moment. I now have a home, a place I belong, and a unit to lead.* A broad smile wrapped his face, uncontrollable and unstoppable.

Chastity continued. "It's a paper unit now. You're going to have to build this regiment up from the ground. But with all of this Clan tech, there's more than enough to rebuild our losses on Wayside, with plenty to spare. The price of Clan weapons on the open market is enough to greatly expand our rank and file."

Loren looked at Chastity Mulvaney and, despite the impropriety and company, pulled her close and gave her a long and loving kiss. She was shocked, and laughed in response as he finally released her. "So, Lieutenant Colonel Jaffray," she said, arms around his neck and smiling into his face. "How do you feel now?"

"At home, Chastity. Home at last."

Smoke Jaguar Khan Lincoln Osis sat down before the box that had been delivered to him and stared at it with suspicion. It had come to him, via merchant courier, marked with the seal of the Nova Cat Khan Severen Leroux. He stared at the rectangular, half-meter-long black container and pondered what it held and what message his foe had sent him. Here, in the safety of his command bunker in El Gitar on Avon, whatever it was could not embarrass him in front of his command. Reaching out, he pressed the stud on the top and the lid opened. Lincoln Osis leaned over the box and looked inside.

There were two objects there. He pulled out one, a small metallic cylinder, and held it in his hand. It was a familiar item, a container used to maintain the giftake, or genetic sample, of a warrior. It was from these genes that a warrior's legacy could be passed on to future generations. A giftake was generally taken only from fallen warriors, those lost in battle. What made this unusual was that it had been sent from one Khan to another.

He turned the container over and cursed angrily as he read the words on the white band wrapped around it. Now he understood why he had heard nothing, now he understood what had happened. In a fit of rage, he cast the giftake container against the wall of his office with such force that it shattered the metallic seal, spilling the frozen contents on the floor in a cloud of white mist from the container's coolant.

"No!" he screamed, then swept everything off his desktop with a violent sweep of his arm. His voice was almost inhuman—beyond anger, beyond hatred. Then he pulled the second object from the box, a Galaxy Baton from the Tau Galaxy. The name on the outside of the baton was Devon Osis. The chip from his codex bracelet had been pressed into place as well, proof of his failure.

Hefting it with two hands, the Khan of the Smoke Jaguars then brought the baton down with all his might, beating it again and again against the desktop until it was nothing more than a mangled piece of worthless metal.

As Lincoln Osis gave vent to his fury, raging at enemies unseen, the essence of Devon Osis's genetic material lay spilled on the floor—lost forever.

About the Author

Manassas
Commonwealth of Virginia
Terran Hegemony
United States of America, Terra
13 March 1996

Virtual Geographic Society Biography:
Blaine Lee Pardoe

Blaine Pardoe was born in Newport News, Virginia, Terra, pre-Star League 1962, but spent most of his life living in Michigan. He attended Central Michigan University and graduated with an undergraduate degree in Business Administration and a Masters in Human Resource Management/Administration. He also became a die-hard BattleTech aficionado and fan.

Pardoe has been writing for BattleTech for the past 12 years, including his first novel, *Highlander Gambit,* published by Roc Books in 1995, which introduced the character of Loren Jaffray. He also has written a number of computer game books for the Brady Books imprint of MacMillan as well. It's a rough job, being forced to play and write about BattleTech and computer games—one that he absolutely loves.

In his "day job" Blaine is a manager for one of the "big six" accounting firms in Washington, D.C., in charge of national training and documentation services. He and his wife,

Cyndi, have two children, Victoria Rose and Alexander William, who lovingly tolerate his nightly trips into the 31st century, where most of his writing takes place. He resides in Manassas, Virginia, just outside of the Bull Run battlefields, and on cool autumn evenings he can be found on Henry House Hill, contemplating what might have been.

What's in the future? Pardoe is already hard at work on a new novel set in the BattleTech universe. At last sighting, he was muttering about the Clans, something called "the Exodus road," and the McKenna's Pride . . .

Celestial Palace, Sian
Sian Commonality, Capellan Confederation
30 March 3059

The office smelled lightly of sandalwood incense and wood polish. It was a comfortable room, with charcoal sketches on the walls and a small aquarium set into one corner. Rosewood gleamed darkly in the room's subdued lighting, its cherry-glow trimming shelves, french doors which opened onto a small balcony, and the desk.

Sun-Tzu Liao hesitated in the doorway, half-expecting to see Candace Liao, his aunt and ruler of the St. Ives Compact, seated behind that desk. The memory of her visit was seven years old. That night Candace murdered his mother, Romano, then-Chancellor of the Capellan Confederation. That night Sun-Tzu ascended to the Confederation's Celestial Throne.

This is an evening for old memories, he thought.

One such memory had disturbed him this evening, rousing him from his bedchamber before he could sleep. To sleep would risk the memory invading his mind in the form of a dream, and Sun-Tzu didn't particularly like dreams. His younger sister, Kali, attached great spiritual significance them, but then she rushed to attach great spiritual significance to all kinds of things that appealed to her various manias. As far as Sun-Tzu was concerned, dreams were half-formed thoughts, nothing more. If he wanted to know the truth about something, he wanted to be wide awake and able to analyze it for its true significance.

He knew only too well that he could not afford the luxury of rash judgments or hasty decisions.

His long robes whispered of heavy silk and his slippers offered only the softest footfall against the hardwood floors as Sun-Tzu moved into the room and shut the door behind him. He crossed over to the aquarium, studiously ignoring the desk. It was an exercise in patience, like any one of several routines he performed throughout a given day. *All good things come to those who wait.*

Leaning over to stare into the clear waters of the tank, Sun-Tzu felt as much as heard the low hum of the pump. Inside, near a small yellow patch of long grasses, a flame-orange Chinese battling fish cruised gracefully. Its overly large fins were tinged with just the slightest touch of violet. A beautiful creature, its aggressiveness matched only by another male battling fish that also occupied the tank.

Sun-Tzu reached into a ceramic pot, kept on a nearby shelf, and withdrew a pinch of food. Opening the aquarium's top, the dull odor of much-recycled water momentarily overriding the sandalwood scent, he sprinkled the food across the waters. The fish rose on strong cuts of its tail, nipping gracefully at the surface to swallow large portions of the food. "That's right, Kai. Put on your little show."

Sun-Tzu smiled thinly. Kai Allard-Liao, his cousin and son to Candace Liao, was one of the greatest threats to his position as Chancellor of the Capellan Confederation. In spite of Kai's self-proclaimed lack of interest in the Celestial Throne, he was heir to the St. Ives Compact and he had taken up the leadership of the Free Capella movement. He ran the movement more as a charitable enterprise, but Sun-Tzu was all too aware of the power base this gave his cousin. Not to mention the backing Kai received from Victor Davion, Prince of what was left of the Federated Commonwealth.

As for the St. Ives Compact, tucked between the Capellan Confederation and the much larger Federated Commonwealth, it had originally been a part of the Capellan state. Sun-Tzu considered it a knife at his back since Victor Davion could pour troops through the small state and be halfway to Sian before news ever reached his ears.

Naming his little pet after Kai was not intended to belittle his cousin, though that was an added bonus, but to remind

Sun-Tzu of the dangerous similarities. Kai was a deadly warrior, one who could move through either political or military circles with a grace everyone envied. And the fish's wide, unblinking eyes reminded Sun-Tzu that every move he made from the Celestial Throne was observed by Kai's steady gaze.

His private smile faltering, Sun-Tzu straightened up and crossed to his desk in a few slow strides. He still did not seat himself. Instead he walked slowly around three sides, tracing a fingernail along the desk's rosewood trim. Gone was the antiquated monitor that had once dominated this desk, now replaced with a screen set flush into the desktop. Right now the screen displayed the Draconis Combine, but would eventually cycle through star maps of all the Great House empires and then a full map of the Inner Sphere. The wood surface surrounding the screen was waxed and polished to a perfect finish. Sun-Tzu demanded that it be kept so, a fitting monument to the past. This had been Justin Allard's desk, as this had been Justin Allard's office.

Sun-Tzu had once vowed to have the office destroyed the day he rose to the Celestial Throne. Too much treachery had been hatched here against House Liao. Justin Allard, known then as Justin Xiang, had crippled the Confederation's military efforts from this very office—leaving the Confederation near-defenseless in the onslaught of the Fourth Succession War. Over one hundred occupied worlds were lost to Hanse Davion and the newly formed Federated Commonwealth, nearly half the realm. Allard escaped with Candace Liao, the two of them later resurfacing in the seceded St. Ives Compact. Sun-Tzu had not yet been born then, but he recalled his mother's description of what that war had done to Maximilian Liao, her father and his grandfather. Allard's treachery changed him into a feeble-minded weakling, the broken shell of a man.

Another old memory.

But instead of having the office destroyed, Sun-Tzu had changed his mind and had it renovated for his own use, determined to oust any superstitions. He accomplished that one short year ago when from this desk he coordinated the offensive that returned to the Capellan Confederation some of the worlds lost in the Fourth Succession War, and left many more under a cloak of Capellan influence he hoped to strengthen. He might have gone further had Thomas Marik of the Free Worlds League not backed out on him, but Sun-Tzu was wise enough to know when to accept a winning hand. The decision to support Thomas's truce was also made at this desk. As with many things in his life, this office served more than one purpose. It reminded Sun-Tzu to be wary of both appearances and complacency, and also that all victories must be guarded.

The memory that had drawn Sun-Tzu to his office so late in the evening had to do partly with the latter thought. Though the Confederation had taken back some worlds lost in the Fourth Succession War, the greater portion still remained as fledgling independent worlds in an area known as the Chaos March. Some were reluctant to accept House Liao rule again, while the hated Sarna Supremacy posed a threat from within his own borders. He had already set plans in motion that might rid him of Sarna, but the Chaos March still remained and Sun-Tzu admitted the fact that he simply did not have the military strength to retake *and hold* all the worlds he coveted. Yet.

An almost audible click sounded within Sun-Tzu's mind as another piece of the puzzle fell into place. *Yes,* he thought, nodding to the empty room, *it all could fit quite well.*

The old memory was of Romano Liao, his mother who had ruled the Capellan Confederation for over twenty years before him. Sun-Tzu had been a child—seven, perhaps eight years old—and found his mother in a briefing room watching holovids of the 3030 invasion of the Capellan Confederation. The boy had already learned to avoid his mother when she was busy, for her uncertain temper would flare without warning into driving rage. She'd noticed him, though, and called him to her. Sitting in her lap, Romano's strong arms wrapped tightly about him, Sun-Tzu's thoughts had cycled between fear over what his mother might do to him in one of her rages and fascination as he watched the holovids of the war.

The Duchy of Andurien had tried to secede from the Free Worlds League. Thinking the Capellan Confederation weakened by the insanity of Maximilian Liao, the Duchy worlds had allied themselves with the Magistracy of Canopus in the Periphery to invade the Confederation. Fueled by her fanatic vision for the state and her hatred of anything that threatened it, Romano had led the Capellan military against them, driving the invaders completely back by 3035. Romano pointed out to her son some valiant stands made by the enemy, even as the Capellan forces routed them.

"Such disorganized states could not hope to win, but what devotion they show in their deaths," she'd said, almost in admiration. "If only they could be harnessed, and driven at our enemies."

Sun-Tzu had never forgotten that idea, that a Periphery state could someday hold a balance of power. Wild beasts broken to a leash could still turn on their masters. But if they were handled properly, given the right prey to bring down, they could be partially tamed.

Sun-Tzu looked down at the screen, now displaying a map of the Capellan Confederation. A few taps against the touch-sensitive screen and the image was joined by the Taurian Concordat and the Magistracy of Canopus, the two Periphery states lying just outside the Confederation's rimward borders. The combined area of the two Periphery states was almost half again as large as his realm and looked very much like the head of a hammer, where his Capellan Confederation was the handle by which it could be wielded.

But where to begin? Political relations with the Concordat could only be described as frosty at best, and the ambassador Sun-Tzu had sent to Canopus IV had recently been expelled for his arrogant behavior toward the Magestrix herself. Diplomatic efforts didn't seem very promising.

Until Sun-Tzu remembered the reports of the Marian Hegemony's ongoing aggression against the Magistracy of Canopus. That placed them in a position to need help. Also, the Magistracy had been the most vocal of the Periphery states in requesting aide in education and technological advancement, two areas they wanted to desperately upgrade. One last memory surfaced, again of his mother Romano and her standard policies when negotiating a deal of any type.

Offer most of what they want.

Give them some of what they need.

Use them for all they are worth.

Reaching out Sun-Tzu tapped the glass over the Magistracy of Canopus, marking long seconds as he sat, and thought.

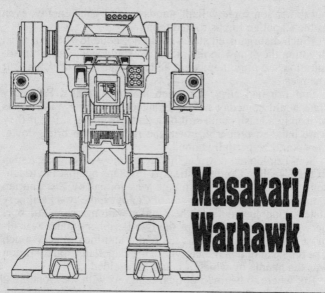

Masakari/ Warhawk

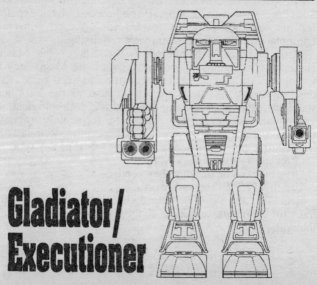

Gladiator/ Executioner

Grand Titan

Hatamoto-Chi

Cerberus

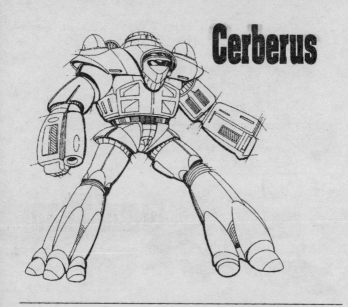

Daishi/ Dire Wolf

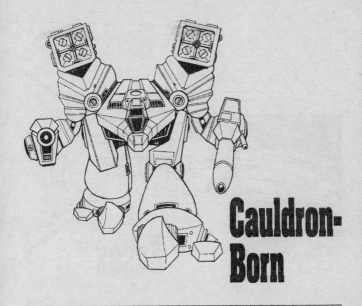

Cauldron-Born

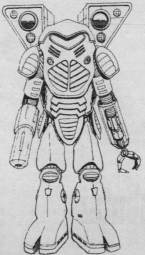

Clan Elemental

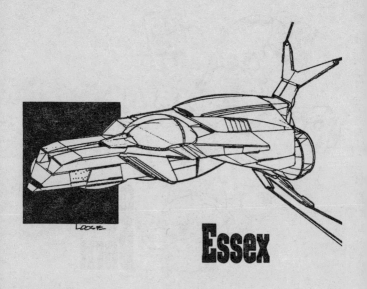

Essex

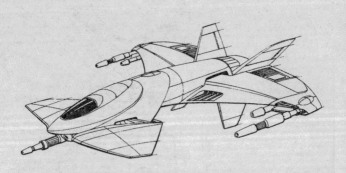

Sabutai

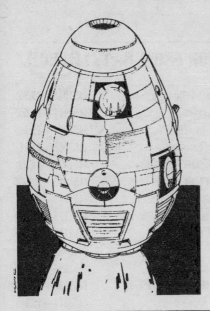

Overlord

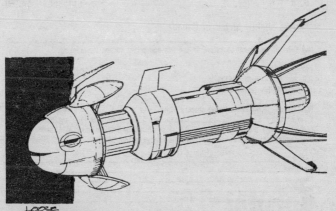

Invader

FASA

RELENTLESS ACTION FROM BATTLETECH ®

ENTER THE SHADOWS SHADOWRUN®

Finally, the answer to the age-old question…
"What are we going to do tonight?"

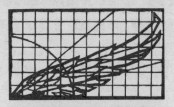

VIRTUAL WORLD®
FEATURING BATTLETECH®
AND RED PLANET™

ATLANTA
DAVE & BUSTERS · 404-951-5544

CHICAGO
NORTH PIER · 312-836-5977

COSTA MESA
TRIANGLE SQUARE · 714-646-2495

DALLAS
UA PLAZA NORTHPARK · 214-265-9664

HOUSTON
DAVE & BUSTERS · 713-267-2629

INDIANAPOLIS
CIRCLE CENTER · 317-636-4204

LAS VEGAS
GOLD KEY SHOPS · 702-369-3583

MONTREAL
COMPLEX DESJARDINS · 514-847-8835

PASADENA
ONE COLORADO · 818-577-9896

SACRAMENTO
AMERICA LIVE! · 916-447-3245

SAN DIEGO
HAZARD CENTER · 619-294-9200

SAN FRANCISCO
CYBERMIND EMBARCADERO · 415-693-0348

TORONTO
CN TOWER · 416-360-8500

WALNUT CREEK
NORTH MAIN ST. · 510-988-0700

OVERSEAS
AUSTRALIA
JAPAN
UNITED KINGDOM

Internet Address: http://www.virtualworld.com

YOUR OPINION CAN MAKE A DIFFERENCE!

LET US KNOW WHAT *YOU* THINK.

Send this completed survey to us and enter a weekly drawing to win a special prize!

1.) Do you play any of the following role-playing games?
Shadowrun _____ Earthdawn _____ BattleTech _____

2.) Did you play any of the games before you read the novels?
Yes _____ No _____

3.) How many novels have you read in each of the following series?
Shadowrun _____ Earthdawn _____ BattleTech _____

4.) What other game novel lines do you read?
TSR _____ White Wolf _____ Other (Specify) _____

5.) Who is your favorite FASA author?

_____

6.) Which book did you take this survey from?

_____

7.) Where did you buy this book?
Bookstore _____ Game Store _____ Comic Store _____
FASA Mail Order _____ Other (Specify) _____

8.) Your opinion of the book (please print)

_____
_____
_____

Name _____ Age _____ Gender _____
Address _____
City _____ State _____ Country _____ Zip _____

Send this page or a photocopy of it to:
FASA Corporation
Editorial/Novels
1100 W. Cermak Suite B-305
Chicago, IL 60608